THE WINGLESS ANGEL

by

FABRICE WILFONG

FROM THE TINY ACORN . . .
GROWS THE MIGHTY OAK

This is a work of fiction. References to real people, events, establishments, organizations, or locales are intended only to provide a sense of authenticity and are used fictitiously. All other characters, and all incidents and dialogue are drawn from the author's imagination and are not to be construed as real.

The Wingless Angel
Copyright © 2020 Fabrice Wilfong
All rights reserved. Printed in the United States of America. For information, address Acorn Publishing, LLC, 3943 Irvine Blvd. Ste. 218, Irvine, CA 92602

www.acornpublishingllc.com

Cover art by Damonza
Interior design by Debra Cranfield Kennedy

ISBN-13: 978-1-947392-63-2 (hardcover)
ISBN-13: 978-1-947392-62-5 (paperback)

For L.B.

CHAP+ER ⊕NE

It is possible for you to survive in Hell long enough to be rescued. Hell is by no means a permanent stay; by all rights, it is a purgatory sentence. If you realize the error of your ways to God's satisfaction, then He can, and will, attempt to save you. Unfortunately, as part of God's bargain with the Devil, He has no divine power in Hell. Instead, only an Angel can rescue you after redemption. Due to the massive amount of people being sent to Hell and the defensive structures the Devil has created, this has become an extremely difficult task. The following guide serves as a resource for your time in Hell to ensure you last long enough to be rescued.

—From "Hell: A Survival Guide"
By Delta-Delius

Silton squared up two thick stacks of fresh twenties on his dresser. On top of one lay a handwritten note in black marker that read: "Sorry for the mess." The other, wrapped in a tight rubber band, barely fit into his jeans pocket.

The liquor store sat across the street from Silton's apartment.

That's why he moved there. This way, when he drank, he only had to hold himself together for a few minutes to get more.

The usual wastes of life dotted the sidewalk in front of the store: Curby, an Asian woman trying to sell plastic bags to everyone who passed; Lester, a wino so hardcore his chapped lips bled purple; and Skinny Chad, the meth head. Skinny Chad was the worst. He might have still been in his teens, but he looked at least thirty years older. The kid's constant scratching left skin craters with tiny scabs that pocked his cheeks, and his clothes hung off his brittle frame like a tarp over unfinished construction. But his teeth were the worst part of him: jagged and eaten away by the meth, they looked like cracked ice. Every time Silton saw them, he had to run his tongue across his own teeth just to make sure they were still okay.

Like everything else in town, the liquor store looked tired. Chipped tiles dotted the ceiling, a water pipe leaked to a stagnant puddle in the corner, and dust lined the bottles of liquor like new-fallen snow. Silton went straight for the good whiskey. His hand fit snugly around the grip of the big bottle. He always thought that meant something, like the stuff was made specifically for him.

Brian, the happy drunk who owned the store, always greeted his customers like he hadn't seen them in years. At first this annoyed Silton, but soon it became comforting, like he belonged to a drinking team and Brian was his coach.

"Silky-Silty, my boy! How the hell are you?" Brian asked.

"Great," Silton droned. "Everything's just great." He plopped the bottle down on the counter sounding like it might have cracked but didn't.

"You know, I meant to tell you," Brian continued, "my

buddy at the VFW wanted me to invite you to the Soldiers' Spaghetti Dinner next week. He said it's free for all vets, put on by the local Presbyterian Church up over the hill." He scanned the whiskey while talking. It cost something, but Silton paid no attention to how much.

"Great, Brian." Silton pulled out the fat wad of twenties, unfolded several from the rubber band, and tossed them on the counter.

"Let me guess, you ain't gonna make it?" Brian asked.

"Nothing gets past you . . ." Silton said as Brian wrapped the bottle in a brown paper bag.

"That's what I thought." Brian smirked. "I'll get you to one of these dinners someday."

"Have a good one." Silton turned, striding toward the door.

"Hey, hey! You gave me way too much!" said Brian as he fingered through the cash.

"It's yours, Brian," Silton said without turning. "You've always been better to me than I ever was to myself." With that, Silton disappeared between the dusty shelves.

"Well, thanks!" Brian said, smiling stupidly with his head cocked to the side as he put the extra cash in the register.

A stiff breeze drifted across town, only interrupted by the occasional dust devil. The idea of the tiny tornadoes used to fascinate Silton, until he moved out to the desert. *Things are never quite what you think they'll be like,* he thought.

Skinny Chad sat up against a rusty newspaper vending machine a few yards down from the store. Silton turned and walked toward him.

The meth head looked half-asleep, in that quasi-limbo state when the high is wearing off. His body, tired and twisted like a soft noodle, shuddered as the breeze blew by. The slow metabolism of chemical junk in his body kept him drifting in the spaces between sleep and wakefulness.

"Hey, Chad," Silton said, kicking him. Skinny Chad let out a grunt, and his eyes opened like he hadn't seen light in years.

"Here you go." Silton handed him a thick portion of twenties. Chad's spine rippled when he saw it, and he sat up straight for the first time that day.

"Thanks, man . . . thanks, man . . . this is gonna . . ."

"Shut the hell up," Silton said. "I don't have time for you. Just promise me something." Silton leaned in close to the stinking kid.

"Sure man . . . sure . . ." Chad said, sitting up as straight as he could.

"I want you to go to the thrift store and buy some clothes. When you're there, you're going to beg the manager for a job. And no matter what job he offers, you're gonna take it. Then go get some food and check into the motel. That should be plenty of money to get you to your first paycheck. Don't you dare buy a rock and smoke it down by the drain shaft. This is all for you man . . . all for you. I'll know if you don't do what I told you. I'll ask around. And if I find out you bought drugs, I'm gonna come back here and kick the rest of your teeth out."

"Oh no, oh, you got it, man, you got it! Don't have to tell me twice." Skinny Chad cracked a smile, showing his shattered-glass teeth. Disgusted but satisfied, Silton stood up and walked away from the kid.

It occurred to Silton that he might have just done something horrible. He figured Chad could buy around thirty grams of meth with that cash, and if he did, it'd probably kill him. Just another junkie offed by his own habit, a morbid set-up for sure. But morality swings to extremes when one is near the end. People either become desperately charitable hoping to create some lasting joy in the world, or recklessly dark trying to destroy everything around them. Silton figured he'd caused enough destruction for one lifetime, so he opted for the former on this, his last day.

Silton had slid down far during the past year, much faster than the three before. It seemed he dropped a peg on the decency ladder with each month that passed. Now he held on to the last rung of his humanity, just a few loose fingers away from becoming one of the dusty, rag-wearing people he passed going to and from the liquor store every day. He divided the rest of the twenties between Lester and Curby. Curby gave him a fistful of wrinkled plastic bags in exchange, and Silton laughed out loud at her gesture.

His apartment, old but clean, wasn't terrible. A small room resting at the top of three flights of stairs held a bed in the corner, a tight bathroom, and a closet with mirrored doors that tried to make the place look bigger, but failed.

Silton had the desk up against the mirrored closet so he could stare at himself while he drank, stare at the man he'd become. He cracked the seal on the bottle and took the first swig. It burned his throat like bleach, and he smiled at the pain.

A quarter of the way through the bottle, Silton looked over at a picture on the shelf. Covered with a thin layer of dust, it looked like everything else did in this town: tired.

A photo of a spouting fountain tucked in a lush park rested in the cheap wooden frame. Silton's smile was wide and toothy in the picture. Kay had that pouty look on her face, like she didn't want to be there, even though she did. The sun sat high in the afternoon, and the sky looked beautiful and still. It had been a perfect moment, he thought. But not for Kay. "Nothing can be perfect," Kay would always say. Her belief was, once you call something perfect, you're on your way to killing it.

Kay thought complacency came with thinking everything was perfect. She thought that perfection let you relax, stop trying, and let your guard down. That's when you stop paying attention to the road for a second; that's when everything gets ruined. So instead she called it "almost perfect." It was her way of keeping life near the middle, away from the extremes that destroy all good things.

"Almost perfect," Silton muttered as he looked back to the mirror. His expression, pained and sad, longed for another time. He looked pathetic, like anyone would remembering a moment so far in the past, a moment so much better than the present. The image of his weakness reflected back into his eyes, and it angered him. Another swig later, and he planted his fist square in the middle of the mirror. It spider-webbed and spit out shards of glass onto the desk and floor, some embedding in his knuckles.

"Damn!" He got up, cracking a few shards under his feet, and pulled up his mattress. His Glock 31 lay there, cold and ready. He loaded it, laid it on the desk, and sat back down. Blood ran down his hand onto the ceramic black handle of the gun. Silton could smell his blood, and he thought the scent paired nicely with the whiskey.

The bottle, half gone, numbed the burning in his throat as his body gave up trying to reject the alcohol with pain. This was the sweet spot, the time when the drunk train hit its long, easy straightaway.

He opened the desk drawer, empty except for one thing: a never-framed commendation letter from his commanding officer. The line he liked most jumped out at him as if typed in bold print:

"For selfless valor in the face of incredible odds, for implicit application of medical skill in the line of fire resulting in the salvaging of three lives."

"Implicit," he thought. Not the right word, and "salvaging" seemed a bit inhuman, but his sergeant was no writer. That didn't matter. Silton understood what he meant. Silton had been there. It wasn't a good memory by any stretch, but one that stuck like stiff concrete in the path of his life. He remembered his hands digging through guts and bone like a gardener would dirt and weeds. He patched bullet holes tight with gauze, splinted bones straight with scraps of wood, and tried to stuff innards back into bellies before they sprung out again. This was Silton's odd gift, the ability to see such trauma to the body just like damage to a car. No emotion, no panic, no hesitation. It can either be fixed, or it can't.

Another quarter of whiskey went away to that place he wanted it to go. The cuts on his fist tried to dry up, but the alcohol had thinned his blood, so they kept a light trickle. His tremors came and went, but mostly went, and soon Silton could hold the gun steady. He licked his lips, tasting the bitter spices of liquor, and figured his last meal had been pretty good, considering. He lifted the gun and placed the end of the barrel to his naked chest. He wanted to save his brain for some future pathologist to slice like lunchmeat. Maybe in death someone could figure out what was wrong with him, and Silton could help save other soldiers.

The gun felt cold, and sent chills across his skin.

In that instant, Silton noticed his rippled reflection in the cracked mirror. So many versions of himself stared back. Silton looked the same in all of them. It wouldn't have mattered which path in life he took, they all ended here. Each one of his reflections could have been another him, another time, another place—but they all looked the same now: drunk with a gun to his chest. This gave him a moment of comfort. Like life wasn't really in his control. Like it never was, and maybe it wasn't supposed to be.

The hammer fell and the gunpowder exploded. The sound temporarily deafened him, pressing a shockwave of air up against the soft inner bones of his ears. The red-hot gas escaped from the barrel and hit him first. It burned a deep cigar stain into his chest. Silton only felt this in an indirect way, like watching it happen to someone else. The bullet cracked his sternum much like he'd cracked the mirror, and the impact started him back off his chair. The shot made its way through a forest of veins and arteries like a mad logging crew. His heart had no argument for the bullet, and its meaty valves folded and spread into odd directions before they exploded out of his back.

The chair gave way and Silton crashed to the ground. His blood quickly sought out the cracks and crevasses on the floor, the dirty rug underneath his bed turned deep brown, and the wall opposite him shone bright red with sticky flesh clinging to it.

Silton turned his head to the dusty picture on the shelf: the park, the fountain, Kay. But he couldn't see it; his view was obscured by his new line of sight from the floor. He'd wanted that picture to be the last thing he saw before he died.

"Almost perfect," he muttered. "Almost fucking perfect."

✠ ✠ ✠

AND watching from above, in the bright blue depths of Heaven's Eye, God frowned.

CHAP+ER TW⊕

It is important to note that part of the Devil's plan in Hell is to malform, or as a function of Hell's design, force you to malform your body. This has been fully and completely orchestrated by the Devil. It is widely known that man has an enduring and sometimes obsessive attachment to his body. In order to successfully survive in Hell, you must endeavor to release yourself from this constraint, as it will only hinder your progress. Understand that you are dead, fully and completely. Although you will feel pain, just as you have felt it in life, the idea of self-preservation from the standpoint of your physical visage is irrelevant. Those who can release themselves from the attachment of their physical selves and embody these principles are amongst the most successful survivors in Hell.

—From "Hell: A Survival Guide"
By Delta-Delius

Montly sat perfectly still on the soft waiting room couch. Supple onyx skin stuffed with semi-hardened fat, the couch almost engulfed her. The cushions, cool and refreshing, were comfortable against her rough, chapped thighs.

"Would you like something to drink?" asked the receptionist.

"Of course," Montly said without thinking. Her mind was elsewhere—paging through her studies, her practice questions, and the stories she'd rehearsed in preparation for the interview.

The receptionist got up from her white, bone-on-bone carved desk while Montly watched in silence. She wore the most exquisite, sinew-netted blouse, so translucent her breasts could be seen through it. Her legs, wrapped tightly in a black-skinned skirt, looked smooth and unlabored. But her shoes fascinated Montly the most. She had never seen their equal: high, thin stilettos, pristine polished white bone on their sides, with heels of pure, whole teeth. As the receptionist walked to get Montly the water she'd offered, the teeth ground on the bone tile so loudly, she thought the floor was cracking.

Montly felt a tinge of jealousy. She wore the only garments she had: an off-white, skin overcoat with a pair of loose fitting, high-water pants held up by a braided-vein belt. Her shoes, a pair of simple, skin-folded moccasins, were old and tattered. Montly wasn't even wearing a blouse. She felt the overcoat was enough, and besides, she didn't have any breasts to speak of. She'd removed them long ago, far too useless for the weight they burdened her with.

The receptionist returned with a small cup made of thinly pressed keratin.

"I just want you to know," the receptionist whispered. "Us girls here on The Sled, we're pulling for you."

"Thank you." A slight wave of anxiety released itself as Montly took the cup. She drank deeply. The cup smelled of finger- and toenails, but the taste of the water overpowered that. It must have been filtered at least twice, as it wasn't salty at all. They had such luxuries here on the Sled, nothing like living out in the Skin-Land with the Herd, Montly thought.

"He's usually late. He likes to make people sit and sweat it out," said the receptionist.

"Yeah, well, it's working," Montly replied.

The receptionist strode back to her desk with the toothy stilettos grinding. "So, you command part of the Herd? That's what I was told."

"I do," Montly said with guarded confidence. She rolled her muscled shoulders back, cracking her spine in a few sore places. The couch had become almost too soft for her, the fat pockets molding too willingly to her body.

"I can't imagine being out there again," the receptionist continued. "It was so long ago for me, but it still makes me shudder." A fearful tone soaked her words. "I got out of the Herd as fast as I could. Up here on the Sled, you just have so many more opportunities, and well, the food's much better." She let out a giggle.

Montly just smiled with a half curl to her lips, counting the long moments between this conversation and her interview.

"I'm actually going to be leaving this position soon to be an assistant for one of the Daughters," the receptionist continued. "I have a friend who is going to get me in. She says I'm sure for it because of my work here, and because I have the right look. Then I'll be invited to all of the dinners, probably meet the Devil..."

Montly had trouble paying attention to what she was saying, distracted by the receptionist's "right look." She had a soft, perfectly skin-stretched face, the work of an expert engineer, no doubt. It was puffed with creamy fat in all the right places, and anchored with cultured bone spurs. But Montly could catch even the tiniest of imperfections in a person, and she could see one such detail clearly in the receptionist. Hidden beneath all of the confidence and the clothes, just below the personality she tried so hard to project, lay a deep fear. Montly realized she could almost see the remnants of a capital H depressed into the receptionist's forehead.

Of course, "Sin follows, it does not lead," Montly thought. It was part of an ancient saying she'd repeated to her Broken slaves in the Herd many times before. Funny how relevant it was here amongst the "civilized" people on the Sled.

A fast, hollow tapping started. It seemed to be coming from behind the reception desk, born from some mechanism beneath the floor, Montly guessed.

"He's ready for you now," the receptionist said.

Montly rose from the couch, straightened her overcoat, and rolled her shoulders back once more to crack her spine.

"Good luck."

"Thank you." Montly walked into the office, her moccasins not making a sound on the tile.

A man sat behind a polished bone-carved desk that made the finest alabaster look cheap. He was writing something as Montly entered, scribbling furiously with a thin blood quill onto stark white-skin parchment. She'd never seen paper of such quality before, with not a tear or wrinkle on it.

"Please, take a seat," the man said without looking up at her, and Montly sat.

This chair was decidedly less comfortable than the couch. The carved backing seemed to curve against her spine, and a large, oval disk sat where the left arm of the chair should be. The disk had a lip around its perimeter made of braided vein, dried to a deep purple-blue. Montly had seen this type of braid before; it was used to make things blood-tight, to corral liquids into any given direction. *Strange it's on this armchair,* she thought. *Everything here seems to be for show, not for purpose like the Herd . . .*

"Good day, Theta-Lopex." Montly used the formal salutation out of respect. "Thank you for seeing me."

"Lopex will be fine. No one in this office uses full titles." He broke himself from his writing, pulled another sheet of dried-skin parchment from a pile off to the side, referenced it, and looked at Montly.

"So, you come highly recommended from your colleagues on the Herd Drive Cantavit. Both the starboard and portside crews have nothing but great things to say about you. What side do you command again?" Lopex asked.

"Starboard, sir," Montly responded.

"Is there any difference between the port and starboard Herds?"

"Well, sir," Montly started. "It seems over the past three years or so, the starboard side has had a bit more terrain to deal with. We encounter Arm Forests every six months or so, and they can be a challenge because we have to keep up with the port side no matter what."

"So, what do you do to keep up with them?" Lopex asked.

"I personally take a party forward and hack through any forest. We take the body parts back to repair our Broken and drive the Herd through it. We don't miss a step, sir." Montly smiled, proud of her achievement, and happy she had the chance to mention that.

"Impressive. I can still remember my days pulling the Sled. Well, it was *much* smaller back then, but it makes you tough being out there. . . . I'll never forget those days."

Montly noticed him reminiscing, fondly it seemed. It

made her feel good, warm, like she might belong here on the Sled. Sometimes she felt looked down upon because she lived and worked out in the open, sleeping under fat green clouds, eating thick bowls of grist with the herd of Broken slaves.

"Let me explain the job, then," Lopex continued. "You are interviewing to be the Sapien Master for the upcoming mandatum out into the Skin-Land Vast. I am the Assistant Praefectus and, as such, the Sapien Master falls under me. This mandatum has been commissioned with thirty Sapiens, not the largest detachment I've had the pleasure of working with, but large."

Lopex paused, picked up a keratin nail-cup, and took a drink before continuing. "As I am sure you know, Sapiens require much work to be kept in good order. They are not like the Broken you care for in the Herd. These are highly complex meat-machines. That's where you come in."

Montly was listening as best she could, fighting the part of her that wanted to drift off into fantasy and imagine driving a group of perfectly honed Sapiens across a deeply tanned plain of rippling skin.

"You will be responsible for all Sapien maintenance and their inevitable repair. Now, explain to me why you think you're qualified for this position."

Montly sat up straight in the uncomfortable chair, looked Lopex confidently in his two perfectly spaced eyes, shook the nerves from her body, and began.

"In the Herd, sir, we do repairs all the time. When the Broken come in, they are rarely in shape to pull the Sled. Many have snapped arms, legs, muscle rips—and none are mentally prepared for their time here. We fix them up, coach them, and reshape their hands to make it easier and more comfortable for them to push on their yokes. I developed a technique where we puncture the wrists with two pieces of bone to create a crossbar." She illustrated the perpendicular format with her hands. "Then we tie the ends of the crossbar to the yoke with vein rope. This is a guide for the Broken so they keep their hands in the right position. They slip less, we get better power, but most importantly, there are fewer injuries." Montly allowed a tight, controlled smile, and a wave of confidence warmed her.

"That is impressive. I have overheard the crews speak of these things. You created that crossbar technique?" Lopex asked, almost to remind himself of the fact, and scribbled it down on the parchment before him.

"The Skin-Land Vast is not like here," he continued. "There is no order like you are used to in the Herd. It's open, dangerous. We don't know what we'll encounter. We make our rules as we go, improvise constantly, and of course, there's the risk . . ."

"Oh, I understand, sir," Montly replied. "Not to understate the dangers of the Skin-Land Vast, but in the Herd we improvise all the time. We don't have the luxuries and resources that you do . . ." She caught herself hearing the insult leave her lips. "I mean, I know that you work hard as well, and that different jobs require different things, like—"

"Just stop, Montly, just stop," Lopex chuckled. "I know it seems like we have everything here." He gazed around his office. "Honestly, I hate it. I prefer to be out in the Vast. Mapping it, taming it, exploring it. I take no offense." Lopex smiled, made a quick note, then put his quill down. "You know who the Praefectus for this Mandatum is, correct?"

"The Delta . . . I mean, Delta-Delius," Montly corrected herself.

"That's fine, that's fine. You can say The Delta to me, but he prefers Delius. Do you know why they call him The Delta?"

"Because he's the last one." She answered with no hesitation.

"Yes, he is the last one. The last Demon from the fabled Delta class. He doesn't need a class surname, because there are no others left. Everyone knows who he is. Do you know your history, Montly? Do you know the legend of the Deltas?"

"Some, sir. But only drunk stories and rumors from my fellow Herdsmen."

"I'd think you wouldn't. Everyone off-Sled is so young." Lopex rose from his chair. Montly could see him fully now. Not a tall man, but his tight-fitting, double-breasted jacket with crisp, white bone buttons made him seem taller. He pulled back a small skin flap on the wall, revealing a portal, and looked outside.

"The Delta is my mentor. I've known him for a century. He dragged me from the belly of the Sled when I was a stupid young Meat Mender hacking away at whatever they put in front of me." He paused and turned from the window to face Montly. "He saw something in me, something more than a dim soul trying to wish his way out of Hell. He saw that I could be something else, something more." Lopex sat. "Can you be something more? Or are you just a century-and-a-half-old shepherd looking to get out of the Herd? Maybe one tour on the Skin-Land, then spend the rest of your days in the luxury of the Sled?"

Montly breathed deeply, feeling the seriousness of the question.

"I too want to be something more, sir," she said. "I don't want titles, or spoils, or comfort, or the dinners. I don't want to be like your receptionist. I just want a chance. A chance to be something more than I am, a chance to learn, to be mentored like the Delta mentored you. It's all I think about. It's all I want, sir."

"Not like my receptionist?" Lopex inquired. "What do you mean by that?"

"I'm sorry, sir. I didn't mean insult to her. She was nice to me . . . she . . ."

"Stop, stop. Now tell me. Hold nothing back."

"Well, she is Hubris, isn't she?" Montly asked.

"Hubris? How do you mean?"

"Her sin, sir. It's Hubris, right?"

"How could you possibly know that?" Lopex said, squinting with interest.

"I can tell, sir. I see Sin Stamps every day in the Herd. I talk to the Broken often. I can guess the sin just by getting to know a person, and by watching them closely."

"How is that?" Lopex asked.

"Well, sir, 'Sin follows, it does not lead.'"

Lopex chuckled to himself.

"So you *do* know your history. We don't hear Alpha Demon quotes around here much anymore. Tell me, what does that mean to you?"

Montly paused, not expecting a question on philosophy.

"You can see what people are through their behavior, through their words. The sin is a trail people leave behind, and if you examine it, you can know a person better. Sin does not lead the sinner, it does not control them. The sinner creates the sin, and the sin follows them." She felt almost embarrassed to be speaking so abstractly.

Lopex stared at Montly for a long minute, and then pulled open a drawer on his desk.

"Do you know what this is?" He showed Montly two smooth bowls—one with a hole in the bottom, a small bone frame to hold them, and a skin-bag filled with something.

"I do not, sir."

"It keeps moments."

Lopex set up the frame and placed the thinly carved bowls into it, one suspended above the other. Then he filled the top bowl with the contents of the bag: finely ground bone dust stained lightly with green bile. The dust filled the top bowl almost to the brim, and a small bone-cork at the bottom kept it from flowing out into the bottom bowl.

"In front of you, you'll see a knob on the desk. Pull it open."

Montly pulled, and a wide, shallow drawer opened. A thin parchment of skin covered the inside, obscuring what lay beneath. Montly stared at it, confused.

"Take off the parchment," Lopex said.

Montly pulled the delicate sheet off the top of the drawer, exposing a collection of technique tools. There were bone scalpels in shapes and sizes she'd never seen, dried vein ropes, sutures with ligament countersprings for clamping, and even crushed bone powder for blood clotting. It was the most exquisite set Montly had ever seen.

"Sir? Do you want me to repair something for you?" Montly asked, trying to act less confused than she was.

"I do, Montly. Place your left arm on the bone plate beside you." Lopex popped out the cork, and a ribbon of green-stained bone sand began to flow, counting seconds. "Remove your left arm from below the elbow, hold it up with your right arm, and then reattach it to its full functionality before this time runs out."

Montly froze. Knowing there could be no argument against

his request, her mind sifted through emotion, logic, and expert surgical technique. She projected herself into the future and envisioned holding her left arm up in the air, perfectly removed, then setting to the task of reattaching it. Montly picked up a heavy, razor-sharp bone-saw and stared at her arm.

Hope has no lungs, yet it breathes. Hope has no heart, yet it beats. Hope has no legs, yet it travels. Hope has no mind, yet it knows all, she chanted to herself in her mind. She relaxed and took one more breath, the electrical synapses in her arms lessening to rhythmic, controlled pulses as her brain slowed to long-wave thought patterns where time seemed to extend.

Montly took the saw and ran a smooth, deep cut just below her elbow, meeting hard, crisp bone. Then she leaned fiercely into the blade with all of her weight.

CHAP+ER THREE

Passage into the afterlife is a rapid, often violent, transport of your physical/mental remains. You will travel naked, as the only items that can pass through the threshold are your physical body, as well as any physical manifestations within it. This transfer will not allow any additions you may have made to your body, including items as benign as tooth fillings and tattoos, or as substantial as breast implants and prosthetics. Any food within your digestive system will be conveyed with you, along with any subsequent bacteria within your intestines. These bacteria represent themselves most impressively in Hell, as they are responsible for the production of methane and other such gasses (see Chapter – Bacteria and Their Uses).

—From "Your Body and How It Has Changed"
By Doctorem Delta-Lindicus

Silton's apartment smelled of spent gunpowder and flesh. A piece of his heart ventricle smoldered gently on the floor, wafting up like burnt barbecue. There wasn't much pain, he thought. Just a tingling throughout his body and the feeling like he'd lost weight. His brain sent a twitch down to his right hand, and his trigger finger pulled again, and again. Disciplined military redundancy even in death.

A feeling of lightness covered his arms and legs as if balloons were tied to all of his joints. He choked a bit on what seemed like nothing, but then spit up some blood. This didn't repulse him at all; he didn't feel queasy, or scared, or panicked. He actually felt the most peace he'd known in recent memory. Maybe this was the last gift he'd be given: an easy moment he could have all to himself.

The lightness started to take over, and away he went. It didn't feel like rising. Instead, his stomach pinched in on him like free fall. The feeling went away after a few seconds as he accelerated, and Silton couldn't help thinking he was traveling in the wrong direction.

His vision went dark quickly, out into some deep, empty place, like the endless stretch of a black highway. Silton floated along completely naked, a realization that under any other circumstances would have preoccupied him, but in the moment, was of minor importance.

He felt another strong tug, only this one hurt. It came from the small of his back, a few inches inside him. It pulled hard in the opposite direction, and a ripple of pain tightened his muscles as he floated through the dark. Something wrenched hard out of his back, through the muscle, the connective tissue, then the skin. It popped out like it was alive and didn't want to be inside him anymore.

"What the hell!" he screamed out loud as the pain hit. A thin ribbon of blood streamed from his back, and the kinetic motion of the thing leaving spun him into a slow rotation. Silton could see what it was now: a nickel-sized glob of metal glistening behind him, floating away, tumbling in slow motion.

"My God," he said. "The shrapnel..."

Silton had forgotten all about it, like everyone forgets about an injury, only remembering when it hurts. He'd caught that molten piece of metal from an IED during his first tour. It wasn't a bad injury, considering the possibilities. He'd actually been hurt more from the fall off the truck than from the shrapnel itself. But when the surgeon tried to remove the metal, he found it wedged in too deep. It had split through the supple fat around Silton's midsection and nestled into a thick ribbon of muscle called the internal oblique. Two weeks of antibiotics later, and the doctor told him he'd just have to live with it. The piece had come in so hot, his muscle had grown around it like a sheath. As long as it wasn't infected, he'd be fine.

Well, I guess now it really is fine, he thought. *Damn, it hurt more coming out than going in.*

As Silton continued his nude spin, he lost sight of the piece of metal he'd carried for the past ten years. This preoccupied him temporarily, until the ink of his tattoos began to leach out of his body. First the chevrons on both shoulders, then his combat medic caduceus. But what hurt most was the deep, saturated black of his *De Oppresso Liber* sword and arrows ripping out of his chest. The dark ribbons of ink flowed like a river into the blackness, and Silton couldn't escape the feeling that he'd been stripped of himself, stripped of his life.

But he was distracted from his thoughts again as two objects, far-off like massive moons, came into sight. One shone a soft hue of sky blue with a bright white center. It stretched out horizontally into an almond-shaped eye. Silton put his hand up to shield his gaze from the blinding light. The second glowed a misty, dirty, out-of-focus beige that made Silton feel like he had something in his eyes as he looked at it.

As he continued twisting, the beige object became clearer. Silton seemed to be drifting closer to this one. Now it looked as if it had a greenish color he could only describe as smog. He kept twisting, floating along, and deduced that he was sprinting past the blue eye, being pulled closer and closer to the beige moon.

Silton's ears popped back from a deafness he hadn't noticed, and he began to faintly hear the soft echo of screams, awkward screams, like wounded birds tucked in a deep forest. He tried to search them out using the echolocation technique all soldiers learn to spot snipers, and that's when he saw them: people. Dozens of people. All of them floating like he was, toward the beige moon, rotating in awkward orbits with arms and legs flailing. Some even had body parts following behind them like anxious pets chasing down their owners. Some twisted and crashed into each other, like skydivers without parachutes, dotting the black sky with desperate packages of drifting flesh.

"What's happening?" He rotated once more to see the blue, almond-shaped eye drifting away. Behind him he could feel the mass of the beige moon pulling on him faster as his rotation began to increase.

This is not good, Silton thought. He had to stop the spinning. He had to get himself into some predictable body position, so he might assess the situation more clearly. The only way he knew to do this was to manipulate the atmosphere with his body, his arms and legs, so he could have some control. It would be just like his High Altitude jump training days. He'd thought that was fun. But this was decidedly less so.

Silton could feel his rotation becoming more pronounced, and his body stressed as the g-forces increased. He tightened his stomach muscles, fanned out his arms, and kept his legs spread in a V for stabilization. The beige moon loomed much larger now and, as he began to reach the edge of the misty green hue, he could feel it burning. Not a heat-induced burn, like a match or a stovetop. This felt like the faint hint of acid, like his body had been sprayed with a mist of bleach.

His most tender parts got the worst of it. The ten thousand nerve endings per square inch of his manhood didn't respond well at all. Silton almost curled up in a ball from the pain, but he knew that would only get him tumbling faster, so he fought it. Just like he'd fought every ounce of pain that had ever crossed his path.

This might be good, he thought. *A little air for me to work with.*

Within a few seconds, Silton was flying face down, in proper position, stabilized and falling to the surface. He hadn't continued to accelerate to terminal velocity. Instead, the green mist had slowed him down to a rapid float. The burning bleach started to feel more prominent as he fell through huge pockets of gas, a terrible stinging pain, but he found it tolerable. That couldn't be said for the other falling people. As soon as they touched the outskirts of the green mist, their screaming became unhinged—some panting, some losing their voices, some speaking unintelligible words.

Gotta keep your head, Silky, gotta keep your head, he said to himself.

A waft of upward wind, and a much denser section of cloud rushed up to meet him. This slowed him down even further, and his eyes stung badly, burning through his thin eyelids. He pierced through the cloud, and could see the ground below him: a skin-colored desert. Even slowed down as he was, he knew the impact would not bode well for his body.

"Face-first ain't gonna work on this one, Silky!" he screamed to himself out loud, getting a mouthful of the green mist as he spoke. It tasted familiar, with hints of metal and acid, and a sourness that he couldn't place. It burned slightly and activated the taste buds on the backside of his tongue. He salivated hard, and spit drooled out of his mouth as he fell.

What is this place?

Silton started a slow, deliberate somersault, the clouds rushing by thick and fast. He positioned his backside to the ground, with his arms and legs out in crab formation. The beige land closed in, the screams of people off in the distance sounding loud and panicked. And then, with almost musical timing, the screams stopped one at a time as the people impacted the surface, until there was only the sound of air rushing past Silton's ears.

Silton's naked backside hit the ground with a slap that lasted an instant. He heard the loud crack of his right arm snap at the forearm. The ground split open immediately and sucked him into a soupy pool tangled with thick, soft noodles. He didn't try to breathe. Silton was smarter than that. Instead, he stretched out as far as he could to help slow his sink, and immediately oriented himself to the surface. It took a few seconds to stop his momentum, his broken arm not helping, but soon he started swimming up, fighting to the surface. The noodles broke apart in his fingers as he swam—their soft, mushy texture almost making him gag.

He reached up, and with a little scurrying, found his entry point. He'd never been trapped underwater before, but he knew how to find a break-through hole from his training. Silton grabbed the lip of the hole he'd made and pulled himself out. It felt like climbing out of a wet burlap sack.

He kept his right arm protected as he moved toward the surface. He knew what a broken bone felt like; he'd experienced it many times before. The compound fracture felt as if his bone had been twisted like a rubber band. To Silton, the pain was more awkward than agonizing.

Silton tucked his arm in as best he could as he climbed out; part of the bone protruded from the skin, and he didn't want to catch it on anything. His naked body glistened with a clear, viscous film, and tiny tendrils, some red, some blue, tangled up his arms and legs. He ripped them off, spit a wad of clear gelatin from his mouth, and took in a deep, well-deserved breath.

As he inhaled, an unimaginable pain shocked through him. The air burned harsh and low in his lungs, like wasps stinging his insides. He coughed to gain relief, taking in another breath that burned right back down into his lungs. He grabbed for his chest instinctually and felt an odd absence. Silton pulled his hand back, confused. It was covered in blood. His eyes went wide as he looked down, and then he saw it.

Any logical argument that he might have constructed to bring sanity to this situation disappeared.

A perfectly round hole gaped in the middle of his chest. The hole went straight through him and out to the right side of his exposed spinal column. Silton could easily reach through himself if he had the courage, but he didn't. He could see his own lungs trembling from the acrid air; wet, pink sacks inflating and deflating. Just below, he could see the scaffolding of connective tissue that held his stomach and other organs in place, all except for his heart.

Silton begged his mind to break him from this dream, but only felt reality in all of its stark, strange, yet perfect clarity surrounding him. He felt the soft ground underneath, looked at the hole he'd just punched through, and watched a pool of fluid slowly accumulate around him. *Strangely familiar, all of this stuff . . .*

"Skin. It's skin?" he said, in a quiet whisper to himself.

He looked to his hand, where a few of the tangled noodles lay unmolested.

"Veins?" Another question. But his subconscious was far ahead of poor Silton. It had already paged through fable and fiction, myths and mores, truth and fantasy, and figured everything out. It was only that childlike resistance, the inborn instinct to deny the facts for the sake of one's own sanity, that kept Silton from acknowledging what this place was.

"My God . . . this is it? This is it?"

He could resist the shock no more, and he let it settle over him like a warm blanket. His mind shut everything else out and desperately tried to help him reconcile with this new certainty.

CHAP+ER F⊕UR

After The Great Fall, Hell was thrust into chaos, forcing the Devil to travel the Skin-Land Vast for eternity. As time passed, Satan employed the secrets he'd learned in the bowels of Hell to repurpose the human body to his will. During this time, the iterations of the Devil's constantly moving home improved. The most recent, largest, and most evolved iteration is the massive city-structure called "The Sled."

—From "A History of Hell"
By Delta-Holt

The bone-carved dining table stretched across the narrow hall. It was thick like a butcher block, the bone warm to the touch from fresh, hot marrow that flowed into the structure through legs molded to the floor. It stood, sharp and silent, a massive, pristine sculpture that looked finer than the cleanest white marble.

The chef hurriedly set the warm table with food: spongy blood cakes accented with beads of bright green bile, a massive hindquarter muscle steak, heaps of tangled capillary pasta, and hot, fat-gravy spiced to perfection with sweat salt. For dessert he'd constructed a delicate confection: tiny lollipops of caramelized brain set atop thin bone stilts.

The chef wiped up a few red droplets from the stark bone table. Like all good chefs, he obsessed over the parts of his work that no one else would ever notice.

"That should do it." He motioned to his Sapien. "Bring the centerpiece!"

The Sapien walked to the kitchen robotically and brought back a hairless human head, immaculate and smooth. Glazed lightly with fat, every facet of the head's mouth, ears, and nose glistened. A masterful patchwork of skin covered the centerpiece, all the way down to the stubby neck. Only the most discerning eye could see that some of the skin-sections were stitched from different tones.

The chef instructed the Sapien to put the head down in the center of the table.

"Ahhhhhh... beau-tee-ful..." the Sapien said in monotone.

"Yes, yes, I know. But you have yet to see its true beauty, my stupid friend," the chef said excitedly. He pulled two tools from his jacket: a pair of thin, bone pliers hinged with springy tendons, and a bone scalpel so sharp its blade could barely be seen when held to the side.

The chef set to work, attaching veins and arteries to a tender quarter-heart he'd assembled, sealing everything up with gummy, sinew putty. The heart consisted of just one ventricle, and was only strong enough to pump a small reservoir of blood into the head, giving it the strength needed for its performance.

"It took me three weeks to procure this tiny quarter-heart. Did you know that?"

"Three weeks," the Sapien responded. "Hearts... not... find... easy..."

"Not find easy at all," said the chef as he wiped flecks of dried skin from his centerpiece. "A true masterpiece worthy of a great hero."

And the feast was set.

Soon after, the guests began to enter. First to arrive were three Master Engineers, all from Demon Design. They took their seats in large, formal wingback chairs skillfully upholstered in moist, red muscle fibers. They were a boisterous and eclectic bunch. The fattest of them chose to wear no pants, just a skin poncho with a large horizontal pocket on the front. The other, rail thin and wiry, wore a welder's cape and bib made of thick hide, much tougher than the supple stuff most Demons wore. And the final engineer, of medium build, had no ears, just two holes in the sides of his head with bone spurs at four points around them.

"A beautiful head, Chef," the fat engineer said as they all sat. "We were wondering what you were up to down on the Engineering Floor, sneaking around, scavenging through our leftovers."

"Yes, thank you," the chef said. "I think you will be very impressed with what I have created for you tonight."

"Enough, enough! We arrived early for the drink, not the decorations!" said the wiry engineer. "Tell us, Chef. What wine do you have for us tonight?"

"Of course." The chef glared at his Sapien standing motionless in the corner. On cue, the Sapien left for the kitchen and returned with a fat bladder of wine.

"I made this fifteen years ago, from an untouched blood pond one of the Cantavits found. They graciously gave it to me." He began to pour the wine into their glasses. "You will notice I added only a small amount of bile to balance the sweetness of the blood. Then I used a sixty-five-year-old bacterium and let it ferment in a special cask lined with the most virgin colon I could find."

The chef finished the pours. "Now, I did add a special ingredient at the end. Let me see if our Master Engineers can tell what it is."

The three smiled and picked up their ornate, bone-stemmed glasses. The wiry one downed his glass in an instant.

"Well, whatever you added, it's not enough! More wine!" he said, and laughed hard and loud, joined by the engineer with no ears who also drank his wine without regard. But the fat engineer drank carefully. He sniffed the wine, sipped slowly, and explored it with his tongue.

"It has a bit of a sting to the finish. What is that? I can't quite place it," the fat engineer said.

The chef smiled, happy to see that he had stumped them. "Adrenal," he said proudly.

The engineers looked at each other, impressed. The fat one spoke.

"I've never heard of adrenal in blood wine. It is truly excellent." He rose his glass to the chef, followed by the other two.

"Now, fill up these damn glasses! We didn't come early for the conversation, either!" the wiry engineer said. The group followed in laughter, and the wine bladder filled their milky keratin glasses.

A large, intimidating Demon entered next, and with a look, he snapped the jovial conversation apart like brittle bone.

Before them stood Zeta-Zaavan, seven feet tall, with layers

upon layers of exposed muscle fiber covering his arms, shoulders, and legs. He wore a tumor breastplate coated in thick, black paste, along with a matching hide tunic laced with bone chips surrounding his waist. But his wings were the most imposing part of his appearance. Even when tucked neatly behind him, they rose a foot over his head. Colored in the most delicate shade of beige, and supple like a baby's skin, when outstretched they'd touch both sides of the hall with ease.

Zaavan sat silent in the unwavering air of intimidation that followed him, observing the displayed food.

"One of your finest meals, Chef," Zaavan said.

"Thank you, Zeta-Zaavan. It's not every day I have the chance to make a farewell feast for Delius, the last of the Deltas."

Zaavan smiled with disdain. *Always this last of the Deltas,* he thought, sick and jealous of the attention Delius still commanded after all these centuries. Zaavan thought of Delius as an old, outdated construct, more reputation than action, an antique that needed to be thrown away.

"So, Zaavan," the wiry engineer said, now under the care of the blood wine. "I hear you had the Acid Sacs installed some time ago. I helped design them. What do you think of them so far?"

Zaavan drank heavily from the cup the chef poured him, smiled at the engineer, and exhaled. A soft greenish mist emanated from Zaavan's mouth in a tight cone. The cloud was so dense, it hung easily around the glass, almost clinging to it. In mere seconds the glass folded in, melting as if being tossed into a fire. Wine spilt over his hand and down onto the pristine white table.

"A better design your team has never made," Zaavan said as a rolling pocket of green mist lolled in his mouth.

The engineers congratulated themselves, and looked at Zaavan in gleeful awe.

"Chef, I will need another glass," Zaavan said, and tossed the liquefied remnants on the table, marring the stark perfection the chef had created.

The group looked up as Lopex entered, elegant as always. He sighed noticeably, seeing that Zaavan had already arrived.

"Well, if it isn't the prodigal son, Lopex. Of course, you're early to your master's farewell dinner," Zaavan said.

"Good evening, Zaavan." Lopex swept his coat beneath him to sit opposite Zaavan at the table.

"I'm actually glad you're early. We never get the chance to talk. You've not taken my advice, I see," Zaavan baited.

"Advice? What advice is that?" Lopex asked.

"Well, to get your legs extended, of course. So you can be as tall as a *real* Demon. I'm sure my recommendation to these fine engineers would be taken seriously. I'd like to do that for you, help you in your desperate need." Zaavan chuckled to himself as the chef poured him another glass of blood wine.

"As always, your charity knows no bounds, Zaavan, but I am fine the way I am. Thank you." Sarcasm fell over the conversation like the sallow light shining from the tallow torches.

"I jest, Lopex. Seriously, though, have you had the chance to speak to Chalt, my candidate for the Sapien Master for our upcoming Cantavit? What did you think of her? You know she did very well during her Demon Trials. This would be a great stepping stone for her."

"I did speak to her for some time. She represented herself well," Lopex said.

"And . . . did you give her the position?" Zaavan asked.

"I've decided to go in another direction. Sorry." Lopex

perused the dinner, trying to escape the conversation.

Zaavan took another sip of wine, never breaking eye contact with Lopex.

"Another direction? And what direction is that?" He slapped the delicate glass down.

"Well, I don't see the Sapien Master job as a 'stepping stone.' I need someone who is planning on staying in the position for some time. There is much to learn with managing Sapiens in the Skin-Land Vast. There is no utility in having someone on for just one Cantavit. We need someone who will be in the job for decades, someone who can train others." Lopex took a false drink from his wine glass. "I wouldn't worry too much about it, Zaavan. Your candidate will no doubt find another position here on the Sled that will set her up perfectly for whatever she wants to do next. Besides, herding Sapiens out in the Vast is dangerous work. It'd be a tragedy if something happened to your pupil, would it not?"

Zaavan held himself at the brink of his control. The meat of his wings flexed on his shoulders, as did the pinching Acid Sacs in his lungs. But he pulled back the temptation to jump across the table, and instead finished his wine with one swallow.

"Yes, you're right, *young* Eta-Lopex, the Vast *is* dangerous. It would be quite a tragedy if *anything* happened."

The fat engineer, boisterous and drunk, interjected.

"So, then, your Acid Sacs have been holding up well? You know we're thinking about making them standard issue for the next Demon Class?"

Zaavan smiled and looked to the three Master Engineers.

"They *are* working perfectly. Better than I could have ever imagined. In fact, I could raise a cloud so dense it could melt someone right across the table from me." He held his glass up to the engineers, settled his gaze on Lopex, and smiled.

The engineers, oblivious to the taunt, drank to their shared accomplishment, as the wiry one started into a drunken rant, detailing the challenges of acid sac design.

Lopex counted long, uncomfortable moments, waiting for his mentor to arrive.

Delius entered the hall quietly and without fanfare. The engineers immediately rose from their seats and clamored around him like children to a parent they'd not seen for some time. They showered him with compliments and questions so rapidly that Delius couldn't answer them all. The engineers examined his exquisite form: seven feet tall, as wide as the dining chairs, with two hunched muscle bands that started at his shoulders and traveled down his back like a thick red cape split down the center.

Delius smiled at Lopex and immediately went to the chair next to him. Lopex pulled it out, more reaction than respect, and Delius squeezed himself into it.

"Can't anyone in the Engineering Guild build us bigger chairs?" Delius said, and silence fell over the engineers, as they froze in mid-drink.

Delius shifted into the seat, settling into comfort. "Well, maybe I don't mind this so much. It makes me feel big, like a Drum Sapien!"

The engineers cheered in laughter at the apparent joke, the fat one wiping a bead of sweat away from his nervous brow.

"Does the chair also make you feel as stupid as a Drum Sapien, dear Delius?" Zaavan said with snide contempt.

"Good evening, Zaavan," Delius replied with a smile. He'd heard the taunt, but let it roll off him with ease. "As you know, intelligence is not the greatest strength of the Sapien. It's loyalty. Loyalty is what makes the Sapiens so valuable, and what binds Demons together. Without loyalty, we are just like the Unbroken men and women the Devil charges us to harvest. You might think of taking that lesson from the next Sapien you meet."

Silence, broken only by Lopex's stifled laughter, drifted across the table.

"Here! Here!" the wiry engineer cheered, and everyone at the table raised their glasses. Lopex raised his as well, smiling at Zaavan's defeat. This time, Lopex did not take a false drink. Instead, he drank full and long, tasting the sweet blood wine along with Zaavan's humiliation.

Zaavan did not touch his glass. He stared at Delius, who ignored him with indifference.

The room filled with a few dozen more guests. Amongst the most distinguished were the lead Watcher, the Praefectus of the Herd, and a few representatives from the Repository. Everyone paid their respects to Delius, some with a knowing nod, others with hugs and handshakes. Soon there were only three chairs left: two for the Daughters of the Devil, and the head chair at the table, reserved for the Devil himself.

The Praefectus of the Herd, Theta-Shelle, a well-appointed and frighteningly acute woman, sat at Delius's other side. She leaned over and whispered to him.

"Do you think he will come to this one?" she asked.

"It doesn't matter," Delius responded quietly.

"How can you say that? You are the last Delta, and this is your last Cantavit. Don't you think he realizes that? Don't you think that's worthy of an appearance for once? For everything the Delta Class has done for him?" Theta-Shelle reasoned.

"Shelle, you're too kind. But that was a long time ago.

Everyone here only knows those days as stories told in the corners of the Sled."

"Delius, but—" Shelle interrupted, with a tint of disdain in her voice.

"*Old, old,* stories Shelle," Delius countered her interruption. "It is time for new stories. There is little place here for me now."

Reluctantly, Shelle held back a response, and drank her blood wine quickly, trying to forget what Delius just said. Instead, she joined the raucous conversations of the Master Engineers.

Lopex saw a natural break in the onslaught of attention given to Delius and took his opportunity to share a quiet word.

"I have completed all of my interviews, and I am fixed on who I want for Sapien Master."

"Good, good. What did you decide?"

"Do you remember Montly? The Watchers recommended her. She works under Theta-Shelle on the Herd." Lopex nodded to Shelle.

"Very nice. I am sure that anyone who works under Shelle will make a fine addition to our Cantavit," Delius said.

"Exactly. So, I've decided to go with her. She's young, only about a hundred and fifty, but she's spent all of her time off-Sled in the Herd."

"That's not a short time in the Herd. How is she? Mentally?" Delius asked.

"Very well adjusted. Montly has a quiet, humble sense to her. She is more than capable of learning the Sapien ways, and she has this quality. It's strange."

"What quality? Explain it to me," Delius said, and sipped from his glass.

"She, well . . ." Lopex was careful to find the right words.

"Montly has this ability in her. When we were talking, she was very enthusiastic, very forthcoming with the fact that she wanted this opportunity. I pressed her of course, trying to uncover if she was using us to get herself onto the Sled. And she said something strange."

"Strange?" Delius asked.

"She said that she wasn't like my receptionist, that she didn't care for the 'luxuries' here on the Sled," Lopex said.

"What's so strange about that? From what I remember, your receptionist enjoys luxury quite a bit. I don't follow," Delius pressed.

"It was what Montly said next. 'Sin follows, it does not lead.'"

"An old Alpha quote?" Delius asked. "I'm shocked anyone so young would even know of that."

"That's not all. When I pushed her on the issue of my receptionist, Montly assessed her."

"She *assessed* her? Right there in the office?" Delius said in disbelief.

"Not in the literal sense, but she said that it was clear my receptionist's sin was Hubris. She just spit it out, like it was a fact, like it was obvious."

"And I am to assume she was correct?" Delius asked.

"Yes. Her sin stamp has long been removed, but I remember when I recruited her from the Herd. Her sin was hubris."

Delius sat back in the muscle-winged chair, his massive haunches flexing behind him.

Lopex asked in earnest, "How could she know that without a full, true assessment with a Demon Stem?"

Delius paused and toyed with his glass, then looked at Lopex.

"It is called empathy, my friend. It rarely survives here over time. In the early days, before all of this . . ." Delius gestured up to the rib cage cathedral ceiling of the hall. "In the early days, we only had guesses as to what this place was and how it worked. Empathy, the way of understanding another through speaking to them, through understanding them, was all we had to know a person. This was long before we could puncture the Unbroken brain with a Demon Stem."

"Empathy?" Lopex repeated softly.

"Search deeply, your first life-memories. We all had empathy once. It used to be much more important here in Hell. But now, there seems no use for it."

The door to the hall opened once more, interrupting all conversation. In walked a pair of perfectly mirrored twins. They walked in unison, step for step around opposite sides of the long table. Each wore a black-skinned robe barely covering their womanly virtues. Their collarbones jutted out like sharply defined bridges from shoulder to shoulder. Embedded into the bone bridges were polished jewels of fat, molar teeth. Each tooth jewel reflected a different color: one, a yellow-green stained with sour bile, the next, a deep red no doubt kept in a blood jar, and in the center of their collar bones, a pristine, natural white tooth reflecting every ray of light from the smoldering tallow torches on the walls.

"Welcome," they said in unison, and sat down at the two seats next to the head chair at the dining table.

One of the women broke into speech alone.

"We are sorry that he could not attend this wonderful dinner tonight. He sends his glory to all of you, especially the ones leaving on the Cantavit tomorrow. And to Delius, as this will be your final journey into the Skin-Land Vast—"

The next twin picked up the speech, not pausing for even a moment after her counterpart finished.

"—he wishes to thank you personally for your intrepid service to him. He hopes that when you return to the Sled, you will find a gentle eternity with your fellow brothers and sisters." The twin daughters lifted their glasses in mirrored fashion and started their toast, speaking as one.

"To Delta-Delius. May no one forget the sacrifices of your class, may no Demon ever pay the price that your class has paid, and may no days be seen like the days burdened on you."

An honest cheer preceded the clinking of all glasses. The twins' words rang with a depth, a poignancy that made this a time for celebration and remembrance.

The chef, seeing the need for mood lightening, responded quickly.

"I have a surprise for all of you!" he said, and galloped to the center of the table.

"Please, our dinner is getting cold!" said Zaavan, and a few spots of laughter spouted from the silence.

"A few more seconds, a few more seconds. The marrow runs hot through the table. Have no concern, your food will be perfect!" said the chef.

The chef double-checked a few valves and veins. Then, with deep concern and attention, he gently massaged the tiny quarter-heart. A moment passed, and all eyes sat on the glistening albino head perched in the center of the table.

The centerpiece twitched, the eyes fluttered, and in an instant it came alive and spoke.

"Tonight, we honor you, the last member of the famed Deltas, the fourth Corps of Hell, Makers of the ancient Blood Palace, and Rescuers of the Devil from the Great Fall. As you go forth into the Skin-Land Vast, we wish you safety and lavish human treasure that you may bring into the Devil's warm fold."

The dinner erupted in applause and awe at the decapitated head's speech; all were amazed and entertained. The guest clamored over the food, and spoke generously of Delius and his accomplishments. It was a glorious celebration for everyone.

All except for one guest. Zaavan sat in silent resentment, secretly hating the Delta-Delius. Camouflaged within the reverie of the dinner, the Demon carefully plotted a coup that would satisfy his envy.

CHAPTER FIVE

If you have the fortitude to withstand intense pain and self-mutilation, there are a great many options that will allow you to not only repair yourself, but also gain an advantage in Hell. Only your creativity and resources will limit you.

—From "Your Body and How It Has Changed"
By Doctorem Delta-Lindicus

Silton sat on the warm ground. The bone protruding from his arm gave up a few specks of jellied marrow, and the skin around the wound flowed easy with blood. He'd done a decent job of ignoring his chest, but it was becoming more difficult. Silton could hear air leaking out of the bottom of his right lung every time he breathed. It sounded like a broken harmonica.

He held his arm up above his heart, just like his Combat Medic training told him to do. He wondered if the absence of this organ mattered, if a magic here somehow kept him alive, or if this missing heart was just a hallucination. Soon the blood from his arm began to pour out of the hole in his chest, and he realized his training might not be entirely relevant in this case. He put his arm back down, thinking it best to try and conserve the blood still left inside him.

Breathing held the most immediate pain. The sharpness of the air was inescapable, and the green haze created a subtle burn that never stopped. It seemed to agitate his internal wounds and fry the flesh of his exposed lungs. He could hear the sizzling within him, and thought he could almost smell himself cooking.

His arm seemed to be the priority. The Combat Medic in him reasoned that he would be better equipped to fix the rest of his body if he had two working hands, or at worst, one and a half. Besides, the hole in his chest, although the most disturbing injury, didn't appear to be having any immediate effects on his functioning.

Although naked, at least Silton was warm. It seemed like the heat rose up from the ground, a sticky wet heat, but heat nonetheless. He could only describe his surroundings as a desert of skin: flat, beige, with white and black patches throughout. He could see some terrain in the distance that looked like stumps or small trees. But he couldn't try for that with an exposed forearm bone. His resources were nil, and only the hole he'd created on landing looked like a promising place to find anything other than skin. Silton crawled back over to the hole with his broken arm cradled in the most careful position he could marshal.

As he approached the opening, his weight depressed the edge of the skin and forced out an ooze of liquid fat and thick red fluid. He peeled back the lip of the hole so he could see inside. Beneath him lay what looked like a tangle of thin, purple and red ropes. Beneath that, the fluid became a deeper red. Silton reached in, careful not to pinch the bone of his broken arm, grasped some of the stuff, and pulled. Most of the tiny strands dissolved in his hands, but some of the stronger ones held, and he yanked on a mass that came out like a knot. He turned over to gain more leverage and pulled the ganglion toward him. Silton sat up and observed his find. He couldn't rationalize what was in his hands. There was no explanation, but there was also no denying it. Silton held a thick knot of veins.

A few of the veins broke from his pulling and leaked blood onto the skin as they collapsed. Silton fingered through the knot, noticing that these veins were quite strong, and tried to find a length that would be useful to hold his bone in place. He pulled a yard of clean vein up to his mouth and bit down on it, cutting the length from its mass. It tasted like iron, a fresh, bloody taste. Holding the end of the vein pinched in his jaw, Silton took the rest of the strip and wrapped it around the exposed bone, making a loop. A few more loops, and he had enough leverage.

He pulled up with his neck, down with his hand, and the bone began to move back into his arm. The pain burned through his body like a blowtorch put to his nerves. Silton broke into a sweat, fighting back screams. The bone popped back into his arm—not exactly where it needed to be, but close.

That will have to do, he thought.

Silton captured the slack on the loops and made them tight. Almost immediately, he noticed some movement in his hand. Even in this shoddy fashion, as soon as he realigned the muscle and bone structure, his right arm seemed to work again. He knew this shouldn't be the case. Normally, the shock of such a break would prevent the lower extremity from being functional.

Silton put that thought aside and went to find something to cover the wound. Milky pus and blood flowed down his arm where the bone had ripped through, and this wouldn't stop on its own.

He reached down to the skin-lip he'd punctured through and yanked. The skin ripped up like a swatch of sod, and he separated it from the rest, flapping it over on the ground. The backside of skin-lip was covered in a spiny tangle of purple threads. He recognized these as capillaries, weaker, thinner veins made to feed skin and other tissues with blood.

Silton cleaned off the bottom, scooping away capillaries and fat until it was bare skin. Using the skin like casting tape, Silton wrapped his forearm carefully, encasing the vein rope that held his bone in place. The skin stuck easily as he wrapped it around his right forearm. He pressed the wrap, feeling the jagged bone pieces inside him grind together. It sent a shock that threw his head back and produced a muffled scream. He took a few more strands of vein and wrapped the ends and middle of the cast as reinforcement. A little blood and pus leaked from his work. Silton couldn't tell if this was from him or the skin he'd just ripped up from the ground.

He took a deep breath and prepared to stand. Again, the air stung deep and low in his chest, stirring up a small coughing fit. Spit and fluid flew from his mouth, and he could see the same fluid eject from the bottom of his punctured lung. The spit tasted like the air: putrid and potent. Like a weak acid, it tweaked the buds on his tongue, and he filled his mouth with saliva to dilute the sour taste.

Silton stood for the first time since the break, careful to hold his wounded arm close to his core. The surface beneath him stretched like a taut trampoline as he put his weight on it.

Silton assessed his situation: broken arm, naked, no resources other than this mass of flesh he stood on.

What have I done? Killed myself to escape that life I thought was so terrible, only to be in this place?

Silton walked slowly and deliberately across the springy skin. His arm ached with every step, the bones inside grinding against their irregular counterparts. He imagined bone chips floating through his forearm, lodging into the underside of his skin, nestling in like grubs.

Silton had brought a few more cords of the vein rope with him in case the bandage fell loose, but he didn't think he'd need them. His wrapping started to feel tighter, not looser. It wasn't uncomfortable, but appropriately snug. Even the vein rope he'd used to secure his bone felt taut, and the reclaimed skin appeared to be hardening to his arm like a leathery cast.

Soon, Silton had full command of his fingers, his wrist turned as it should, and when he flexed his right bicep, the reinforcement of the bandage protected the movement. Unfortunately, this did nothing for the pain, and the sharp aching hindered his every step.

Silton surveyed the landscape. From what he could tell, it was midday moving to evening. The sky looked opaque, overcast with the same sickly greenish-yellow he remembered from the fall. He couldn't see the sun, and deep down he suspected it might not be there.

But the others. The people he had watched screaming and tumbling. *Where were they? They must be close,* he thought. What option did Silton have but to search them out? For what reason, he could not rationalize, other than the need to seek out others who shared in this disaster. Maybe he could even help them too.

Silton walked toward what looked like a tree stump. It only stood a foot-and-a-half high. He thought he saw other stumps in the distance, some grouped together, but the haze made it hard to see anything clearly. Growing nearer, he could see that it wasn't a stump at all; it was an arm sticking out of the ground.

Silton bounded toward the arm, the springy Skin-Land almost assisting him in his gait. As he got closer, his steps depressed the ground, and it wavered like a waterbed. The arm, pocked with pronounced veins and track marks, looked sickly, but came alive as the vibrations of Silton's steps shook the skin. The fingers flexed, the wrist shook back and forth, and underneath the Skin-Land it looked as if the body attached to the arm was writhing.

Silton grabbed the hand, and it gripped him back hard, so hard Silton thought it might pull him over. Silton set his feet, protected his broken arm to the side, and pulled. The ground around his feet pooled with blood and congealed fat as an awful suction sound came from the hole, like a massive birth separating itself from the womb. The sickly arm barely had any muscle to it, and made a poor tool to extricate the body. Soon, though, he could see a head and matted hair appearing near the top of the Skin-Land. He pulled harder with the excitement of progress, but then felt a crack.

A splinter-break in the forearm, he thought. *That's no problem, it should hold.*

A face emerged. A man's face, wet with blood and viscous fluid. The eyes were closed, the mouth open and choking. He vomited as Silton held his arm as still as he could. Fluids ran over the man's mouth and face as he tried to form words. Silton heard the arm crack again, more pronounced this time, the weight of the writhing body too much for the bone's brittle construction.

"Hellllp . . ." the man yelled, his face still covered in fluid. Silton carefully kept the head above the skinline so he could breathe.

"Stay calm! Stay calm!" Silton implored. "Your arm! It's going to break! You need to be still!"

The eyes opened up wide with attention as soon as Silton spoke. The man looked straight into Silton's face, as if he'd heard something familiar. He coughed up the rest of the phlegm and fluid in his lungs.

"You! Youuuuuuuu!" the man screamed. Silton stayed his pulling, trying not to break the fragile arm. "Youuuu!" the man screamed again, and the writhing became panicked, strong, reckless.

Blood and fluid ran off the man's head, and Silton, confused by his screams, kept him up above the skinline as best he could. Minute cracks and skin-slits riddled the man's arms. And then, Silton could see them: the tiny imperfections and lines that make one person's face distinguishable from another.

It was Skinny Chad . . . the meth head.

Silton fell back in shock, his weight snapping Chad's brittle arm at the elbow.

"Youuuuu! You did this! Youuuuu!" Skinny Chad's struggle became more frenzied, twisting back and forth against the broken elbow. Silton had no time to think, to rationalize, to understand why Chad, the meth head from across the street, was here in this horrible dream, but not a dream.

"Why? Why!" Skinny Chad said, pulling away from Silton, back into the hole. The broken elbow, only held together by tendon and skin, began to tear against Silton's strong grip.

"Stop! Stop, Chad, stop!" Silton screamed, hoping he could stay the addict's fury long enough to pull him out.

The skin around the arm and elbow ran white with stress, and Silton felt himself starting to slip on the liquid fat covering the ground. He had to try with one good pull to get Chad out and over the lip. Silton steadied himself as best he could, took in a painful breath, and pulled.

Chad's arm ripped off at the elbow, sending Silton rolling away from the hole. Blood and bits of torn skin scattered from the joint.

Silton dropped the arm and scampered back to the hole. But there was nothing. No sign of Chad. Only the deep tangle of veins, arteries, and ripped skin that formed a dense murk beneath.

Shock washed over him, thick like the blood and fat that covered his body. Silton panted, breathing deeply, not even noticing the coarse air. There were no words. No thoughts he could muster. Just the stark vision of Skinny Chad's needle-ridden arm still alive, still gripping and pulsing on the ground in front of him.

CHAP+ER SIX

A Demon is not some mystical creature separate from man or indigenous to Hell. A Demon was once a person, resigned to his punishment, just like every other person in Hell. What separates Demon from man is the fact that the Demon is a willful participant in Hell. The Demon has no intention or desire to leave Hell; he has succumbed to it and is a part of it. Hell is the Demon's permanent home.

—From "Hell's Inhabitants"
By Doctorem Delta-Lindicus

Zeta-Zaavan sat, waiting silently in his dark office. Only one fat tallow brazier in the corner offered light. But that didn't matter to him; sometimes he felt more at home in the darkness. His office was cramped, a tight square with no architectural character to speak of, no sculpted bone pillars, no bleached skin wallpaper. It didn't even have blood-plumbing. These were things Zaavan could have had, things that would have been given to him for his accomplishments, his position. But no. He, like all Zetas, denied himself such comforts.

As Zaavan sat, he quietly repeated his class mantra.

"A Zeta uses covet to drive him, a Zeta lets covet burn inside him, a Zeta turns covet to hate, and uses hate to fuel the only true lust: the lust for power."

Zaavan sat on his only possession of note, an antique, skin-banded chair with matching footrest. It was made in the much older baroque style, well before the sleek modern upholstery that filled most of the rooms on the Sled. His chair's style was designed to mimic the natural human form. The armrests of the chair were clean, hairless arms with fists clenched at their ends. The back was an open chest cavity with twelve, individually skin-wrapped ribs that gently curved around to form the wings. The legs of the chair were human legs, each one a different color: black, beige-tan, soft yellow, and albino white.

He preferred this old style. It made him feel more at one with his environment, and reminded him of where everything really came from. Not like the modern interpretations that made the Sled look so immaculate, so non-flesh. Even Zaavan's door expressed his philosophy: a gated horizontal network of arms, each made perfectly straight with locked elbow joints. The arm door slowly opened toward Zaavan like a lattice of interwoven fingers, and his Artifex entered, carrying a heavy bucket filled with steaming blood.

"Are you ready for your blood down, Sir Zeta?" the Artifex asked.

"I've been ready," Zaavan responded.

"Of course, sir." He put the bucket down next to the antique chair.

Zaavan's Artifex was an older man, hunched and crippled from his own life-times. He had descended into Hell during the twilight of his life, and amazingly he'd survived the fall, as well as his mandatory time in the Herd. This was why Zaavan had chosen the old man to be his servant; he was a determined specimen, and something of an antique himself. Others in Zaavan's position had younger, skin-sculpted, well-quaffed assistants. Only calcium bone braces and lumps of skin twine held this old man together. One slip, one tear, and he'd fall to the ground in a sack of fluid and shattered bone chips. But the Artifex was obedient, Zaavan could not deny that. The old man acted almost Sapien-like in his attitude. He took whatever abuses Zaavan could deliver.

The Artifex gently placed a piece of porous bone into the bucket of steaming blood and took it dripping to his master's shoulders. He rubbed the exposed muscle braids with care, slow and deliberate, allowing the blood to seep into the deep striations beneath. In response, Zaavan's muscles drank and swelled, returning to a bright red color, plumped back to their intended form. The Artifex continued the blood down, dipping again and again into the bucket, wasting only a few drops as he ferried the bone sponge back and forth to his master's body.

"I heard the dinner was quite impressive," the old Artifex said.

"Quite." Sarcasm draped Zaavan's tone.

"I trust the wine flowed, and the food was no doubt exquisite?"

"No doubt." Zaavan wanted the conversation to end, but the Artifex continued.

"A friend of mine said he ate a piece of leftover blood cake. He said it melted on his tongue . . . delicious." The old Artifex curled his mouth to a toothless smile, fantasizing about the taste.

"And what of it? Is that what you do? Ponder rumors and second-hand stories? Is that how you spend your time? Is that how you plan to spend eternity here? Thinking about what others do? What others taste? Pathetic." Zaavan pushed his Artifex's hand away, disgusted.

"Well, no, Sir Zeta. I don't plan on spending my time that way. I don't plan on spending eternity here, either." The Artifex carefully continued his work.

"Then you are more a fool than you look." Zaavan chuckled to himself. "You will serve me and the Sled until you aren't worth repairing anymore. And then one day, when your joints are ground down to dust, you'll be tossed overboard like the rest. You'll sink down into the thick bowels of Hell to dissolve into the meat of this place. You'll drift off into the mass of jellied innards just like the million, million before you. That's what you have to look forward to. That's what your purpose is: to add a few pounds to Hell."

Without reaction, the Artifex went back to the bucket and started on Zaavan's wide, thick legs, making them bright and red with blood.

"You are probably right, sir. One day I will sink, just like the million, million before. My body stretched out into the innards of this place. But one can always hope," the old man said.

Zaavan laughed again, this time loud and hard. "Hope was a distraction for people in the life-times; it has no purpose here." He stayed his Artifex's hand and looked directly at him. "Haven't you ever wondered how many people make up this place? The endless stretches of Skin-Land? You ever think about that? What did hope do for them?"

"The fact is undeniable, Sir Zeta," his Artifex responded. "But one does not use hope as a tool for gain. Hope *is* what you gain."

"I never understood how deep a fool you were. Talking in these stupid riddles. If you weren't so good at your job, I'd make a desk out of you." Zaavan chuckled and shook his head.

Just then, the hinges of Zaavan's arm-woven door creaked open again. In the doublewide entrance stood one of the Devil's Daughters. Her patchworked skin cleavage bustled in a seductive fashion, and she clutched a small purse made of dried stomach clasped with tiny pink cartilage.

"Have I interrupted you, Zaavan?" she said in the most delicate of tones.

"He was just finishing. Leave us," Zaavan said, and the Artifex grabbed his bucket and closed the arm door behind them.

"You are looking quite fresh, Zaavan. As strong and full as the day you were made Demon."

"Thank you, Daughter. Your compliments are always a gift, as is your presence."

She moved easily, almost floating around Zaavan's small chamber, circling his chair, observing the antique style.

"Baroque furniture, interesting. Most people find it revolting," she said, daintily caressing the back of his chair as she walked behind it. "This style is so before my time. I rarely get the chance to see it anymore."

"I don't like to be separate from the natural world. I like to be reminded of where we are. What we are. Why we are."

She smiled, showing her set of precious teeth.

"Yes, I am sure you do like to be reminded of that. That's one of the reasons he likes you."

Zaavan perked up, sitting straight and tall in his chair. "He speaks of me?"

"Oh yes, Zaavan. He speaks of you," she said, completing her circle around his tight chamber. She placed a hand on each of the arms of his chair and leaned in toward his face, dipping her perfectly mismatched breasts so that Zaavan could see the fine molded stitching of her soft skin patches. "He speaks of you. He sees you in a possible future. He sees much potential in you. Much strength."

"Ahhh, I'm flattered," Zaavan stammered, stuck between confusion and compliment.

The Daughter retreated and stood straight, hand on hip in front of Zaavan's massive form. "He is very interested in your Mandatum tomorrow. He is very much looking forward to your journey into the Skin-Land Vast."

"Yes, yes. I am confident that we will fill our quota. Very confident," Zaavan said.

"He is sure that you will, but that is not exactly why he is looking forward to it."

Zaavan's interest piqued.

"He needs something of you. He needs you to do something for him," she said.

"Anything. Anything, of course!" Zaavan replied.

"He needs you to make sure that Delius does not return."

Zaavan smiled deeply, a few of the inner bones within his chest cracking audibly as muscles contracted hard and firm at attention.

"It would be an honor to sink that old wingless blood sack," Zaavan said.

"I am sure he will be very happy to hear you feel that way."

"He is no match for me. I will rip every layer of muscle from his bones. I will remove his organs and leave him a skeleton with eyes so he can stare helplessly for eternity."

"That won't be necessary, Zaavan. In fact, the more discrete you can be, the better. We don't want a scene, something that we will have to address back here on the Sled when you return. It will just be better if you can do this quietly," the Daughter instructed.

"No matter, quiet or not. He will not return. This *will* be his last Mandatum!" Zaavan said.

"There is one thing." She unlatched the cartilage clasp on her purse and reached inside, pulling out a small, jellied ball. She held it in her palm, where it seemed to flatten out by its own weight, as if it were full of fluid.

"When you have him subdued, place this sack into his brain, through his Demon Stem entry. It doesn't matter when you do this. But it *must* be put onto his brain. It must absorb completely."

Zaavan took the small gland-sack into his hand. It was a dangerously delicate thing. He'd never seen its equal, so small, so seemingly full of purpose.

"What is this? Why do I need to put this in that old Demon's brain? If you want, I'll crush his brain, scatter it into pieces."

"No! He does not want that! He wants you to do what I told you. Do you understand?" The Daughter's voice turned to an uncomfortable sternness.

"What is this, then? Is it poison? I don't need to poison Delius! I can kill him myself," Zaavan returned.

"It is not poison." She clasped her purse shut and placed her hand back on her hip. "This is a collection of allylamine that took the Master Engineers years to accumulate. It is very precious. One of a kind. It cannot be replaced. Be mindful of that, Zaavan."

"I've not heard of this before—allylamine . . ." He looked at the gland-sack, a deep pink-blue, round with no seals he could see on its surface.

"It is the forget-chemical, the eraser of minds. Place this into Delius's brain, and his life-times, his Hell-times, all of it will be gone. This is of utmost importance to the Devil. He will have you do this for him, under your own free will."

"Of course. It will be an easy pleasure," Zaavan committed.

"We are glad you feel this way. He knew you would not disappoint him."

The Daughter turned, and her cloak wisped around, profiling her perfect, womanly shape in the singular sallow light of the fat brazier.

"Once done, I will want an audience with him," Zaavan said.

"Of course. Once you have completed this duty." The daughter exited, leaving Zaavan in the shadows to contemplate this new Mandatum.

CHAP+ER SEVEN

Like a fractured skull that heals into an oblong shape, or a scar that grows over the eye, your body will try to make sense of an injury and heal it the best way it knows how. Only in Hell, this process will never stop. If not attended to, the injured body will heal itself into the most crippled of fashions.

—From "Your Body and How It Has Changed"
By Doctorem Delta-Lindicus

Silton remembered the hospital with perfect clarity: stark, clean, but surprisingly disorganized, as though saving lives must be something new to them, a process they were still working on, still ironing out the details.

The car had hit Kay while she walked across a poorly designed intersection. It was a known place, a death trap that the local community had complained about for years.

She had two black eyes, a broken nose, and a bruise on her forehead that swelled up like a purple balloon. He'd brought the picture of them at the park, the one of her pouting, the "almost perfect" day. He planned on leaving it there, on the end table, so she'd know he'd been there. When she woke up, he imagined she'd have this full epiphany that life was precious and fragile. She'd realize you don't throw away a marriage because of idiosyncratic differences and selfish wants. She would want to work on the bad parts of their relationship and make them good. She would enjoy playing the part of wife and enjoy him playing the part of husband. But that never happened. She never had that epiphany.

He held her hand that day in the hospital. It felt clammy, but warm. Kay was still alive, but an uninterested alive. He could almost feel her soul, distant and bored, trying to move away from her body. She waited somewhere, tethered to this world, with those pissed-off folded arms she had while impatiently tapping her feet. She'd always told him playfully, "You can't keep up with me. Do yourself a favor and don't try, Silton."

Maybe Kay was right. Maybe she couldn't even keep up with herself.

This memory went through Silton's mind as he watched the arm he'd ripped off Skinny Chad sink into the skin. It too felt clammy, but warm. Once the arm stopped pulsing, the skin beneath it became moist. The moistness turned to wetness, and the wetness turned to a shallow pool of liquid fat and blood. The ground swallowed up Chad's arm like fleshy quicksand, then hardened back to solid ground, pale and beige. Silton wondered if the arm was on its way to catch up with the rest of Chad's body, just like Kay had been trying to catch up with her soul.

Silton walked east, away from the Skinny Chad incident, for what he figured was an hour. Keeping time wasn't the hard part; he'd always had an uncanny, automatic sense of it. But knowing what direction he walked seemed almost impossible. The light source, the bright white and blue, almond-shaped eye he'd passed during his fall, was obscured by the greenish haze of the sky. This made it difficult to tell exactly where it was. Even if he could see it clearly, he didn't know if it was a stable light source. He didn't know if this place spun on an odd axis that made east and west irrelevant. He didn't know anything.

Instead of worrying, Silton figured it best to try and find the other people he'd seen during the fall. He had to talk to someone, fulfill the human need to verify an experience, to shed the feeling that this was all a dream.

His injured arm radiated a painful warmth. Silton should have felt the pulsing of it, the sensation of a heartbeat pushing blood to an injury in that familiar rhythmic fashion. But that wouldn't happen, not with this odd vacancy in his body, this clotted, jellied hole in his chest.

The fact of his absent heart wasn't the most concerning part; Silton accepted what he'd done to himself. The feeling of air wafting through him as he walked and the tickling he felt on the frayed edges of his hole didn't bother him much. What troubled Silton, what his mind and medical knowledge wouldn't stop reminding him of, was that his blood couldn't move anymore. He walked, his brain worked, and the broken arm seemed to be healing by the second. The marrow inside his bones was reaching out, creating a spongy raw bridge between the broken pieces. And as the skin around his arm grew into a leathery cast, it made a perfect, blood-tight seal. But his blood felt like it had thickened without a heart to move it around, and he could feel a sense of rigidity starting to creep in. Although things seemed to be working for now, Silton couldn't escape the thought that having no heart would eventually catch up with him.

In the distance, he could see more stumps clustered together at the top of a hill, like a grove of stunted trees. Now that he knew what they were, the limbs of the half-sunk, he quickened his steps to a slight jog, just enough not to cause pain in his arm.

As Silton scaled the hill, the ground became stiffer. The skin, parched, cracked, and flaky, felt almost like stone. This made sense. The bodily fluids underneath the ground would pool at their lowest points, leaving higher elevations dried out, just like skin. A bitter wind bit Silton as he neared the top. The acrid air stung his eyes and howled against his ears so he could hear little else.

Silton reached the first stumps: a pair of black hands reaching up out of the skin. He grabbed both, hoping this would provide him more leverage. He pulled, but it didn't feel like Chad. The ground around him didn't give even half an inch. This part of the skin was rock hard, and the hands didn't answer back, either. He felt a slight warmth in the palms, but nothing else, no response, no answer to his efforts. Silton leaned in, stiffened his back and prepared to give a strong heave. But then he froze, finally taking in the full view from the top of the hill.

Below him, gently sloping into a shallow valley, lay a tangled swamp of no less than five hundred arms, legs, and bodies, sticking out of the ground. The wind stopped for a moment, and Silton could hear soft moans wafting up. He could see twitching, writhing, an orgy of struggle with hundreds of body parts in spasm. They looked like desperate insects fighting against a sticky trap.

CHAP+ER EIGH+

Sapiens are defined as people in Hell who have been physically altered to serve the Demon Class as slaves. Sapiens are constructed with specific purposes in mind, and often the alterations are not in the person's best interest. If you encounter a Sapien, know that it cannot be reasoned with. All Sapiens are lobotomized, rendering them ignorant of everything except for their designed purpose. It is best for you to regard them as animals, or as the old Demons called them: Meat Machines.

—From "Hell's Inhabitants"
By Doctorem Delta-Lindicus

A quietly eerie silence pervaded the morning as Montly walked through the long expanse beneath the Sled called Sapien Bay. The high, arched ceiling supported by carved bone trestles was the largest she had ever seen, and Montly wondered where they'd found so much bone. The thick air in the bay almost seemed to have a weight to it. It smelled like feces, skin, and blood, boiled in a bath of sweat. Strangely, Montly found the smell comforting. It reminded her of the Herd: driving the thousands of Broken men and women across the pristine stretches of Skin-Land.

Gated pens holding groups of Sapiens dotted the massive expanse of the bay. The Sapien constructs always amazed Montly. Some were small, built for speed and stamina with dog-like faces. Others were large, at least five times the size of a man, with massive legs so they could balance their bulk. Sometimes Montly could easily see where the pieces of men and women were stitched together to make the beasts.

But some of the Sapiens looked completely alien. Amalgamations that Montly couldn't fathom, shapes and figures that looked entirely inhuman, masterfully constructed flesh architecture that only the most talented Engineer could have imagined.

Montly carried everything she possessed with her: a thick sleeping roll, a spare set of pants, her favorite set of technique tools, and a necklace holding a small charm. This was her most prized possession, given to her by the Herd Praefectus, Theta-Shelle, on the day of her first promotion.

Shelle had told her it was quite an accomplishment when a member of the Broken Herd moved directly to a Herdsman, and she made sure to commemorate the occasion by giving Montly the gift. The charm had just been a small piece of tumor then, an ugly thing that most would consider useless.

"But within all things is the potential for greatness," Shelle had said to her. "Inside this ugly, twisted tumor is the ability to create any of the beautiful and complex structures of the body."

And she was right. The tumor piece had sprouted a smooth and polished fingernail on one side, and on the other, short black hair, coarse to the touch. It was a truly rare possession.

"In the life-times, this was something that would be thrown

away, cut out, shed from the body. But look at it now: beautiful, unique, and desperately fighting to find its purpose in this place. Just like you, Montly," Shelle had explained to her.

Montly kept those words close to her for the next century as she worked the Herd, slowly making her way from Herdsman to the Commander of the starboard side. She'd always seen herself as that little tumor: forgotten, written-off, discarded. But inside herself lay something special, a power that would let her become anything she wanted.

Lopex waited beside one of the gated pens near the far side of the bay.

"Good morning!" he yelled to Montly across the cavernous expanse.

"Good morning to you!" she yelled back, a huge smile stretching across her face.

"Your first time down here, I suspect?" Lopex asked.

"Yes. It is," Montly replied.

"Pretty impressive isn't it?"

"I would say so. I had no idea we had so many Sapiens down here," Montly remarked.

"Well, we go through them pretty quickly. We always seem to need more than we have."

Montly closed the distance to Lopex and grasped his hand in greeting. He wore a different overcoat now, not as nice as the supple bone-button one he'd worn during her interview. This coat was worn, tattered, and fitted for field use, much more like the one Montly wore.

"So, what can I do first?" she asked anxiously.

"Eager. Very nice," Lopex said, and smiled. "First thing—turn around."

Montly knew what he wanted to see: the results of the

operation she'd had to have before going out on the Mandatum. Lopex put his hand on the back of her neck and observed the Engineers' work. A small orifice had been dug into the base of her skull. Lopex gently explored the circular valve, making sure it opened wide enough for its purpose, but remained small enough so that nothing unwanted could enter.

"Very nice work by the Engineers, as usual. Our Demon Stems will have no issues connecting with you," Lopex said, approving.

"Thank you. I mean, that's great. I'm flattered that you think I am ready to administer a Demon Stem already."

"Hold on, Montly. No one said you're ready to do that yet. But Delius demands that everyone who goes out on his Mandatum have a portal for a Demon Stem. It's more a precaution. In case we lose our designated Scrotters. But..." He paused and looked at his pupil with pride. "But who knows? Maybe I can get Delius to let you merge with an Unbroken... maybe. If you do a great job out there, that is."

"Of course, Eta-Lopex, of course," Montly said, using the formal title. Her mind filled with excitement.

"We need to get acquainted with the Sapiens now." Lopex unlatched the waist-high gate to the pen. The ground inside was covered in a thick blanket of dried skin flakes, comfortable bedding for the beasts. A large trough ran down the side of the gate, filled with a viscous and lumpy reddish-brown mash.

"This is their grist," Lopex pointed out. "They get food all day and night a few days before we leave. This fattens them up. But once we're out in the Vast, they only get fed once a day."

He dipped his hand in the trough and pulled up a dripping handful of the stringy stuff. "We have to make our own grist out in the Vast. Our chef takes pride in our grist, too. It's not like this swill." Lopex slapped the rest of it back down into the trough.

Montly cringed, chuckled, and smiled.

"Our Cantavit will consist of ten Canem, ten Drums, and ten Mauss. It's the same combination we always take out. Delius chooses this. He's very committed to his habits. I would rather have more Canem than so many Drums, but it's not my decision."

Lopex turned, his back to the group of Sapiens huddled in the corner of the pen, and faced Montly.

"The most important job of the Sapien Master is Sapien maintenance, and the most important part of Sapien maintenance is the blood down. Do you know why?"

"Blood downs keep the Sapiens moving," Montly said automatically.

"Correct, but how?" Lopex pushed.

Montly responded in textbook fashion, "Sapiens are only given half a heart, no matter what their size, because the Devil collects as many hearts as possible. Sometimes, half a heart isn't strong enough to saturate their muscles and organs with the blood they need. The blood down gets fresh blood directly to the muscles and organs, allowing them to work better, faster, and with less injury. We use the same technique for some of the Broken in the herd. It works well for the ones with damaged hearts; it keeps them moving, at least for a while."

"Good . . . good, Montly," Lopex said. "You are used to using the traditional technique for blood downing, and that's fine. But out in the Vast, you will find it much easier to cut open a blood pool in the Skin-Land, and then just let the Sapiens bathe in it. It will save you so much time."

Lopex walked into the group of Sapiens, and they moved

away from him in fear, splitting a path. He reached out fast, grabbing one of the smaller, dog-like Sapiens, and dragged it back to Montly.

"These are our Canem. We'll let these run ahead of us once we clear The Sled." Lopex pushed the thing to its side and it lay down for inspection. "The Engineers make them with four legs." He lifted up one of its back leg. "They reinforce the joints of the back leg and give it a balled heel foot so it can turn fast when running, see?"

He rubbed his palm against the course traction on the Canem's heel. "They also add hands on the front two legs. This lets them climb up steep slopes and trudge through fat bogs." Lopex let Montly feel the Canem's front fingers.

"Why are its fingers so stubby?" she asked, holding the short digits.

"Full fingers break too easily," Lopex answered. "When they first developed these, all we were doing was fixing their broken fingers. Once, on a Mandatum, a Sapien Master decided to cut off the fingers at their middle joint. Then, no more broken fingers. Once they got back to The Sled and showed the Engineers, it became standard for the Canems."

He flipped the Sapien to its back. "Who knows, maybe you'll find an improvement for the Sapiens while we're out in the Vast," Lopex said.

Montly smiled, imagining such a success, such an honor.

Lopex continued, "Next, I inspect the vocal cords." He opened the long mouth of the Canem. "They add in another set of vocal cords, so they can scream louder and longer when they find the Unbroken. This way we can hear them far off. Sometimes the extra vocal cords don't take to the throat, or get loose, so we need to make sure they're attached securely."

Lopex reached into the Canem's mouth, deep up to his forearm. The four-legged thing writhed and twisted and choked out an inhuman scream. "Yeah, this one's fine. You just need to feel both sets; they should be one on top of the other. Go ahead, you try."

Montly looked at Lopex with apprehension.

"Don't worry," Lopex said. "They won't bite you."

Montly shook off the slight fear and reached deep into the thing's mouth. She could feel the tender ruffled flaps of specialized skin that made up the vocal cords. They were taut, and connected firmly to the sides of the Canem's throat.

"Yes, I feel them. I feel how they're attached," she said.

"Good. There's no Unbroken man or woman who can outrun a Canem." He patted the beast on its stomach and let it go.

"Next, I'd like to take a look at the Drums. They require a much more delicate touch to inspect."

Lopex went over to one of the Drums. They were huge, and looked like a mass of body parts melted together. Montly couldn't tell where one person began and the other ended.

Lopex grabbed underneath one of its arms, leaned hard, and pulled the massive Sapien away from the group.

"These are our muscle, our crowd control, and our guards," he said, while leaning to pull the massive thing along. Montly could see more details now. It was made of no less than three people mashed back-to-back in a triangular form. The backs of their heads were merged together into what looked like one oddly shaped skull. It had six legs, which made it move in an ungainly, stumbling fashion.

"They're much more graceful than they look," Lopex started. "You can't knock one of these down, and you can't sneak up on them." Lopex pulled it up to Montly for inspection.

The Sapien must have weighed seven hundred pounds, with six arms jutting out in all directions like a human octopus. The skin was a patchwork of stark color changes: a tanned woman, a black man, and a white man, their skin meeting at neatly sewn capillary thread stitches that joined their bodies together. Montly ran her fingers down one of the intricate stitches. It felt perfectly strong and smooth.

"Sometimes I think the Engineers make the Drums in colorful combinations on purpose," said Lopex as he slapped the Drum on its side. "So, we only need to make sure of one extra thing on these: the Adrenal Gland placement."

Lopex spun the huge, awkward mass around to one of the seamed meetings. "Between each section of the Drum, just below where they fuse the shoulders together, is a nerve trigger—three to be exact—one under each pair of arms." He lifted the two arms that shared the fused shoulder of the Drum. "Right here."

He gently touched the underarm, and the Drum jumped slightly in response.

"Easy, my friend, easy..." Lopex said. "They are very sensitive here, but they have to be. When we depress this ganglion of nerves, it triggers a gland placed below it to release adrenaline into the bloodstream. The other two glands will activate as well. If you gently press the skin, you can feel the gland, just below the surface here."

He took Montly's hand and slowly depressed the area. She could feel a pocket under the skin.

"I feel it. It's like a little lump of muscle," Montly said.

"Yes, that's it. It's important that the Engineers place it exactly under the arm, so it doesn't get pressed by mistake." He let the Drum's arm back down. "Now, I need you to understand something, Montly. You have to be prepared if you're going to push this. Once you hit this, the Drum will go berserk, and you won't be able to stop it. I've seen plenty of first-timers come away from a triggered Drum without an arm."

He stared into Montly's eyes for a moment to emphasize his point. "It can be real messy, and we have enough work to do out there without having to reattach our own people's limbs. Got it?"

Montly got it. She could still feel the seam where she'd reattached her arm in Lopex's office, and had no interest in doing that a second time.

"So next, you will need to check the position of the off-gland." Lopex pulled the massive Drum down to its six knees. "This is located on the top of its skull, the soft spot."

He pointed to a slight depression in the middle of where the three heads were merged together. "It basically puts the Drum into a coma. Sometimes it causes some brain damage, but generally it works pretty well."

Lopex slapped the Drum to rise. "Every Adrenal Gland on every Drum must be checked. Be careful; it's the most danger-ous part of the inspection." He gently leaned into the Drum, pushing it back to the corner of the pen.

"Finally, the Mauss. There's not much to inspect here. It's just important they get to know you."

Lopex went over to his own Mauss, a majestic construct standing three heads taller than him. Four muscular legs came down from its long, thick midsection to sharp heels of pressed keratin. A long, stem-like neck extended from its body and ended in an oblong head about the size of four fists. The head was clean and smooth, with none of the normal cavities. No mouth, no nose, no ears, just four eyes set in a semicircle around its spotless head. On the underside of the long neck were six openings set two-by-two. They looked like cut-off noses with cartilage stems segmenting each hole in half. It was the most graceful and elegant Sapien Montly had ever seen.

"This is mine," Lopex said. "You'll need to pick one too, just not this one. Don't pick any Mauss with a brand on its side, see?" Lopex pointed to an E-L on the side of his Mauss. "This will be your transport, your guide, and your friend out there in the Skin-Land Vast." He caressed the back of his Mauss. It huffed out of the six orifices on its neck and shook its oblong head up and down. Lopex smiled.

"It's beautiful," Montly said. "We use them out in the Herd sometimes. I've always thought them to be so stunning."

"Yes, and smart. They have great instincts. The Engineers make sure they leave enough brain so that they have some personality. They can be quite a lot to handle sometimes. Isn't that right?" He slapped his Mauss hard, sending it back to the herd of Sapiens. "Okay, Montly, inspect the Sapiens. Pick out your Mauss, and make sure you brand it. Take all of them over to the blood port for one final soak, then bring them to the front of the bay to join the rest of the Cantavit. We leave tomorrow morning, so you should have plenty of time. Be thorough."

"Of course, Lopex. And thank you so much."

Lopex nodded, turned, and walked away.

Montly smiled and stared at the crowd of Sapiens milling around the pen. She gently rubbed her necklace, feeling the coarse hair on one side, the smooth nail on the other. A single proud tear fell from her eye, and her smile grew for an instant. Then she went to work.

CHAPTER NINE

As Hell is composed completely of human bodies, the skin surface of Hell is varied in its tension and consistency. Where the skin is soft and pliable, people will fall through, often sinking. When this happens, many of them become solidified into the Skin-Land. On many occasions, one or two of their extremities will remain above the surface. This phenomenon is called an Arm Forest. It is wise to stay as far away from these areas as possible, because the Skin-Land is so delicate. Arm Forests are amongst the most dangerous land constructs in Hell, and are extremely common.

—From "Hell Geographica"
By Doctorem Delta-Lindicus

From the top of the hill, Silton could see for several miles before the haze obscured his vision. There were other rises and falls in the distance across the land, a rolling expanse of multicolored skin covering the viewable geography.

Silton choked on the slow and gentle steam drifting up from the shallow valley in front of him. It smelled like hot, melting flesh, and he could taste the salty fumes in his mouth when he inhaled. The swamp valley stretched out about one city block in size and shape, and looked like a massive swimming pool of liquid fat.

The scene was a riot of bodies flailing in the muddy soup. Dozens of people struggled, most of them sunk almost completely into the fleshy marsh. Many of their bodies were broken, shattered, or twisted horribly from their fall. Along the drier, slanted sides of the valley, Silton saw what looked like people who'd exploded on impact with the land, like insects on a windshield.

Silton's instinct told him to rush into the fray, to explode into rescue mode, to start pulling people from the swamp. He could triage the most endangered, build a team from the capable, and save all of these poor souls. This was the Combat Medic in him. Everyone can be saved, everyone *will* be saved, no matter the circumstances. But the experience with Skinny Chad had shaken Silton's confidence and all but stolen away his resolve. Most of these people were lost, too far sunk into the fat, blood, and skin. Most were up to their shoulders or worse. He knew he'd have to be careful, deliberate, and investigate this forest of arms.

You don't run into a minefield either, Silky, he said to himself.

Silton made a cautious descent, moving sideways to capitalize on his traction. Although the hill was dry and hard at the top, as he made his way down closer to the pit, the ground became slicker. The skin seeped fluids, sweating out a milky stuff that ran down the hill into the fat boil.

As he got closer, the voices became much more clear. He wondered if the thickness of the air had muted them before.

Silton could hear moaning, screaming, some unintelligible speech. He could even hear what sounded like a conversation in the distance.

Silton made his way around the edges of the swamp. Here, the taut, dry-cracked skin felt safer, more stable. The ground transitioned sharply into the fatty swamp, and Silton could easily see where the danger spots were. He stared at the mess of exposed body parts as he walked the perimeter. There was no prejudice in this place. All likes of people floated in the pit. He could see black, white, and every shade in between. Old and young. Large and small. It was as if someone had overturned a cemetery so Silton could see the roots of bodies underneath.

The sound of voices grew louder, clearer, until Silton could make out two people: one male, one female. He walked in a wide circle, away from the edge of the swamp, so he could observe the conversation from afar.

The woman lay near the edge, where Silton determined the break point between the soupy fat and the solid ground began. She was up to her hips, but bent over at the waist. Her stomach lay flat against the muck as she stretched herself toward the center of the liquid fat pit. She spoke to someone in that direction, though it seemed more like screaming.

"Hold on, Mr. Halpern! Hold on!" the woman screamed. "Try to reach out to me! Try!"

Silton could hear someone trying to respond, but the voice sounded muffled with wetness.

"I can't move my legs!" the woman screamed. "I can't move my legs. I can't get to you! I'm sorry, I'm so sorry..." She started to cry, heaving hard in resignation.

The woman was young, about Silton's age, maybe younger. She had a soft smooth hue of brown to her skin, and although globs of white fat congealed on her body and face, Silton could see that she was fit and attractive, with a thick mane of flowing black hair.

Silton hoped he'd have better luck this time. The woman was only up to her legs, with her whole torso exposed. He had to try.

Silton walked closer toward her, his hands outstretched and open in a non-threatening position. Silton knew from Combat Medic training that he had to approach like this. When injured, people react more like animals than in any other situation. They panic, thrash around. There was no escaping this instinct, no matter how rational a person was. The woman would be scared, and Silton had to get past that fear quickly, because she was starting to sink.

Bubbles of gas began to pop up around her, like a pot of thick stew coming to boil. The skin seemed to respond to her, taking advantage of her resolve to give up. When she saw Silton, she froze, maybe from fear, shock, or the elation of seeing someone else. He didn't know what she felt, but her face mouthed a silent "Help Me" with every pained contour and nuance.

"It's okay, try to stay still," Silton said, and slowly dropped down to his stomach. The woman stopped struggling, calmed herself, and leaned in his direction. Her arm stretched out sideways, trying to close the distance.

They gripped, her fingernails cutting into Silton's hand.

"Okay. I'm gonna pull a bit." Silton used a hushed voice, calm, soothing. As if being quiet would help somehow.

The woman nodded, letting Silton know she was ready. He stiffened his stomach muscles, dug his feet into what he could of the surface, and pulled. A deep suction noise came from her waist, and she winced hard at some unseen pain. Silton pulled again, gaining some leverage, and her body started to move, sliding out of a sleeve of congealed fat. She fought back the urge to scream, but it didn't work, and her voice joined the other cries around her.

Her legs popped out as they emerged, and Silton dragged her away from the swamp to the hard, dry, skin. She trembled, shock rippling down into her arms and legs like an earthquake. Now Silton could see why she had screamed when he pulled her out: it was her legs, her poor legs. The bones were twisted into unnatural positions. A broken shin served as a tent pole pushing her skin up at a sharp angle, and Silton could see at least one of her knees was dislocated.

"Are you . . . are you okay?" Silton asked, staring at her disfigurement.

"I can't feel them, they're numb," the woman said between rapid breaths.

"You're in shock, so you need to—"

"I know I'm in shock!" she screamed defiantly. "My legs are broken, and I've been stuck in a hole for two days! Of course I'm in shock!"

"My . . . my name is Silton," he said, placing his hand on his chest, reminding himself of the gaping hole there.

"Am *I* okay?" she said. "Look at you! Are *you* okay?" She almost gagged looking at Silton, but glanced away quickly.

The woman pulled herself up into a more respectable position, still shaking but settling in. She moved her legs so they lay side by side and covered her breasts with one of her arms.

"I'm sorry for that. I don't mean to be rude. My name is Mariella." She sighed, exhausted, and extended her hand in a formal manner. They shook politely, and both of them realized the absurdity of the greeting. Silence crept in for a few long moments.

"I should look at your legs," Silton said.

"Don't bother. They're both broken, compound fractures. My knee joints are both dislocated. I think the left one's completely blown out. ACL is torn for sure. But the hips are still in place. At least I have that going for me." She cringed in a hum of pain and pounded the ground around her.

As far as Silton could tell, Mariella was right. Her legs were compound fractures, and not the clean type like Silton's arm. One leg had two breaks in the shinbone; the other he couldn't tell. Silton didn't know a lot about knee anatomy, but Mariella seemed to be right about them too.

"How can you be so exact about your injuries?" Silton asked.

"'Cause I'm a nurse!" she said, raising her voice. "We're the ones who actually *have* to know everything!"

The pain edged her personality to anger, Silton could clearly see that.

"I can wrap your legs up, push the bone back into place, and cast it. I did the same for my arm here, and it worked, it's healing."

Mariella cut Silton off sternly, huffing between breaths of pain.

"And why would I want that? Do you think I care? Don't you see where we are? What difference will any of that make?"

Silton suspected that was the shock talking. He ignored Mariella and went to a tender part of the skin covering the ground. He pierced the surface with his fingers and started to pull up a sheet. He brushed off as much of the fat and capillaries as he could, walked back to Mariella, and motioned like he was going to throw it over her shoulders. An improvised shock blanket. The wide swath of flesh was dripping with fluids as he approached, and she started to coil away in disgust. But she knew what he was trying to do.

"Thank you," Mariella said, taking the warm skin sheet over her shoulders. "I'm sorry, I just . . . the last two days, have been . . ."

"I understand, really. Don't worry about it," Silton replied. "I heard you talking to someone when I found you. Where is he? Is there any chance we can get to him too?" Silton asked, looking out into the swamp.

"You go out there, and you're not coming back," Mariella said. "I've been here two days, and all I've seen is people falling from the sky and sinking into this pit over and over again. No one gets out."

"But you didn't sink. How did you make it?"

"Some people struggle for a few hours, like Mr. Halpern. Then they sink. I don't know how I got lucky landing near the edge, but the ground was harder there, hence my legs. But he was such a good man, he didn't deserve this." She shook her head.

"Didn't deserve this?" Silton said, confused. "What do you mean, he didn't deserve this? Do you know him?"

"I did," Mariella said as the warmth of the skin blanket forced the shock to fade. "He died five days ago at my hospital. I was there. I saw him die. I was the charge nurse when he passed. I even called the Code Blue. I watched him be pronounced. I pulled the sheet over his head. Had his body taken to the morgue . . ."

Silton processed her words. Thoughts of Skinny Chad invaded his mind. *How could she know someone here too? What sense did that make?*

"I saw someone too, someone I know," Silton said. "This drug addict kid I used to see in my neighborhood. He fell into this place. He was really messed up. He didn't make it either." Silton paused and sat down next to Mariella. "But how could he? I mean, what a coincidence that you would see someone you know . . ."

"It's not a coincidence," Mariella said, her shock now slowing down to a trickle. "We all died. I work at the hospital. Mr. Halpern died in the hospital. So did all of the people in this pit! We all fell down here, like straight down in the same area! Don't you get it? I've been watching patients from my hospital fall into this pit for the last two days! This is just like some underside of death, a mirror of where we were in life. That's why you saw someone you know. And that's why this is a goddamn swamp! Everyone who dies in the hospital falls directly down into this. It's a sinking pit of everyone I knew!"

Silton tried to wrap his head around the idea. This "underside of death," Mariella called it. He got up and walked a few steps away from her, toward the steaming, melting fat.

"I don't know about that, I just don't . . ." Then he heard a distant scream closing in.

They both looked up and saw a dot falling through the sky, ribbons of the green gas trailing off the edges of flailing arms and legs. The scream filled the air as the body ripped through the sky, then it hit the swamp, sending out a wave of hot fat that splashed over the two of them. The man landed head first, up to his chest with his back bent against the natural hinge of his spine. His exposed arms and legs twitched along with the hundreds of bodies and limbs that dotted the Arm Forest.

"Another Code Blue at the hospital. You get it now?" Mariella said, speaking to Silton like a dumb child.

And Silton got it.

CHAPTER TEN

Concentrated Digestive Acid can, and will, render flesh to liquid. Muscle will last for a time, and one should survive most contact. A healthy layer of fat smeared onto your skin may provide some protection. Other protections from acid are stomach/digestive lining robes or blankets. The interiors of the stomach and digestive linings have inherent protective properties against acids. Although this will work, it is not recommended that you expose yourself to Concentrated Digestive Acid for an elongated period of time.

—From "Hell Geographica"
By Doctorem Delta-Lindicus

Eta-Lopex snapped heel to toe on the bone tile floor of Sapien Bay. Around him, workshops of every type thumped with early morning activity: tanners stretched and dried skin sections to make thick hide flaps, sculptors pared down large, awkwardly shaped pieces of bone into more manageable forms, and weavers braided yard upon yard of dried vein rope. But what Lopex needed today was very special and could only be found at the Clorix Basin, the place where acids were distilled. The Clorix Basin lay on the far end of Sapien Bay, and he anxiously pushed his pace to get there.

Lopex found much joy in his work. He had a place in Hell with a true sense of purpose that he'd never known before. During the life-times, he was a man consumed with eternal boredom, forever sitting on the sidelines, waiting for life's meaning to impose itself on him. But this never occurred, and soon he forgot what he was waiting for. How could he have known that his purpose patiently waited for him in Hell?

The Clorix Basin was a known dangerous place. The workshop, tented with thick layers of skin, was sealed at the sides with Ossein Paste, so no acidic fumes could escape. On white hooks near the entrance hung oddly shaped hooded cloaks, the Basin robes. They had simple skin ties around the waist so one could wrap themselves up completely. The Basin robes, constructed from stomach linings, had a moist pink color with blue capillary thread that made a stylish contrast. Otherwise, stomach linings did not lend themselves naturally to clothing design due to their oblong shape. When Lopex put one on, it felt very uncomfortable and looked even more awkward.

Lopex pushed through several layers of heavy skin drapes and entered the cramped workshop. Long, shallow tables filled with fluorescent, steaming fluids stretched from one end to the other. Sapien Tenders used special bone brushes to gently stir the acids, ensuring their consistency. Along the side of the workshop sat Digestive Tanks that produced the acid. These long systems of digestive organs were daisy-chained in a zigzag fashion back and forth along the wall: stomach, small intestine, large intestine, stomach, small intestine, large intestine. They snaked one after the other in a long, tangled line of pink chambers and tubes. A few heads could be seen tucked into the lumps of visceral tissues. These were the Sessile Sapiens, their brains supplying the electrical impulses needed to keep the stomachs and intestines working to produce acid.

This is where Lopex found his friend, Eta-Hotund, a round man, cinched into a Basin robe that barely covered his body. The exposed skin of his bald head and face had been completely bleached out by the acidic fumes, leaving it a sickly, almost artificial, white. He wore goggles with vitreous jelly lenses reinforced with liquid cartilage. The goggles didn't allow for perfect vision, but they did allow Eta-Hotund to work in this caustic environment for long periods of time.

Lopex tapped him on the shoulder, and Hotund jumped and turned, startled. When he saw Lopex, his face broke into a wide, bone-toothed smile.

"Ha ha ha!" He laughed deep and low. "My old classmate! Down here slumming again!" he yelled. The Sapiens looked up at the noise made by their master, but seeing no direction from him, turned back to their robotic mixing motions.

"It's good to see you, Hotund. You're looking well."

"And you're becoming a great liar now that you've spent so much time on the 'upper' levels of the Sled."

They laughed hard and slapped each other like brothers. Hotund led Lopex to a small room, a sloppy storage area filled with technique tools, rolls of tanned skin, and sealed bone buckets filled with various fluids. The crowded space also doubled as Hotund's office.

"Pull up a bucket," Hotund said, and plopped down on one, the banded bone flexing as he sat. Lopex did the same. "It's great to see you in a Basin robe, brother. You look like you actually work for a living again," Hotund joked. He pulled out a small square piece of dried skin, dashed some dusty skin flakes onto it, rolled the thing between his stubby fingers, and handed it to Lopex.

"No . . . no, thank you, brother. I quit after we graduated," Lopex said.

"Oh." Hotund took the skin roll back. "I see. Not appropriate, huh? You have to keep up appearances when you get stationed on the 'upper' levels," he said loaded with sarcasm. Hotund joked, but part of him was saddened by the judgment.

"Well, us Demons down here in the Bay, we've got to spend our time doing something." He dipped the end of the skin roll into a small pouch of highly potent acid. It began to sizzle immediately, and Hotund sparked it with a Synapse Trigger he kept in the front pocket of his robe. The roll smoked, Hotund inhaled deeply, and soon the small storage room was filled with the drifting scent of smoldering skin.

"So, I hear you're leaving tomorrow," Hotund remarked. "Delius's last trip out there to the Vast. Must be pretty special for you."

"It is. This makes almost two dozen trips out into the Skin-Land with him. A long time," replied Lopex.

"Then you'll take over as Praefectus, I'd guess? You were always such a climber."

"Maybe. Delius will probably recommend me, but you know how that process goes. There's no telling who the Daughters will pick. Sometimes there doesn't seem to be any reason to what they do."

"You're being modest. That always annoyed me about you." Hotund took in another deep inhale. "But then again, just about everything about you annoyed me." The two laughed again. "Are you still doing that 'take off your arm and put it back on before the time runs out' thing?"

Lopex almost blushed as he put his head down in a chuckle.

"You are!" Hotund accused. "Do you tell your little Minions that you stole that idea from me? I bet you don't! Do you, scum? You keep all that credit for yourself, Eta-bastard!"

Lopex lifted his head, a smile of deep reflection stretched across his smooth, unblemished face. "I remember when we came up with that idea. We were preparing for the group torture final and drinking way too much that night."

"Yeah," Hotund said, long and low, joining his friend in the memory. "It was Crishon who made that Blood Beer for us. He had such a talent for that. What ever happened to him?"

"He fell," Lopex replied.

Hotund hadn't expected that, and he froze. "He fell? What happened?"

"I only heard stories," Lopex began quietly. "He was on a Mandatum about eight years back. I heard they encountered a large settlement of Unbroken, one where they actually had developed a town, buildings, defenses. Anyway, they went in to start the Scrotting and, to no surprise, there was much resistance. The Unbroken took out about half the Cantavit. Eta-Crishon was among them. By the time reinforcements arrived, they'd torn them all apart and sunk their remains into the Skin-Land."

Hotund let the silence stretch out once Lopex finished, continuing to smoke his skin roll.

"He's with Hell now," Hotund said low and reverently. He lit one more roll to fill the empty space.

"I did have something else I needed to talk to you about, old friend," Lopex said.

"Of course, what is it?"

"I am a little concerned about this Mandatum."

"Concerned? What's there to be concerned about? I mean, other than the usual things."

"I don't want to involve you, so please don't press me on this. But let's just say that I feel like there's some tension in the group going out," Lopex said.

"Tension, eh?" Hotund pulled long and hard, smoldering skin looping off the roll. "So, what can I do to help you with this 'tension' problem?"

"Just answer me this. The acid you make for the Demons Sacs, the ones you load into the Zetas, how potent is it?"

"It's the most potent. It's filtered eight times at least. It's reprocessed for months through the digestive links I have out there. When that stuff comes out, it can burn through most anything. Why do you ask?"

"Your Basin robes, will they protect against it?" Lopex asked.

"Protect? For the most part, the robes are made of the same stomach material as the Acid Sacs, so it should." Hotund kept smoking, thinking about the layers under Lopex's question. "But if you're asking me if it will protect from this acid being sprayed onto you, that I can't tell you. There's a lot of force behind a Demon's Acid Sac spray, and the Basin robes are designed for spills, accidents. Not deliberate contact."

"I know, but for the most part, it will protect me, right?"

"Yes, for the most part. But why do you need protection from—" But before the question left his lips, Hotund's smile broke, and he understood the implications of his friend's question, understood why he couldn't press him on the issue. Silence invaded the cramped storage room for a third time. Then Lopex broke it.

"So, can I borrow the robe?"

Hotund gave him a knowing look, a look that spanned their friendship, linked it, and held it together like mortar. "Of course you can. Anything for you, Brother Eta." Hotund paused. "You be careful out there, Lopex. You hear me?"

"Yeah, I hear you," Lopex said. He reached over, taking the smoldering skin roll from Hotund's hand.

"For old time's sake," Lopex said, putting it to his mouth and inhaling deeply.

CHAP+ER ELEVEN

Broken bones are a common occurrence in Hell. It is wise to understand how bones work and practice how to fix them. A broken bone can, and will, fuse itself into whatever shape it rests in. This can create problems if bones are not set in their desired positions. A bone in Hell will eventually fuse itself to any bone it rests upon. If you do not address broken bones, they will fuse together into broken shapes. You can repair any bone by setting it in its desired place, making sure that the marrow within the interior is exposed to either a bone surface or another section of open marrow. This will force fusion of the bone and the healing should be complete in a few days.

—From "Your Body and How It Has Changed"
By Doctorem Delta-Lindicus

Mariella dreamed of water: cool, clean, and tasteless. She dreamed of a wet cascade in a vividness that she'd never known. The thirst plagued her, and in the dream, it drove her mad. She dreamed of the pain in her legs, twisted and searing hot, with cells bouncing back and forth in places that they should not be. She begged for relief. She screamed toward a sky that refused to hear her, that refused to help her. In the dream she turned her head to the ground and begged once again. Relief from the thirst. Relief from the pain. Then the dream shifted, and she galloped fast and free on four legs across flat-pressed skin. She could hear herself breathing, feel great foreign slabs of muscle driving her forward. She stopped next to a pristine pool of water, bent down her neck, and lapped from it without pretense like an animal would. And in this awkward, malformed dream, Mariella felt at peace, finally at peace.

Mariella awoke in a pool of sweat, her mouth parched and dried out from the acrid air. The skin had acted like a loose waterbed through the night, and she found herself resting in a depression made by the weight of her own body. Her face was damp, clammy, and stuck to the ground. She peeled her torso away and found water pooled in the depression. She stretched out her tongue and licked. It tasted warm, salty, and of someone else's flesh. The thought of this made her gag, but she fought the nausea, and licked the surface dry.

The pair had slept outside, a hundred yards or so from the Arm Forest. Throughout the night, they'd heard at least four more people splash down into its soupy mess. Each time the same thing: a desperate scream far off, increasing as it closed in, a muted splash, then nothing.

Mariella turned to right herself and leaned up to look at her legs. Silton had wrapped a piece of skin around the bone protruding from her fracture, a meager attempt to heal the injury. The skin he'd wrapped around it had grown taut through the night. She could still see the bone protrusion, but the skin seemed to join itself to her without prejudice, without the rejection she'd seen so many times with hospital skin grafts.

As she rose, she noticed more sweat-water had accumulated around her waist and legs. Her eyes opened wide with anticipation. She tried to lean forward to put tongue to skin, but the pain in her legs wouldn't allow her.

"Silton, Silton!" Mariella said. "Wake up!"

Only half-asleep, Silton woke quickly. "What? What is it?"

"Careful, careful . . . look where you're lying. There's water on the ground."

Silton shook the grog from his head and immediately noticed what Mariella was talking about. He too licked up the moisture near his upper body, and winced at the taste.

"It's like sweat," he said. "It's coming up from the ground." When he pressed down the skin to his side, it glistened with dampness.

"I know. There's more. I can't reach the water around my waist and legs. Help me. We need to get it."

Silton lifted himself up carefully and scooped a hearty handful of the sweat-water he lay in, taking it to Mariella. She drank hard, fighting her reaction against the fleshy taste. Silton did the same, and Mariella could see part of his pink esophagus pulse like a worm as the water moved from his mouth to his stomach.

Before long, the shallow sweat pools were dry.

The night hadn't gone completely dark; the sky was still a sad yellow color lit from a distance by the blue almond eye far off on the horizon somewhere. But it had gotten dark enough for them to know it was night, to know that there was some kind of daily rhythm here.

The greenish haze of day hadn't moved in yet, only steam rising from the boiling fat pool tainted the air. Silton assessed himself. His arm seemed to be doing well; it still felt awkward and a bit like part of someone else, but the pain was slight and fleeting. The hole in his chest had gone from a congealed blood hole to a crusty, dried, almost hardened form. Like his body had tried to bypass the injury as best it could. But the missing section of chest still felt wrong, and when Silton stretched long and hard, his muscles ached with an unusual tightness.

"It's clear now," he said to Mariella. "The haze. It must dissipate at night. I want to get back up on that hill to look around. See if I can find anything, anything at all. We can't sleep out in the open like this."

"Yeah, good, go do that. I'm not going anywhere," she said, with more than a hint of sarcasm. "And you were right about wrapping the skin around my leg. Look." She tugged at her left leg, showing Silton the drying skin cast.

"Good, but we still need to splint them, or they are going to start to heal wrong."

"If we're going to do it, we need to do it soon. They're already getting stiff. I can feel it. I think you're gonna have to break a few of the bones again," Mariella said.

"Let's hope it doesn't come to that. I'll be right back." Silton jogged off toward the hill as fast as his stiff muscles could take him.

From the top of the rise, Silton could see much farther than before.

The blue light crested on the horizon, and he immediately oriented himself to it.

"That will have to be east," he said to himself. The muted light glimmered for a moment, reflecting off something white in the distance, some type of formation about twenty or so miles away. Silton squinted, and saw shadows pocketed around the formation. He thought the shadows could be overhangs of some sort. Maybe they would provide them some cover. To the west he could see a smooth sea of deep red. Blood, undoubtedly. A thin ribbon of red moved from west to east across their north to the general area of the glimmering white land formation.

"Shelter," Silton said out loud, and then jogged back down the hill as fast as he could.

Mariella sat patiently. She kept trying to move her legs, her feet, her toes, triggering electric jolts that ran up her spine and tensed every muscle in her body. In response, endorphins leached out of her brain and tried to help her with the pain. She wanted to be saturated with the stuff; she wanted to feel like these legs were in some far-off place, or like they weren't hers at all. She saw Silton jogging toward her, running with purpose.

He must have found something, she thought.

"I think I see some cover," Silton said, panting. "It's not far, maybe fifteen or twenty miles."

"Okay, that sounds like something good. But I'm not going to make it *one* mile like this."

"Don't worry," Silton said, and went over to a clean section of skin. "I've already thought about that." He felt along the ground and searched out a weaker, dryer section of skin. Then he dug into the skin with his fingers. He methodically walked and pierced, walked and pierced, making a perforated square in the skin. "I'm going to drag you on a gurney flap. It's not ideal, but the ground is smooth and moist in most places. You should slide. It'll work."

"A gurney flap? Can't say we had those at the hospital."

"No, you probably wouldn't. It's something we learn to

make in the field."

"In the field? You're military?"

"Ex," Silton replied. "I'm pretty much ex-everything."

"Really. You wouldn't happen to be an ex-pharmacist then, would you? I'm dying over here."

"I know. I know you are," Silton said, and started to rip up the skin. It tore along the perforations he'd made with ease. "All I can tell you is that once I set my arm and cast it, the pain was more manageable. It hurts, don't get me wrong, but at least I can use it." He finished ripping up the skin sheet, cleaned it off, and approached Mariella. "I need to try and scoot you onto this flap."

"I get it. I'm ready," Mariella said with careful confidence.

Silton moved her as quickly as he could. She fought the screams her body demanded and breathed deep and hard, almost crying by the time they finished.

"I know you're hurting, but I think we need to get moving as fast as we can. I'm not sure how much daylight we'll have."

"Then let's go," Mariella said, and she slid her legs close to each other. "I'm no slouch. I've been hurt before, and I've always hated patients who complained about pain. So, you won't hear it from me, Silton. But I'm a talker. When I'm stressed, I talk constantly. It keeps me calm. You okay with that?"

"I'm okay with that. Now let's get moving." Silton gripped the skin sheet, faced forward, and dug his stiff legs into the skin, careful to keep the cresting blue light in view as he pushed toward the glistening, bright white formation.

CHAPTER TWELVE

A Minion is a member of Hell who has by their own free will decided to serve Demons and the Devil. Sometimes called an Artifex, a Minion is not at all like the mindless Sapien, as they are not lobotomized. Because of this, they play a critical role in the day-to-day management of Hell. Minions can also eventually be selected for promotion to Demon (see Chapter – Demon Trials). In this way, they are treated more equally than Sapiens, but still hold a second-class position to Demons.

—From "The Demonic Encyclopedia"
By Delta-Haldon

The day crested toward morning, and once again Sapien Bay throbbed with activity. Montly had worked late into the evening, inspecting and blood downing her Sapiens. Now finished, she leaned, exhausted, against a skin-banded half-wall at the front of the bay. Her Sapiens, calm and obedient, meandered in the pens next to her. A trail of spotty blood covered the bone tile floor where she had led them from the blood downing pool to the staging area. Several of the working Sapiens had taken to cleaning up her mess with dried vein mops. Montly was used to cleaning up her own messes. But for some reason, having these Sapiens clean up after her made Montly feel like she was part of something greater—that *she* was something greater.

A stout man approached the staging area followed by a Mauss. Though wide as he was tall, he moved with a nimble gait. He wore an albino skin jacket set with white bone buttons, and as he walked toward Montly, he extended his hand.

"You must be Lopex's new lackey!" he said boisterously.

Montly felt surprised, confused, and a bit shy, but she reached out anyway.

"The name's Reese, Eta-Reese. I'm the Inspector, and I do the cooking for the Cantavit as well." He cocked his head to the side, as if playfully impressed with himself. "Lopex and I go way back; we graduated in the same class. He speaks very highly of you, says you took your arm off faster than he's ever seen." Reese slapped her on her recently amputated left arm and laughed. "You know he didn't make that test up! Don't let him tell you that was *his* idea."

Montly didn't get the joke. Taking her arm off during the interview with Lopex was one of the most intimidating and frightening moments in recent memory. Worse than that, in the rush to join her arm back to her shoulder, she'd mismatched a few of the nerve links, and now she had an odd twitch in her left hand. She didn't find it funny at all, and it showed.

"Aw, lighten up kid. We've all done worse."

A naked Sapien arrived, interrupting the conversation. It dragged a small-wheeled cart topped with a bundle of supplies.

"It's about time!" Reese said. The Sapien was of typical construction, the basic bipedal form, only this one was missing several fingers and had horrible burn marks on its arms. It lifted the large bundle of supplies and placed them onto Reese's Mauss like a set of saddlebags.

"Nothing more for you," Reese said to the Sapien. "You're off for few weeks. Don't go into the kitchen while I'm gone, you got it?"

The Sapien heard what Reese said, but gave no outward response. Its lobotomized brain had no capacity for social decoding.

"I'm trying to teach it to cook. To be my assistant chef. It isn't working out so well." Reese lifted one of the Sapien's burnt arms and chuckled.

Montly forced a laugh, not wanting to be rude to her commander's friend and classmate. He was a bit odd, she thought, casual and silly, very different from any other Demon she'd met.

Lopex arrived moments later, looking rushed, carrying a bundle of skin-scrolls tucked under his arm. No doubt they were the requests for supplies from the Sled's different departments. His mind seemed to be off somewhere else, paging through some long, invisible inventory.

"Perfect, you've met Reese," Lopex said.

"Yes, and I was just explaining to her how you steal everyone's ideas and pass them off as your own." Reese slapped Lopex on the back, almost dislodging the scrolls from under his arm.

"Of course you were, Reese. You've brought everything I asked for?" Lopex said.

"I did, you stinking orifice, I did. I even brought my finest blood beer bacterium. It packs quite a punch." Reese patted the saddlebags straddling his Mauss.

"Good, I want Delius's last Mandatum to be special, maybe even a little fun." Lopex walked to his Mauss, tucking the scrolls into his own saddlebags.

"So, who else is on the Cantavit? Who is our Scrot crew?" Reese asked.

Lopex stopped fiddling with his supplies and turned to Reese. "I don't know. Zaavan's Defensionem for the Cantavit, so he's picking them."

"Zaavan? Oh, great. That waste of skin is coming? Damn Zetas are no fun at all. But I do love giving that particular Demon a hard time."

Lopex walked over to Reese. "I know you like to pick on him, but let's take it easy this trip, okay?"

"Take it easy? On a Zeta like him? You've got to be kidding me."

Montly could see that Reese wasn't going to be controlled. He was wild, brash, and unforgiving in his humor.

"Reese, I just don't want to push Zaavan this time. This is Delius's last Mandatum. I don't want any incidents. We have to manage Zaavan. You know how he is, so just take it easy. Got it?" Lopex implored.

Reese barely responded. He huffed, went to his Mauss, and busied himself retying a saddlebag that had already been tied tight by his Sapien.

"They look good," Lopex said, changing his attention to Montly. "The Sapiens, I mean."

"Oh, thanks," she said, surprised by his sudden focus on her. "I only had a problem with the Drums. One almost got away from me. They're a lot faster than they look."

"Yeah, when they get all those legs working together, they're almost as fast as a Mauss." Lopex put his arm on her shoulder. "But they all look good. Great job."

He paused, making sure Reese was out of earshot. "Reese is

a great friend, one of my best. I knew him even before we went through the Demon Trials. But he's got this way of . . . it's a way of pushing people."

Montly listened to him intently, nodding her head.

"One of the many lessons you'll learn when it comes to Mandatum and the Skin-Land Vast is that you can't have internal conflict amongst your own, not in the Cantavit. Things are too hard, too unpredictable out there. We need everyone to be doing *exactly* what they need to be doing. We don't have time for squabbles."

"I understand. I do," Montly said. She could sense some new feeling coming from him, a deep concern she'd not sensed before. She thought it must be the stress of preparation, all of the hundred things that Lopex needed to do for the last Mandatum of his mentor Delius.

Loud unison footsteps could be heard against the crisp bone tile floor of Sapien Bay. Lopex broke eye contact with Montly and looked to the source of the sound.

Zaavan and his team approached. Zaavan, the lead Demon, was dressed formally in his textured tumor breastplate, forearm slats, and matching black hide tunic, all accented with polished bone chips. His wings were tied and tucked behind him, encased in supple skin-sleeves.

Two Demon constructs followed him. To his right, a woman dressed head to toe in an exquisitely polished black skin-suit. It was so tight, Montly couldn't tell if it was clothing or her skin. The material glistened with a newly applied layer of fat that accentuated the feminine curves of her hips and the two perfect breasts jutting out of her chest. Her arms were slight but strong, and a braided length of blue and purple veins twisted from her scalp into a thick ponytail behind her. Montly thought that she was all at once both beautiful and terrifying. Exactly the type of Demon she wanted to be one day.

To the left loomed a massive Demon, standing the standard seven feet tall with an extended frame. He had no visible skin, just thick red muscle covering his entire body. Instead of a nose, he had a custom-made bone plate resembling a shovel. It extended from the middle of his face to just above his skull. Montly could see no eyes, but that didn't mean they weren't there. Something else odd about this Demon caught her eye, a shimmer about him. The rising light of day bounced on his massive form and he seemed to almost sparkle. Montly couldn't make out what it was. She leaned to Lopex.

"The large red one, he shines. How is that?" she asked.

"Bone dust," Lopex said. "It's embedded into his muscles. It causes agitation to the outer fibers, makes his muscles incredibly tough. You won't ever see greater, or stranger feats of Demon Engineering than with the Zetas. They actually volunteer for experiments, no matter how radical or odd. They're proud of it. I guess you'd call them pioneers."

Montly stared. She couldn't break her eyes from them. She'd never seen their equal.

Zaavan stopped at the pens and spoke to his two Demons.

"This is your Cantavit, Zetas," he said in a dismissive tone. "These are the Demons, Minions, and Sapiens you will help protect." He spoke as if the rest of the Cantavit could not hear him. "You may find this group unusually weak, unusually inept in the Skin-Land Vast, but this does not alter your charge." Arrogance bled from his every word. "You will protect them without regard for yourself, as is the maxim of the Zetas."

Zaavan turned to his right, now addressing the rest of the Cantavit. "This is Zeta-Chalt." He motioned to the black-coated woman. "She was the first in her class to swim the entire length of the blood tunnel. She is the most formidable woman Demon on The Sled." Zaavan paused. "To my left is Zeta-Bore. He could not be moved during the Drum Push portion of his Demon Trial. There has never existed a Demon stronger than him. So, know this, Cantavit: We will keep you safe on this, the last of Delius's Mandatums. You have nothing to fear from the Skin-Land Vast now that we are here."

"Well, I feel better already," Reese said sarcastically. "We were all here just trembling with fear until you and your team showed up in those stunning costumes."

Lopex couldn't control the escape of a chuckle.

"Ah, Eta–Reese," Zaavan said, staring at his plump, white-coated form. "Zetas," he turned to his fellow crew, "Reese is an example of the great diversity in the Eta Demon Class. They made all sorts of odd Demons during that time," he said with disdain. "What was your purpose again? I can't remember, it was so obscure."

"Inspection," Reese said, staring intently at Zaavan.

"Ah, yes, inspection. Well, Zeta Brothers, where would the Devil be without an inspector? Your contributions to the Sled are invaluable, to be sure."

Zeta-Chalt laughed at her master's joke. Bore did not seem to understand the sarcasm. Montly almost involuntarily smiled widely, enamored with Zeta-Chalt.

Reese wiped an invisible fleck of dust from his short white coat, like he was wiping off the insult. Then he walked up to Zaavan, face to face.

"Just remember, Zaavan, we won't get credit for any Unbroken who are so injured they can't work. You got that? I know your class likes to show off all of your little 'additions.'

But that won't mean anything to the Sled, or our quota, if all we bring back are body parts. You understand that, Zavy?" Reese said.

Zaavan fumed at the twist to his name, but Reese continued. "I've heard the stories about your team. Keep those *beasts* of yours under control. I won't let pass what other inspectors have let pass for you."

Seeing the situation rising, Lopex interjected.

"Enough! We're leaving as soon as Delius gets here. Everyone needs to be set, gear settled and ready. No time for this belly-fat rubbing!"

Reese and Zaavan stared at each other for a moment, then dispersed accordingly. But their tension did not dissipate with distance.

Zeta-Chalt went to her Mauss, which happened to be next to Montly's. Montly saw a chance to befriend the impressive Demon, and she took it.

"Hello, Chalt, is it? My name's Montly," she said, with a hopeful smile.

"Montly? What is your *class* name?" Chalt responded.

Montly felt hot with embarrassment.

"I . . . I don't have a class name yet. I'm not a Demon. I'm from the Herd, from the Starboard side." She used the most formal terms she could muster in an attempt to impress, but the words felt odd and clumsy as they left her mouth.

"A Minion, then?" Chalt said.

"Well, yes, but we were all Minions once, right?" Montly searched for some common ground.

Closer to Chalt now, she could see her outfit for what it truly was: a giant tumor covering her body. It was thick, black, and impossibly malformed. In awe, Montly went to touch it.

Chalt gave a piercing look and retreated.

"How did they—" Montly was too amazed to finish the question.

"The Engineers can do many things that only a few privileged Demons get to experience," Chalt said with arrogance as she mounted her Mauss. "The Zetas get the best work done."

Montly reached into the neckline of her coat and pulled out the tumor necklace to show Chalt the similarity they shared.

But Chalt kicked her Mauss and rode over toward Zaavan and Bore, cutting the conversation short.

Montly watched her move away, still wide-eyed. Lopex interrupted her thoughts.

"Delius approaches. Mount up, and be ready!" he said, formal, stern, and a bit nervous. The disparate group came to attention. Montly ran over to her Mauss and climbed onto it.

Delius walked, unaccompanied, through Sapien Bay. Demon and Minion conversations hushed as he passed. He seemed not to notice any of this, as though his thoughts were in that place where those with great responsibilities dwell. His muscle ribbons lay closely against him, wrapped in a long flesh overcoat. He was not adorned with polished bone buttons or shiny tooth jewels, nor was his coat accented with purple or blue vein stitching. He just wore beige on beige, the most common color of skin found in Hell. His seven-foot-tall Demon frame seemed larger when wrapped up in the coat. He looked like a pillar of flesh that could hold up an entire level of the Sled by itself.

Delius walked directly toward Lopex. Lopex stood stiff and professional, with his arm outstretched holding a skin-scroll. Delius took it from his hand, and silently nodded to his pupil. He went around to the wagon where the Drums were lashed, patted one on the side, and smiled. Then he climbed to the top of the wagon and unfurled the scroll.

A moment passed as Delius read, then he wrapped the scroll up, surveyed the Cantavit, and spoke.

"Demons, Minions, Sapiens! Brothers and sisters of the Sled! We have been given a steep quota by the Daughters this Mandatum. But do not worry. The Skin-Land has always provided for the Sled. And I have no doubt that we will fulfill this quota." The Cantavit all nodded their heads confidently.

"The Unbroken will no doubt resist our gift to them. But we will be gracious when they resist, and we will not add undue suffering. For Hell is suffering enough." Delius looked toward the Zetas.

"We are here to serve the Devil. We have chosen this, and we serve him in all his needs in his rule over Hell. Never forget that this is a righteous task. God has commanded that the Devil rule Hell. This then is God's work that we do, and one must be humble when doing the work of God." A silence pervaded the Cantavit, punctuated only by nods of quiet agreement as Delius spoke his mantra.

Then the large doors of Sapien Bay opened onto the Skin-Land Vast. The morning air seemed tame, and the first blades of light crested an unknown horizon. The Sled slowly sliced across the Skin-Land like a ship across the sea. Delius mounted his brown Mauss and held up his right hand in a fist.

"From God's hand, to Hell … to the Devil's mouth!" Delius yelled, and he strode out onto the thick Skin-Land Vast. His Cantavit cheered as they launched their beasts behind him. The motley group of Demons, Minions, and Sapiens, all full of terrible things, furious hopes, and secret intentions, charged screaming behind their leader on this, his last venture.

CHAPTER THIRTEEN

The biggest problems facing God in this time are two-fold:

1. *People are completely inept at following the rules set forth to allow access to Heaven.*

2. *Most people do not believe that they are going to Hell, and are therefore entirely unprepared when they arrive.*

Unbeknownst to most, God is not interested in what interpretation you follow of His word. With very little, almost trivial variation, His core principles are the same from religion to religion. God allows, and even finds it endearing, that man has defined many iterations of His word both through culture and individual interpretation. But what He finds most interesting, and most to His dismay, is that even amongst all of these man-made rules, sub-rules, exceptions, and ceremonies, man still seems incapable of controlling his appetites to the point where he can put himself on a direct path to Heaven.

—From "God Worries"
An essay by Delta-Delius

Mariella ached, pain-drunk as the nerve endings in her body neared overload. Impulses fired up through her legs to her brain, demanding chemicals to block the pain, setting her mind off into a surreal loop of hallucination and epiphany.

"I deserve to be here. I know I deserve it," she mumbled. Her words drifted off into a strange hum of sound, then the next sentence would start abruptly. "I know what I've done. He knows what I've done. It's okay, though, it's okay."

Silton did a fair job wrapping her legs up in the sheet of skin. With no thread or needle, stitching the skin together was impossible, so he had to tie the sheet in large awkward knots that made a loose hammock he could drag her in. Mariella screamed when Silton tied the first knot. It pushed down on her ankles, the most fragile and broken part of her legs. The other knots seemed to hurt her less, but this was due to Mariella's endorphin-soaked brain. It made her seem intoxicated, tipsy with the chemicals that tried to edge over the pain. Silton started walking, dragging her in the skin hammock across the ground, off toward the white formation in the distance while Mariella grunted in pain and tried to talk.

"So, I'm a nurse. I'm a charge nurse. You know there's a difference, don't you? I don't take orders from anyone!" She slurred her words, wincing every once in a while from an involuntary leg jolt. "I float from department to department. Wherever they need someone, I go there. I'm good at everything. Maybe that's why everyone hates me." She laughed at herself. "I guess there's no point in hiding from that now. Funny how in life you lie to yourself all the time, every day it seems . . ."

Her eyes rolled around in her head. She could see nothing but a large, beige blob in front of her, set below a deep, yellow-green sky. "I lied to myself all day, every day. Different lies, the same lies. But I don't think lies matter much in this place."

"You don't have to tell me, Mariella. All I did in life was lie to myself," Silton interjected. "Blowing a hole through my chest was the most honest thing I've ever done." He kept pace, trudging toward the goal without regard, like any soldier would.

"Wow, you killed yourself. Is that hard to do? It sounds like it would be hard to do." An insensitive question perhaps, but her inhibitions were nil. She didn't seem to mean anything by it.

"It wasn't really that hard. All you need is a quick finger, some whiskey, and a picture of your wife."

"Ah, the wife, of course. So why did she leave you?" Mariella said, finishing the sentence with a sort of hum.

"You assume she left me?" he said. "Funny, but you're not entirely wrong. I wasn't good enough for her. I was always a step behind her for some reason. I guess I married up too far and couldn't cut it."

"Married up? She was a rich bitch, huh?"

"No, not really at all. Just smart, or more like a smart ass. She just acted like she had the whole life thing figured out before anyone else did. Definitely before I did."

"Mmmmm, sounds like a fun person to be around," Mariella said sarcastically.

Silton felt where the conversation was going, so he veered it into another direction. "So, what else about you? Tell me about you and the hospital."

Mariella hummed in response, a stiff popping sound, like she had lost control of her vocal cords. "I was the one you didn't mess with. I was great, NIC-U, ONC Ward, Surgery, you name it. That's the great thing about a small-town hospital;

you can get your hands into everything. There's never enough people, so you get to do things you'd never be qualified for anywhere else."

"Comforting," Silton responded.

"But the best was the ER. Most nurses will say that, because they think they have to say it. But most nurses don't mean it. They'd rather have something more predictable, a job where they can sit down. I can't blame them for that. I get it. I totally get it." Mariella grunted as Silton went over a small hump of hairy, irregular skin. "But not me. I really liked it, kept it fresh. But after ten or so years, even the ER gets tough."

"Yeah, seeing all that blood. All those accidents, I understand," Silton interjected.

"No, not that. Blood and guts and you name it dropping out of a person, that never bothered me. Still doesn't, not even in this place. No. What starts to get to you are the patients. You realize that we aren't going anywhere as a people anymore, as the human race, I mean."

"I don't follow," Silton admitted.

"Evolving, you know? In the most Darwinist way of thinking about it," Mariella said. "You ask any doctor, any of them. You ask if we're still evolving as a species, and they will tell you no. That's *if* they're being honest," she rambled. "I mean, we save everyone—at least most people. Darwinism, evolution . . . it needs death. That's the point of it. People have to die, and that just doesn't happen to a lot of people when it's supposed to."

"You did say you were a nurse, right?" Silton said playfully, dragging toward the white object on the horizon.

"Don't make fun," she slurred. "Anyone in healthcare who's worth their salt will tell you the same thing. When a guy comes in who blew his hand off with an M-80 on the fourth of July, we tourniquet his arm, give him a few pints of blood and stitch him up. We take care of it. When a woman comes in on an overdose from heroin, she's pumped full of Narcol. We take care of it. When a four-hundred-and-fifty-pound man has heart failure . . . and you know what I did once?" She paused as if she might have forgotten what she was talking about. "The doctor cracked open his chest and made me hold open the clamps, and he jumped on top of him and massaged his heart back to beating. That's what he did. Now why should anyone do something like that on a four-hundred-and-fifty-pound guy? Why?"

"Because you're a nurse, and he's the doctor, and it's the humane thing to do," Silton said firmly.

"The humane thing? I don't think you understand what that word means. That's a stupid idea that's screwed up our evolution for centuries. We don't have any more predators, we killed them all. Now even when we try to kill ourselves, some do-gooder puts a stop to that, too. No more evolution, that's it. We ain't going any further."

"Well, no one stopped me from killing myself," Silton countered.

"Yeah, because you did it the right way, Silton. You should be proud of that."

"Proud—well, somehow I don't see this place as a reward."

"It sure is for me. I deserve to be here," Mariella said.

"You deserve to be here? Why would you say that?" Silton asked.

"Why wouldn't I say that? Why do people constantly try to wiggle away from what they deserve? That's part of the problem."

"I just think it's harsh. It's like you want to be here, Mariella."

"Me *knowing* I belong here and *wanting* to be here are two different things."

Even in her compromised state, Mariella could tell that her callous words, words that were really meant for her, had inadvertently hurt him.

"I'm sorry. I told you I talk too much, Silton."

"No, it's okay," Silton said. He stopped and turned to face her. "I think I needed to hear that. You're right. This is no place for lies. I mean, what difference will they make here?"

Mariella still wasn't happy with what she'd said. Her constant impulse to steal away people's hope, no matter how much they needed it, was part of the reason she was here, and the reason she was so unpopular at the hospital. Maybe Mariella didn't belong in a place where compassion was the medicine most needed.

"I was the know-it-all who told you how it was," she continued. "Explained to you that if you didn't take your antibiotics on time, the infection would spread and we would have to amputate your arm. Or that if you pressed the morphine button too many times, you'd become addicted and it would ruin your life. I thought that telling the truth, the brutal kind of truth that people say they like to hear, made me better at my job. But people really don't want to hear the truth. I'm sorry, I shouldn't be so . . ."

Mariella stopped herself again. Instead, she focused on her own brutal truth: the twisted mess of bones and veins that were her legs. It had been three days since her fall, and the breaks should have been set by now. They should have been fused together with stainless steel pins, and a flat, curved ridge of surgical steel should be holding her shattered shinbone together. And the whole thing should have been wrapped up in a compression cast.

Instead, tiny calcifications were growing where they shouldn't be, blood was pooling where bone once was, and precious tendons floated around the whole mess like seaweed in the ocean.

"I think it's just the pain talking, Silton. I'm going to shut up now. So, tell me, your wife, don't you think she misses you? She probably does, right? Now that you're gone?"

"I don't know about that. She passed away three years before I did. Actually, the last time I saw her was in your hospital. The Coma Ward. She died there after about three months. Who knows, maybe you even treated her. You ever work the Coma Ward when—"

"No. Never. Sorry." Mariella answered quick and curt, and then kept quiet. She didn't want to talk anymore about her time at the hospital, especially not the Coma Ward. So she just stared at the beige blob in front of her, tried not to move, and wondered if maybe lies did have a place here in Hell after all.

CHAP+ER F⊕UR+EEN

In Hell, Demon construction is considered art, as they are perfect in both form and function. Centuries ago, the Devil discovered the mysteries of Hell, (see "The Devil's Great Fall") and because of this discovery learned how to manipulate Hell's resources to his advantage. The Devil has used all of this knowledge to experiment with the human form, thus creating the Demons we know of today.

—From "The Demonic Encyclopedia"
by Delta-Haldon

A trail of red depressions filled with blood followed the Cantavit as it strode across the Skin-Land. The sharp hooves of the Mauss pierced the upper layers of skin easily as the group cantered at a medium pace. The dog-like Canem could barely be seen in the distance. They ran as a pack, awkwardly sniffing out every crevice, every knoll, every feature of the geography before them. Once in a while, a pair of Canem would steal a moment to pounce on each other in vicious play, then they would return to their work.

Delius rode at the head of the Cantavit, Lopex at his side.

They spoke without looking at each other, always with their eyes on the horizon. High above, Zaavan sliced through thick green clouds on his huge skin wings.

Bore and Chalt rode a distant second, along with Zaavan's unridden Mauss. They didn't speak to each other, but between them lay a knowing, much like the knowing between brother and sister. Montly and Reese rode in the rear with the waddling Drums trailing behind them. It seemed to Montly that Reese hadn't stopped talking since they'd left the Sled. And if Montly was being honest, she had no idea what he'd been talking about. Maybe something about the special bacterium he used for the blood beer. Montly didn't know. But Reese spoke in a way that didn't require a response. He didn't seem to need anything other than a somewhat willing subject.

Instead, Montly stared at Chalt and the thick braids of blue and purple that hypnotically swayed back and forth as she strode. Her cobalt black skin glistened wetly in the light of morning, just like Montly's necklace did sometimes. Montly was slowly building up the courage to talk to Chalt, secretly wishing for a friendship that might quench her envy. But how could she not be rude to Reese, who'd now moved on to a full lecture on blood beer fermentation? She didn't want to offend him, but there were no gaps in his speech, no slight pause that would allow her to break out of this one-sided conversation. So Montly just interrupted him somewhere between reducing blood froth and alcohol yields per batch.

"I should go check on Zaavan's Mauss. Make sure it's okay without a rider," she said. It made no sense in her mind, and made even less sense as she said it. But it did disrupt Reese just long enough for her to smile, heel into her Mauss, and stride up to Chalt.

"Hi," Montly said and nodded to Chalt awkwardly. "Just wanted to check on the Sapiens, make sure everything is okay." She turned and inspected Zaavan's Mauss for a moment.

"Everything's fine," Chalt said with a sharp edge to her tone.

"Oh, of course," Montly responded. "I just want to make sure the muscle under Zaavan's Mauss's front left leg is okay. I noticed the area took a bit less blood when I was soaking it. The joint might be a little rigid." A lie, but it was all Montly could muster to create some type of conversation, a way to show concern and perhaps interest.

"I *said* everything's fine," Chalt responded again, still with that blade in her tone.

Having found no anchor for the conversation, Montly decided to change the subject. She looked over her shoulder to the ever-shrinking Sled in the distance.

"So, the Sled. It looks so different from here, but it gives you such an appreciation for its size, seeing the whole thing at once, you know?" Montly said uneasily.

"And how long have you lived on the Sled? A week, maybe two?" Chalt asked.

"Almost a week," Montly said, a bit embarrassed.

Chalt chuckled, but Montly pressed as if she'd not just been insulted.

"I just wanted to say that I think your skin is beautiful."

"Thank you," Chalt said, and looked at Montly for a moment, then pushed her scowl to a smirk.

"I never thought about it until I saw you, but tumor *would* make the perfect skin out here. I mean it's flexible, it can really cover any shape or surface of the body, and yet it's still so hard and durable. It's really genius on the part of the Engineers."

Montly rambled on. "I actually have a tumor necklace . . ."

She pulled it out from underneath her coat, leaning over to offer Chalt a look. She didn't stop talking, not for a second, fearing the conversation might end otherwise. "It was given to me by the Praefectus of the Herd during my graduation from Broken to Minion Herdsman. It's pretty rare. I've never seen anything like it. Well, until you."

Montly held it out, beckoning for Chalt to look. Reluctantly, Chalt turned her head and observed the necklace for a moment.

Montly smiled, also looking at the necklace as they both trotted along. "It's pretty close to your skin. I mean the smooth side, that is. I think it's almost identical. I'm thinking one day I can—"

"That's nothing!" Chalt interrupted, and Montly fell silent. "That is a reject. A piece of tumor spit out of someone. There's no order to it. There's no structure to it. It's disgusting. It's nothing like my skin!"

Chalt paused to let the words sink in. Montly froze with shock as she continued. "This was engineered. This was fitted and grown for *me,* and only *me.* What you have around your neck was made for no one. Some crusty old Herd Praefectus picked it up, put a vein rope on it, and gave it to you—a weak and blistered Broken she needed to help her run that mess of blood and bones that pulls the Sled." Chalt's voice rose, and Lopex turned his head to see the commotion. His attention quieted Chalt to a whisper.

"Listen to me, *Minion Montly.* I don't need you to tell me how perfect my skin is. I know how perfect it is. And I don't need you to tell me about Zaavan's Mauss and the flexibility of its joints. I know! *I* was supposed to be the Sapien Master on this Cantavit! You understand? I've been preparing for this Mandatum for months. And some nobody Minion like you comes along and takes *my* position? *My* promotion? You're not even a Demon. Just some Herd worker. You haven't even lost that smell. You stink like the feces the Herd marches through every day."

Chalt turned up her sharp, black nose. Bore, who'd remained silent, chuckled at the insult. Montly heard him, and his laugh only magnified her embarrassment. She found no response, and slowly placed the tumor necklace back under her coat, heeled her Mauss to a slow trot, and let the Zetas move ahead.

Soon, Montly strode side by side with Reese again.

"They ain't worth a thought," Reese said, trying to comfort her. "Such a distempered bunch, the Zetas are. No one gets along with them. You know that?" Although Montly heard his voice, she was deaf to his comfort.

Montly looked back over her shoulder at the Sled once more. Its massive structure stretched out long across the Skin-Land. Its huge blades sliced into the ground, splitting the skin, creating two blood canals that flowed like a red trail behind it. Even so far off, she could see Demon, Minion, and Sapien alike, bustling with activity. The Devil's bright white tower stretched high above the moving city, like an arm reaching for the sky.

And then Montly looked to the Herd: the lines of tens of thousands of Broken, all pulling against harnesses and bone yokes. They kicked up a cloud of skin flakes, feces, and blood as they marched. She could see the Herdsmen climbing on top of them, whipping and screaming the Broken, pushing them to pull ever harder. It was a symphony of pain, toil, and fear that Montly knew well, and now missed. She thought of the putrid smell that Chalt had spoken of and sniffed herself. Chalt was right—she still smelled of the Herd's rancid magnificence.

CHAP†ER FIF†EEN

Bone Catacombs can be a very useful land feature in Hell. This is an area where large deposits of bone have jutted upward from the Skin-Land by way of flesh tectonics. Bone in these structures is often much larger and stronger than the bone found lying on the surface due to the pressure placed on them over time while submerged in Hell. This makes them excellent for shelter and construction materials.

—From "Hell Geographica"
By Doctorem Delta-Lindicus

The miles passed slowly, and Silton's muscles seemed to get stiffer with each step. The blood in his thighs thickened and settled like soup left on the stove too long. Mariella had fallen asleep in mid-sentence a few hours ago. The exhaustion of pain had lulled her into a feverish dream state where she only mumbled to herself every once in a while. The absence of her voice made Silton feel lonely, and the loneliness made each step more difficult.

The bright white form on the horizon began to take shape,

and like everything else here, it wasn't what Silton had first thought. He'd suspected the white mass to be a large hill, maybe even a small mountain, but instead it looked more like a series of caves stacked jaggedly one on top of the other. The walls of the caves were juxtaposed and random, filled with holes and depressions. It was as if a rainforest had been bleached white and stripped of all its leaves, leaving only a pallid maze of thick trees.

Although not what Silton expected, it was better than he could have hoped for. There must have been a hundred cubbies, overgrowths, and shade spots for them to find cover in.

"Mariella, Mariella. Wake up." Silton jostled the skin hammock, hearing his voice echo behind him in the catacombs. He pushed his voice to a whisper, bent a knee, and moved closer to Mariella.

"Hey, hey..." He caressed her face, feeling the still warmth of her cheek. "We made it. It's time to get up now." No response. Silton adjusted himself to get a stance so he could examine Mariella more closely, and noticed that his knees were wet, his shins were sticky. He reached his hand down to the ground. The skin had changed from solid to a viscous liquid, like smooth, beige-colored oil. Immediately his mind went to the fat pit and the drowning people from the hospital, and to Skinny Chad, with his arm sucked into the ground like quicksand.

"Mariella!" he said louder, panic rippling along the edges of his voice. But still, not even the subtlest movement from her. Silton debated striking her—not something within his character, but he could feel the skin around them starting to depress, sinking like a weak trampoline canvass. The meat of his hand squared perfectly with her cheek, and the fleshy pop of the strike echoed into the caves.

Mariella's eyes flashed open, and she grunted a guttural sound from the base of her vocal cords. "Huh... wha... shhhhh... no!" Unintelligible words formed a sentence even she could not understand.

She shifted back and forth, moving her legs as she tried to get up. Audible cracks came from her ankles, and tears burst from her eyes as the broken bones in her legs ground against each other. A clear cry of pain brought Mariella back to full consciousness.

"Oh God, oh God...."

"I know, I know. Just breathe. Try to stop moving so much," Silton implored.

She started to sob, a stark departure from the hard-nosed charge nurse she'd described herself as only a few hours earlier. The skin around them was still very sticky, wet with liquid skin and fat, but seemed to not be worsening.

"Hey, we made it. We made it, and it's better than I thought." Silton held her face in his hands, a tender counterpoint to his harsh slap. "We can sleep here, Mariella. We'll be safe in these caves. We can start work on your legs."

She smiled, took in a snotty mucus-ridden breath, and started to chuckle with a deep, almost insane laugh.

"Work on my legs..." Mariella said to herself. "Work on my legs?" Her maniacal voice echoed into the bleached caves. "Screw this!" She pulled herself to sit upright. Anger filled her voice, and she started to come back to her strong, forceful self.

Silton noticed the skin beginning to harden around them, and the looseness of the ground became taut again. Even the beige oil on his hand crusted, lost its moisture, and became dry. Silton couldn't ignore the causality of the situation, the natural rules this place seemed to command. If you give up it will try to take you.

"I'm fine now. I'm fine . . ." Mariella said. "Thank you for getting us here, wherever that is." She looked wide-eyed at the fantastic maze of white lattice around her.

"Yeah, let's get inside. We need to get to work on those legs. And I'm gonna need your help. I hope you're as good a patient as you are a nurse," Silton said.

"Awww, Silton. Don't you know nurses make the worst patients?" she said harshly, knowing it was painfully true.

They both smiled—a forced smile, but a smile.

Silton and Mariella gripped hands, paused to garner strength, and heaved up to stand together. The bones in her knees cracked, and the muscles in his thighs strained deep and long. They merged, becoming one person who might be able to walk, and moved into the maze of choppy white caves step by step.

Behind them, the skin where Mariella had lain moved as if alive, as if it had its own consciousness. It waved, became taut, and the moistness reabsorbed. Soon it was solid and dry-cracked, just like the miles of skin around it.

CHAP+ER SIX+EEN

When found by a patrolling Demon Cantavit, expect to experience a series of protocols before being taken to the Sled. These protocols are gruesome and painful, so prepare yourself as best you can. Demons are singular in their drive, and have been hardened through their existence in Hell, so it is recommended that you not struggle. Although you may at first feel these protocols to be torture, understand that these methods create a larger sense of order which will ultimately translate into a safer, more fulfilling experience for you in Hell.

—From "Hell: A Survival Guide"
By Delta-Delius

L opex stared intently at his master skin scroll as his Mauss lolled back and forth. Listed on the sheet was a bevy of items demanded by every department on The Sled: twenty-three orders for vein lengths, twelve orders for palatable blood, ten orders for bone, etcetera. Then the requests became more specific: five orders for gall bladders, three orders for gallstones, two orders for perfectly shaped Medulla Oblongatas, and one order for an unmolested nerve ganglion. Finally, there was the standing order for intact hearts. It was completely unnecessary for this request to be written down, as every Minion and Demon who went out into the Vast knew to collect intact hearts. The order came directly from the Devil himself, yet no one knew why. Some said he used them as trophies, a way to remind himself that he'd stolen man's heart. Others said he dined on them exclusively, having a taste for only the toughest of muscles. And others still had even more imaginative theories, but these were scant rumors born more from tattered drunk conversation than fact.

What concerned Lopex the most about his master list was the quota for Unbroken. The quota demanded twenty-five intact, fully to semi-functional Unbroken. Although a Cantavit wouldn't necessarily be judged negatively if they didn't find some rare organ or gallstones, they would be judged for their ability to find and bring back the necessary quantity of Unbroken. The Unbroken were the backbone of the Sled and, as many would say, the backbone of the Devil's power in Hell. Without the Unbroken, there would be no Broken to pull the Sled; without the Unbroken, there could be no Sapiens to do slave work; and without the Unbroken, there would be no pool from which to select Minions and create Demons. Everything started with them. They were the most precious resource in Hell.

Lopex felt it necessary to bring this to his master's attention, and although he considered Delius a friend, Lopex always found it difficult to start conversations with him. Perhaps the constant air of preoccupation Delius embodied made Lopex feel like he was always interrupting him. But Lopex fought this feeling of intimidation, sometimes successfully.

"So, I am a little concerned about this request," Lopex started. "Twenty-five Unbroken? That's not a small amount. In fact, I can only remember one other time when we were asked to bring back this many. And that was only after we'd found a settlement."

"You worry too much, Lopex," Delius dismissed.

"I didn't say I was worried, just concerned. It would be quite a task to round up twenty-five Unbroken, even if we knew where they were. But to just stumble upon that many? I'm concerned that the request is unrealistic based on what we've seen out here."

"Of course you are concerned. Of course you are paging through the historical Cantavit quotas in your mind. Of course you realize that the request might be out of reach. That's what makes you so good at this. You see the Cantavit and its place here in Hell as a whole. You don't just focus on your own responsibilities. You care about not only our success, but the success of the Sled," Delius said cryptically.

"Well, what else would I care about?" Lopex asked.

"Exactly."

Confused by Delius's vague response, which seemed to brush off his original concern, Lopex pushed again.

"Right, Delius. So, as I was saying, I think we need to speak to the Daughters about this request, and make them understand that we can only—"

Delius held up his hand, motioning for Lopex to be quiet. Lopex stopped mid-sentence. Delius turned and looked straight into his eyes, pausing for a moment before speaking.

"You know that I'll be requesting that you take my place as Cantavit Praefectus, don't you?" The brevity and sincerity of the question shocked Lopex to silence, but he pulled himself from it.

"Well, I had hoped that perhaps one day I could—"

"Hoped? Hoped, Lopex? You don't need to hope that one day you could do this job. You've done it for the last six Cantavits. I'm only a figurehead, a name. I've watched. I've seen you coordinate the Scrottings. I've seen you marshal the items for quota. I've seen you keep peace between the Demons. You *are* a Praefectus. You just haven't realized it yet."

"You honor me. You, the last of the Deltas, have given me so much—"

"Enough," Delius said dismissively, almost annoyed. "You and I are more than teacher and pupil. We've exceeded that many, many Cantavits before. You always talk about what I have given you. Well, you are going to give me something, now."

"Anything," Lopex said.

"Peace."

"Peace? How can I give you peace?" Lopex asked.

"By taking this Cantavit," Delius said.

"Taking this Cantavit? I don't think I understand."

"You will." Delius reached into a skin flap pocket in his coat and pulled out a small pouch lumpy with something inside.

"There is a tradition, a secret tradition, only between Deltas," Delius continued. "One of the reasons why the Deltas have been so strong is that we pass all of our knowledge on to one another before we sink. We've done it for centuries, even before The Devil's Great Fall. In this pouch is a small piece of brain tissue. I've placed my entire memory into this tissue, as well as the memories of the entire Delta Class before me. As there are no more Deltas left, I am in a quandary. Who do I give it to? Do I just let the memories of the Deltas fade away? I think not."

Delius handed Lopex the pouch. "Once I'm gone, you will

take this brain tissue and merge it with your own. Then you will have the combined knowledge of all of the Deltas, including mine. This is not a gift, Lopex; it is an obligation."

Once again, Lopex froze, silenced by his teacher. The pouch, a rough hide covering, protected something tender inside.

"I didn't think it was possible to put so much memory into such a tiny bit of brain tissue," Lopex managed.

"Well, the Zetas aren't the only ones who benefit from our industrious Engineers," Delius countered.

"Of course." As the shock wore off, Lopex snapped back. "Wait, why are you giving this to me now? You said you only give these before you sink. But how do you know that you will fall? That doesn't make any sense . . ."

"Silence, Lopex! I don't want you to think about that. I don't want you to worry about anything except this Cantavit, this journey, this time right in front of you. You will keep that brain tissue safe, and when the time comes, you'll know what to do with it. Do you understand?" Delius asked. "Say yes to your Praefectus!"

"Yes, Praefectus, I understand." Lopex put the hide pouch into the pocket of his coat.

But Lopex did not understand.

CHAP+ER SEVEN+EEN

In Hell, your body and the bodies that compose Hell are the only materials you can use to your advantage. Therefore, if at all possible, and with your utmost resourcefulness, you must keep your body intact and in relative working order. In many cases this will require you to attempt self-repair. This is an intimidating task, but one that should be taken with resolve. Understand that your body is still alive, and if left unchecked, it will simply push the healing process along on its own. Many individuals who have had relatively simple injuries find themselves completely crippled because they did not take on the painful obligation of repairing themselves.

—From "Your Body and How It Has Changed"
By Doctorem Delta-Lindicus

T he inside of the bone caves smelled moist and milky, with hints of iron from the rich marrow that ran through the walls. Parts of the floor were hard, with flat white expanses. Other parts were soft, flushed with blood-rich muscle. The forced march from the fat pit to the bone caves had taken most of Silton's strength and made his legs horribly stiff. Massaging his quadriceps helped to get some of the blood moving again, but not much. For the first time, he allowed himself to notice his stomach growling, desperate for food.

He laid Mariella's head down on a soft, springy lump of muscle and moved her legs onto an elevated patch of bone. He didn't mention why he'd chosen this deliberate positioning of her body. He didn't want her to know he planned to re-break her legs.

"There are about twenty ways you can break a bone, but only one way to put it back together," Silton's Combat Medic Trainer would always say. Bone was resilient and had a knack for healing well. But if not done correctly, the effects could be worse than the initial injury. Silton wasn't sure if he was about to make things better or worse for Mariella.

"So, what's next? I assume you've made plans for dinner?" Mariella asked, trying for a grin but wincing in pain at the end of her sentence.

"Funny, I was just thinking about that," Silton replied. "But I'm afraid you can't have anything to eat before surgery."

Mariella laughed, jolting herself so hard her ankle joint cracked, and she grunted.

"Damn you, Silton! You military types are just as twisted as us nurses."

"Yeah, staring at death day in, day out will do that to you," Silton replied. "Well, here's one you might like. If I can get you laughing hard enough, maybe you can re-break all of these calcifications yourself, so I don't have to do it for you." Silton forced an awkward smile.

Mariella didn't laugh this time. She knew what was coming. She knew that the bones in her legs were busy trying to repair the injuries by themselves, and doing a terrible job of it. She knew that there were at least three breaks that needed to happen. Her left femur was off by about two inches, looking like she had an extra hip on that side. Her left shinbone was only off by an inch and a half, but it was twisted inward by over forty-five degrees. And then there was her right ankle; it might have only been a hairline crack, but the swelling told her it could be broken, too. All of these would need to be cleanly snapped and separated from the calcifications that jellied around them.

Ironic that the compound fracture of her right shinbone sticking out of her skin was the cleanest injury. It would need to be set, but not re-broken.

Done with her self-analysis, she gave her medical opinion to Silton.

"I would suggest a surgical hammer and pin for the left femur and shin. Then put me into a spatial brace for the ankle. With a steel rod inserted into my right shin, I should be good to go. Then call in the orthopedist so he can look at my knees." She said this as a joke, but Silton didn't respond to the attempt at humor. He knew all too well the pain waiting for Mariella in the moments to come.

"Yeah, I'm thinking the old grab and yank technique is what we're going to go with," Silton said as he went to his knees next to Mariella. She tried to be calm, but the tears came hard. She knew he was right. No amount of dark humor could distract from that.

"So, I do have something I want to ask you," Silton said, slow and deliberate.

"Go ahead," Mariella said.

"Would you like me to restrain you?"

Mariella responded with sobs as she covered her face.

"It's nothing to be ashamed of. About half of the guys I ask take the option. The other half tell me afterward that they wish they had. I only ask because I'm not going to be able to do these breaks quickly and hold you down at the same time." Silton tried to be professional, doing his best to hit that Warrior Switch all combat soldiers have that turns them into well-trained machines. But this was different. Mariella was no soldier. She wasn't prepared for this.

But Mariella was also no fool. She knew she'd probably punch Silton with all her strength, if not during the first break, definitely the second. She'd seen this before: a one-hundred-and-fifteen-pound girl knocking back a two-hundred-and-fifty-pound orderly during a re-break because the damn intern didn't wait for the anesthetic to take hold.

But to give up one's power so utterly and completely in this horrible place would be difficult. Luckily, Mariella was smart enough to know the right thing to do and trusting enough to let Silton do the job.

"Get it done, Silton."

Silton ripped apart the skin-gurney into long flat strips. He put her arms parallel behind her back and wrapped them over and over again, until they were immovable. Next, he fashioned four wide sections of skin: two as long as her upper legs and two as long as her lower legs. These would be the castings. He spied a patch of splintered bone bowing out from the wall, leaking fresh marrow. He ripped off eight pieces the same length as the skin he'd prepared.

"I know it looks sloppy, but this technique worked for my arm. It sounds hard to believe, but I'm actually really good at fixing people up when I don't have what I need. It's our specialty as Combat Medics," Silton said, trying to make light of the situation as he positioned all of his splints.

"You'd get along great at my hospital, then. We never have what we need, either," Mariella said, chuckling as she squirmed a bit against her bonds. "So, one more thing before you start, Silton."

"Anything. Anything at all."

"I'm going to ask you to put a blindfold over my eyes, okay?"

A brief moment of silence pervaded between them, and only the flat sound of blood dripping off the ceiling and landing on bone could be heard.

"Right. Of course." Silton ripped another long, flat piece of skin from what he had left and showed it to Mariella.

"Good luck, soldier. You do me right—you got it?" Mariella said as she closed her eyes.

"Yes, ma'am." Silton tied the skin blindfold tight across the back of her head, then placed a small round of bone in her mouth between her teeth.

Silton positioned his hands above where he would make the first break: the ankle twisted to the side. Hopefully, Mariella wouldn't anticipate this, and the surprise would steal away a few seconds of pain.

An instant later, he twisted her ankle back to its correct position. A humming howl of pain curdled out of Mariella's mouth. Without waiting, and without placing the splints, Silton moved to the femur. With a tug and a strong push down with all of his weight, a grinding crack vibrated through Mariella's body. She lost control of her bowels, spreading warm liquid across the ground. Her shoulders slumped down like a marionette with cut strings, and she lost consciousness.

Silton took his time with the rest of the breaks, snapping

each one with the focus and technique of a primitive surgeon. With the hard part over, soon he was placing the splints. The skin casts molded nicely to each length of her leg, and he used some of the ragged capillary on the ground to make tight ties around his work.

Without an x-ray, it would be impossible to tell if he'd lined everything up correctly, but things looked much straighter than before. He massaged the cast work with sweat, hoping to dry the skin out quickly so it would set hard like his forearm.

"Maybe she'll walk now, if her knees hold together," Silton said to himself, hearing his voice echo through the white caverns.

"And now . . . to dinner."

CHAPTER EIGHTEEN

The first step a Demon takes when encountering an Unbroken is to apply a Scrot. A Scrot is an arm's length piece of petrified bone ending in a U shape that has the sole purpose of mutilating your sex organs. Before being applied, the Scrot will be dipped in a highly acidic mixture strong enough to melt skin but not damage bone. When you are Scrotted, it is important to limit struggling, as this could cause other injuries. Please note: The Scrotting is one of the most important steps toward your survival and becoming a productive member of Hell.

—From "Hell: A Survival Guide"
By Delta-Delius

A quiet covered the Cantavit. An easy, natural quiet only interrupted by the occasional sound of suction as a Mauss pulled its sharp hoof up from pierced Skin-Land, or a squeak as the bone wheels on Reese's wagon begged for more fat to lubricate its axle.

High up in the yellow-green sky, Zaavan glided like a kite tethered to the ground. His eyes, a deep hazel brown, kept track of the Canem. The pack of dog-like Sapiens scampered across the Vast, sniffing out every nook, every hill shadow, every potential hiding place. Far off in the distance, a pair of Canem grouped around a small outcropping of bone covered in sloppy skin. They'd been there longer than usual. Zaavan tweaked the muscles in his eyes, pushing the lens of his cornea so the light focused behind the retina. This allowed him to see much further and more clearly for a few seconds.

Suddenly, Zaavan snapped his wings straight and spun in tight barrel rolls. He dove swiftly toward the Canem with all the force and intent of a hawk closing in on its prey.

Chalt saw this move immediately and kicked her Mauss hard and sharp with the long bone spurs at her heels. "He's found Unbroken!"

And she was off, pouncing past Delius and Lopex, charging to where Zaavan had dove. Bore, who seemed confused for a moment, shook off his stupidity and quickly followed her as fast as his Mauss could run beneath his massive weight.

"It begins," Delius said, more to himself than anyone else, and moved his Mauss to an aggressive canter.

Lopex went into action, turning to Montly. "No need to break your Mauss under speed. The Zetas will get there first. Just make sure you don't lose the Drums or Reese behind you."

"Yes, yes, of course," Montly responded, her heart fluttering.

"You never forget your first encounter with Unbroken, kid. Just remember to enjoy it!" said Reese as he pushed his Mauss and wagon to a stride. Montly moved to a canter next to him, and the Drums began their awkward run, six legs moving like a clumsy, but capable, insect.

As Montly got closer to the skin outcropping the Canem had found, she could see that this was no natural formation. A tall piece of bone jutted out of the Skin-Land, acting as a shoddy tent pole where a large swath of capillary-ridden skin hung over it. There was much commotion at the site: the Canem howled uncontrollably, the Zetas spoke loudly to one another, and then there were the screams—high-pitched, desperate screams of confusion and terror. Screams that could only come from one such entity in Hell: the tender Unbroken.

Three men, stark naked and bathed in fear, sat huddled together under the makeshift tent. The men screamed at the Zetas to stay back. Their arms extended up and out in an aggressive posture, trying to protect their skin tent. Zaavan stood at the rear, his wings outstretched and intimidating. Chalt and Bore stood at the forefront with the Canem keeping the Unbroken men corralled.

"Bore!" Zaavan yelled, and the red giant moved toward the closest man in the group. Seeing the monster approach, one of the Unbroken sparked uncommon bravery and lunged at Bore, throwing himself into his chest. The Unbroken man bounced back onto the ground, dizzy from striking his immovable form. The Demon bent over to get closer to the man, and he kicked upward toward Bore's shovel-shaped, bone-plated head. Bore caught the man by his ankle and snapped it like a twig. A shock-pause rippled through the man before he screamed in both pain and disbelief.

One of the other Unbroken men sprinted out into the Skin-Land away from Bore. Zaavan took in a deep breath and expelled a cone of acid onto the Unbroken's back. The man's skin melted off of him like a cloak dropped off his shoulders. His knees buckled as the pain crumpled him into a puddle of blood.

The rest of the Cantavit arrived quickly. With a look, Delius quieted the Canem and kept mounted while observing the scene. Lopex appeared next, with Montly and Reese close behind.

"Take the Drums around to make a perimeter, then get back to my side. Quickly, Montly. Quickly!" Lopex said.

Montly took the herd into a wide arc around the entire Cantavit, commanding one Drum at a time to stop, until they made a circle around the ordeal, staring dumbly at the still-screaming Unbroken men at the center.

Chalt and Bore hogtied the two injured men first, then worked on the third. He struggled less, but talked more. No one paid any attention to him, but this didn't stop him from talking.

Soon after, the three Unbroken men sat on their knees in front of their tent, shaking, screaming, and sobbing.

"The Drums are set, sir," Montly said, meeting Lopex at his side.

"Perfect. Very nice job on the spacing. You have a good instinct with them, and they seem to like you."

"Thank you so much," Montly replied loudly over the screams of the Unbroken.

Reese dismounted and walked aggressively toward Lopex.

"I don't want to start an argument, but this is exactly what I'm talking about, Lopex! That one is going to need a new skin-sheet for his back, and the other one won't be able to walk on his own! Who's going to fix that? You know the Herd Praefectus won't accept them as they are."

"First of all, Reese," Lopex started, "the Herd Praefectus will accept whatever we bring her, because she needs them. And secondly, we have Montly. She's well versed on repairing the Unbroken. That's one of the reasons why she's here."

Reese, although unsatisfied with the explanation, quickly realized it was the only explanation he was going to get. He folded his arms around his fat belly, and resigned himself to observe quietly.

Delius, still mounted, had yet to say a word. He looked over at Zaavan. Their eyes met, and Delius gave a nod. Zaavan, in turn, gave a silent nod to Chalt. Chalt cracked her knuckles and neck, walked to the Unbroken, and began to speak.

"You must always remember this moment. You must commit this to memory, your first true memory of Hell. In time you will look upon this day as the beginning of your life here, and this will provide you some comfort." She said this with open arms and the perfected voice of a master orator.

Montly watched, impressed. She so wanted that skill.

The man with the broken ankle spoke. "Look, I'm a cop. I'm the Chief of the Yuma County Sheriff's Department, and the Head of the Southern District Special Regimen Task Force. I don't know who you people are, but—"

"Titles, always the titles. They seem to get longer with each Mandatum," Bore interrupted. Zaavan put his finger to his lips, motioning to hush Bore like one would hush a small child ignorant of their place.

The Unbroken man continued, full of courage. "I don't know who you people are, but I'm a powerful man. I am a God-fearing man. I go to church. I donate! I've helped countless people! I don't belong here! I belong somewhere else. I have authority. I can help you people. If you let me go, I can—"

"Silence!" Chalt's voice shattered the air like a hammer to glass. Even Montly covered her ears, the sound so deafening. Obviously, Chalt had extra vocal cords and a reinforced diaphragm to speak at that volume. Montly's admiration grew ever further.

Chalt continued, "Understand this, Unbroken man: It is

not we who put you here. *God* has placed you here, and you are now staring into the eyes of God's servants. Your time to bargain is over. *He* made a bargain with *you*. A bargain where *He* gave you your life and in return asked for your love. It is this bargain that you have broken. And this place, Hell, is your punishment for breaking that agreement with God. There is no one here for you to negotiate with."

The man shook his head, squinted his eyes, and began to speak again, but Bore struck him in his mouth. Seeing this, Delius cleared his throat hard and loud. Bore looked at him, then to Zaavan, who silently motioned to the massive red Demon to calm down. Bore took two steps back, and like a child, hung his head.

The uninjured man saw this as his opportunity.

"Look ... look, listen. I'm like you," he said in a comforting tone. "I know where I am, I want to be here. I'm a Satan Worshiper. I've prayed for this. I worship every day ... I had tattoos! I had a pentagram on my thigh, and the devils face on my arm! They're gone now, but I promise you, I had them! Look at my shoulder ... please! Come here and look at my shoulder! I have a brand! An upside-down cross! I'm a Satanist. I promise. I'm like you! I'm on your side!"

Chalt looked back at Zaavan, almost for permission, and Zaavan nodded. Chalt approached the Unbroken, bent down, and looked closely at his shoulder. There, in the center of the joint, was what looked like a swollen, upside-down cross welted into the skin. Chalt looked back to Zaavan once again, and Zaavan held out his hand in response. Chalt turned back and ripped off the skin from the base of the man's neck to his mid arm. It peeled from his body like thick sod from the ground with thin capillaries instead of tiny roots.

The man wailed in pain and wretched a dry heave in shock as he slumped to the ground. Staring at Lopex, Reese shook his head in silent protest. Lopex sighed.

Chalt took the bloody skin patch to Zaavan, who quickly examined it. Then he walked it to Delius and handed it to him.

"Chalt has never encountered a Satanist before," Zaavan said. "I yield to you, if you'd like to address them."

"Of course." Delius dismounted, holding the flap of skin in his hand. He walked toward the men and spoke. "To worship the Devil? To this you have committed your life-times?" Delius shook his head. "Well, I am sorry to say that in this regard, your life has been a waste."

Delius stood tall and straight, casting a wide, dark shadow over the man. The man looked up at him in silent fear. "It is a sad thing, that for you, history has been so manipulated, so falsely taught to you."

Delius bent down and gently cupped the man by his chin. "Now that you are in your new home, you must understand something firstly and immediately: *The Devil hates you.* He hates everything about you. But what he hates more than you is the fact that God *chose* to make you. The Devil doesn't understand why God would make something so imperfect, something that had the choice to love him or not. The Devil doesn't understand why something so flawed as you should exist. To worship him, to dedicate your life to him, to speak of him in such a way, the Devil finds this as the most egregious of insults. He blames *you* for the rift between him and God. He despises every day he spends here, not because of the solitude, but because God made him rule over that which he hates the most: You."

He held up the skin-flap with the branded cross. "You should thank Zeta-Chalt for ripping this off your arm. Your fellow Broken would not look kindly on this image. And a little advice. Never again speak of your imagined loyalties to the Devil, but instead cherish this fact: If it is truly your wish to serve the Devil here in Hell, you may get your chance. But serving him will require much more of you than some silly skin-decoration."

Delius threw the bloody flap down on the ground next to the man. "Zaavan. You and your team may begin the Scrotting." Delius walked away.

Chalt and Bore went to their Mauss and grabbed their specially carved bone Scrots. Each of the tools held personal customizations with artistic carvings, dried vein grips, and jeweled teeth. They dipped their beautiful Scrots into a large stomach bladder of acid until they sizzled. Then the screams of the Unbroken men truly began as the Zetas melted off their tender parts like fleshy ornaments.

CHAP+ER NINE+EEN

Muscle Ponds, although difficult to find, are an excellent resource in Hell. They are created beneath the surface due to shifting flesh and muscle's inclination to always try to adhere to other muscle. This phenomenon can be particularly useful during injury repair, as fresh muscle will strengthen and even replace damaged muscle. Demons have utilized this technique for centuries to enhance themselves with increased strength (see "The Demonic Encyclopedia" – Chapter – "Enhancements").

—From "Hell Geographica"
By Doctorem Delta-Lindicus

Mariella lay unconscious. Her chest rose and fell, rhythmic and gentle, like deep ocean waves. The caves stood silent, except for odd noises that could be heard soft and far away: the sound of meat slapping against meat, or bone scraping against bone. Silton pulled his mind away from these noises and worked hard not to add any noise of his own.

Silton had crafted a small watering hole and filled it with the excess sweat that accumulated under him during his sleep.

The warm water tasted much better than the batch he'd had a day ago, but he drank it sparingly. Next, he ripped up six arm's-length strips of muscle from a shallow depression in the ground. The flesh was tough, like flank steak, but with the help of a thin piece of bone, Silton scraped off much of the sinew and tendons that ran through the slabs. Soon he had two piles: one of translucent connective tissue, and one of rich, red muscle flaps. He carved off a small ribbon of muscle, slicing it easily between its rowed striations. He looked at it for a second and, feeling no hesitation, popped it into his mouth. His mind may have had an argument for not eating the stuff, but his stomach had long ago given up on such philosophic luxuries.

He chewed once, twice, three times, just to get it soft enough to swallow. It was odd to feel food travel down his throat for the first time in days: a large lump in his esophagus, then no feeling as it passed the vacancy in his chest to his stomach. Once there, desperate acids greeted the meat with pleasure. He ate the rest of the muscle with a ferocity found only in wayward animals. It tasted of deep iron, a flavor that was almost alive. He would have to soak the next piece with sweat water, and imagine eating a plate full of oiled Carpaccio.

Silton took another of the large bloody steaks and slapped it across his thighs so he might have better leverage while slicing it. The muscle bled a bit as he worked on one of the tendons, and immediately Silton became overcome with a feeling of lightheadedness. He looked down at the muscle steak lying on his thigh and noticed the blood had stopped dripping from it. In fact, the blood that leaked out was gone, as if his thigh acted like a sponge and drank it up. He felt dizzy, euphoric, and a tingling ran up his spine like his flesh had taken in a deep breath. The feeling invigorated him, and without thinking, Silton pressed the meat down on his thigh, squeezing out more blood from the steak. His skin soaked it in desperately.

Soon, the meat was exhausted of fluid. Silton went to remove it from his thigh, but it wouldn't budge. He pulled a bit harder, and it tugged back at him as if glued to his leg. He pulled harder still. Hair, and even a bit of skin, peeled off his leg as Silton ripped the muscle steak off and threw it across the cave. He got up to investigate the meat parasite and immediately noticed the stiffness in his leg was gone. He flexed, bent his knee a few times, and was in awe. His thigh felt completely normal. All of the muscle cramps were gone, and he felt no more heaviness in his foot. He realized that he'd taken something from that muscle, from that blood, and added it to his own.

"That good, huh?" Mariella said. She'd been quietly awake for some time. Silton turned to her, surprised.

"The meat, the muscle, it . . . I think it tried to attach to me. And the blood, it . . ."

"Attach?" Mariella interrupted.

"I'm telling you, it's like it's alive."

"Yeah, well, I think technically it is. But I don't care, what did it taste like? I'm starving, and in case you're wondering, I'm already over the whole cannibalism thing."

Silton grabbed another steak, cut it as thinly as he could with the crude knife, and they ate for what seemed like an eternity, tearing away at strip after strip with anxious teeth, washing the food down with swallows of warm sweat water.

"Look at us huddled here, bloody, naked, squatting in a cave eating human flesh. And loving it! It's like we've lost every bit of humanity we ever had," Mariella said between breaths.

"No, not even close," Silton said with his mouth full. "Losing your humanity has nothing to do with what happens to you, or what you do to yourself. Trust me. I know. I've been there before. Losing your humanity has to do with how you treat other people. It's a choice, like quitting a club. We can't let that happen to us. Though, from what I hear, there's a certain freedom in it. Once you lose your faith in humanity, people can never disappoint you again."

Mariella thought his comment revealing. It gave her a glimpse into a portion of Silton's personality she thought attractive, a dark realness that made them more alike.

"Tough words, coming from the patriotic Army Medic," Mariella said with shadowy flirtation.

"Not everyone who joins the military does it because they're patriotic," Silton said.

"So, you're saying you're not?"

"No, I'm not saying that at all. I'm just saying that I had other reasons, too."

"Like . . . ?" she asked impatiently, wiping blood from her chin.

"I was damn patriotic. I paid my taxes. I served my country. I was good at it too . . . but I got lost. Forgot what I was working toward. The day-to-day just got automatic, and when I thought of doing what I originally set out to do, it scared me. So, I just stayed in the Army. Kept doing what I was good at: killing people and saving people."

"So, what was it? Let me guess, you wanted to start your own private security firm. That's what you people do, right?" Mariella meant it as a sarcastic slight, but the comment was lost on Silton.

"If you have to know, I wanted to go to Med School. That was the whole point of joining the Army. I wanted to be a doctor, work in a hospital like you. I figured if I could save a guy with his arm blown off, rolling around in the desert, with rounds flying past my head, I could do pretty good in a fully staffed emergency room."

"Hmm. Cliché, but you're probably right. I've worked with a couple of ex-military doctors. They've always been worth their salt, and real down to earth."

"Yeah, well, like I said, I forgot about all that. There's a thrill to active duty. It makes normal life look black and white. That's what she used to say to me. That I only saw her in black and white."

Mariella chose not to respond. She sipped a bit of sweat water and secretly begged for a subject change.

"Maybe that's why I have no heart," Silton continued. "Maybe I never did. Hell's supposed to be ironic, right? She always told me I didn't know how to love her."

"Would you please stop with the self-pity garbage? It's making me sick. Maybe she just didn't love you as much as you loved her. You ever think of that? God, you're even starting to sound like her."

The conversation froze. Seconds seemed like hours as Mariella's words organized themselves in Silton's mind.

"What do you mean I sound like her? How do you know what she sounded like?"

There was a shuffled pause.

"I just meant you sound like a typical girl, that's all." She chewed hard on her muscle steak, stuffing her mouth full.

Silton pushed the strange comment away. "Maybe you're right. Maybe there wasn't enough love on her side. At least she was kind to me, like she was doing me a favor. She was smart enough for both of us. I did my best to understand her, but she always seemed to be ahead of me in everything, even our marriage. But it's funny when you lie to yourself. It either works permanently, or it doesn't work at all, like me telling myself I was a good husband."

"Yeah, well, some would say that the ability to lie to yourself is a virtue, Silton."

Silton huffed. Although he might have agreed with her, he decided to put the whole conversation away.

"Forget all of that. Let's look at these legs of yours." The two chuckled morbidly, but Mariella winced, thinking of the pain to come.

Much like Silton's arm, the skin had begun to seal itself to Mariella's body. It banded stiffly in the sections around her calves and thighs, and very tight around her ankle. Both of her knees still held heavy bruises in a deep purple slowly changing to an awkward yellow-green. But the shinbone protruding from her leg remained tucked nicely where it belonged.

"It looks as good as I hoped. I want to push on your heel, okay? I want to see what kind of pressure you can take." Silton said.

Mariella squealed as his palm pushed up against her heel. Even the slightest amount of force compacted the swollen fluids against her distended skin. The pieces inside her body, bone chips, tendons, congealed blood, were all still lost, trying to find their way back to where they belonged.

"You're gonna need a few more days, I think," Silton concluded. "My arm feels much better after about two, but with the weight you'll be putting on these, you'll need more time."

"Yeah, soon I'll be ready to put weight on it," Mariella said reluctantly. "But it would be nice to have some crutches."

"I was thinking the same thing." Silton looked around the bone cavern again. "There's a few pieces of bone I could rip off the walls that would be long enough, but nothing strong enough to support you."

"So, we just sit here and wait?" Mariella asked.

"No. I think I might be figuring this place out. That muscle, I'm telling you, if I left it on my leg, I think it might have attached itself just like the skin did to my arm. And the blood . . . I haven't felt that strong since I got here. My body soaked it up like a sponge."

"You can't be serious," she said.

"Look at your leg, Mariella. You think that skin I wrapped you up in is going anywhere? It's getting stronger by the hour. That's a fact, a sick, demented fact of this place. You can't argue with that."

"Unfortunately, I think you're right," Mariella said.

"My idea is this: Tomorrow I want to get to some open skin, maybe cut a hole and get some fresh blood, a bunch of it. I think it would help us feel better. With this no heart thing, I feel sluggish, like my veins are full of mud or something. Tonight, I want to try to make a bag with the leftover skin from the gurney. If I can make a pouch or something, I can bring back some blood for us."

"I'll need some time to get that straight in my head. You get us what you need. But let me think about this 'soaking in someone else's blood' plan of yours."

"Sounds fair, but we should eat our fill for now. There's no telling where our next meal will come from."

"I've got a strange feeling I know exactly where it's coming from," Mariella said, and slapped the ground with a wry smile on her face.

Silton smiled with her, feeling a strange, morbid connection, then went to work piecing together a blood sack from the leftover skin that surrounded them.

CHAP+ER TWEN+Y

The Demon Stem is a construct that allows Demons a general mental connection to the Unbroken. It is composed of an entire spinal column, including the cerebellum, which is attached to the base of a Demon's spine through their engineered orifice. Demons use this connection to assess an Unbroken and discern their major sins. After the administration of a Demon Stem, most Unbroken become exhausted and will lose consciousness. This is often viewed as a beneficial side effect, as the acid branding of the Unbroken's "Sin Stamp" onto the forehead is the next step.
—From "The Demonic Encyclopedia"
By Delta-Haldon

Evening closed in fast on the Cantavit, and Heaven's bright blue eye fell to the horizon, shining through some of the lighter portions of the Skin-Land. Montly could see veins and soft red blood through the ground of slight hills as the light of Heaven shone through the translucent skin.

Camp was set for the night. Taut skin tents and larger

pavilions created a circle around the newly Scrotted Unbroken. The Mauss lay next to a hastily made blood pond, the immense Drums kept guard around the perimeter, and the Canem lay asleep, exhausted. Near the center of camp, in a makeshift kitchen, Reese prepared dinner for the Cantavit.

Montly walked to Lopex, who sat outside his tent in a cleverly made folding bone-chair.

"The Drums are all blood downed, the Mauss are taking turns in the pool, and I figured I'll get to the Canem tomorrow morning, as the ones who got back have eaten and are already asleep," Montly reported.

"That sounds perfect. Any injuries?" Lopex paused, just understanding what she had said. "Wait, what do you mean by 'the ones who got back?'"

"Well, by my count, two Canem are still out there. Only eight came back so far."

"Damn!" Lopex rose. "Follow me!"

Montly's stomach dropped, and she immediately felt the sensation of nervous failure. How would she have any idea where all of the Canem were?

Lopex approached Delius's tent and tugged on the entry skin flap. "Delius, a moment?" Lopex said.

Delius came out, his muscles shining a bright, strong red, his skin cloak shed for the night. "What is it, Lopex?"

"Two of the Canem haven't made it back to camp yet. We only have an eight count."

Delius paused for a moment. "That's not an issue. Sometimes they bed down if they're too far out before Heaven-fall. Zaavan?" Delius yelled. "Zaavan!" he repeated loudly.

Zaavan came out of his tent, near naked without his matte black tumor armor.

"Delius?"

"Two of the Canem haven't returned to camp yet. Did you see anything while you were in flight that might give us an idea of where they went?" Delius asked.

Zaavan's face changed to a glaze of honest concern. "Really? Strange." He thought for a moment, searching his memory. "I did see a mass of Bone Caves on the horizon just before I circled back. I was going to suggest at dinner that we make for them tomorrow. That must be where they are. They must have gotten lost in them."

"That makes the most sense," Delius said. "Something similar happened a few decades ago. Our whole team of Canem got lost in a set of Bone Caves."

"I can leave now," Zaavan volunteered. "I'll make it to the caves before full dark and find them."

"No. No, I don't want to lose my Defensionem in the caves as well," Delius said, as he patted Zaavan on the shoulder in an unusually compassionate gesture. "We make for the Bone Caves first thing in the morning. Zaavan, you can fly ahead and scout them out for us. You'll lead the Canem; they will sniff out their brothers. That's the plan."

Zaavan nodded, as did Lopex. Montly followed, more out of a confused mimic than anything else.

Delius continued, "Lopex, make sure Reese is going to be ready with dinner soon. I want to administer the Demon Stems on these Unbroken tonight so they'll have enough time to rest before we march them to the caves tomorrow. We don't have much more light left."

"Of course," Lopex said. "I'll make sure Reese is ready."

"Zaavan, prepare your team," Delius said, before returning to his tent.

"It will be their pleasure, Delta," Zaavan said snidely as he walked away.

Lopex hurried toward Reese. Montly followed, anxious and apologetic.

"I am so sorry, Lopex. I had no idea about the missing Canem. I just thought they were late, or still scouting," she said, her voice tender and shaking.

"Stop, Montly." Lopex halted, putting his hand on her shoulder, looking her straight in the eyes. "Your job is to make sure the Sapiens are in working order, and that they're fed and comfortable, that's it. You've done what you needed to do. But next time, when you realize the count of Sapiens is off, let me know immediately, all right?"

"Yes, all right. I'm really sorry," Montly said.

"You have nothing to be sorry about. Now, let's make sure Reese is on time. He tends to embellish when he cooks."

Reese sat next to the three Unbroken men. They'd finally stopped sobbing about their castration and knelt on the ground with their heads hung low. Reese had opened up the Skin-Land and created a ground pot full of pristine blood and his thick, meaty grist. He turned it over with a bone ladle, and Montly could see the chunks of meat, no larger than the tip of a finger, floating in the viscous red broth. This grist wasn't stringy like back in Sapien Bay. It had depth, complexity. The signs of a chef's efforts ran through every detail of the stew, and Montly, who was famished, thought it looked delicious.

"Reese, are you almost done with dinner?" Lopex asked.

Reese looked up with disdain at his friend. "It will be done when it is done. You can't rush the process, old friend," he said coyly.

"Well, Delius is starting the Stemming now, and then dinner right after, so get moving."

"Not even the last of the Deltas can make my grist cook any faster," Reese responded.

"Just get it done, Reese," Lopex said, in a defeated tone.

"'Just get it done, Reese,'" Reese mimicked, and continued to gently stir his masterpiece.

"Alright, Montly," Lopex started. "I want you to pay close attention." The pair positioned themselves in front of the three Unbroken men. "The Zetas will handle the Stemming. That's part of their job in the Cantavit, but there is learning in every corner of experiences, even the ones you don't take part in. Got it?"

"Of course," Montly responded.

Chalt and Bore approached the center of camp, and like most Zetas, they looked battle-ready. Chalt shone in her skintight, deep latex black, and Bore's skin shimmered like diamonds floating in blood.

Montly smiled wide at Chalt as she approached, but as she caught her gaze, Chalt rolled her eyes.

Bore bent down and pulled one of the men away from the group, dragging him on his knees. He struggled against Bore, like an infant fussing with a parent, but soon he was in position.

Zaavan and Delius approached, observing the scene. Chalt stood front and center and addressed the Unbroken for a second time.

"Unbroken. Revel in the next stage of becoming a part of Hell. Tonight, you give to us what every Unbroken, what every Demon, what every inhabitant of Hell must give: your sins."

Chalt whipped her head, and the bony vertebrae of the Demon Stem snapped into her hand.

"Be at ease, Unbroken," Chalt said. "Soon you will be released from hiding your sins, and you can use that effort to become a productive member of Hell. Once again, cherish the memory of this time, as it signifies your leaving behind the useless tool of deception that you so relied on during your life-times."

One of the men shook so hard, he'd barely heard a word Chalt said. He tried to speak in response, forming awkward sentences, inept and confused.

"I . . . I . . . I'm not a sinner. I . . . I . . . I'm a cop . . . I'm a good cop! I was a good cop! There's been a mistake. I've saved lives, countless, many . . . helped people, rescued people. Risked my life . . ."

"Come now, Unbroken. Are you suggesting that God is in error?" Chalt asked, shifting to one side, embellishing, enjoying her position.

"No! No, no, no, I'm not at all. I mean, okay, okay, maybe I wasn't the nicest guy in the world, but that's all. I've saved dozens of people. I was a good cop! People loved me! They needed me—"

"Silence!" Chalt screamed, her double-ribbed vocal cords striking the Unbroken man's ears like a punch. "Understand this, Unbroken: God does not use scales to measure your sins. He is not a merchant looking to trade your atrocities for good deeds. After centuries, you people still do not truly understand Him? Well, your education has begun, and we are to indoctrinate you into eternal tutelage."

Chalt approached the man, holding the knife-edge of her Demon Stem tight in her hand. Then she thrust it into the base of his skull. Bore held his arms back as he roiled in the pain. The Unbroken twisted his head back and forth, but the depth of the Demon Stem allowed Chalt to control him completely. A few seconds later, the man went into a vapid hypnosis, his eyes rolling back into his head, his body calming to subtle shakes and twitches.

Chalt too went into a hypnotic trance—not nearly as severe as the Unbroken, but she looked preoccupied to be sure. Her mind scraped against the man's consciousness, unrelenting in its search for the memories of his sin. She held no regard as she stepped through the history of his life-times, hacking away at his personality like a thick forest until she found what she needed. A few moments later, Chalt pulled the Demon Stem from the back of the man's head, wet with cerebral fluid and caked with small chunks of pinkish-gray brain. She stepped back, a bit weathered from the experience.

"He's an adulterer. He's cheated on his wife and often breaks promises to the Almighty," she said, turning and looking at her master. "Sin-Stamp 'A,' please, Zeta-Zaavan."

Zaavan went to a large ring at his side. A seemingly infinite amount of bone brands no larger than keys clattered as he fingered through them. He separated one out, a carved and pristine white skeleton brand: A. He took in a deep breath, sprayed a small cloud of highly concentrated acid from his lungs onto its surface, and approached. Zaavan pressed the sizzling brand deeply into the man's skin, to the bare bone of his skull.

The man screamed and spasmed. The other two men whimpered, vomited, and collapsed in fear.

When Zaavan took back the steaming acid brand from the man's forehead, there remained in its place a letter surrounded by a perfect circle: a capital A.

Montly looked in awe, her mouth smiling from ear to ear.

"I can't wait till I get to do that," she said in a hushed voice, barely able to contain her excitement.

CHAPTER TWENTY-ONE

The clearest and simplest definition of an Angel is a member of Heaven, who through teaching and a deep concern for his fellow man, has volunteered to exercise God's will outside of the confines of Heaven.

An Angel is endowed with the perfect human form: virile, strong, and devoid of physical imperfections. Also, God has granted Angels with full and capable wings that allow flight. These are the only gifts that God can equip his Angels with, as any outside material not completely and wholly part of the body will not pass beyond Heaven.

Angels can only exist in Hell for short periods of time, as they are not imbued with the immortality of those who are condemned. In Hell, an Angel will suffer when breathing the acidic air, will not be able to eat or drink, and if injured, the Angel cannot take advantage of the repair techniques that Hell's inhabitants find so valuable to their existence.

—From "Hell's Inhabitants"
By Doctorem Delta-Lindicus

Silton woke early and started his trek, moving easily through the bone caves. At first, the jagged formations seemed to have no order to them, but as he traveled, he began to notice similarities. The bone built itself into a coded pattern, growing to about eight feet before curving to meet in an arch. Many of the caves formed ravines, as they had no ceiling, but this allowed Silton to use the light and shadows they created to stay hidden. With every turn, he etched a slight mark on the side of the bone wall to create a trail that he could use to find his way back to Mariella.

He couldn't help replaying some of Mariella's comments in his mind as he walked. Although harsh, there seemed to be no deception in her, no manipulation. Maybe she was right, maybe he'd loved Kay more than she loved him. This idea made the feelings about his wife and her death seem fresh. And though he had no physical heart to take this burden on, the rest of his body responded to the stress as he recalled the depression he'd struggled with after her death. He was happy to have Mariella in this horrible place, and strange as it was, here in Hell, Silton finally didn't feel alone anymore.

The caves became less developed as he progressed through them, like an old, thick forest opening up to a newer field of saplings. The light shone through the top of the bone ceiling as morning moved to noon, and even the walls turned porous and transparent with light. As he traveled to the edge of the caves, Silton could see through to an open expanse of skin. Something there caught his eye: a deep, razor-flat expanse of blood that backed up to a wall, a huge boulder of bone. The tall slab cast a shadow over part of the blood lake, which made it difficult to see.

"Perfect," he said to himself. "That will work!" Silton

surmised this to be the end of the blood river he'd seen while traveling to the bone caves. The natural world he knew so well during life replicated itself here with morbid perfection.

Excited that he'd found what he needed so soon, Silton unfurled his blood sac and ran out of the caves to investigate. His enthusiasm had overpowered his training, as he naïvely exposed himself to the open space.

"Don't be scared," said a voice from the shadow of the boulder. Caught off guard, Silton jerked his head quickly to the side. And there, up against the boulder, sat a man unlike any that Silton had seen before. The two stared at each other in silence. The man had thick curls of black hair, pale, perfectly consistent skin, and lumps of chiseled muscle that would be the envy of any Special Forces soldier. But his most predominant feature overshadowed all of this: a pair of massive wings. Thick and white, they overlapped with huge feathers larger than any bird Silton knew of. Even while hinged down to his sides, Silton could see that this man's wings easily stretched to twice the length of his body.

The man didn't get up at first; he just continued to stare at Silton.

"Don't be afraid of me, friend," he said again in a soft whisper that beckoned Silton closer.

Silton's eyes darted next to the man, where two piles of ripped flesh lay with sloppy organs spilled out of them. They looked like mutilated dogs, stitched together from graveyard leftovers.

"They won't hurt anyone anymore," the winged man whispered, his voice calm. He reached his arm up to Silton in a welcoming motion, and Silton could see a horrible injury. Underneath his left shoulder, the white wing dripped with blood.

Silton assumed the dog-things had bitten him. The irregular marks of teeth and shredded flesh made that apparent to anyone with even a minor knowledge of traumatic injuries.

"What are you?" Silton asked.

"I am not here to hurt you," he responded.

The man seemed delirious, exhausted from loss of blood. But Silton didn't need him to answer. Religion, no matter the skeptical theories of fiction or fable, seemed meaningless now. An Angel sat in front of him—every man, woman, and child from the civilized world would know that. The realization stunned Silton to a silence where logic and faith met.

"Are you going to be okay?" Silton asked and, against his judgment, walked closer.

"No, brother. I won't be okay. But there is nothing that can be done about that."

"You're an Angel?" Silton asked.

"I am," he responded.

"What are you doing here?"

"Ah . . ." he said with surprise. "So, you know where you are?"

"Of course I know where I am. I'm in Hell," Silton said.

"How long have you been here, brother?"

"A few days."

"Wonderful. Wonderful," the Angel said. "We often think that you don't know where you are until it's too late. We lament that you become so confused when you first arrive here. This is a good thing, that you have no illusions about this place. He would be happy to know that."

"*He* would be happy?" Silton asked.

"Yes, *He*. God." The Angel rose, pushing himself up the bone boulder. He stood as tall as a normal man, but his muscular form rivaled that of even the most fit. A thick ribbon of blood escaped from under his wing, ran down his pale leg, and dripped onto the crisp white bone beneath him. The Angel winced.

"You're badly injured," Silton observed.

"Yes. I won't be going anywhere, but you need not worry about me, brother. My name is Tragen." The Angel extended his hand, and they shook.

"I'm Silton. I'm sorry, but I have to ask. Can you help me? Can you take me—us away from here?"

As if pondering Silton's question, Tragen stretched his injured wing.

"I am afraid there is nowhere I can take you, Silton. But I am here to help. In a small way I've helped everyone here. But to find your way out of this place, you must answer the question of why you are here. And I cannot know that. Only you and God know that."

"Where is He now? Why does He not help you? Help us?" Silton asked.

The Angel smiled. "He *is* helping you, brother. He is."

Silton shook his head, frustrated with the conversation.

"I'm sorry, brother," Tragen continued, "but there is much confusion in your world." He paused and gathered his strength. "Our wonderful and loving God has no power here. That was the bargain between He and the Devil. This is the way it has always been. You being here is the cost of not loving Him. God loves you so much, and if He had a choice, He would never want to see you in this place. But you are here, and I promise you, it pains Him."

"Well, it doesn't seem like it." Silton covered his head, disappointed, lost in thought. "So then ... so then that's it? I'm stuck here? Forever?"

"No, no, not forever. I was here for over a thousand years, and I survived. I became redeemed, and was pulled from this place to live with Him where I always belonged."

"A thousand years? *A thousand years?*" Silton would not let himself believe it.

"Yes, a torturous and horrible time that was erased in the first seconds I entered Heaven. But this may not be your path. My life was a terrible one, one that deserved a millennium. You may be different."

"Your life was terrible? What were you? A murderer?" Silton pushed rudely.

"Well, yes. I was a murderer. I was a Roman soldier, brother. I was a Roman soldier in the time when the Romans thought they held the world in their hands. And as a Roman soldier, I manipulated the Word of God the way many Roman soldiers did back then. And that is one of the most difficult sins to redeem," Tragen admitted.

"I'm a soldier too. So, this is all measured out? How long do I have? Tell me!" Silton yelled.

"You have as long as it takes, but don't concern yourself with that. We don't have much time together." The Angel scanned the sky, ensuring the shadow still hid them both.

"Why don't we have much time?"

"These pets . . ." Tragen pointed to the jellied piles of bone and blood to the side. "The absence of these beasts will not go unnoticed by their masters. No doubt they are on their way."

"Who's on their way?" Silton asked.

"Demons, brother. Demons. The stewards of this place. The teachers of Hell's most intimate lessons," Tragen said.

"Demons? I don't believe you."

"Belief is secondary at this point, brother. We don't have

much time. But I can impart a few things to you that may help."

"What would help is if you'd fly me and my friend out of here," Silton said.

Tragen shook his head. "I am only a scout. An injured scout who couldn't fly if I wanted to."

"A scout for what?" Silton pressed.

Tragen took in a breath, considering whether he should answer him or not. "You are a fellow soldier. You know of tactics and strategy. Before an attack, any attack, what do you do?"

"Prepare, get intel on the target, and scout the area," Silton responded.

"Yes! Exactly. I am just a soldier sent to help prepare for a massive battle."

"A battle? A battle for what?" Silton asked.

"A battle for the souls of the redeemed. The only thing worth fighting for here in Hell."

"And God can't just take them?"

"No, as I said, He has no power here. But *we* do. *You* do. There is a place here. A horrible place that you've not seen, for if you had, you and I would not be speaking. It's the Devil's lair. A giant moving beast called the Sled. Here the Devil and his Demons enslave thousands and thousands of people, some of whom God has redeemed. Yet they still remain trapped. It is our job to take them to Heaven, and so a rescue Mandatum is to take place in two days. I've scouted for their arrival. They're on their way, more Angels than have ever descended to Hell before. And they're going to rescue the many souls trapped here by the Devil in his massive construct."

"Then let me help you." Silton's military prowess and tactical knowledge leapt to the forefront of his instincts. "I'm a medic. Look how I fixed my arm, Tragen! We can do this! I can help you scout this place!"

"You honor me, Silton. And I truly hope that you become redeemed. But I cannot be helped. You are a part of Hell, part of its immortal self. Maintain yourself here as long as you can. Keep your body together. No flesh of Hell can become flesh of Heaven without redemption, and no flesh of Heaven can mingle with the flesh of Hell," the Angel said.

"Then what about me and my injured friend? We just sit here and rot? Rot away until God decides when we can leave, if we happen to survive long enough to run into an Angel like you again?"

"No, brother Silton, you don't sit here and rot. You thrive here. You make yourself strong. It is not God who decides when you leave. You do."

Silence again crept over them as thoughts bent around words.

"*He* does not want this. *He* does not want any of this. This place . . ." Tragen paused, visibly uncomfortable. "This place has become something that He never wanted. The Demons, the Devil, they've become too powerful. If they find you, they could change your time here forever. Hide from them. Stay strong. Help your friend. Be selfless, and contemplate your sins so that you can become redeemed, and maybe, maybe one day you will be rescued."

"But—"

"You must leave now," Tragen interrupted Silton's objection. "It is only a matter of time until the Demons get here, and once they arrive, there will be nothing I can do." Tragen reached up deep into the layers of feathers on his uninjured wing and plucked hard. "Take this."

Tragen handed Silton a thick, pristine feather. "Let this be a reminder to you that hope is the only weapon you have against them, against this place. It is the only thing they can't take from you, and the only thing that will stop this place from swallowing you whole."

A deep howling horn broke the silence. A sound so inhuman and loud, Silton could not fathom where it came from.

"They are coming, brother. You must leave me now," Tragen said. "If they find you, your days here will change for eternity. There is no stopping them. You must believe me."

Silton tried to find words for Tragen, but he couldn't. He reached out, placed his hand on the Angel's shoulder, and looked deep into his eyes. There he saw the grace of Tragen, a grace that was of a man, not of some fantastical religious construct. A grace he had seen many times in the eyes of his own combat brothers. And with that, Silton darted off to the blood lake, where he quickly filled his sack, splashed some of the rich, pure, red on his legs, and made for the caves. But before he entered, he turned back.

"Fight well, Tragen," he said, then retreated into the cavernous depths of the caves.

"I have fought well, brother," Tragen said. "I have."

The terrible sound of the inhuman horn cried out again, rising ever louder as it closed in.

CHAP+ER TWEN+Y-+W⊕

The historic relationship between Angels and Hell has always been a complex one. Although God has no direct power in Hell, He is able to send Angels across the threshold, where they collect redeemed souls and return them to Heaven. For thousands of years, this process continued uninterrupted, until one day when an Angel did not return. In response, God sent several Angels to investigate, but again none returned to Heaven. This marked an important change in the relationship between God and the Devil named: "The First Heavenly Disobedience."

—From "A History of Hell"
By Delta-Holt

Zaavan flew high but slow, so that the Canem could keep pace. Heaven-rise crested over the curve of Hell, and the white bone caves glowed brightly in the distance.

At allotted intervals, Zaavan held his arms out straight and dipped into a circle, signaling for the Canem to stop and howl. With their multiple layers of vocal cords, their howls could be heard for miles, and if one of their fellow Canem heard that howl, they would respond in turn, giving Zaavan its location.

The Demon compressed his eyes to see farther across the horizon, farther into the uncharted Skin-Land Vast. To the west beyond the caves, an ocean of blood cut its way across the skin. To the north, Zaavan could barely see a dot that must have been the Sled slicing across open skin. But most interesting was the phenomenon to the south.

Difficult to see even with his enhanced eyes, Zaavan could make out bodies falling one by one, sometimes in clusters, down from the sky. To find one or two Unbroken falling from the sky was not a rare thing, but to discover an area where many fell at once? This was a very rare phenomenon indeed. He would have to tell the Daughters of this. He would also have to hide this from the Cantavit and take credit for the discovery himself. Perhaps the Daughters would alter the direction of the Sled based on his information. At the very least, Zaavan could lead a Cantavit to investigate. This find would no doubt ensure his upward mobility.

Unfortunately, these thoughts would have to wait; the missing Canem remained the priority. Zaavan spied a tall hill overlooking the entire span of caves that would be a perfect place to regroup with the Canem and scout the landscape.

He perched himself on the hill and looked back at the dog-Sapiens in the distance, then to the caves. From the top of the hill, he could see their entirety: a cramped outcropping of bone, adjacent to a blood lake fed from the ocean.

"Bizarre that our Canem got lost here. The caves are so small," Zaavan said. It could mean that they were hurt or trapped somehow, or perhaps they'd found food. Zaavan decided to draw out the missing Sapiens with a series of howls from their fellow Canem.

Zaavan waited as the band of Canem joined his side one by one. He pet their misshapen heads and gave their legs a once over to ensure they'd not bitten each other too badly. Seeing all in order, he lined them up side by side, and commanded them to howl.

The deafening sound struck across the late morning, echoing off the bone walls in waves of sick noise.

The Demon waited. Nothing. No movement. No screaming Canem running back to meet their brothers. He motioned for them to howl again. Louder still, the sound cracked across the Skin-Land and bounced off the white formations. Zaavan stressed his eyes to see anything.

"Where could you be?" he said to himself. "Are you hurt? Both of you? Drowned maybe?" He peered as hard as his eyes could to see the edges of the lake. And that's when he saw it: ripples.

Zaavan took flight in a hard stride up and out, staying close to the land, close enough to touch it if he wanted. The Canem followed, far behind him, as fast as they could. A large boulder obscured the lake, but Zaavan knew something must have made those ripples. The light of Heaven cast a shadow of winged Demon, so he kept close to the Skin-Land. And then, at the last moment, he arched his back, curving up and over the bone wall and dove into the opening below.

Standing in the shadow of the boulder, at the base of the lake, Zaavan saw him: a pristine, feather-white Angel with thick, black hair. Zaavan could barely hold back his joy.

"Well, let me fall with the Devil. I've found myself a lonely Angel."

Zaavan kept midair as he circled his find, flying across the blood lake. He swept behind the boulder, waiting for the Angel to take flight in escape, but as he rounded the bone, he saw nothing. Zaavan knew there could be only one reason an Angel would not take flight when seeing a Demon: It couldn't.

Zaavan landed atop the caves, directly in front of the Angel. He saw two mutilated Sapiens—the work of the Angel, no doubt. Zaavan could hear the other Canem closing in. Not wanting to upset them with the sight of their dead brothers, Zaavan signaled for the dog-men to stop.

Zaavan jumped down from the top of the caves, gliding down to the Skin-Land just in front of the Angel. Tragen rose to his feet, using all the strength he had to push himself up against the bone boulder.

"What have you done with my pets?" Zaavan demanded, arms folded.

"I've released them from their service," Tragen said.

"Pity. There must be compensation for destroying them. They are precious to me. What do you have to give me in exchange for them?" Zaavan asked.

"I'll give you your life. I'll let you live out your terrible existence here without interruption," Tragen responded.

Zaavan chuckled at his arrogance. "I don't think that will do. My life is not yours to give me. It belongs to someone else."

"I know who it belongs to," Tragen said. "And I am sure *He* would find the bargain I have offered you acceptable."

"We speak of different people, I think," Zaavan said.

"No, Demon brother. You are mistaken. You can only belong to God, no matter where you place your loyalties. If you search in what is left of your heart, you will see that to be true."

"Perhaps instead I will search in your heart. I know mine far too well." Zaavan smiled.

The threat fell over Tragen like dark mist. "I was once like you, brother, strong and fulfilled by this place. But I've changed. I've been redeemed."

"You were *never* like me, brother. There is no one like me. Allow me to show you."

Zaavan took in a deep breath and spewed out a cone of acid, covering Tragen from wing to wing. Tragen dropped to his knees, grunting hard to hide his screams. His feathers wilted in seconds, melting to a green slop. The skin on his chest sloughed off in ribbons of gray-black, and Tragen gagged as he inhaled the acid into his delicate lungs.

"How you so embellish evil here," Tragen said, choking. "Do you even know why you—"

"I've so often wondered about you Angels," Zaavan said, interrupting him. "You come here, to *my* home, and try to take *our* souls. You must know what you are up against. You must know our singular devotion to this place. And yet you come here, so inept. So unprepared."

Zaavan stepped closer to the melting Angel. "Why is that? Why would God, seeing that He is all-powerful, send you here, defenseless, against me?" Zaavan asked, toying with Tragen.

Insulted, Tragen panted hard and wiped a bit of acid from his black hair, regaining his composure. He got up from his knees, proud and unyielding to Zaavan.

"Why should I need to defend myself from my brother? There is no reason for you to stand against me. No reason."

"Hmm..." Zaavan curled his lips. "Maybe that was the way long, long ago. But after The Great Fall, after what *He* did to him, breaking *His* own rules.... Well, as you can see, things have changed here. Now, Hell is the way it always should have been."

Tragen struggled to stand, his feet sizzling in a pool of melted feathers.

"It's not supposed to be like this. It doesn't have to be, brother."

"I have a friend," Zaavan started, ignoring Tragen. "Well, not really a friend. I actually hate him more than I hate you. He feels the same way. He's always talking about the old times, the time before The Great Fall, and the way things should be here."

Zaavan brushed some invisible dirt from his tumor chest plate. "I think I'll give you to him as a gift. A parting gift on this, his last Mandatum. A small reminder that things are different now, and that they will never be like they used to." He bent close to Tragen. "Now, I know that this will be a useless question. But protocol when finding Angels is very strict. Tell me, why are you here? How many are you?"

Tragen gave no acknowledgment that Zaavan had even asked the question. He just smiled as much as the pain would allow.

"Yes, yes, Angel on high," Zaavan whispered. "How you so wish to reclaim these souls from Hell, only now to become a permanent part of it. Ironic, isn't it?"

And with a flash, Zaavan's muscles twitched, and he had Tragen by his thick, black hair. The Angel tried to struggle, but the Demon lifted him off the ground and expelled another blast of acid directly into his chest. His flesh fell off in hot curls of liquefied skin, muscle, and tendon, until the weight of Tragen's body began to separate his head from the rest of himself. Clutching onto Zaavan's shoulders, Tragen screamed until his neck and vocal cords melted in a tortuous cacophony of guttural anguish.

Tragen's body fell to the ground, sizzling into a pool of melted organs.

"'Brother,' you call me? Any brother of mine would have put up a better fight." Zaavan took off into the sky, holding Tragen's head by its dripping hair.

And in the shadows, soaked in sweat, Silton could not believe what he'd just seen.

CHAP+ER TWEN+Y-+HREE

Redemption should be the central preoccupation of your mind, second only to keeping your physical form in working condition. Unfortunately, this book cannot guide you to redemption, as this is a private endeavor. For many, the self-reflection needed for redemption is the most intimately private process they have ever embarked on. For some, this process takes months, for others, years, and others still, centuries. But understand that no inhabitant of Hell is divorced from God's redemption, which is why this author suggests you begin seeking it immediately.

—From "Hell: A Survival Guide"
By Delta-Delius

Panicked, Silton ran. The new blood invigorated him, thickened his muscles, and he felt as tireless as a thoroughbred horse. The blood sack sloshed over his shoulder, and the feather lay securely tucked into the hole where his heart once belonged. He had little trouble following the markings he had left, but his feet, wet with thick blood, lost their grip a few times, sending him hard to the floor.

Panting heavily, Silton returned to Mariella. She lay exactly where he'd left her: legs straight out, sitting upright next to a pool of stale urine. Her eyes, wide with anticipation, were sprinkled with a healthy dose of fear.

"What's wrong?" she asked.

Silton laid the pregnant blood sack down, caught what he could of his breath, and spoke. "We have to leave! We have to leave now!"

Mariella's fear ebbed higher. "Why? What happened? What?"

"There are other things here; it's not just us. They're going to come for us. We have to go now! Please tell me your legs are feeling better," Silton said.

"Better? Better than what? They're better than they were yesterday, but I haven't even tried to walk yet," she said.

"Yeah, well, we're gonna try. I'm gonna soak you with this blood. It'll help, but we have to go now."

"You've got some explaining to do, Silton. So, get to it!" Mariella said.

Silton knelt down next to Mariella and carefully opened the blood sack. The blood had jellied a bit, becoming viscous like red gravy.

"An Angel, I met an Angel." He scooped out a handful of the blood and rubbed it on her legs.

"An Angel? You were hallucinating. You didn't see an Angel."

"Yeah, well then, what's this?" Silton pulled the feather out of his heart hole—long and white, tinted with flakes of red.

Mariella's eyes locked on the thing as if hypnotized by its beauty. She reached out and held it to ensure it existed.

"You've got to be kidding me," she said as she turned it over in her hand. "What did she say? What did she say!"

"It was a he, and he said a lot of things. He said that we *can* get out of here. He said that once we get 'redeemed,' Angels come down and take us up to Heaven. He said God wants us to get out of here, that this place isn't permanent, that we can escape."

"Okay, okay, so let's go. Get me up and let's go!" Mariella started to scamper upright, ignoring the pain in her legs.

"He's dead," Silton said, without looking at Mariella.

"He's dead?" She paused, the words not registering for her. "He's dead? How does an Angel die, Silton? It can't!"

"I am telling you, Mariella, he's dead. I saw it with my own eyes."

"No . . . what can . . . who . . ." she stumbled.

"This thing came out of the sky. It was huge. It was . . . it had wings, it was horrible, it was a . . . a Demon, I think. They talked for a while. I couldn't hear what they were saying. And then this *thing* killed him, tore him apart, took his head, and flew away."

"My God," Mariella said, looking down at her legs. Helplessness crept over her, and she realized how little control she had over the situation. This place had her at its mercy. She looked to the blood sack and furiously began coating her legs.

"Careful, careful, we have to make this last," Silton said.

"What else? What else did he say?" she asked.

"His name was Tragen, and that he's been here in Hell, like us, for a thousand years. He got right. He did what he had to do. He got 'redeemed,' he said. And then he was rescued by an Angel," Silton explained.

"Got right? How did he do that?"

"He said you have to learn about your sin, make amends, and just be better. I don't know exactly."

"And that takes a thousand years?" Mariella asked.

"No, he said it's not about time, it's about you, your sin, and getting yourself redeemed on your own."

"So, he didn't take you? Why didn't he take you?" Mariella asked.

"He couldn't. He was injured. His wing was torn up. He was bitten by these ... these things. Things that looked like a mutated dog, or I think they were like—"

"Did he say anything else?" Mariella interrupted him. "About getting out of here, Silton! Are there more of them?"

Silton took in another breath, leaned the blood sack up against Mariella, and sat back. "He said that in two days, more Angels are coming. A lot more. He said that they are going to a place called the Sled. That his job was to scout out this place and report back. But that didn't happen, because he got injured."

"So, they'll send someone else to do the job, right?" Mariella pushed.

"Do the job?"

"Yeah, do the job, Silton! Isn't that what they do in the military? If someone goes out to do a job, and they don't come back, they send more out to see what happened? Right? I mean, that's how you Army guys do it. No man left behind, right?" she said.

"That's how we work. I don't know anything about Angels."

"Well, obviously that's how it works!" Mariella finished coating her legs, her new skin drinking in every drop of blood. Then she began testing herself.

"Help me up. I feel strong. Help me up," Mariella said.

"Wait, maybe you should—"

"Don't tell me to wait! I'm done waiting! I'm done being helped, Silton! It's time for me to get out of this place."

She struggled, bent her knees, and tried to get her feet under her. She slipped on the stale urine, and found no grip to stand. As her frustration settled and her breathing calmed, she looked at Silton sincerely.

"I'm sorry. I didn't mean for it to come out like that. I'm sorry." She brushed her legs, distracting herself from the shame of yelling. "I just feel helpless. And I don't take to helplessness very well. I need to get out of here. *We* need to get out of here. And if you're telling me that you found an Angel, and more are coming, then we have to get to them. We have to make them get us out of here."

"I know, but he told me that you need to be redeemed first. He said it takes time," Silton explained.

"Maybe for you," Mariella said under her breath. "Look, Silton, I don't know why you're here. Maybe you don't even know. But I do. I know exactly why I am here, and I've made amends for it. I've paid my price, in life, and here, and I know what I've done wrong. I am redeemed. I deserve to be out of here!"

"Mariella, how could you know that?"

She looked down at her legs, cursing them, cursing her fall. She became calm, holding her eyes still. "Listen to me. There is a reason we met, this isn't coincidence. We're here to help each other. I believe that. You've helped me so much, and now I want to help you. Those Angels are coming back. I know it. They're going to come back to look for their dead friend. And we are going to be there when they come. I think I can walk. I think I can try now. I feel strong. I feel—"

"Mariella! You didn't see what I saw. You didn't see this thing. You didn't see these dogs that tore the Angel apart. We can't handle these things. Not now, not in our condition. I don't know if we ever can. The Angel told me. He told me specifically to get out of here, to get away and never come into contact with those things. He said that it could change our life here forever. That's what he said," Silton implored her.

"Did he? Or did he say that *you* aren't ready yet? That *you're* not redeemed? So, what difference would it make to you if we found more Angels?"

The division between them was stark and plainly in the open.

"Instead, you just troll along with me, right? Running off into this terrible wilderness where we have no idea where we're going? That's the *plan*, Army boy?" Mariella pushed on, not wanting an answer. "Well, I don't think so. I don't think you *want* to find any more Angels. I don't think you do. Well, *I am redeemed,* and I am going to go back to where you saw that Angel, and I am going to get out of here, with or without you. Now help me up, damn it!"

Mariella extended her hand and stared hard at Silton. He reached out, gripped, and hoisted her up. Her accusations took a bit to settle in. He couldn't figure if it was this place, paranoia, or Mariella's days of pain that made her turn like that.

She took a step, holding onto Silton's arm and wincing as a shot of pain ran up her ankle, through her spine, to the base of her neck. But the leg held. She took another step. This time the pain came straight from the compound fracture. She felt it almost slip out of place, but the skin bandage compressed the bone hard, and she put her full weight on it.

"You see. I'm okay. I can walk," she said ambitiously. Silton knew it pointless to try to convince her otherwise. Mariella took another step, and the knee buckled. She shrieked as Silton caught her by the waist. "Damn it!" she said.

"You're better. But you're going to hurt yourself if you don't let me help you. You know that."

"I do. I do know that. So, listen to me, and let *me* help *you*. Take me back to where you found that Angel, and let's wait there a while. Wait and see if they send more. I know I need you, and I'm thankful for what you've done. But maybe you met me so I can do this for you. Change your mind about this, go meet the Angels and get us both out of here."

"Mariella, you didn't see what I saw."

"We have to have faith, Silton. We have to have *hope*," Mariella said tenderly.

Hope, Silton thought. The words from the Angel reflected in his mind like so many shards of light: Hope. Maybe she was right. Maybe the Angels would seek out the remains of their fallen brother. That's exactly what Silton would do for his fellow soldiers, and exactly what his fellow soldiers would do for him.

CHAP+ER TWEN+Y-F⊕UR

The greatest hurdle you will face as you move from Unbroken to Broken is the memory of your former life. At first you may think that your memories will bring you comfort or give you a sense of attachment to your humanity. But this is false. The memories of your life-times will only burden you in Hell. They will create a painful wanting of something you will never have again, and force you to see Hell in the terms of your old reality. Behaving in Hell like you would behave in the life-times is inappropriate and will most likely lead to your destruction. The sooner you forget about your old life, the more successful and productive member of Hell you will be.

—From "Your Body and How It Has Changed"
By Doctorem Delta-Lindicus

H eaven crested to the highest point in the sky, allowing Montly to see far across the skin landscape. The bone caves stood in view a few miles off, shining so bright she could barely look at them directly.

Montly rode in the back of the Cantavit again. Although

she knew she had to ride in the rear to keep pace for the slow Drums, it didn't stop her from imagining being at the lead, riding stride for stride with Delius and Lopex. All Montly had for company was her Mauss and the sad Unbroken being pulled along behind them. Even Reese and his wagon rolled a few lengths in front of her.

One of the Drums started to become distempered, its three heads grunting with each step. She turned and looked at the beast, six arms, six legs, all mashed back-to-back. It seemed fine at first glance, but then Montly saw the problem. One of the Unbroken was refusing to walk, forcing the Drum to drag him across the skin. Montly heeled her Mauss to slow, until she was side by side with the Unbroken.

"You'd better get up and start walking," Montly said.

"I . . . I can't . . ." he whimpered.

"Yes, you can. Now get on your knees, then get up. We aren't going to stop for you."

"I can't. I can't walk anymore. I'm in too much pain," the Unbroken said.

"Come now. You exaggerate. Just get up and walk like the others. They've been through the same as you have, and they aren't complaining."

The Unbroken looked at his companions. They didn't make eye contact with him, terrified to speak. "I'm not. I can't," he said, sliding on his back, arms stretched full and long behind the moaning Drum.

"You know this is only the beginning of your journey, Unbroken. Soon you'll be at the Sled. Working where I use to work, on the Herd. You will meet many, many, Unbroken just like you. They will bring you comfort. Don't you want that?" Montly asked.

"I can't . . . I can't . . ." he whined.

"The Herd is an incredible place. Thousands of Unbroken, all working together, all pulling the Sled, it's beautiful. It's really quite a sight to see."

"But my wife, my children . . . my life, I can't do it."

"Don't worry about the life-times anymore. That's what the Herd is for. Once you spend fifty or so years pulling the Sled, you'll have forgotten all about your life before. Soon you will be Broken, and then maybe you'll be ready to become a strong Sapien like our Drum here, or maybe, just maybe if you're smart enough, you can become a Minion like me. And after that, who knows? One day you could be a Demon just as strong and proud as Delius himself! Anything is possible. But none of that matters if you don't get up and take that step. It all starts with taking that first step." Montly's tone was kind and empathic. The words filled the Unbroken man's ears.

"Fifty years? Fifty years!" He began to cry, twisting and moaning, rolling back and forth on the Skin-Land. The Drum moaned louder, laboring to keep pace while dragging its unruly prisoner. Behind the Unbroken, Montly could see a moist strip creating a trail across the land. She looked to the ground beneath the man and saw it becoming spongy and wet. Angry, she took in a deep breath and spoke firmly.

"Now, you listen to me, you weak blood bag! If you don't get up and start walking, that skin is going to swallow you up! Do you hear me? And when my master gets back here and sees two of you instead of three, he's going to blame me! So, you have two choices: You get up and walk like the rest, or I will cut off your arms and legs so you can roll behind the Drum!"

The Unbroken stared with shock in his face.

"Which is it?" Montly pulled out a large, hand-carved bone blade with a translucent sinew grip.

The Unbroken scurried to his feet, desperate to get up. He slipped a bit on the Skin-Land, but soon walked alongside the rest. The Drum wheezed a relieved sigh, and Montly gently patted the Sapien on one of its heads. Then she kicked her Mauss to retake the lead.

"You got everything handled back there, kid?" Reese yelled from his wagon.

"Yeah, yeah, yeah. I've got it."

"Good. Well, look sharp. Zaavan and the Canem are back." Reese pointed to the head of the Cantavit, where Zaavan had returned. Delius seemed to give a few commands, and Zaavan to agree with him. He motioned to his fellow Zetas, waved his arm wide, and took flight toward the caves. The other Zetas charged off to follow their master, with four Canem in tow. Montly stood up in her stirrups and could see they headed south, to the back side of the caves.

Lopex pulled his Mauss to the side and stopped, waiting for Reese and Montly to catch up. "It looks like we may have gotten lucky," Lopex said to the two of them, then kicked his Mauss to keep pace.

"How's that, Brother Eta?" Reese asked.

"Zaavan said that the caves are small, and they abut a blood lake fed from an ocean, so it will be very fresh and more than we need. He also said there is plenty of new and old bone, huge amounts of the pure stuff. We're to make camp on the north side and start harvesting. The Zetas will search the caves from the south side, flushing anything out to us at the blood lake."

"Wow, ocean blood! I've never made beer from ocean blood!" Reese's mouth watered.

"Well, let's not celebrate just yet," Lopex warned. "We need to set camp and do at least a half-day's harvest. Got to make sure everything is as perfect as Zaavan says it is."

"And the missing Canem?" Montly asked.

"Killed apparently. He doesn't know how, probably from some Unbroken hiding in the caves. At least that's the thought. Who knows? Maybe we make our quota tomorrow!" Lopex smiled and nudged Montly.

The three laughed and kicked their Mauss to a slow canter as the Drums jostled to a run, and the Unbroken desperately tried to keep up.

CHAPTER TWENTY-FIVE

Two schools of thought exist on the relative value of coming into contact with Demons. Mainly out of fear, many wish to avoid Demons at all costs due to the torture they will experience once coming under their care. But there is an opposing view: Being captured by the Demons will absolve you from dealing with many of the environmental dangers in Hell. Demons will want to keep you in good working order on the surface of Hell where they enslave you. Demons have many uses for people in Hell, and some have determined that the security of this relationship is worth the anguish.

—From "Hell: A Survival Guide"
By Delta-Delius

Silton held Mariella up as they slowly walked through the caves. The bone, sheer and slick, proved difficult for Mariella to navigate. Her knees popped out of joint every ten steps or so, causing excruciating pain so rhythmic that Silton could almost predict it. Afterwards, Mariella would stop, lift her leg, and her knee would slip back into place.

Silton followed the markings he had laid out before, never imagining he'd be following them again back to the blood lake. Each cave they passed reminded him how terrible the idea was. As they rounded a corner, Mariella lost her footing again, and her knee popped out.

"Damn!" she cried louder than Silton would have wanted. Her voice echoed through the catacombs. "I can't even walk ten steps!"

"I know, but..." Silton hesitated, not wanting to chastise her while in pain. "But you have to try and be quiet. We don't know what's out here."

"Sorry," Mariella said. "It's not the pain, I'm just so frustrated."

"I know," Silton responded. "I wish I knew how to build a knee. The tendons and muscles are so small."

"Rebuilding knees is tough, everyone knows that." Mariella labored on.

The echo from Mariella's frustration made Silton more aware of the noise they made. He tried his best to be silent and stop shuffling his feet across the ground. During the silent steps, Silton became aware of distant sounds, fragmented echoes through the caves. He couldn't make them out, but they didn't sound like anything natural. Silton suspected the sounds came from other people.

"If only I had a nerve block. Damn!" Mariella said. "What I wouldn't give for some opium or a dopamine vial."

"I'm afraid that'll be a tall order, Mariella. Maybe you shouldn't think about it. We can rest at the lake, and more fresh blood will help," Silton assured.

"Is it a tall order? I mean, really? Don't you think we can find something, some substitute for a painkiller here? The body makes its own, you know."

Silton tweaked his eyebrow, intrigued by the idea. "I think we should just get to the lake and have you rest. And hope this theory of yours holds up about the Angels."

"Yeah, well, if they don't show up, we're gonna have to think of something else. I'm not going to have you dragging me around this place for eternity, Silton. You know that, right?"

"What are you talking about now, Mariella?"

"You ever help one of your fellow soldiers only to realize he wasn't going to make it? I know you must have experienced that before. What do you do? Tell me, what does your training tell you to do then, Silton?"

"No, Mariella. That's never happened to me before. I know what you're getting at, and no, we don't leave anyone behind."

"Well, you're either a fool, Silton, or you just haven't seen what I've seen." Her knee slipped out of socket again. She winced and shook it back into place. "I've seen it bad. People who don't have a chance, who bit off more than their body could chew, or people who've just reached the end. It's a big problem in hospitals these days, keeping people alive longer than they should be. It's cruel to everyone involved—the family, the person, the staff."

"So, we're talking euthanasia now? You're not in that world anymore, Mariella, and we're gonna push through. Besides, you're probably right. More Angels will come. Then we'll be okay." Silton didn't believe what he was saying, but he needed Mariella to keep walking. To stop now, stuck in the depths of these caves... Silton didn't know what would happen to them.

"Sure, euthanasia, like good old Mr. Halpern. You remember

him, right? The old man in the swamp? I knew him. He had Alzheimer's. He didn't know who he was, and he'd just been diagnosed with lung cancer. It had already spread to his lymph nodes," Mariella explained.

"Yeah, so?"

"So, what's the point of keeping him alive? He's not the man he was, he's in unbelievable pain, he can't even remember his loved ones, and it cost a ton of money just to keep him breathing."

Silton stopped and looked Mariella square in her eyes. "A ton of money? *A ton of money?* What's that supposed to mean?"

"Don't go getting all high-horse on me, Silton. You know exactly what it means. Don't act like you don't." Mariella pushed him away, trying to walk on her own. "You think that doesn't matter? I've had patients tell me that they don't want anyone to help them anymore. Tell me that they feel guilty for all that they cost their families, in money, and stress, and pain—"

Her knee popped, and she gripped the wall. Silton grabbed her arm and tried to help her.

"That's what Mr. Halpern said to me. That's what he said. Do you think that after his long life, a wonderful life full of sacrifice and success, that he should go to the afterlife feeling guilty for putting his family through his own drawn out death? Do you think that's fair to him? Or anyone else for that matter?"

"That might be what you and your nurses talk about at happy hour, but that's not the way the world works, Mariella."

"Isn't it, Silton?"

"No, it isn't."

"It worked that way for Mr. Halpern. He wanted to die, so I helped him get what he wanted," she said sternly.

Silton halted, shrugged from under Mariella's shoulder, and leaned her against the wall. "Helped him get what he wanted? A man delirious from Alzheimer's?"

"Oh, Silton, the brain might wilt away, and you might forget this or that, but the wish for self-destruction, those thoughts are clear, no matter how old you are, no matter if you're an addict, or crippled lying in bed. It's an evolutionary thing. People know when they need to die. Even animals know when they're being a burden to the herd and it's time to move on."

"What exactly are you saying, Mariella?"

She looked at Silton resentfully for making her explain it. "You want to know? Big man-patriot you-don't-do-anything-wrong? I'll tell you what I did. When it was time to give the oncology ward their pain meds, I took five vials of morphine instead of three from the vault. Then when it was time for Mr. Halpern's dinner, I spiked his IV with both extra vials, and he went to sleep. That's what happened. And while he drifted off, he never looked so happy."

No words stretched between the minutes that passed.

"You're a killer?"

"Yep. So you're in good company, Soldier Boy." Mariella methodically put her weight on him, walking a few steps before speaking again. "Oh, I see. So, *I'm* the bad person, right? You kill during war and it's okay, but I kill when someone *wants* to die, and I'm evil. Odds are we're here for the same reasons, Silton. The only difference is that my killing wasn't out of anger. It was out of mercy. That's why I want to find the Angels and you don't. They'll save me. But you? Well, I guess we'll just have to hope that the Angels are ex-military, huh?"

"So, you're saying what you did was selfless? That you did a service for him?"

"You're damn right I am! You'd be surprised who asks for death. Old, young, men, women—" She stopped herself mid-sentence.

They walked for a few more minutes, only stopping to shake her knees into place. Silton's mind ricocheted with thought. He thought of his wife, Kay, and if she had felt the way Mariella described, even in her coma. He thought about what he'd done to the meth head, Skinny Chad. But mostly he thought about putting the gun to his chest. Was that the same thing? Did he do what Mariella did, but for himself?

A scream, stark and clear, cut Silton's introspection short. Bellowing from the caves behind them, it sounded close, and getting closer.

"Be still," Silton said, and they both huddled together, listening.

Heavy footsteps echoed through the caves, then a stiff thud that sounded like someone fell.

"They're coming this way," Mariella whispered.

"I know. Stay quiet." They slowly sunk to the floor.

The wet slap of footsteps grew louder, and Silton could make out the voices of at least two people.

"Come on, come on. It's getting closer," the voices said, closing in.

Silton kept his eyes focused on the opening of the cave. He pushed Mariella against the wall, slowly got up, and readied himself. He put up his hands, positioned himself between the entryway and Mariella, and drew in a deep breath.

Darting around the corner ran a stark-naked woman, moving full tilt. Behind her, two men followed, running as fast as they could.

The woman stutter-stepped, startled to see Silton. With

wide eyes and panting breath, she slowed a bit, and the man behind her almost plowed her over.

"Keep going!" the man said as he grabbed her arm and pulled her back to a run. The man in the rear never stopped his pace. He sprinted past all of them without even looking.

Before disappearing into the caverns, the woman only got one word out to Silton: "Run!"

Mariella got up, scurrying against the wall, and one of her knees popped out again. Silton moved quick enough to catch her and pulled her up against him.

"Ok, we can do this," Silton said, before a deafening howl echoed through the caves so strong it almost knocked Mariella back down.

"What was that?" she said, her eyes watering with shock.

"Doesn't matter, let's—"

"Oh, my God!" Mariella said.

A four-legged beast scampered into the cave, stopping just short of the two. Covered in a patchwork of mismatched skin and dotted with hairs coarse like wire, it howled, and Silton covered his ears as Mariella dropped to the ground.

Silton backed up against the wall, trying his best to protect Mariella. Tense seconds passed, but the creature didn't advance.

What is it waiting for? Silton wondered. And then, in the shadowed entrance of the cave, a huge, shimmering, blood-red wall of a monster appeared.

"More?" it said in a deep, guttural voice. The dog-beast looked up at its master and whimpered obediently, and the red giant pointed to the exit and grunted. In response, the creature ran off howling through the caves once again.

Silton didn't think. He didn't want to. His instincts took over, and he lunged at the red monster.

His fist hit the red flesh hard, and immediately he felt a sting in his hand. His next shot, a strong half fist to the neck, felt the same way. Silton spun on his heel, curled his elbow, and struck the giant right where the kidney should have been. He stepped back, hoping he hurt it, or knocked it off balance, only to see his arm and fists pocked with tiny cuts, covered in blood.

With a flash quicker than he could see, the red giant backhanded Silton across the face. He flew into the cave wall, slamming his back hard against the unforgiving bone.

Silton ignored the pain, pushed off the wall, and launched a fist straight at the red monster's face. His knuckles landed square in the middle of the flat white plate that covered its head. The red mass stumbled back, stunned for a moment, and Silton pulled back his aching hand.

As the red monster regained its senses, Silton bent his legs and charged forward with all his strength. He flew himself at the midsection of the giant, marshaling every ounce of weight he could for the tackle.

With blinding speed, the giant sidestepped and grabbed Silton midair with one hand. It lifted him three feet off the ground so the two were face to face.

"Bad Unbroken," the red monster droned, pulling back its massive head. Silton could clearly see the flat white bone plate covering the thing's brow. It looked like a shovel that started at its nose and ended a foot over its head. The red monster pummeled Silton over and over again with headbutts to his face, until the thing's white shovelhead dripped with his blood.

Pain swelled across Silton's face, and a soupy fog crept into his vision as his consciousness evaporated. A red and white blur filled his eyes, and all Silton could hear were the sounds of Mariella's screams ringing through his ears.

CHAP+ER TWEN+Y-SIX

As stated in previous chapters, the art of Stemming the Unbroken to uncover sins is a trying task. Many Demons find that entering into an Unbroken's mind is disorienting, distasteful, and potentially damaging. Although all Demons are required to have proficiency in Stemming, there are those that have an innate skill and talent for carving through the Unbroken's mind. Often this task falls to these individuals.

—From "The Demonic Encyclopedia"
By Delta-Haldon

S ilton woke from a restless sleep, his head heavy with pain, his body soaked with sweat. A lump a quarter-inch high rose on his forehead, and when he touched it, pain ripped down his spine. His vision came back slowly in a wet blur of beige and green, and Silton could see that he lay on a warm pile of bodies. His throat, too dry to speak, ached for water. Silton rolled off the pile to the ground, and sucked some of the morning sweat off the Skin-Land. The moisture soothed his throat, and the salty taste sparked his eyes to open.

A large shadow blocked the morning light from view, and when Silton's weary eyes squeezed into focus, he saw something very strange. There, on the ground in front of him, were six pairs of mismatched feet, twisted in odd, crippled directions. His gaze moved up to the long, stilt-like legs. Silton scampered back, slipping on the sweat-soaked ground beneath him, pushing back to the warm pile of bodies. Then he saw the source of the shadow: a monster covered in meaty ground flesh. It stood six and a half feet high, with three heads, six legs, and as many arms. It looked at Silton with dumb, hampered eyes, as if it'd been drugged. Silton clenched his fist out of instinct, but little could be done without a weapon against a thing three times his size. Looking closer, he could see the thing more clearly: three people melted together as if by some terrible accident. Catching movement in his peripheral vision, he turned his head and saw six, eight, ten of the giants. Surrounding Silton, the flesh monsters stood like statues, unmoving and stolid.

Footsteps squeaked across the morning sweat of the Skin-Land, and a figure grabbed the massive beast in front of Silton, tugging on it.

"Come on. Be good like your brothers and sisters," Montly said. "You're going to love this fresh lake blood. Come on now." The beast moaned in a sick combination of three voices as Montly pulled.

As the Drum walked to the opening of the pen, Montly saw Silton, awake and silent.

"Oh, perfect. Another one's up." Montly counted the Unbroken, numbering the ones who were almost conscious.

"Who are you?" Silton asked.

"My name is Montly," she smiled.

Silton looked her over. She had a slight form, strong but feminine, with a smooth, glossy face. Her clothes were made of a dried skin-leather two shades darker than her own skin. She wore a short jacket, cinched at the waist, and a pair of tattered pants rolled up tight to her knees. Bright red blood covered her legs, and crimson footprints showed a trail from where she'd come.

"What is this? What are you doing to us?" Silton demanded.

"Calm yourself. We're taking you home. Don't worry. It won't be long. Are you hungry?" Montly asked, leaning her head to the side. "I know you're confused, but don't worry. Everything is being taken care of. Everything. Just rest and drink more. You and your fellow Unbroken have a big day today." Montly smiled, showing a mouth full of straight, polished bone where her teeth should have been.

Montly snapped a look at the two Drums to her side and gave them the command to close ranks. She kept view of the Unbroken man for a moment as she walked away, and saw what looked like a dried skin casting on his arm.

Strange, Montly thought. *How could he have a cast?* Montly would have investigated further, but she had little time, and far too much work to do.

Montly walked the Drum into the lake. The thick, fresh blood rippled soft and slow, and shone tender highlights in the morning light. To her left, a few of the Mauss stood knee-deep in a shallow pool of blood, while others grazed on some wild hairs that grew from the skin further away. She led the Drum away from them until they were both waist-deep in the lake, then gently splashed the Sapien with blood and looked over the busy morning camp.

The night before, they'd set up all of the skin pavilions and tents. Reese, of course, didn't help at all; he was too busy readying his makeshift kitchen. He made quite a spread as usual: two grist pits—one for the Cantavit and one for the Unbroken, a large flat bone plate for acid grilling, and a cauldron chipped from the huge bone boulder that shadowed camp. That, of course, would be for the blood beer he'd make later.

Across the lake at the caves, Montly could see Chalt and Bore ripping and hacking away at the walls. They harvested the bone like wheat—Bore ripping away a strip, and Chalt hacking it to a standard size before dropping it onto a pile.

Delius worked a mile or so in the distance with a few of the Canem, sniffing out precious organs and glands from the rich, blood-soaked ground. So far, Montly thought Delius a bit strange. She'd heard so many stories of him, how he was a great leader, how everyone loved him, but she'd barely shared more than a few words with him so far. She knew Demons of his position had many responsibilities and couldn't be bothered to speak to a lowly Minion like her. But deep inside, in the place that housed her empathy, she couldn't help but feel that something else consumed Delius, something complex and terrible.

But what could it be? Montly resolved that she might never know.

Lopex bounded toward her, close to the edge of the lake, but not close enough to get wet. He seemed unusually happy, and Montly had to smile as he waved her to shore.

"Yes, Lopex?" Montly said enthusiastically.

"Right… right. Good morning to you. Good. You're blood downing already?" he said.

"Yes. The Mauss are grazing, and half of the Drums are done. Once I've downed all of them, I'll start the Canem in small groups."

"Perfect, perfect. You'll be done ahead of schedule then." Lopex said.

"Yes, I will. So, what's on the agenda today?" she asked.

"Well, I think you're going to like it." Lopex smiled, almost giddy with excitement. "This place is rich. Rich with bone, blood, organs from the ocean to the west. But this find, these Unbroken we've found in the caves—if we can harvest all of them, we'll be almost halfway to quota! I can barely believe it!"

"I know, that's great. But what does that have to do with me?" she asked, splashing blood across the Drum's side.

"Well . . ." Lopex dragged. "I've spoken to Delius, and because we have so many Unbroken, I suggested we spread the Stemming burden across some of our other brethren. Namely, you."

Montly bit her lip hard. She didn't believe him.

"You'll let me Stem? Really?"

"Delius said it was the most prudent thing to do. He said that we couldn't expect the Zetas to stem all twelve Unbroken in one day. It's just too many too quickly, and too much stress."

"Oh, thank you! Thank you so much, Lopex!" Her head swam with anticipation of the day to come.

"Don't thank me yet. I told Delius that you'd have all of these Sapiens done early, so I can show you a few tips before it all starts."

"Oh, it *will* be done. I promise," she said.

With that, Lopex turned and walked away.

"Master," Montly said. "Thank you again."

Lopex didn't turn around, but he couldn't help but yield a small smile, sharing in Montly's joy.

CHAPTER TWENTY-SEVEN

It is generally accepted that the most treacherous construct in Hell is the surface of Hell itself. Hell is responsible for the destruction of more souls than any Minion, Demon, or even the Devil himself. Estimates reveal that upward of seventy percent of those who descend into Hell are consumed within the first few moments of reaching the surface. Many who remain do not last more than a few days before being absorbed. This explains the phenomenon of so many people being relegated to Hell, but so few being present on its surface.

—From "Hell Geographica"
By Doctorem Delta-Lindicus

The camp roiled heavy with activity as Heaven's eye crested toward the late morning. Zaavan sat perched atop the bone boulder, surveying the land, pushing his compound eyes to scout the surroundings. To the south, far in the distance, he saw a drip of bodies coming from the sky, splashing down into Hell. Earlier that day, he'd seen a group of at least ten make their fall. But none of them survived to pull themselves to the surface. All were absorbed into Hell's fleshy bowels.

Zaavan always thought that the Skin-Land's appetite for consuming souls was a major flaw in Hell's design. Tens of thousands of people were lost every day to Hell's insatiable hunger, and this fact hampered all of the Demon's plans.

"Twelve Unbroken, we've found," Zaavan said privately. "I watched ten times that fall to Hell last night alone. It's a shame." He dreamed of keeping all of the souls he'd seen drop into Hell. He dreamed of commanding them as a huge army of his own, conquering Hell, and bringing back the old times when the Devil ruled every corner of skin—a time that he'd heard of only through stories. Now the Unbroken were so few, so feeble, and took many resources to find. The harshness of Hell's nature worked tirelessly against Zaavan's dreams, tirelessly against the past to which he so wanted to return.

Zaavan reached into a flap on his belt and took out the tiny organ given to him by the Daughters: the Allylamine, the forget chemical. He squeezed the gland between his coarse fingers, wondering how and when he would apply it to Delius's brain. But the why of it confused him. *Isn't killing him enough?* he wondered. *What does Delius know that terrifies the Daughters? What terrifies the Devil enough to procure such an organ that could erase the last of the Deltas' memories? Something about the past? Some secret of Hell that only that bastard Delta knows? But what could it be?*

Zaavan thought hard on this as he watched Delius return to camp. He still hadn't mentioned his encounter with the Angel. The head lay hidden in his tent, wrapped in skin parchment to keep it moist. Perhaps Zaavan would present it to him during dinner. Delius did so like centerpieces.

✛ ✛ ✛

S I L T ⊕ N wandered the outskirts of the group as some began to wake. A few of them cried, realizing they weren't in a dream, that the same realities of yesterday faced them today. Silton counted six men and eight women. He searched for Mariella, and found her lying in a depression of skin, sipping sweat water from her cupped hand.

"Morning," she grunted.

"Are you okay?" Silton asked.

"I was going to ask you that."

"My head is throbbing, but other than that—"

"I thought that thing killed you," Mariella interrupted. "He hit you so hard. I've never seen something move that fast."

"Neither have I," Silton admitted.

"Oh, my God!" shouted a naked white man. "Your chest!" The man walked closer to examine Silton. "How? How..." He bent slightly, staring bewildered through the hole in Silton.

"Well, you have some explaining to do, don't ya?" Mariella said, mocking Silton.

"I was injured," Silton said.

"But you can't be alive," the man said.

"I'm not. And neither are you. None of us are," Silton explained.

As the rest of the group came awake, they watched groggily. Some gasped when they saw Silton up and walking around.

"We thought you were dead!" yelled a woman as she rose from her sleep. "We thought that thing killed you in there."

"I'm afraid not," Silton replied.

"Yeah, he's one tough cookie!" Mariella said, adding only sarcasm to the fray.

"You two know each other?" the naked man asked.

"Oh, yeah. We're old friends, Silton and I. Partners you could say," Mariella responded.

"My name is Tremmel, Patrick Tremmel. I'm a doctor." The naked white man moved closer to investigate Silton's injury.

"It's fine . . . it's fine," Silton said, protecting his chest and stepping back.

"Tremmel? I know that name," Mariella said. "I've seen your name on orders before. I work at the hospital, Cook County."

"What? Cook County? How . . ." Doctor Tremmel said.

"This phenomenon, this place," Silton started. "It's local. It's like the underside of the real world. We've figured that out for sure. We're all from the same general area, we think."

"Yeah, doc," Mariella said. "I landed in the dead swamp that's right under Cook County Hospital. It's like a big dumpster for everyone who dies there. And let me tell you, if you thought the hospital was messy, you ain't seen nothing."

"What are you talking about?" the doctor asked. "Swamp?"

The rest of the Unbroken crowded around the conversation.

"You know where you are, right?" Silton asked him.

"No . . . no, I assumed I was hallucinating. I mean, I don't know . . . I can't—"

"You're in Hell, doc," Mariella continued. "Straight up Hades, afterlife, purgatory, or whatever you want to call it."

"What are you talking about?" the doctor asked.

"Yeah, what are you saying?" said a female voice. "We were abducted, right?

And what are these things?"

The voice came from an older woman of about sixty,

observing the conversation. "What do they want? Why are they just looking at us?"

"Listen," Silton began, "I don't know how to tell you this gently, but this is Hell. You're dead. All of us are. And this is what happens next. This place. And these things, I don't know, but they're... they're Demons. They're just here to keep us in one place. They won't let us get by. I tried."

Sobs came from the crowd. The older woman collapsed, but the group grabbed for her before she hit the ground, gently laying her down.

"You're crazy. What are you saying?" the doctor continued. "Don't go spreading panic like that! We have to approach this calmly. We don't need that kind of nonsense."

"It's not nonsense," said a man's voice from the side.

Everyone turned a head to see a man sitting cross-legged on the ground near the edge of the circle.

The man stared blankly, almost in a trance. "I've been here two weeks, maybe three. I can't tell anymore. I met those two when I first fell into this place." He pointed at two other men who lay adjacent to him.

"And then, then this group of things found us. I guess you're right," he said to Silton. "Demon is the best word for them."

"Why are we naked? Who took our clothes?" the older woman lying on the ground said. "What are those things? They look... they look like mashed up people." She rolled to her stomach, hiding her eyes as if it would make them go away.

Several of the women tried to comfort her with pats and rubs on the back, while covering themselves as best they could.

But the doctor just stared, perplexed, at the man sitting near the edge of the circle. "What happened to you?" he asked.

"What happened to your . . ." He pointed to the man's crotch.

"The same thing that is going to happen to you. That's the first thing they do." The man pulled his hair back from his forehead. "And this is the second thing." He showed the branded capital A on his forehead and twisted his neck, revealing the puncture hole in the back of his head.

Seeing the injuries, the older woman sobbed hard in chokes and tremors. A few of the others desperately looked to Silton and Mariella.

"Is he right? Are they going to do that to us?" the younger woman asked.

"Of course they are, honey," Mariella said. "You see these things guarding us? Keeping us in here? What do you think they are? You ever see anything like that? Maybe in a movie, I don't know. You're dead. I'm dead. They're dead. This is Hell, and these things are Demons. Silton here even saw an Angel yesterday. Tell 'em."

Silton had hoped not to broach that subject, and he gave Mariella a stern look in response.

"You saw an Angel? You saw one? Where?" a younger woman asked.

"Look, I . . ." Silton thought of pulling the feather out of his chest hole, but didn't. "Look, I saw what I saw. But . . ."

He hesitated, not wanting to tell the group what had happened to Tragen. "The Angel told me that we're in Hell. He told me that most people don't believe it at first, but that's what this is. He said it's important for us to understand this quickly."

"I don't believe you," the young woman said. "Hell? How could I be in Hell? *I'm a good person!*" She continued to caress the sobbing older woman. "I've never done anything to anyone! I'm a mom. I loved my children. I . . ." She paused mid-sentence and squirmed. She seemed off-balanced, confused.

"My God!" interrupted Doctor Tremmel as he walked toward another man, severely injured, still lying on the ground. "His arm. It's . . . it's gone."

The group curled in around the deeply tanned man and investigated the charred remains of his left arm. His eyes, pinned open, stared into the sky, and his mouth formed silent words as if he spoke to someone not there.

"What do you think happened to him?" the doctor asked.

"It looks like his arm was blown off," Silton suggested. "These burn marks are typical of explosives. They cauterize the veins, stop the blood flow. It's a painful but clean amputation."

"You're a doctor too?" Tremmel asked.

"No. A Combat Medic. Unfortunately, I've had experience with these types of injuries, a few times. I . . ."

"Silton!" Mariella screamed.

"What?"

"Look!" Mariella pointed to the ground next to the two women. A viscous fat seeped from the Skin-Land that surrounded them. Mariella scampered back, dragging herself and her crippled legs away.

Silton jumped to action. He grabbed the young woman and tore her away. Then he knelt down into a shallow pool of milky fat and turned the older woman over. Beneath her, the moist Skin-Land was rendering to liquid, covering her face in warm fluid as she flailed and choked. The people standing around her were ankle-deep in fat, and they pulled up their feet from the skin quicksand as they moved back. A silent shock ebbed through the group while they watched Silton and the woman slowly sink.

"What's happening!" screamed the young woman.

"Stay back! Stay back!" Silton yelled, the swampy flesh creeping up his mid-thigh as he tried to keep the woman's head upright.

The group pushed back to the perimeter of the Drums. A few tried to squirm through, but a bevy of arms kept them in. One of the Drum's heads began to moan, a sick, haunting sound. Then the rest of the heads joined in, screaming out a deafening cry.

Silton struggled to keep the old woman's head above the fatty liquid. She stopped moving and didn't cry—just stared up at the green-yellow sky and the almond blue shape of Heaven's Eye.

"Come on, come on! Don't give up! Don't!" Silton slapped her in the face, hard like he had with Mariella. But no response. "Come on!"

The fat rose up to Silton's waist, and he felt his legs tangling in a stringy mesh. Instinctively, he lurched to drag her away from the bog beneath him, but he couldn't. With each movement, each effort to stay afloat, the ground melted away further, and they both helplessly sank into the Skin-Land.

CHAPTER TWENTY-EIGHT

The Sinking Harvest Technique is one of the most dangerous tasks a Demon can master, because it involves harvesting Unbroken while they are being absorbed by Hell. As is known from earlier chapters, the fresh, still intact, operating organs of the Unbroken are amongst the most precious items a Demon can harvest. Due to the value of these items, Demons will often attempt to harvest from an Unbroken even after they have lost all hope and are in the process of being consumed by Hell. Please note that this technique is only to be attempted by Master Demons, as the risk of being pulled into Hell is extremely great.

—From "The Demonic Encyclopedia"
By Delta-Haldon

Delius heard the deep howl of Drums clear and stark across the expanse of camp. He compressed the lenses of his corneas, looking to the source of the sounds, and saw Zaavan diving down from his perch into the Unbroken holding pen. Immediately, he sifted through his intuition and experience and concluded that Hell was trying to take one of their Unbroken.

Without proper care, hope would evaporate amongst them, and Hell would no doubt take advantage of that.

Delius dropped his sack of organs and bounded toward the Drums. His legs bounced on the elastic Skin-Land, pushing him fast, and he reached the gathering crowd in seconds. Zaavan, now in the center of the Drum circle, corralled the Unbroken into a cluster on the far side, away from the sinking skin. Delius crashed through the Drums, easily pushing their bulk aside with his strength. Lopex and the rest of camp arrived moments later, and all looked to Delius for direction.

"Lopex, fetch my technique tools and an organ tray! Zaavan, keep the Unbroken back!" They both nodded. Lopex ran off, and Zaavan expanded his boney wings to hold the Unbroken against the perimeter of the Drums. The rest stared at the scene, realizing the growing danger of the fragile Skin-Land.

"No one enter this circle!" Delius yelled. "Stay back no matter what happens! No matter what!" Delius removed his tanned cloak and tossed it away, revealing the thick, red mass of muscle that hung from his back like a split red cape. He moved slowly and methodically to the liquefying hole, watching the two Unbroken struggle to keep their heads above the soupy skin-line.

Lopex arrived, holding a shallow, bone-carved box and a tray with dried vein handles on the sides. Delius motioned for Lopex to enter the circle, still keeping an eye on the sinking Unbroken pair.

"Hand me the large scalpel and a pair of gripped tongs!" Delius commanded.

Lopex slid open the shallow box, ferried out the requested tools, and handed them to Delius. He took them in each hand and thrust them into the flesh of his shoulder muscle, where they stuck out like stubby branches. Then, Delius slowly walked into the liquefying fat and skin until it reached his thighs. He held his arms out straight and rolled his shoulders, the two long strips of muscles on his back rippling with motion. Delius flexed some unknown set of nerves, and the muscle mass came alive as a set of thick red tentacles. Delius plunged them into the Skin-Land behind him, sinking them deep below the surface as an anchor. He walked slowly into the fat swamp, his technique tools stuck into his shoulder, his muscle tentacles extending behind him.

Silton struggled to keep the woman from sinking, but the screaming of the Drums made it difficult for him to concentrate. Below him, the semi-solid surface melted to a thick wax that he couldn't push up from, and he sunk into the soup as thick veins encircled his legs. Silton coughed as he swallowed a mouthful of liquid skin and realized that soon he'd be submerged. Luckily, he found a small foothold of solid flesh and pushed up, momentarily pulling the older woman's head above the skin-line. Her eyes opened wide, full with fear and confusion. She looked at Silton like a desperate child.

"You've got to move!" Silton screamed, spewing fat from his mouth. "You've got to try to push up and swim! Don't give in! Don't lose hope, or this place will swallow you up! You can't lose hope!"

Silton could tell she heard him, but her anguished mind didn't understand. Just then, Silton felt a strong hand on his shoulder and a massive tug of inhuman strength. The hand pulled the pair sharply, and they drifted a few feet back, where Silton found a platform of semi-solid footing that allowed him to keep both of their heads above the skin line.

"Stay still!" a voice rang in Silton's ear. He looked back to see a massive Demon construct wrapped in muscle holding him by the shoulder. "Can you pull her closer to you?" the Demon asked.

"I think so." Silton turned his head back to the woman and pulled her as close to him as he could.

"Good," said the voice. "Now wrap your arms around her waist, lock your hands, and don't let go."

Silton reached hard and strong around the woman's thick waist, and eventually got his arms around her completely, interlocking his fingers.

"Done!" Silton yelled back, as he felt the ground beneath him starting to give way. The liquefied Skin-Land seemed to be following the hopeless woman wherever she went.

"Hold!" the Demon said, and Silton felt a bone-wrenching pain through his shoulder as inhuman strength pulled him out of the skin. Silton thought for a moment that his shoulder might dislocate under the power, but it held. Silton and the woman rotated to the side, and he could fully see his rescuer: a skin plated, seven-foot-tall Demon anchored by muscle ropes to the Skin-Land behind them.

"Let go! Let go of her and crawl over me to dry skin!" the Demon yelled.

"She'll drown! She doesn't understand what's happening! She'll drown!" Silton screamed.

"It's too late! Let go or drown too! Climb over my back! Climb to dry skin! Do it now!"

Silton reluctantly complied. The woman's despair wouldn't stop, and no matter how hard he tried, he couldn't save her. Silton swam into the thick fat, under the Demon's arm, and up to his massive red muscle masses. As soon as Silton gripped them and started to pull himself away, the ground became more solid. Soon he lay on dry skin, soaked with viscous fat and covered in soft blue veins, gasping for breath.

Zaavan observed the commotion: the screaming Drums, the Skin-Land folding in on itself, and Delius engrossed in the center of it all. He reached into his belt loop and fingered the Allylamine sac. *I could easily pounce on his back, crack open his skull, add the chemical, and push his head below the Skin-Land,* Zaavan thought.

"Drums! Grab the Unbroken!" Zaavan yelled. Without having to hold the Unbroken back, he'd be free to attack Delius, to put an end to his legacy once and for all. But as the dumb Sapiens reacted to his command, they grabbed Zaavan's extended wings along with the Unbroken. The massive Drums held the Demon at his most brittle point. Zaavan couldn't escape their strength without tearing off his own wings, which would put him at the mercy of the Skin-Land, just like Delius.

Delius set to work quickly. He lifted the woman up with both hands so her body lay near the top of the liquefied skin. He could see her chest, her abdomen, and her legs through the murky fat. He grabbed his technique tools from inside his meaty shoulder and slashed a huge incision from her throat, down between her breasts and past her stomach, ending at the base of her pelvis. The woman screamed so loud, it drowned out the howls of the Drums.

Delius inserted his tongs, and with both hands, pried the skin away to reveal her rib cage. He pulled the skin back as far as he could, and the cavity filled with as they both sank below the skin-line. Delius flexed his thick, red tentacles, and the meaty anchors pulled them up slightly so that he could see her innards.

I have no time, Delius thought, and despite the sloppiness of her organs, he began to harvest as fast as he could. First, he cut the major aortic valves, releasing the thick muscled heart. He ripped it from her chest and tossed it to the dry skin, where Lopex snatched it up. Next, Delius cut enough of the vascular tissue around her liver to wrench it from her, and tossed it out with the bright green bile duct still attached. He ripped out the kidneys, one by one, and threw them to Lopex. Delius lifted his arms, and with one swift blow, shattered the woman's rib cage. The force of this sank them faster, the liquid skin creeping closer to the base of Delius's neck. Blind, he dropped his technique tools into the murk and grabbed a lung with each hand. Then, with a huge flex of muscle, he tore himself out of the sinking pool, twisting off the breathing organs like brittle branches.

The woman sank swiftly, and within a moment, Hell had swallowed her up completely. The Skin-Land began to harden. A thin gelatin surface appeared, and soon the deep beige skin morphed back to its dried, cracked origins.

Delius nodded and tossed the lungs to Lopex, who nodded back and took the full tray of organs away. Delius wiped a tangle of soft blue veins from his legs and shook the glistening fat from his chest and back. Annoyed with his own disheveled state, he looked to the Unbroken, still being held at bay by the Drums.

"Drums, release!" Delius said.

All of the Unbroken collapsed to the ground, and Zaavan, silently enraged, slowly pulled his wings back in.

Delius took in a deep breath and looked at the terrified Unbroken.

"This!" He pointed to the ever-hardening pit where the woman had sunk. "This is the fault of physical pride!" he screamed. "This is what happens when you think that you are your body! You are *not* your body! You are not the flesh and bone that you once knew! You are much more! In this place, your body will change. Your body will hurt. Your body may even join with another! If you hold on to your physical pride, if you hold on to the sense of self you knew in the life-times, if you hold on to the thought that your visage is what makes you who you are, then you will suffer the same fate as she did. Only adding a few more pounds to Hell."

Delius paused, surveying the Unbroken as they stared in awe. "Know this, and know this well: *We* will offer you mercy! *We* will offer you a chance! But you will get no such offer from *Hell!*" And with that, Delius paced off, wiping the rest of the fat from his body.

"Zaavan!" Delius screamed as he left.

"Yes, Delius?" Zaavan snapped.

"Ready the Unbroken for Scrotting!"

CHAPTER TWENTY-NINE

To your Unbroken mind, the concept of Scrotting may seem ruthless, cruel, and without merit. This is a normal reaction, as you are like a newborn child of Hell. Before the advent of the Scrotting protocol, Hell was a treacherous place, full of forceful copulation and self-pleasuring. The Devil demanded this be put to an end for several reasons. Firstly, as a new resident of Hell, you should not be subject to torture by other Unbroken. Put simply, Unbroken do not know how to torture in an appropriate manner. Therefore, rampant, mindless raping cannot be allowed. Secondly, the usage of your sex organs in Hell is considered an enjoyable experience and also cannot be allowed. Without sex organs to cloud your mind, you will become more accepting of your surroundings, and generally be a more productive individual. This is why Scrotting remains the first step in your indoctrination to Hell.

—From "Hell: A Survival Guide"
By Delta-Delius

C halt set the Scrot line parallel to the blood lake. She placed a thick branch of ten-foot-long bone across the ground, anchored by two Drums on each end to fight against the eventual struggle. Chalt set the entire apparatus up on a gentle slope down. She thought this particularly ingenious of her, as the bodily fluids would simply flow down to the lake. She hated cleaning up after a Scrotting; it was by far the worst thing about the job, and she took any advantage to make it easier.

Bore tied each of the Unbroken to the bone branch. Although he wasn't the brightest Demon, he had a knack for tying knots. Neither Chalt nor Zaavan could recall a time when Bore had tied a knot that failed. Often, they would press Bore about his uncanny skill, ask him how it was that no one could ever break a bond he tied. But Bore would always respond in the same way: with a thin smile and a soft shrug of his shoulder. Zaavan suggested Bore had been a master of tying knots during his life-times, and somehow, after all his years in Hell, this extraordinary skill stayed tucked within his simple mind.

The nine men and women, bound at the hands and ankles, knelt along the Scrot line with a small piece of bone wedged between the knees. This held their legs open, exposing the most tender parts of the human form. The three men who'd already been Scrotted sat in the pen guarded by the rest of the Drums, sweltering the time away.

Zaavan walked the line with Chalt in silent observation. "What's this? These pieces of bone that keep their knees apart?" he asked.

"It's an invention of mine," Chalt said. "I thought that with so many Unbroken, we could reduce the time we have to hold their legs open to apply the Scrot.

"That's very good, Chalt. You are dedicated to your work and a fine example of the Zeta class," Zaavan said.

"Also, did you notice they are set on a downslope, so any

fluid rolls into the lake? I thought that . . ."

But Zaavan ignored her and walked away, having no stomach for self-praise.

The Unbroken squirmed against the tight bonds of dried vein rope. They knelt staggered, male to female, down the line, with the stark Eye of Heaven pressing onto their backs as it reached midday. Mariella sat near the center of the line, her crippled legs twisted into position. She breathed short and shallow, trying to hold back the pain wafting up from her lower body. Silton shifted uncomfortably at the end of the line, where he could look down and see the Demons' preparations. A few of the Unbroken had taken to crying, others were semi-conscious with their heads lolling back and forth, and two of them lost control of their bowels, sending streams of yellow and brown down the slope to the blood lake.

"What are they going to do to us?" the woman next to Silton whispered to him. She was middle-aged and fit, with a deep tan that soaked her skin.

"I'm not sure," Silton replied.

"I always knew there were Demons. I remember feeling them when I was young, when I was a little girl. They always called to me. Made me do bad things. But I never thought . . . I never thought I would . . ." She choked on a sob and looked to Silton for some comfort.

"Calm down. We just need to look for a weak spot. It may take time, but just keep your head, okay? Keep your head." Silton said this as much for his own confidence as for hers. He knew there wasn't a Prisoner of War protocol here. These things weren't going to abide by any laws, or listen to pleas, or make exceptions. But that wasn't his biggest problem. Even if Silton could escape, how would he fight these things? One swat from the red one had almost shattered his skull. There seemed no way something that big could move that fast. It just wasn't physically possible. *How did he do it?* Silton wondered.

The Cantavit began to gather in front of the Unbroken. Chalt and Bore stood near the blood beach admiring their elaborate Scrot sticks, Zaavan fingered the ring of near-infinite bone brands on his belt loop, and Lopex walked with Reese from the shanty kitchen.

"So, for dinner tonight, I think I'm going to sear the liver steaks we found. They should turn out great," Reese said, mid-conversation with Lopex.

"As always, brother, that sounds delicious. Your dedication is second to none when it comes to cooking. Everyone says so," Lopex replied.

"Really? Well, that's... that's great to hear," said Reese, taken off guard by the compliment. Lopex and Reese stepped over the creek of excrement as they walked to the center of the line.

"Ahh, whose great idea was it to set up the Unbroken facing downslope?" Reese yelled. "Great work. Now we can all stand in their stench while we watch the show. Nice!"

Chalt glared at Reese from the blood beach, embarrassed that he made light of her miscalculation.

Montly rushed to blood down the last of the Canem. She could see the group gathering on the far side of the beach and knew the Scrotting and Stemming would begin soon. Tingles shuddered up through her spine and out to her skin in excited anticipation. She finished with the Canem and waded out of the blood lake, leading the soaked Sapien. In the distance, waiting at the Canem pen, stood Delius. Montly hesitated for a moment.

Is he waiting for me? she wondered nervously, then heading quickly on to the pen.

"They're all done, ahead of schedule. All happy and healthy," Montly said to Delius as she opened the pen and led the Canem in.

"I can see that. They look well," Delius replied. "Can we walk together? To the Scrotting?"

Montly was astonished that Delius would even ask such a question. "Yes. Yes, of course!"

"Good, please . . ." Delius motioned with his arm for their departure.

An odd silence filled the first few steps. Montly racked her brain to find something to say, but everything that came to her seemed inane. *The blood lake is so fresh, Heaven's Eye seems less bright today, or isn't this patch of Skin-Land unusually smooth? Ridiculous conversation starters,* Montly thought.

Luckily, Delius broke the silence for both of them. "So, are you enjoying your time with us in the Vast?"

"Oh yes, Delta-Delius. I am enjoying it."

"Good . . . good. I hoped so. And please, there is no need for class names out in the Vast. In the Skin-Land there is no class. No one is better than anyone else in such a dangerous place. Class was invented only for the civilized world on the Sled, a thing that the Devil created so that he can more easily keep track of his ever-growing Demons."

"I see," she said, thrilled to be speaking to Delius.

"There are a great many things you're going to learn in the coming years working with Lopex," he said. "I should think it will be a very exciting time for you."

"Yes, of course. But I should also hope to have a chance to learn from you as well, Delius," she replied.

"Hmm." Delius laughed at the compliment. "You want to learn a lesson from me?" He paused. "You'll be doing your first Stemming today, no?"

"Yes, Lopex said I might be able to Stem today," Montly said.

"Well, then, here is my lesson on Stemming: The Unbroken mind is a cloudy place. No doubt you will feel that immediately. There are many techniques for Stemming, for getting to the heart of an Unbroken's mind to fully understand and classify their sins. That is the point of Stemming. You know that. Demons like Chalt move through an Unbroken's mind with a scythe, slicing through strands of memories until they find the ones most dominant and dark. It's a very effective technique—fast and sloppy, but effective. This is why she excels at Stemming."

"Yes, she *is* very effective," Montly agreed.

"But there are other techniques, other ways of learning of an Unbroken's sins. Softer ways. Ways that will allow you to see so much more. Not only about the Unbroken, but perhaps even about yourself."

"Myself?" Montly asked.

"The Unbroken, no matter the reason they are here and no matter the purpose that we set them to once they arrive, are our only link to what we remember in the life-times."

"I don't understand. Why would we need to be linked to the life-times?"

"You may not remember them. Maybe you've been conditioned over these hundreds of years to forget them so you could be a better citizen of Hell. But you do remember that the life-times did offer you knowledge, experience, perspective?"

"Well . . ." Montly thought, "of course they did, but that was so long ago."

"Long ago or not, the fresh, Unbroken mind allows you a window into that world. Don't destroy that window like Chalt. Don't ignore it. Instead, look through it. You may find that you learn much more than simply an Unbroken's sins. You may, in fact, see something that helps you know your own sins better. Do you understand?"

"I think so. Yes, I think I do," Montly said, her mind still swimming in his words.

"Good. Then you've received the lesson you've sought from me?" Delius asked.

"I have. Thank you, Delius."

"Now, in exchange for that, there is something I need you to do for me."

Montly tweaked her head, inquisitive. "Anything, Delius."

"Lopex, your teacher . . ." he started.

"Yes."

"He is going to need you, need you more than he realizes. You will stand by his side, undying in loyalty. You will not simply be his servant to wash and mend the Sapiens; you will be his confidante, his advisor. You will listen to him, support him in his decisions. But you must know when to question him if he needs such questioning. That is the true power of an advisor, of a friend."

"Of course. But Lopex has friends, friends he's known for hundreds of years longer than he's known me. Like Reese. Reese was in his class, and . . ."

"Ah, ah, ah." Delius shook his hands, interrupting her. "Reese's loyalty is to his craft. First and foremost, he is a chef. A good friend to Lopex, yes he is, but one who can see a situation from a different perspective? To bring thoughts to a conversation that perhaps Lopex has not considered? This is not Reese. Lopex will need to get this from you, Montly."

It was the first time he'd used her name. She felt the words heavy on her mind, and although she did not completely understand Delius, she hoped that in time she would.

When the pair joined the rest at the blood beach, Chalt had already started her speech. She told the Unbroken of the importance of remembering, of how this moment was so important in their indoctrination to become productive members of Hell. She went on and on, waving her hands, preaching with furor and dominance, embellishing much more than she had a few days ago. Montly thought that this time Chalt looked a little ridiculous.

Bore and Chalt dipped their heavy Scrots into a deep bowl of acid and began moving down the line, melting off tender-lings and sealing up orifices that had no purpose in Hell. The flesh drizzled down the gentle slope of the beach and landed at the feet of the observing Demons. Cries of pain and torturous begging pervaded the acrid air. Montly watched, observing the surgical precision of both Chalt and Bore, but her mind was lost in thought from her conversation with Delius. She considered his words, wondering what there was to be found inside an Unbroken mind that could possibly help her.

Montly stared into the gentle Unbroken faces as they turned inhuman with pain, and imagined what secrets lay inside their heads.

CHAPTER THIRTY

To step into the Unbroken mind is to step into someone else's past. There is no doubt that you will see memories very similar to your own, and in this way, you might draw a glimpse of yourself. Understand this, Demon: Your past is what has condemned you to Hell, so beware—you revisit your own sins when you visit the sins of others.

—From "The Demonic Encyclopedia"
By Delta-Haldon

The group of Unbroken lay exhausted, lashed to bone, bound by their hands and feet. A putrid rainbow of the most awful kind slid down the easy slope in front of them. Silton came out of his pain-haze and found what he already knew to be true, that the gentlest part of him had been sizzled off, replaced with a flat scar of drying flesh.

"I can't... I can't believe... I can't..." His mind roiled with the new reality. Was he still a man? Was he still himself? Was this the "Breaking of the Unbroken" they spoke of?

Silton shook the thought.

De Oppresso Liber.

He remembered the tattoo ripped from his arm when he fell to this place, the tattoo that all Army Special Forces soldiers had, the tattoo that held their brotherhood together. He remembered staring at that symbol, stark and black, on his comrade's arm while he lay crippled in a hospital bed. His friend's legs were blown off at the hip after a brutal explosion, and Silton had been just barely able to save him. After his recovery, his friend went on to lead a full and happy life: Still husband to his wife, still father to his son.

Who am I to sulk? Silton thought. *I've lost nothing compared to him. Nothing.* It took some time, but soon Silton convinced himself.

The rest of the group didn't share this revelation. The line of people lashed to the bone pillar still sobbed. Some screamed hard with broken voices, others hung their heads low, passed out from the pain. A few of the Demons were being fitted with something. Silton thought it looked like a rope, a cord—or even a tail coming from the backs of their heads.

"Most of them have come around," Zaavan said. "Chalt, after your Stem is set, check to make sure they're all awake. And Bore, try to clean some of this mess up."

Chalt inspected the Unbroken as she walked, sloshing through their released fluids. She checked them over, lifting their weak, sobbing heads, slapping the unconscious awake with violent strikes. Bore went to the mess at the base of the slope and kicked mounds of sloppy flesh into the blood lake.

Lopex busily fitted Montly with her Demon Stem.

"Now, don't be nervous," Lopex said. "Just take it slow. You're going to see the Zetas go quickly, very fast through these

Unbroken. Don't feel like you have to do that. Take your time. Understand?"

"Yes. Yes, I do. It feels weird. The Stem tickles a little . . . like my mind is reaching out for something, grabbing, but nothing's there."

"Very good. That's a very good sign," Lopex replied. "You're going to do great. Just concentrate on your breathing. You have some time yet. We'll wait till the end, okay? I think Chalt is going to give another one of her speeches first." They both smiled.

"In the life-times . . ." Chalt began, melodrama sweating from her dark tumor plated skin, " . . .you were known by *so* much." She paused. "You were known by your skills, by your personality, by your size, your shape, your ability to accumulate things. Here in Hell, none of that matters. Here, you are free from all of that. Here, you will not be known by the illusions you created in life, not by the visage you hid behind. Here, you will be known by your sins!"

There were gasps from the terrified Unbroken, the perfect audience.

"*But* . . ." she continued. "As we know, you will not volunteer this, nor are you capable of even knowing yourself deeply enough to identify your sins. So, we are going to help you."

Chalt walked over to the first woman on the far side of the Scrot line and stepped behind her. She lifted the knife end of her Demon Stem and thrust it into the back of her skull.

Silton watched from the far side, and even from that distance he could see the woman jolt as if being electrocuted. The woman didn't scream, only hummed a low, guttural sound as if in a trance. A few moments later, Chalt withdrew the stem.

"Lust—Adulterer!" she yelled, then moved to the soft man next to her and again thrust in the Demon Stem.

Zaavan quickly sorted through his vast chain of brands and found the capital A: a large brand, green and sticky from overuse.

"I may need to make a new one of these soon," he said under his breath as he inspected it. Zaavan took in a breath, puffed out a cloud of acid, and drove the brand into the woman's forehead. The sizzling pain drew much more than a low hum from her, and the woman convulsed in screams as the skin of her forehead smoked.

"Greed—Thief!" Chalt yelled after a short time stemming the soft man. Zaavan went back to his chain, looking for the appropriate brand. But Chalt hadn't taken out the Demon Stem. She looked to the sky, concentrating, pushing through the weeds of the Unbroken's mind.

"Ahhh . . ." She pulled out the bone knife. "This one's a doctor." Chalt smiled at Zaavan, who nodded at her confidently.

"Good job, Chalt," Zaavan said, as he looked through his brands again.

Lopex leaned to Montly. "It's always good to find medical people. Sometimes they make the best Engineers."

Zaavan branded a thick T onto the doctor's forehead, then took another brand and melted a D into the middle of his chest. He leaned in heavy, holding the doctor still as he pressed the body brand, signifying his medical expertise. The doctor howled and howled, leaking out his remaining fluids until he finally passed out.

Chalt walked behind Mariella. She sat in an awkward position, her misshapen legs not allowing her to kneel straight. Mariella hadn't let out more than a few screams, even during the Scrotting. Silton watched from the end of the line as Chalt took Mariella's hair in hand, positioning her head for better leverage. Silton couldn't help himself.

"Mariella!" he screamed. "Mariella, be strong!"

Mariella turned her head slightly and looked at him with sad, defeated eyes, silently mouthing a word. Silton strained his eyes to see.

Sorry. Over and over again, she mouthed *sorry* as she closed her eyes in tears.

Chalt thrust the Stem into the back of Mariella's skull, and they both went into a trance. Mariella didn't convulse like the rest. She sat with her head arched back, connected to the Demon's mind. A few moments went by, and Chalt ripped out the Demon Stem.

"Wrath—Murderer. A Murderer of many! A Murderer of the helpless!" the Demon screamed, and took a step back, weary from the Stemmings.

"Also . . ." Chalt paused. "She's a nurse," she said with a decidedly lower tone, as exhaustion crept in.

Silton hung his head. Mariella, a murderer of many. A murderer of the helpless. *How many more people had she killed?* he wondered. *How many people had she sent to Hell?*

Chalt stepped to the next man in line, who'd been praying silently ever since the Scrotting. Chalt palmed the top of the Unbroken's head and could feel the eyes of her fellow Demons upon her. Watching her, they silently wondered how far she could go, how many could Chalt Stem in a row?

Chalt thrust the Stem in hard, holding the man's head as best she could. She wandered in his mind as the man screamed over and over and over again, "No, God no! No, God, no! Noooooo!" The deepest parts of his psyche were being perused for the first time, the eyes of a Demon searching his soul like one would page through a book.

Chalt pulled back the Stem, taking in another deep breath. Zaavan watched his pupil closely, fearing she neared exhaustion. The entire Demon Cantavit silently waited on her assessment.

"Manipulation of God's Word!" Chalt said as if relieved, and smiled, throwing the man's head forward. The crowd of Demons hummed and shook their heads in acknowledgment, waiting for any further details as Chalt caught her breath. "He's a Priest!" Chalt said, and the Cantavit broke into a roar of laughter, clapping their hands furiously.

"Another Priest, huh?" Zaavan said, with an air of gleeful sarcasm. "Well, we have a special brand for you, Father." Zaavan pulled up the heavy chain on his side, flipped a few dozen brands over themselves, and yanked out a strange looking device.

He held a stubby bone column, vein rope banding the handle, with a circle at the end of the shaft. The circle had a hinge at the halfway point, and when Zaavan opened it, he carefully sprayed a thin coating of acid around the inside. Chalt held the Priest as Zaavan approached, his bone-plated teeth gleaming with a smile as he slapped the apparatus around the Priest's neck and held him fast. The Priest started to scream, a bellowed yell filled with words about God's mercy and forgiveness. As the inside of the Unbroken Priest's throat melted in on itself, his vocal cords dissolved.

"You'll manipulate God's word no longer, Unbroken fool!" Zaavan said as he unclasped the brand, revealing a deep black collar of scar, perfectly uniform, surrounding his neck.

Montly leaned to Lopex. "Why that special brand for him? Why not just a sin stamp?"

"The Daughters want any clergy specially identified," Lopex said.

"I see that, but why?" Montly asked.

"It's important for the other Unbroken to know that men of God don't escape the Devil's wrath. Also, by taking away their ability to speak, they can't preach."

"Really? I never knew that," Montly replied.

Chalt, dizzy from rummaging through so many minds, steadied herself.

"Chalt!" Zaavan yelled from the beach. "Fine work, Chalt! Work reminiscent of the Gamma Class Harvesters. The Devil would be proud!"

Chalt smiled in response, still half-dazed, and marshaled herself. She took two short steps to the next woman, and went to grab her by the hair. Chalt's hand slipped off the Unbroken woman's sweat-soaked head, and she almost stumbled over her. The trembling woman started to speak, a whisper, almost to herself at first, but then her tiny voice crept higher.

"Liar. I'm a liar, and a cheat, and I..." the Unbroken woman said meekly.

Chalt could barely hear the woman as she steadied herself, shook off a dizzying haze, and again grabbed her by the hair.

"I said I'm a liar." The Unbroken woman pushed her voice to courage. "I'm a liar, a cheat. I lied about being hurt. And I got money. I lied and said I couldn't work! It wasn't true. I was even..." She coughed. "I was even proud of it." The tears rolled down her cheeks, tiny trickles of guilt releasing themselves. "Please, please don't hurt me, please."

"Good... good," Chalt whispered in her ear with an

almost drunken slur, petting the woman like fat livestock. "That helps me, weak one."

Chalt punctured the back of her skull, sending the woman into a convulsion that almost snapped her spine in two. Having a lead on her sin, Chalt moved easy and high over the landscape of the woman's mind. She dropped herself into the woman's weak psyche only to make a few slashes, like drawing in the sand or skipping stones on a pond. Chalt didn't explore, didn't delve into her mind as she should. She only spent enough time to make it look like a full Stemming. The black tumor-coated Demon was completely exhausted, her mind nearing fragmentation, a confused place where a Demon could forget who they were.

She pulled out the Stem, and a spurt of fluid spit out of the woman's brain: the sign of a sloppy Stemming, a teasing of the mind that yielded damage, not information.

"She is a Liar—Greed—and took Pride in her falsehoods," Chalt said.

Zaavan quickly grabbed the brand, soaked it in acid, and marred the forehead of the shattered woman.

"That was a fast one," Reese said to Lopex under his breath. Lopex looked at him with deep, emotionless eyes, knowing all too well what his friend implied.

"Montly, get ready. We may need you to jump in soon," Lopex said, and a ripple of queasy excitement ran from Montly's toes to the base of her neck, where the Demon Stem lay.

Chalt stepped to the next man in line, the silent man with only one arm, his shoulder stub lined with charred flesh. She took in a deep breath, resolving that she could Stem at least one more. She violently pulled back his dark hair and thrust in the Stem, then held very still, deeply searching out the man's sins.

Suddenly, her hand twitched and gripped the Demon Stem as if she wanted to pull it out, and her eyes squeezed tight as if she were fighting to keep them closed. She shook her head like invisible pests circled her.

Moments passed, and Chalt's chest began to heave, as if being hit by some unseen force. Chalt stumbled back, catching her balance by the hilt of the Stem. She opened her glassy eyes and stared blankly out over the flat, blood lake.

"Wrath—Murderer, Killer, Suicide . . ." Chalt said, lost in the ripples of her own mind. The Unbroken, only half-stunned by the brief Stemming, yelled out.

"I'm not a murderer! Not a murderer! I'm a soldier for Allah! I fight for God! I'm God's soldier!" he said. His eyes drifted unfocused, and his mouth drooled as he spoke.

"Ahhhhh!" Chalt, Stem Drunk, screamed, pouncing on his back and striking him over and over again in the back of the head. "*God* does not need your help! *He* does not need you! You don't serve *Him! Never speak His name again!*"

Chalt pounded on his head again and again. The many minds she'd bonded with had taken their toll, and Chalt, now fragmented, was unable to separate the reality of this Unbroken mind from her own.

The Cantavit watched, patient and silent. Zaavan looked over at Bore, a long, hard look. Bore didn't seem to understand.

"Bore!" Zaavan clapped his hands.

Like a dumb pet, Bore shook off his confusion and jumped to action. He bounded to the Scrot line, and with one leap cleared the kneeling Unbroken, grabbed his comrade Chalt, and cradled her to his chest. The Unbroken man fell forward in an unconscious bloody lump.

"Okay. It okay, sister, okay . . ." Bore said in the low soothing tone of a speaking beast. He carried Chalt back to Zaavan, who inspected her.

"Are you back? Are you with us, Zeta?" Zaavan said sternly, holding Chalt's chin in his hand.

"I am, master. I am," she replied, visibly exhausted.

"You've done very well. Six in a row. You are now amongst the best Stemmers in Hell."

Chalt smiled, a woozy smile, and took to her feet uneasily, working to shake the fragmented feeling from her mind.

"Bore, you're up!" Zaavan said, and pointed to the woman next to Silton.

Lopex arched his brow, confused.

"Zaavan, I was under the impression that my pupil, Montly, would have a chance to Stem today."

"Your pupil can have a chance if my team can't handle the Stemming load. Is that not correct, Delius?" Zaavan asked. "Is Stemming not solely the responsibility of the Defensionem?"

Reese couldn't hold back.

"Seriously? You're gonna let Bore Stem? The only thing you're going to find after he gets done with her brain is soup."

"Silence!" Delius commanded. "Zaavan is in command of Stemming. This is done at his discretion. But as any good Demon leader knows, in the Vast, one always uses the *best* tools at their disposal, no matter rank or class."

"Right, the *best* tool, my dear Delta," Zaavan replied snidely, and motioned for Bore to ready himself for Stemming.

Bore bounded back to the Scrot line and positioned his bulk behind the last woman in the row, right next to Silton. The scene, silent now that most of the Unbroken were unconscious, allowed Bore needed concentration.

Bore took the Stem, careful to make sure it didn't tangle,

and placed the tip of the bone knife to the base of the woman's skull. She cried and begged, speaking of her family, of her devotion to God. Silton looked on, helpless.

Watching Bore try to line up the bone knife with the back of the woman's head reminded Silton of his medical training and classmates who felt squeamish around cadavers. "Nervous Medics are more dangerous than the enemy," his teacher would always say. This beast, this red Demon, looked nervous to Silton, a brain butcher with a shoddy tool. *What will he do to me?* Silton shuddered to imagine it.

As Bore thrust the Demon Stem into the back of the sobbing woman's head, Silton heard a crunch that must have been one of her vertebrae being crushed. The woman's left arm started to shake, then her whole left side went limp. Silton looked at her face, vapid and lost in some distant horror. Her left cheek, eye, and chin all looked to be sliding off her face, the muscles beneath giving up.

She's having a stroke, Silton thought. *That thing is causing her to have a stroke.*

✛ ✛ ✛

B⊕RE kept the Stem in deep, searching, searching, lost in the forest of her thoughts. Soon he found a trail, a well-worn trail, a memory he could follow. He walked down the path, admiring the fragments of thought reflected off so many leaves of her Unbroken mind.

Beautiful, Bore thought, *so beautiful.*

The path edged to the left. It looked a bit overgrown, but inviting, so Bore took it. He strode down the poorly lit memory, observing days long forgotten, experiences lost to time. It was so serene, so quiet. No one here to yell at him. No one here to tell him what to do.

Bore's eyes grew heavy, and he considered lying down in this peaceful place. *What Bore doing here anyway? No matter, Bore sleep*, he thought, as he lay down in the soft memory.

�֍ ✖ ✖

B ⊕ R E awoke to Zaavan slapping him in the face.

"What are you doing? What are you doing, you bloated blood sac!" he yelled.

It took Bore time to come to. Zaavan held Bore's Demon Stem in his hand. The Unbroken woman now lay slumped over with a steaming hole wafting smoldering brain matter from the back of her head.

"Well, she ain't gonna be good for anything other than Sapien parts. What a waste. See, I told you," Reese said, shaking his head and scratching his round belly.

"What happened?" Montly asked Lopex.

"He got lost," Lopex said. "You can never get lost, Montly. If you feel that you're lost, you have to leave immediately. It doesn't matter where you are, just concentrate and try to pull the Stem out. Stemming too long will cook the Unbroken mind. It can even cook your own. Luckily for Bore, he doesn't have much to cook."

Zaavan dragged Bore back to the front of the Scrot line, scolding him the whole way. Bore hung his head, his shoulders low, saddened to be back where people yelled at him, where they told him what to do, where the Demon could find no peace.

"So, then I assume my pupil can Stem the last one?" Lopex

asked in Zaavan's general direction. "Zaavan . . . Zeta-Zaavan? Am I to assume that we can now set my pupil up for the last Stemming? That is unless you want to do this one yourself," Lopex said sharply with disdain. No Demon of Zaavan's stature and authority would Stem. Although it required deft skill to do right, it was seen as a menial job to step into the Unbroken mind.

"Fine, fine!" Zaavan yelled, tending to his worn-out pupils. "Do as you will, Lopex!" He turned back to the beach.

"Are you ready, Montly?" Lopex said, with a deep, white smile.

"I am. I'm ready," Montly replied, fighting the excitement welling in her body as she looked across the beach to Silton, bound and kneeling in front of her.

CHAPTER THIRTY-ONE

The phenomenon of Backwash Stemming is rare and not fully understood. It occurs when an Unbroken, either willfully or accidentally, gains access to the memories of the Demon. This could lead to the Unbroken attaining sensitive information that could upset the natural order of Hell. Therefore, the Demon must move quickly and efficiently through the Unbroken mind so that this risk can be reduced.

—From "The Demonic Encyclopedia"
By Delta-Haldon

Montly walked toward Silton, Demon Stem in hand, as the long spinal cord itched at the back of her head. Lopex followed close behind, and as the pair rounded the end of the bone line, Montly and Silton locked eyes for a long moment.

She'd thought that she'd have no feelings about the Unbroken, that like Chalt, she'd see him as a dumb Sapien: simple, lost, and desperate for help. But that's not how she felt when she looked into Silton's eyes. She felt sadness for him, like one would for a wounded animal. She felt Silton's fear, palpable and thick like the blood lake that stretched out in front of them. Thinking of the pain she was about to cause shaved off the excitement Montly felt, and only nervous apprehension lay in its place.

"So, first you need to grab the head. From the top is best," Lopex said as he guided Montly's hand.

She took up a thick tuft of Silton's hair as gently as she could.

"Now, tilt his head forward," Lopex continued. "And lean in with your hip so you can lock his chin down tight."

Montly complied. Against his own logic, Silton struggled a bit, shifting his hips back and forth as he pushed to get up. But realizing struggle was pointless, he forced himself to stop, and tried to save his strength for the torment to come.

"The Stem will slide in much easier than you think. You don't need to stab like Chalt does. Besides, this will ease your consciousness into the Unbroken's. It's very important to ease in, as they will be less apt to try and hide their thoughts."

Lopex took his hand away from Montly's. "When you're ready." He stepped back, with the rest of the Cantavit silently watching.

Montly pressed the blade of the Stem into the base of Silton's neck. The boney edge of the knife slid past the skin into the warm meat of his brain like soft mud. For a moment, there was nothing. Montly felt herself reaching out, reaching for something solid, the handle to the door of Silton's mind. Then, all at once, she heard a sharp crack as she surged into him.

✝ ✝ ✝

INSTANTLY, Montly found herself standing on the high precipice of Silton's consciousness, below her a valley thick with chaos and clamor. The scene looked reminiscent of war: she could see pockets of fighting, light splashing from end to end across his life, and deep pits of darkness that light could not penetrate. Montly crept closer to the edge, her legs trembling with fear. She marshaled her courage, and dove into Silton's memories.

A soupy disoriented mess greeted her in the valley. Voices yelling, screaming from all directions, objects flying past her with terrific speed, and grand explosions blinding her from distant origins. A dark mist cleared, and Montly found herself standing over Silton as he knelt on the ground, tending to someone. His hands frantically moved around a twitching and tortured body. She thought it looked like a Harvest, like the ripping of organs from an Unbroken, but instead of taking organs, Silton tried to put them back. His hands, soaked in rich red, pushed and shoved intestines into an empty cavity and desperately tried to hold them there. The body settled to shudders, and soon only the mouth moved as it spewed out inhuman sounds of pain. A voice came from the body as it slowed to death. The throat full of blood only let out distorted words, but Montly could still make them out.

"Thank you, Silton, thank you, brother . . ." the body whispered, and then it faded away, leaving only a shadow on the ground.

His name is Silton, Montly thought, *Silton.*

The commotion surrounding her faded away like the night, and Montly saw Silton sitting in a chair in a lonely room, staring at his reflection while the world moved around him swiftly. For days it seemed he sat in the room. Montly watched patiently behind him, his only action: drinking. He drank, and drank, and drank. He left for a flash in time and then he was back again, drinking. Silton's body became elastic and stretched out, and he clumsily fell to the floor where he lay for some time. And then back to drinking again as the world spun around him. Montly kept guard, waiting to see, waiting to interpret his sin. *Gluttony perhaps?* Montly thought. A minor sin, but maybe that was all to be seen in his mind.

And then, abruptly and without warning, Silton struck the mirror in front of him. His image shattered and floated around both of them like flat raindrops. He pulled out an object, one that seemed strange to Montly, and put it to his chest. It exploded with a flash that burned Montly's eyes, the sound startling her, and she jumped back in fear. Across the room, an arc of red painted the air. It seemed to come from his chest in an endless flow.

A suicide. He must be a suicide, Montly lamented.

Montly waited until the red faded slowly to dark shadow, satisfied that she'd seen his mortal sin. She turned to walk out of his mind, but in the distance, in a dark plot where she'd not been able to see before, a light shone, a warm glowing light that pushed comfort and peace from its soft rays.

The fresh Unbroken allow you a window into that world of the past. Do not destroy that window. Do not ignore it. Instead, look through it. You may find that you learn much more than simply a person's sin. Delius's words echoed in Montly's mind, and instead of leaving, she floated to the soft light and entered the hole from where it came.

The sun shone bright and high in this other place. Montly could barely remember what the sun looked like, and she had to cover her eyes as the light bled warmth onto her face. A fountain of purest water shone in front of her, fresh water like Montly hadn't seen in hundreds of years. It made her mouth salivate with envy. This is what Delius must have meant: this beautiful memory of the life-times that only exists in minds of the Unbroken.

She could see Silton on the far side of the fountain. He walked easy and free, his hand holding another's. Joy caressed his face, and laughter echoed through the air against the background of splashing, fresh water. Montly pushed forward to see a woman by his side, a fair-skinned, neatly dressed woman edged in shadowed darkness. They kissed hard and long at the base of the fountain, and warmth exploded through the memory. Montly smiled, feeling the pleasure of the scene, and stared into the face of the woman with envy. Her features shone clean and beautiful, but Montly felt a distance in her.

His wife, Montly's empathic skills told her.

She walked toward them and looked closer still. Something about the woman's face felt familiar, something she'd seen before. But soon the memory faded, evaporating up into the sky of Silton's mind, along with so much glistening water.

Thrust through to the next memory, Montly stood over a bed with Silton's back to her. He sat hunched, jolting with sobs of sorrow in a stark white room that glowed sallow with artificial light. Again, Silton held the hand of the woman from the fountain. She lay there unmoving, with eyes closed tight like thin ribbons. Silton clutched her, squeezing her hand as he cried, "Wake up, Kay. Please, give me anything. You have to wake up so I can make this right!"

Montly felt a wash of emotion come over herself, a deep sadness that she'd not felt in hundreds of years. It pained her. It pushed her toward a part of humanity she'd thought lost a long time ago.

Was this an effect of the Stemming? Why should I feel this way?

Montly's emotions, unearthed from so long ago, forced her to reach out to Silton, and she gently touched his back. Montly could not control this. Her empathy demanded consolation, and the woman lying in the bed looked so familiar to her.

✦ ✦ ✦

S I L T ⊕ N felt a sharp yank on the back of his head, and fell backward through a tunnel of shadows and light fighting to gain position over one another. His eyes tried to focus, and he found himself standing in a stark white hospital room. Quickly, his consciousness came together like a jumbled puzzle, and he remembered clearly where he was: the hospital room where his wife Kay lay in a coma. This was the last time Silton would see her alive, the saddest, most desperate moment in his life.

But something seemed different. He could see the memory clearly: at her bedside, holding her hand, crying, trying to wake her. But something else he couldn't make out drifted in the room. As the misty hue of light dissipated, he could see it. Someone else, *something* else, was there with them.

Silton shook his head and blinked his foggy eyes to clarity. *What was it?* He took a few steps forward, and it all rushed to him. *The Demon. The Demon torturing me!* he thought. *It's here, in my mind!* It leaned over him and Kay, vandalizing Silton's most precious and delicate memory.

"What are you doing here!" Silton screamed. But his semi-muted voice formed words that even he did not understand.

"What are you doing!" Silton screamed again. "Leave! This is mine! Mine!" He reached out and gripped Montly's shoulder, his hand sinking deep into her skin.

Then, deep in Silton's memories, in the shadows of the

reality that Montly and Silton shared, something happened. Silton touching Kay, Montly touching Silton, and Silton's fragmented self grabbing Montly. Somewhere in the electric current of consciousness running through the Demon Stem, an error occurred.

As if pushed by a tremendous force, Silton's mind crossed a bridge busy with sickly yellow and green clouds. The threshold between his and Montly's mind ripped open, and Silton found himself standing on a hill of deeply tanned skin. This was Hell, but not the stark Hell Silton knew of. This place was softer, more deliberate.

Silton held still, at first thinking he had escaped. But the lofty edges of the horizon, the artificial feel of the light, and the shadowy details in the objects around him told him that this was still a dream. But not his dream.

In the distance, a slow rumble began, and the image of a thousand, thousand people rushed toward him. A herd of men and women, strapped in like cattle, pulling a huge sled the size of an office building. The masses started to pass by him, ignoring Silton as he sat observing the scene, invisible. The herd of people looked hacked to pieces. Some absent arms and legs, some just fleshy forms being dragged along by the white yokes and vein ropes that held them in place. And then he saw her. The Demon who'd invaded his own memories, riding tall and fast on a majestic horse-beast.

I'm in her mind, Silton thought.

The Demon screamed frantically while pointing to her cohorts. "It's coming apart! It's coming apart! More rope! Quickly!"

She rode strong, keeping pace with the herd of people, and Silton could see what she was so concerned about. The lashings had come loose on a portion of the yokes, and like oxen pulling in opposite directions, it shredded the remaining ropes, setting free a dozen people from their restraints.

"We're losing it! We're losing it! The Sled will sink if we stop! Push harder!" the Demon yelled again, and her fellow companions swiftly set to fix the split ropes.

The freed people, running fast and slipping on the wet Skin-Land, scattered in all directions. A young, frenzied woman, naked and wet with flesh, scampered in front of the mounted Demon. Without hesitation, the Demon rode her down, scooping the naked woman off the ground and straddling her weak body over the horse-beast. The Demon started riding back to the chaotic herd, and as she passed Silton, the captured woman lifted her head in struggle.

Through the mess of blood, hair, and fluids, Silton saw the face of the woman clearly.

It was Kay.

CHAP†ER THIR†Y-†W⊕

When an Unbroken is given access to a Demon's mind during the accidental phenomenon of Backwash Stemming, the effects can be disastrous. In the few recorded incidences of verified Backwash Stemming, it has been found that exposure to a Demon's mind eventually drives the Unbroken mad, or gives them access to information detrimental to the process of breaking them. Therefore, it is recommended that once an Unbroken has been identified as being exposed to Backwash Stemming, they be destroyed after a detailed interrogation.

—From "The Demonic Encyclopedia"
By Delta-Haldon

The Cantavit roiled with celebration as Reese labored heavily over his outdoor kitchen. His rotund form, deep in concentration, bounced from one cooking station to the next. He covered the flat bone plate he'd made with a thin veil of acid, and began to sear thick, liver steaks. The purple slabs were beautifully crusted in a mixture of bright green bile salts and dried skin flakes. They sizzled as he flipped them on the hot surface. A thick grist boiled in the ground pot next to him, and he dashed it with a healthy handful of cartilage bits to stiffen the stew. But all of the chef's precision was lost on the other Demons as they recklessly indulged in his dark, blood beer. Every Demon had a cup, and every cup was drunk over and over again. So much so that Reese had to start a second batch.

"What makes your beer so good?" asked Lopex, salivating as he tasted the deep bitterness on his tongue.

"I can't take all the credit; it's this fresh blood. It makes all the difference, Eta brother," Reese replied. "The fermentation process can be completely different from bacterium to bacterium. That's why I always use my own special breed. I'm used to making beer with filtered blood, the wretch we siphon out of the Skin-Land on the Sled. I've never made it with fresh blood from a lake. There are fewer impurities, less fat. It changes the taste a bit, makes it stronger for sure, but the best part is that it ferments so fast. I just want it to be perfect for Delius. Do you think it will be okay?"

"Of course it will. He'll love it, I'm sure. And at worst, it looks like the Zetas are liking it."

"Yeah, I know. But who gives a stump about them? You'd better drink what you can before they come back. The next batch won't be ready for a bit," Reese said.

"Good idea." Lopex dipped his keratin cup into the dark bone bowl of beer.

Lopex walked to the gathering pit, where a set of bone rolls for sitting surrounded a pile of smoldering bone chips and marrow. Montly sat there, stoking the marrow until it glowed deep red.

"Here, take this." Lopex handed her the beer. "You're quiet."

"I know. I'm sorry. I just... never mind." She stopped herself and took a sip from the cup.

"What? Tell me," Lopex said.

"It's just..." She paused, apprehensive as her thoughts formed words. "The Stemming, it's not how... It's not how I thought it would feel. I didn't think that..." Montly stifled herself.

"You didn't think what?" Lopex pressed.

She took in a breath, stole her eyes from the bone fire, and locked on Lopex.

"I didn't think that I would care as much as I did. When I was in him."

Lopex silently thought on his pupil's words, looking for the right balance of criticism and compliment.

"The first time is never quite what one expects. We think the Unbroken to be just another means to our ends. Body parts for Sapiens, beasts to pull the Sled, food. We forget that they exist independent of us, that they have their own thoughts, their own needs. We forget that we were once just like them. That we came from them. Stemming the Unbroken brings these feelings out. Makes us think more of their lot here. But you have to remember: This is the way. This is the only way to condition them so they can survive here. It may seem cruel, it may seem that we take something away, but it's not. What we do is mercy. You'd think nothing of ripping a loose tooth from a Canem. Or if a Drum had an injured arm, you'd amputate it without thinking twice. Wouldn't you? This is the same. That's how you should feel about it."

"I know. I know what you're saying. And I know you're right. It's just..." Montly stammered.

"Tell me."

"No, you're right. It's probably just because he was my first, that's all." Montly turned back to the glowing bones, as did Lopex.

But that wasn't what Montly thought. What she thought scared her. It scared her so much she'd not had the courage to tell her mentor. Montly knew that somehow the Unbroken had entered her own mind. She didn't know how, but he had. She could feel the film of his consciousness still in her, a sticky sense that someone had rummaged around her memories. Montly didn't know what that meant, if it meant anything at all, but she knew deep inside her that it wasn't normal.

Chalt, already drunk from the blood beer, perused the guarded pen where the Unbroken rested. Curled up into groups, holding each other for warmth, they lay exhausted from the ordeal of Stemming.

The priest sat by himself, itching at the scar around his neck.

"Now, don't scratch it. That will make it bleed and ruin the scar. Then we'll have to do it all over again. Satan is very specific about you 'Men of God,'" Chalt said, leaning on a post for support.

"Satan has no power over me. Satan has no power . . ." the priest whispered, the only sound he could make with his mutilated vocal cords.

"Oh well, you'd better revisit your teachings. Satan has all the power. Don't forget that God gave Satan dominion here. God can watch, He may even listen from time to time, but have no illusions—you are in the Devil's territory now."

Chalt started to walk away from him. "Oh, and don't forget that *God* sent you here. Remember to thank *Him* in your prayers."

She continued over to the man with the blown-off arm.

He knelt silently, eyes closed, rocking back and forth slowly.

"And let me guess, you're praying too," Chalt said, slurring her words. The man didn't respond, but she didn't care, and continued her ridicule. "Do you really think that He is ready to listen to a man who killed dozens of His children in *His* name? Do you really think he cares that you're having a bad time? You should worry more about that arm of yours. You know we're going to sew another one on to you? An arm from another person. They probably won't be from your religion. In fact, it could even be a woman's arm. I know men in your religion are *real* sensitive about women, right? They're the lesser class, right? Well, how about this: I'm gonna *make sure* you get the arm of a woman. What do you think about that?"

Chalt took a deep swig from her cup. The man looked up at her, his trembling, tanned skin fading to pale. Chalt whispered, mimicking the kindest tone. "You're going to see this is all a gift one day. It might take you a thousand years, but you'll see." She stumbled away. Once out of sight, the man broke down into tears.

Three of the women lay in the corner huddled together. Two of them busied themselves consoling the one Bore had accidentally lobotomized, her blank eyes staring past them into nothingness. Chalt approached, walking with a loose swagger in her hips.

"How is she? Has she spoken yet?" Chalt asked.

The women looked at her with terror, then their eyes moved to slits of disdain.

"What did he do to her?" the liar woman yelled, with some force to her words.

"Oh, that?" Chalt responded. "Well, that shouldn't have happened. That was a mistake. You see, my friend, Bore, he's not very smart." Chalt chuckled to herself.

"It's not funny!" the liar yelled. The capital L brand, sweaty with pus, shone on her forehead.

"No, you're right," Chalt replied. "It's not funny. She'll probably be taken off our quota because she is so damaged. That's no good. But look at the bright side: She won't have to spend any time in the Herd like the two of you. She'll probably have an easy life working in the kitchens or cleaning, or maybe she could even be a Daughter's Artifex."

"What the Hell are you saying? She needs help!" the enraged liar woman yelled.

Chalt replied quickly, "No, you've got it backwards, my pretty little friend. *You* are the one who's going to need help. She's going to be fine now that she's Broken. You, on the other hand, have about fifty years to go, pulling and pushing and trudging through the blood mud with the rest of the Herd. You'll see. I bet in two years you'll be wishing you were her. I bet . . ." Chalt laughed out a burp as she stumbled away.

The three men first found by the Cantavit lay sleeping in one of the corners. Chalt reached over and poked the self-proclaimed Satanist with her Scrot. His shoulder, still thick with pus from where she'd ripped off his brand, jumped involuntarily. But he didn't rouse to her torture. They were wise to Chalt by now. They knew the only way to survive was silence. Bored, Chalt walked on to the corner where Mariella and Silton lay knotted together. Their brands ached with pain, Silton with an S for suicide, Mariella with an M for murderer, and both with Capital Ds on their chests.

"Here she comes," Mariella said. "I can't believe I'm saying this, but I think she's drunk."

"Yeah, she is," Silton replied. "Just keep your cool, try not to agitate her. Who knows what she's capable of?"

"I'll do my best," Mariella said.

Chalt lost her footing walking toward them and had to use the side of the pen to catch her balance.

"So, what are you two talking about?" Chalt said with a slur.

"Oh, we were just remarking how classy you look, so ladylike," Mariella snapped. The slight was lost on Chalt, either due to her inebriation or the hundreds of years in Hell.

"You know, I don't think you're so bad," Chalt said to Mariella. "I think that killing off the weak and sending the dying to the next life is a good thing. I like that. If I were back in the life-times, I think I'd do that too. God is cruel for sending you here for it."

"So glad you approve," Mariella said. Silton nudged her sharply to stop, and Mariella reluctantly obliged.

"But you . . . you're the only one I don't know about, aren't you?" Chalt said to Silton, putting her chin to her fist as she leaned heavily on the fence. "Well, I guess I don't know the lobotomized girl, either, but there's not much to know about her anymore, right?" Chalt laughed at her joke so hard she choked. She took in a last deep swig of beer, wiped her face with the back of her black tumor-covered hand, and settled into a serious tone.

"But really. How was it with her? I'm curious, did she do a good job?" Chalt asked.

"It wasn't great. If that's what you're asking," Silton replied.

"She was probably sloppy. You know she's not even a Demon. She's actually a Minion, a laborer. She ran the Herd. A dirty job, in a dirty place. I can't imagine what it must have felt like to have someone that filthy crawling around inside your head." Chalt stared hard at Silton, spoiling for a response.

Silton refused. Instead, he shrugged his shoulders like he didn't care.

"Fine, you don't have to answer me. You'll see what the Herd looks like. You're both going to be part of it for quite a while. You'll spend every day and night pulling the Sled for the next fifty or so years," Chalt said in a scathing tone.

"Yeah, I know. We pull it so the big city behind doesn't sink into the skin, right?" Silton jolted out.

The comment stunned Chalt to silence. Her head twitched to the side as she processed what the Unbroken had said.

"How could you know that?" Chalt said in a disbelieving tone. "How could you—"

Just then, Zaavan and Bore stumbled out of the darkness, drunk to their bones.

"Eat!" yelled Bore, slapping Chalt on the back as he grabbed her and ripped her off the lip of the pen.

"No, wait. That one . . . he . . ." Chalt tried to get her words out.

"Never mind the Unbroken, Chalt," Zaavan interrupted. "I have a little surprise for Delius tonight." He lifted a sack he carried. "You don't want to miss this!"

"Surprise Delta. Surprise Delta," Bore mimicked.

And before Chalt could interrogate further, she was whisked away from Silton and the disturbing knowledge he possessed.

CHAPTER THIRTY-THREE

Backwash Stemming also can have severe side effects for the Demon who's been exposed to the Unbroken mind. When the Unbroken's consciousness Backwashes through the Demon Stem, massive amounts of the Unbroken's memories follow. This exposure leads to the potential fragmentation of the Demon's mind. Therefore, it is recommended that once a Demon has been identified as being exposed to Backwash Stemming, they be destroyed after a detailed interrogation.

—From "The Demonic Encyclopedia"
by Delta-Haldon

Everyone dined well under the hue of a pale, yellow evening. The Cantavit chewed on thick liver steaks, munched on crisp, brown skin chips heavily seasoned with sweat salts, and washed it all down with a second batch of warm, tart beer. Even the Sapiens reveled as they slopped up meaty grist with such ferocity they actually remained silent for once.

"You are second to no one, Eta-Reese," Delius said as he

finished his steak. "I've never had such a meal out in the Vast. I don't know how you do it."

"I couldn't imagine a higher compliment. Thank you, Delius," Reese replied.

"To Chef Reese!" Lopex said, and raised his cup.

"*TO CHEF REESE!*" the Cantavit cheered, and drank.

The beer ran heavy through their blood, and conversations scattered across the group as they sat around the glowing bones. Night slowly took over the sky, and soon only the soft smolder of marrow and the faces of drunken Demons could be seen. A hush drifted across the group as the talk crept naturally to silence.

"Tell us a story, Delius," Lopex said. "Tell us a story of the old times."

"Yes, Delius, why don't you tell us a story," Chalt said, drunk and sloppy. "Tell us one of your great Delta battle stories. Of how you defeated the Angels! Crushed them."

Delius shifted uneasily on his seat. He scanned the group, all of their eyes on him, and knew they'd accept nothing less than what they demanded.

"A story of battle? Are you not bored of such tales? Have you not heard them a thousand times before?" Delius said.

"Maybe so. But not from you," Zaavan said snidely. "Not from the last of the Deltas."

Delius paused uncomfortably. "Fine then. I will tell you a story." He set down his cup, feeling the beer warm his tongue a bit more than expected, and began.

"About a thousand years after The Great Fall, we were well on our way to a full recovery. Although the Blood Palace remained abandoned, destroyed, the Sled had been built, and was working quite well, better than we thought it would. Of course, it's not like the Sled we have today, but still, it was very impressive for back then. The Angels must have thought us still weak, thought that we'd never get back to the strength we had before. They must have thought that they could come down and take the redeemed from us at will, without a plan, without scouting us first. When I look back on their first attack after The Great Fall, their terrific failure... terribly overconfident the Angels were then, not like now. Not at all like now. We must have had at least five thousand Unbroken pulling in the Herd at that time. It might not sound like a lot, but after The Great Fall, we didn't even know if there *were* five thousand Unbroken left in Hell. The Angels saw us as a prime target, and one day, early in the morning before Heaven's Eye crested, they descended. What they didn't know, what they could not have known, was that every Demon on the Sled had already been fitted with Compound Eyes. I know it's a simple addition now, but back then, Compound Eyes were revolutionary. Our scouts had no problem seeing the cracks in the sky, the break in the void where the Angels descended. They must have thought they'd have surprise on their side. That we wouldn't know they were here until they started plucking redeemed from the Herd. But we saw them. We saw them even before they crossed. The Deltas were sent to meet them, and we flew, our entire class, straight up to the cracks. We didn't have the weapons we have today, no. We were only armed with bandoliers, and nets soaked with Ossien Paste."

"But why?" Montly asked, catching herself immediately, embarrassed for interrupting Delius.

"Because we were not to fight them in the air. The Devil instructed us specifically on that point. We were only to tangle them. Only to make them fall to the surface. It wasn't even important to get them all. We were just told to tangle up as many as we could and return to the Sled."

Delius hesitated, and against his judgment took another gulp of blood beer from his cup.

"They were caught by such surprise, seeing us right there to meet them as they crossed. None of them had any idea what to do. I'll never forget the shock on their faces, all of them, almost frozen, like they never expected to see Demons in Hell after The Great Fall. We tangled most of them easily in the nets, the others who escaped were knotted up by the bandoliers. They fell swift and clumsy. It was such a strange sight to see: Angels with grand white wings so bright you could barely look at them dropping into Hell like the Unbroken do." Delius took another drink.

"They were met on the ground by Canem. It was the first version of Canem, back when they had full hands and legs. We'd only made about fifty by then, but that was more than enough. By the time we got back down to the surface, feathers and flesh covered the skin, and only a few Angels were left struggling under heaps of hungry Canem. The Canem ate them. Ate them to the bone. It was a shame, too. We had to destroy all of those Canem. That's when we learned to train them not to eat the Angels. The fight lasted only until morning crested, and the Skin-Land shone bright with a thick snow of white feathers. Thick up to your ankles." Delius retreated sadly into his cup, finished with his story.

A soft silence flowed over the Cantavit as each member reflected in their own way. Bore broke the silence.

"Story great. Story good. Angel snow," he said.

"No, Bore, my fair Demon. It's not a great story," Delius replied.

The group arched their necks in silent quandary.

"And *why is that,* Delta-Delius?" Zaavan pressed.

"Because that is *not* what Hell is supposed to be!" Delius yelled, the beer now sharpening his emotions. "*We* are not the ones who decide who is saved and who is not. *We* are not to be a barrier between God and His redeemed. That is *not* why we are here!"

"Then tell us, oh great Delta, *why* are we here?" said Zaavan.

An uneasy pause filled the scene, and Delius stared hard across at Zaavan.

"We are here to serve the Devil. We have chosen to serve the Devil," Delius said in a reluctant tone.

"Then if the Devil wants us to kill Angels, to protect *his* Unbroken, *his* Broken, *his* Minions, *his* Demons, redeemed or otherwise, is that not our charge?" Zaavan said, reasoning in the most patronizing tone he could muster.

"Of course it is. We serve him in all of his debauchery. That is the Mandatum of the Demon," Delius resigned.

The uncomfortable silence seemed like it would never end. The bones smoldered and cracked, the Sapiens snored full and asleep, and even the soft sobs from the Unbroken pen could be heard on occasion.

Zaavan broke the silence he'd created.

"Enough of this! We are Demons of the highest class! We've had a wonderful day full of harvest! We have a fat, Unbroken crop! We must continue the celebration! And I have the perfect thing."

Zaavan reached behind him and pulled up his sack. "Perhaps this will remind us all of why we do this. Why we toil out here in the Skin-Land Vast under dark skies in the unrelenting open Hell!"

Zaavan reached into the sack and pulled it off, exposing Tragen's head. The Cantavit gasped, stealing every breath the acrid air had to offer. All except for Bore, who laughed without abandon. Zaavan smiled bright and bone-toothed white as he stared into Delius's shocked eyes.

"Zeta-Zaavan!" Delius screamed, throwing his cup to the ground, shattering it into pieces. "Where did you find this!"

"Relax, dear Delius. I found him on my scout here. He was alone, injured, stranded. Two of the Canem took a bite from his wing before he destroyed the poor things. So, in turn, I melted the Angel into soup. But I kept the head. I thought you'd like it as a prize. A memento for your last Cantavit. A trophy to remember your *undying* service to the Devil."

Delius rose. "You know that no part of any Angel can be kept on the surface of Hell, Zeta!"

"That is an old rule, Delius. A stupid rule that everyone breaks from time to time. Stop being so honorable for once. Look at it. I've melted it off in perfect condition. Would this not look wonderful perched in your chambers? A reminder of how we aren't supposed to be a barrier between Angels and the redeemed, perhaps? Or a way you could be closer to the Angels you seem to care so much for?"

"You twist my words, Zeta-Zaavan." Delius walked over to stand face-to-face with the winged Demon. "To keep such a thing perverts all that we risk out here, and insults every Demon in this Cantavit."

"You make too much of this, Delius," said Zaavan.

"Lopex, dispose of that thing. The Devil's instructions on Angels are clear!" And with that, Delius stormed off into the night.

Zaavan watched him leave, gripping Tragen's head by its dark hair.

"Great job, Zaavan," said Reese, as he rose and began to clean up dinner.

Lopex got up, shaking his head. "Give it to me, Zaavan."

"And if I don't?" Tension tethered the two together. Lopex extended his hand, and slowly Zaavan handed over Tragen's head.

"I think that does it, Cantavit," Lopex said. "We have a busy day tomorrow. We still need to harvest more bone, and camp has to be broken down so we can keep moving." Lopex walked off with the head. "Montly, you're with me."

The party broke. Bore helped Chalt rise, so drunk she could barely stand. Zaavan kicked the smoldering bones to smoke, smiling deep and wicked.

Montly walked fast to keep pace with Lopex. He seemed angry, stepping hard and swift into the darkness outside camp.

"What was all that about?" she asked.

"It's just Zaavan. He makes light of Delius and his story. He always takes it too far."

"But what does it matter? Who cares about some Angel head? Why wouldn't Delius be happy to keep it?" Montly asked.

"Delius has some strange ideas about this place. You have to understand that. He's been here for thousands of years. He's seen things that you and I will never see. He knows things about Hell that we will never know. You can't hope to understand him unless you've had his experiences." Lopex thought of the tiny piece of brain Delius had given him, the piece that held all of the Deltas' memories.

"It doesn't make any sense to me," Montly replied.

"It doesn't have to. Look, I know this is a low job. But I need you to butcher this head, then cut open a hole and press it down to make sure it sinks, okay?"

"Of course, but one more question. Why can't we keep this? Why does every part of an Angel have to be destroyed?"

"The Devil doesn't want the Unbroken to know that Angels exist. He doesn't want them to think that they *can be* redeemed. He doesn't want them to know that there is *any* way out of Hell."

"And what do you think?"

"I think I do what my mentor tells me to do. You should think the same." Lopex handed the Angel head to Montly and she grabbed it with both hands.

"Of course, Eta-Lopex. Of course."

"I'm going to go check in on Delius. I think that wraps up the day. I'll see you tomorrow morning."

Montly nodded, smiled uncomfortably, and watched Lopex walk away.

"So much tension," she muttered as she put the head on the ground and started to split the Skin-Land open with her knife. *Things are never quite what you think they'll be like,* she thought. Montly had assumed all Demons got along, that brotherhood bound them together. Not this conflict, this constant bickering that penetrated everything.

She flipped the Angel's head to face her and gripped the knife to begin butchering it through its brilliant blue eyes. Eyes that glistened blue like the water she'd seen in the Stemming of Silton's mind. *The water was so pure in his memories,* she thought.

Montly's mind sparked as it flashed to Silton's Stemming. His memories rushed over her like ropes of rain filling her head.

And suddenly, Montly recognized the Angel's face.

CHAPTER THIRTY-FOUR

Being resigned to Hell may lead you to believe that your actions in the life-times have been so horrible that you are imprisoned here forever. This is not correct. Ascension from Hell, although difficult, is possible for almost everyone. Morality being the execution of God's law is recognized in Hell just as it was in your life-times. Therefore, if ascension is your goal, you must balance your actions to ensure that you do not continue to sin in Hell. To do so will only elongate your time here.

—From "Hell: A Survival Guide"
By Delta-Delius

Silton couldn't sleep. The vision of Kay helpless somewhere in this place plagued his mind. Over and over again he replayed the scene, the Demon scooping her up off the ground, returning her to some sick slavery. Silton couldn't escape the vision. He knew her body—her perfect breasts, her hips just a scant wider than her shoulders. He knew it was Kay. But how could she be here, in this place? How? She was a much better person than he. He couldn't make any sense of it.

But if she was here, he had to find her. There was no question in that.

Mariella slept deeply next to him on the warm, soft ground. Her breathing, relaxed and rhythmic, made Silton wonder if she'd finally found some peace. The Drums towered over the pen like sentries, one of their deformed heads always awake, always keeping watch. How could they possibly escape? Taking Mariella would be tough, but the fight in her seemed unstoppable, and Silton couldn't stomach leaving her to these maniacs anyway.

Silton was fingering the brands on his head and chest as they dried to coarse scabs when he heard the rubbery sound of feet walking toward him. He stressed his eyes to see, but they offered nothing. The sound got closer and closer still, then out of the darkness, a hulk of muscle wrapped in a cloak of skin appeared: Delius.

"You're awake, Unbroken?" Delius whispered. "You're not exhausted from your day?"

"I guess not," Silton answered.

"Today was almost your last day above skin. That was very brave of you, to try and help that woman," Delius said as he looked Silton over, slowly taking in all the details of his form and peering into the gaping hole through his chest.

"What can I say, when people need help, I help," Silton replied.

"Of course you do. Tell me, Unbroken, what is your name? What did they call you during your life?"

"Silton. My name is Silton."

"Silton," Delius repeated. "I am Delta-Delius."

"I wish I could say it was good to meet you, but being a prisoner here and all . . ."

"You're not a prisoner. I know you can't understand that now, but ..."

"Stop. Please. I've heard enough garbage from you people already today. I don't need to hear any more. If I'm not a prisoner like you say, then let me out of here."

"And what if I did? Do you think you'd survive?" Delius asked.

"I'll take my chances," Silton snapped.

"You saw what happened to the woman you tried to save. You know that can happen to you too. Do you want to sink into this place and swim in these bloody bowels for eternity?"

"That will never happen to me," Silton replied.

"How can you be so sure?" Delius asked.

"Because I have hope."

Delius fell silent. A long moment passed.

"What do you know of hope?"

"As long as I have hope, this place can't destroy me. And neither can you," Silton said defiantly.

Another long moment of silence. Delius smiled and squinted his eyes at Silton.

"How long have you been here?" Delius asked.

"A week, I think."

"And when you were sinking with that Unbroken woman, what exactly did you say to her?"

"I told her not to lose hope, or this place will swallow you up. I said hope is the only thing you Demons can't take from us. It's the only thing that can get us out of here."

"That's very insightful for an Unbroken who's only been here a short time," Delius commented.

"I catch on quick," Silton quipped.

Delius stood up next to the Drum closest to them, reached

his arm over to the top of its head, and patted it a few times. Instantly, the eyes of the Drum closed, and the thing went to sleep. Delius quietly did the same with the two other Drums closest to them. Silton watched, perplexed. Then the huge Demon reached in with both arms, motioning for Silton to get up, to come toward him. In awe, Silton obliged, and Delius hoisted him up and over the pen, resting him gently on the Skin-Land.

"Her," Silton whispered. "Her too." He pointed to the sleeping Mariella. He didn't know why Delius was doing this, and he didn't care.

"The Skin-Land will be hard enough just for you. Are you sure?" Delius whispered back. Silton nodded his head in response, careful not to rouse the Drums.

Delius gently jostled Mariella awake as he held a finger to her lips, ensuring silence. Confused, Mariella woke with bright, startled eyes. Seeing Silton on the other side of the pen, Mariella realized the situation instantly, even though she did not understand why.

Delius gently lifted her out. Mariella winced a bit as her legs dangled, and the three of them walked into the solid darkness to the far side of the lake.

"Thank you," Silton began. "I can't thank you enough. Where do we go now?" Delius help up his hand, silencing him.

"Listen closely, Unbroken. Advice is not given often in Hell." He paused, looking across the lake toward camp. "Keep yourself coated with fresh blood as often as you can. That will stave off the stiffness of having no heart. Her legs haven't healed correctly. If they aren't fixed soon, she will need to have them replaced. Stay away from outcroppings and caves like these, as they attract Demons. And never tell anyone of our conversation. Never tell anyone that you saw me tonight."

Delius let his words sink in before continuing. "In exchange for this, for your freedom, you will do something for me."

"What could I possibly do for you?" Silton asked.

"The next time you see an Angel, tell them that Delius has been destroyed. Do you understand?"

"What?" Silton asked, perplexed.

"You tell the Angels that Delius, the last of the Deltas, has been destroyed. That is my bargain with you, Silton."

"What makes you think I'll ever run into an Angel?"

"Because they gave you that feather hidden in your chest for a reason, and they will seek you out to fulfill that reason."

Silton looked down at his chest hole, as did Mariella. The feather, tucked deep inside him, could not be seen.

"What feather? What . . ." Silton started.

"When I pulled you out of the Skin-Land, pulled you off that woman, I saw it."

"Now run," Delius continued. "Try to survive, and reflect on what has brought you here. You don't need these Demons to help you realize your errors. They serve themselves now, not God. And remember, tell the Angels—Delius is destroyed."

Delius held out his flat palm to Silton. Silton gripped his hand, and the two held eyes for a moment. Then Delius turned and walked toward the beach, wading slowly into the thick blood. The pair strained to see Delius as he swam further out. The Demon took off his long coat, flipped over to his back, and stretched his arms. His face looked to the acrid night sky, his dark eyes wide open. Silton and Mariella, stifled in nervous fear, watched as Delius slowly sank into the blood lake, drowning himself in its thick depths.

CHAPTER THIRTY-FIVE

The rules governing structures in Hell are clear: All structures are off-limits to any Sapien, Minion, or Demon. This mandate was set forth after The Devil's Great Fall in hopes of avoiding the circumstances that led to that horrible time. Many of these structures still exist, their purpose and uses unknown to all but those who constructed them. When these are discovered, they are to be documented so future Cantavits can avoid them. The Devil has decreed that there are to be no exceptions to this rule.

—From "Hell Geographica"
By Doctorem Delta-Lindicus

The endless darkness of the Skin-Land rippled under Silton's feet as he carried Mariella, step after step. Mariella strained her eyes, but saw nothing. So, she lay there, a lump of helpless flesh heaped onto Silton's back as they pushed further away from the Demons' camp into emptiness.

Her dislocated knees rested in the grip of Silton's sweaty arms, and as they walked, insects of pain crawled up her spine. The agony was so familiar, so ever-present, that the brief moments when it disappeared seemed strange and alien to Mariella.

There is no end to this, she thought. *There is no way my legs will ever be strong enough to walk.* The idea made her cringe. It wasn't the realization of being crippled or the vision of cartilage floating around her insides that bothered her most; it was the helplessness, the understanding that her prison in Hell was permanent dependence on this man. The thought itched at Mariella's psyche, and it became almost too much for her to bear.

I'm just like the patients I murdered, just like their bodies shackled by disease or injury, she said to herself. Mariella had always thought she knew the dying mind so well, that she knew how and why a person came to the realization that they couldn't go on without destroying the lives around them. But now, trapped neck-deep in the depression that leads to self-destruction, Mariella concluded that her murders were not ones of mercy. Instead, what she'd destroyed in those people was the last semblance of who they were, the last of what made them good. Like crushing a flower with only one petal left, her killings weren't an act of compassion; they were the heinous vandalism of a person's soul, the bright center of humanity.

Heaven's Eye peeked over the Vast, forcing beige tones to pink as it shone through the skin. Sweat glistened as far as she could see, and while the morning drew on, the soft smell of metallic blood drifted into her nose.

"How much farther?" she asked, pain woven into her voice.

"I can go another mile or so, I think," Silton said, parsing his words out carefully, like every syllable stole needed strength.

"Good, I want to lay down for a while. We should look for a place soon."

"I agree. I think we've gone as far as we can for now. Hopefully, it's far enough."

"Do you think they'll follow?"

"Probably. They might think that the three of us are together. But I don't know."

"Why did he let us go?" Mariella asked.

"I don't know. A last act of kindness? Maybe he was trying to make right. That's all I can come up with."

"Are you still thinking we need to find the Angels? When they come back, I mean?" she asked.

"I don't know what to do now. When that Demon connected to my mind, I saw things. I saw . . ."

"What do you mean, you saw things? I don't even remember what happened. What did you see?" Mariella pressed.

"I . . . I saw . . ." Silton hesitated, worrying that the words about to come out of his mouth would sound foolish. "I saw my wife, Mariella. I saw Kay. She's here. She's here captured, like we were."

"How could you know that?"

"When that thing was reading my memories, I think I got pushed into her head. I saw a different place. A place where there are thousands and thousands of people like us. That's where I saw Kay. She tried to escape. It was like watching someone else's dream. I didn't think it was real. But that Demon, the one covered in black, she said we were going to be slaves in a place called the Sled. I'm telling you, that's what I saw in that Demon's head, that's where my wife is, and that's where I need to go."

The idea swam in Mariella's mind like a frantic fish tethered to a line.

"So that's where more people are? And they're all trapped? All slaves? And you want to go *there?*"

"I'm sorry, Mariella, but if Kay's here, I have to find her."

"Of course you do. You still love her. Love makes you do stupid things," Mariella said, knowing this to be true even for herself. This man, Silton, a man Mariella grew closer and closer to in the silence between steps, would not let her fill his empty heart. A foolish idea, she thought, falling in love in Hell.

"And where is this place? Where she's being held?" Mariella asked.

"I'm not sure."

"You're not sure. You see where we are, right? You see it's basically endless, right?" Mariella scolded.

"I know, but those Demons, they had limited supplies. They can't have traveled far from their home base. It can't be more than a few days from here." Silton hesitated. "In the vision I had, when that Demon attached to me, I saw this thing, this Sled. It's huge, like a moving city, and as they drag it, it makes cuts in the ground, into the skin. And the cuts bleed. It's a trail, an unmistakable trail wherever it goes. If we can get to high ground, maybe we can see the trail . . . and then . . . well."

"We? And where do I fit in, in this new plan?" Mariella asked.

"You're coming with me, of course."

"Right. Take the woman who can't walk to the home of these things. The place where they have thousands and thousands of people enslaved. You're really something else, Silton . . . *Soldier Boy,*" she said with a sarcasm that guarded her feelings.

"We'll figure something out. We will. We have to," Silton said as he dragged the dead weight of conversation to an end.

Mariella, silently locking away her feelings, felt a small drip on her back. Before she could register it, she felt another, then another.

"Is it raining?" she asked.

"Huh?" Silton lifted his head.

Before them, a slow freckling of red spots dotted the Skin-Land. Silton stopped, and they both watched as the rain fell. He felt a drop on his shoulder, and turned his head to see it.

"It's blood," he said, the thick, crimson blot unmistakable. Concern washed over his face, and he picked up the pace. But to where, Silton didn't know. The land simply rolled out in front of them: slender hills peppered with stringy hair, and slight depressions pooled with sweat.

The yellow sky darkened above them and obscured Heaven's Eye. A few pieces of new skin splashed down on the ground. The fierce impact of flesh on flesh made the sound of a man being beaten to a pulp.

The blood and flesh came down harder, until a red hail filled the sky above them. Then the body parts began to fall: arms, legs, pieces of torso in chunks. Silton hobbled to a run, hoping chance and movement would help them avoid being hit. But to no avail; a thick leg glanced off Mariella, knocking her off Silton's back. She screamed from the impact, and Silton slipped on the blood, toppling next to her.

"We've got to find cover!" she said, pulling her legs close and screaming in pain over the pounding sound of flesh rain.

"If we can," Silton cried, as a flap of meat slapped him on his head, stifling his words midsentence.

Neither of them tried to speak again, the sound too loud to hear anything else. Silton grabbed Mariella and hoisted her up, and they shuffled slowly across the blood-drenched ground. Pieces pelted them as they moved, and their stinging eyes tried to see forward, to see anything. But only the misty red of falling flesh stretched out before them.

Silton slipped again, the uneven surface of the land working hard against him. In the distance, he saw a deep depression, a wide valley in the Skin-Land. He could see it clearly, beyond the blood shadow created by the storm. He ran, sloppy and fast, dragging Mariella along with him. The ground, a buffet of body parts, proved unmanageable, and he tripped again, landing on a stark white leg that looked like it'd been blown off its owner.

"Ahh!" He fell on it with his full weight, Mariella falling down on him. He felt the pinch of a cracked rib, and heard the snap echo through his trunk and out of his chest hole. "We have to crawl... that way!" he screamed over the sound of flesh on flesh, and pointed to the small valley.

"I can see it!" Mariella screamed, and arm over arm she crawled past Silton to the respite.

"I can't... Mariella! I can't see... blood in my eyes!" Silton yelled, as his hands made a mess of the fluid covering his face.

"Hold on to my legs!" Mariella shrieked.

With one hand, Silton grabbed her foot as a guide, and the pair crawled through a soup of muddy blood and body parts all the way to the edge of the valley. Once there, Mariella inched over the rim, and they slid down a long, slick ridge, splashing through blood and sweat, with body parts following them down the red flow. They slid for what seemed to be an eternity, gasping for breath, holding on to one another, tumbling and sliding fast out of the brunt of the storm. Finally, the slope graded easier, and they slowed to the soupy floor of the valley.

Breathing hard, spitting out blood, and wiping off indiscriminate pieces of this and that, they shuddered in the terror of the ordeal. The fury of the storm broke, and Heaven's Eye reappeared. The flow rushing down the valley slope eased to a trickle, and the Skin-Land crept back to silence.

The pair sat in a horrid mess of flesh and bone, body parts in all manner of disarray. They threw the pieces off of themselves as quickly as they could.

Silton tried to regain his vision, his eyes still blinded with blood.

"Silton, Silton open your eyes, you've got to see this," Mariella said, tapping him.

Silton blinked the bloody fog out of his eyes and looked around him.

They both sat at the edge of a perfectly round pool of blood. As if manicured by the most careful craftsman, a short wall made of solid red bricks surrounded its circumference. In the center of the pool, a small mound of flesh rested like a soft pink island. And if not for the fact that the two were in Hell, they would have thought the architecture looked beautiful.

CHAPTER THIRTY-SIX

For the past three thousand years, a strange phenomenon has occurred with the oldest existing class of Demons constructed in Hell, the Deltas. This class methodically and with no exception has completely disappeared from the Sled. Many theories abound about this phenomenon: Some say that the Deltas, having been in the service of Hell too long, give themselves up to the Skin-Land in return for solace. Others say that the Devil himself commands that the Deltas exile themselves, fearing that their long-standing influence could eclipse his own. And others still believe that the Deltas have a more sinister plan that seeks to usurp the Devil and his rule over Hell.

—From "A History of Hell"
By Delta-Holt

Lopex rose early, just before the crest of Heaven's Eye bled soft light onto the Skin-Land. He'd always liked that about himself, his sense of automatic timing. No matter on the Sled or in the Vast, whether in the confines of his dark chambers or lying out on open skin, he always woke moments before the crest of Heaven. He often thought that this must be a mental remnant of his own life-times, some skill he'd procured for some meaningless reason, and only now, in the afterlife, was he truly able to enjoy the spoils of the ability.

The Demon camp still slept. Canem snored against one another in piles, the majestic Mauss slumbered alone, and the Drums stood right where they were left, a walled sentry around the Unbrokens' pen.

Lopex liked these settled moments. Moments when the blood lay flat and unmolested, when the skin stood still like ice, and far off sounds from unexplored corners of the Skin-Land cried out for attention. He walked quietly past the gathering pit, the burnt marrow lying crusted and jellied, then past a few tents, down to the beach. Lopex crouched down to the blood, the sound of his knee joint popping as he squatted.

"I'll have to have an Engineer take a look at that when we get back," he said to himself. Lopex cupped his hands, dipped them into the lake, and took in a full draught of fresh blood. It felt thick moving down his throat, congealed slightly from the coldness of night, but he liked it that way. The albumin, the metallic accents, even the tangy plasma could be discerned with blood this fresh. He let out a relaxing breath and reveled in the tranquility of a day in its infancy.

Across the flatness of the lake, Lopex saw something—a distortion, a bubbling of sorts that interrupted the serenity of the blood's smooth surface. It perplexed him. It looked like a huge sheet of skin, or a mass of yellow fat congealed on the surface. Lopex stood to get a better vantage. It wasn't fat, that was for sure, and he'd say skin, but it looked so uniform, like clothing almost. Perhaps someone lost it during the revelry of the previous night.

"Oh, well. We can't leave anything behind," he said, and peeled off the tight layer of skin he wore as a shirt.

Lopex waded out into the lake. The waist-high blood invigorated his muscles, and for a moment, he felt jealous of the Sapiens who had this treat almost every day. He pushed closer to the object, leaned out, and grabbed it. A garment for sure. The long-stitched skin was pruned and frayed, flaked off in some sections and making it difficult to see exactly what it was. He dragged it back to shore, twisted as much of the blood out of it as he could, and shook the skin out.

"What?" Lopex said out loud. There was no mistaking it—this was Delius's cloak. The bone buttons that cinched it closed were from another time, so old that they'd lost all of their white color. "This doesn't make any . . ." Lopex muttered, then darted to his master's pavilion.

"Delius?" No answer.

"Delius?" he asked again. Still, no answer.

"Delius!" Lopex yelled, and pulled the flap open.

Delius's cot lay empty, his personal effects still in their places, the bit and bridle for his Mauss hanging in the corner—but no Delius. Lopex stood perplexed for a moment, then a queasy itch filled his stomach.

"No . . . no, he wouldn't! Not to me . . . he wouldn't do that to me!"

Lopex ran, cloak in hand, to the Canem pen, hopped over the bone fence and grabbed one of the four-legged Sapiens by the collar. He gripped its throat, and the beast let out a monstrous howl that deafened the area and started the other Canem howling in turn.

The camp violently roused awake. Montly leapt out of her tent, thinking the Canem in trouble, and Zaavan burst through the flap on his pavilion in midflight, assuming an attack. Bore, Chalt, and Reese rushed from their tents as well. The Cantavit stared at Lopex, beckoning him for an explanation.

"Delius is gone! He's gone!" Lopex yelled. The Demons gathered quickly around him.

"What do you mean, he's gone?" Reese asked, confused.

Lopex held up the long, skin cloak. "I found this in the blood lake, out near the middle, just floating there. And he's not in his tent!"

The expectant silence persisted.

"So then, the legend of the Deltas is true. They do all commit themselves to the innards of Hell," Zaavan said sharply, and without care for their leader.

"No, he wouldn't leave us. He wouldn't do that!" Lopex was disbelieving and frantic.

"It looks like that is exactly what he did. Tired of his years of service, taking the coward's way out. I'm not surprised," Zaavan said, dismissive.

"You bloated blood sac!" Lopex made for Zaavan in a deft leap. Reese took his huge bulk, grabbed Lopex, and stayed his friend.

"Calm down, Lopex. Calm down. You're not helping. This isn't helping at all."

Chalt shook her head. "I'm not surprised either. He was too old, too much with the ancient ways. He's better off in the bowels of Hell with the rest of his Delta brothers."

"Say that again and I will peel your skin off your bones!" Lopex said, struggling against Reese's strength.

"Okay, okay . . . everyone calm down," Reese said. "I can't believe I'm the voice of reason here, but we should all fan out for a bit, look around. Maybe he just took a walk or something."

"Right, he took a walk," Chalt continued. "And he's not here after that Canem howl? Sure, that's possible. The only way he didn't hear that is if he's underskin."

"Just do it!" Reese said. "Zaavan, you know that's the protocol. Get your Demons in line!"

Zaavan smirked and nodded to his group. Bore, confused about all the yelling, had to be told what was going on, twice.

Lopex regained his composure, shook off the aggression, and calmed himself.

"Montly, mount up and take the Canem on a run around the back side of the Bone Caves, then push them through, just like when we flushed out the Unbroken. Zaavan, get up in the air and let me know if you see anything. Bore and Chalt . . ." He paused. "Take a Drum each, and dredge that blood lake. I want to know if there is anything else in there."

Bore and Chalt shared a look of disgust. To dredge a blood lake was the lowest, dirtiest of chores. They looked to their leader to abort the command.

"Is that really necessary, Lopex?" Zaavan asked.

"It's standard. If anyone were missing from a Cantavit, we would do the same thing. Even if it was you, Zeta-Zaavan."

Unable to argue with standard Cantavit protocol, Zaavan nodded to his Zetas, and they reluctantly started toward the Drums standing guard at the Unbroken pen.

"And what will you do to help, Lopex?" Zaavan asked with insincerity.

"I'm going to search his tent, try to figure out where he is, or why he left. Reese stays with the camp."

"So, *you're* in charge now?" Zaavan asked.

"Zaavan, that's not what this is about!" Lopex yelled.

"Isn't it?" the winged Demon responded, his question finding no answer.

"Zaavan! Zeta-Zaavan!" Chalt screamed.

The group turned to her attention.

"Two of the Unbroken; they're gone!"

CHAPTER THIRTY-SEVEN

Sessiles, one of the rarest inhabitants of Hell, are sentient beings permanently rooted into the Skin-Land. In the early times of Hell, before The Great Fall, Sessiles were constructed as conscious and stable markers across the Vast, often serving as guides to Demon travelers. But, in the aftermath of The Great Fall, construction of Sessiles became a way to permanently exile an undesirable or treasonous member of the Devil's legions. Therefore, the Devil has decreed that Sessiles are to be avoided at all costs.

—From "Hell's Inhabitants"
By Doctorem Delta-Lindicus

Mariella watched as Silton slept pressed against the curved wall of blood bricks. She could hear him wheezing through his chest hole, and assumed there were tiny puncture holes in the fabric of his lungs. But even so, he slept deeply, exhausted from carrying her. Mariella leaned on the short wall that encircled the pond and stared out at its perfectly flat surface. The bricks felt warm to her, as if veins fed them fresh blood. She lay her head on their rough, red masonry, and let the warmth pulse through her skin.

Silton is a good man to have helped me so much, she thought. For the first few days, Mariella had been sure she'd end up stuck in that pit with the rest of the patients from the hospital. If not for Silton, she'd be in the bowels of this place, drifting endlessly in the depths of Hell. Unfortunately, she had to admit she hadn't made much progress since then. Her legs, wrapped up tight with the hard skin cast, didn't feel much better, and nothing could be done about her knees. To have no mobility, no power, to be dependent on Silton for everything was a situation alien to her, and the thought wouldn't stop turning over and over again in her mind.

The pond seemed to be almost a gift to her. An answer to the only question that remained: *How do I get out of this situation?* She looked over at Silton once more, and allowed herself to admire his handsome face and fantasize about meeting him in another place and another time. She wiped a tear from her eye, and gently pressed it to the side of his mouth.

"Goodbye, Soldier Boy," Mariella said in a whisper that even she could barely hear. Then she lifted herself up, grunted against the pain in her legs, and lay herself slowly into the velvet red pond.

She drifted easy on her back and stared up at the green clouds while Heaven's Eye, stark and blue, stared down on her.

"I'm sorry. I'm so sorry. I didn't know it was all real," Mariella said as she exhaled, letting blood fill her mouth. Her body, floating and buoyant, finally felt at ease as the rich red penetrated her skin, flowing into her and out of her. She imagined herself dissolving: her skin separating from muscle, her fingernails melting off into clear fluid, her brain oozing out of her ears like jelly, all helping her become one with this place. She welcomed the warm feeling of release, the final fragments of soul leaching from her body, the thought that she'd finally found where she belonged . . .

And then, Mariella felt something grab her by the hair.

She reached up and found an incredible strength in the hands that gripped her. She tried to yell, but only a thick stream of blood escaped her mouth. She struggled, flapping her arms and kicking her crippled legs, but to no avail. Quickly, she felt herself pulled up, out of the blood. She coughed and coughed, desperately wiping blood from her eyes.

"Oh . . . my . . ." Mariella heard from a deep, inhuman voice. "Oh, little Minion, you are not well."

Mariella opened her eyes in a glaze of sticky blood, her view of the sky now obscured by someone holding her, someone cradling her.

"Oh, my little Minion, can you speak?" the voice said, and Mariella could hear it more clearly. It sounded deeper, masculine. She felt bony fingers reach into her throat and scoop out thick globs of blood and mucus. Mariella gagged, still half-blind, and reached out to the arm. When she gripped it, she felt no flesh, just hard bone and warm sticky muscle.

She looked up to see a skeleton wrapped in red muscle. Mariella tried to scream, but choked halfway through the sound.

"Be still, Minion, be still. You are damaged," the muscled skeleton said. Mariella focused, and the face came fully into view: a man with no skin. Thin bridges of yellow-white tendon circled his head, ropes of tensed muscle pulled on the joints of his face, and two perfectly spherical eyes stared down at her with no eyelids to allow a blink.

"Can you speak, Minion? Can you speak?" he asked again.

"Let me go!" Mariella screamed.

"I am not your captor. You must calm yourself. You are damaged," he repeated.

"Silton! Silton!" Mariella tried to yell across the blood pond, but still half-choking, she managed little more than a murmur. Mariella scampered away from him on the blood-wet skin island, and her knee gave way, an audible pop cracking as it came out of joint.

"Your knee is dislocated. Let me see it, young Minion." The creature lay his hands on Mariella, dragging her closer to him. Mariella tried to kick, but his immense strength made short work of her struggle. She could see his body fully, now. He was only half a man. He had arms and shoulders rippled with muscle that led to a bony rib cage and chest, then to a tendon-covered midsection tethered to a spine that burrowed directly into the Skin-Land. It was as if he'd been grown there, like a tree.

The horror of the scene startled her, and she screamed louder than before, writhing with all of her strength.

"Minion, you will damage yourself further. Stop!" He took one of his bony fingers to the back of Mariella's head and fingered it into the orifice made by the Demon Stem. He stuck his finger deep into the back of her skull, and with a few motions, Mariella felt instantly at ease. A tingling wave rushed down her spine like warm milk, and for the first time since being in this place, her legs didn't hurt anymore. Nothing hurt. She let out a low hum, her head swimming deep with endorphins that relaxed every muscle in her body.

"Now, let me help you, Minion." The muscled skeleton removed his finger from Mariella's head, and with the razor edge of his hand, sliced through the skin of her left leg like paper. Then he went to work, diving his thin fingers into the muscle of her thighs. He pulled out elastic tendons, and like needlecraft, began to stitch her knee joint back together.

Silton roused from his deep sleep, having heard something far off, something distant in a dream calling for him. He shook himself to consciousness and immediately noticed Mariella gone. He scanned in a full circle, and then he saw it. Mariella was lying on the island in the middle of the blood pond with a horrible mound of bone and muscle hovering over her.

Silton didn't speak, he just reacted. He hopped up on the short brick wall, and with both feet pushed himself off, diving headfirst into the thickness of the blood pond. Silton arched his back, pulling himself up to the surface, and began heavy strides with his arms. The blood flowing through the hole in his chest tickled as he swam.

Silton muscled arm over arm onto the short beach. "Get off of her!" he screamed, rising to his feet, covered in a sheet of blood. The mass of hunched muscle and bone twisted its head in surprise, seeing Silton.

"Stop . . . no, Silton, stop!" Mariella said in a drifting voice. "It's okay, he's—"

But none of the words registered to Silton, and he launched himself at the skeleton man, ripping him off Mariella. She slid off to the side, and Silton straddled his opponent, lifting his heavy, skin-casted arm to strike.

"Silton, no!" she yelled. "He's helping me! Stop." Silton looked to Mariella, his hand clenched, ready to shatter the thing's skull with a drop of his clubbed arm.

"What?" Silton responded, confused.

In the moment of distraction, the skeleton man launched Silton off of him, his strength incredible and magnified by his rooting into the Skin-Land. Silton landed squarely next to

Mariella, where she grabbed hold of him hard. The pair watched the thing recover from Silton's assault, its thick spinal column becoming stiff as he got upright.

Silton took in the entirety of the man and stared in awe. Covered in perfectly symmetrical muscle, with not a single piece of skin to speak of, he looked like a terror. His organs, suspended beneath his rib cage by translucent netting, pulsed with a perfectly disgusting rhythm.

"Are you okay?" Silton asked.

"It's not what you think. He's helping me! Look!" Mariella pointed down to her leg. Silton looked at her open knee joint, the area he dared not try to fix, and saw tiny strands of tendon reattached to the sides of her kneecap. The opening of her skin looked surgical, smooth and deliberate, only disrupted by Silton's tackle.

"What is this? What's going on, Mariella?"

"I don't know exactly. But he did something to me, and I'm not in pain anymore. For the first time here, I'm not in pain!"

The half-man stretched himself, looking more annoyed by the ordeal than anything, and shook his head, clearing it from disorientation.

"What are you doing to her?" Silton asked.

The half-man stood upright, his spinal column fully erect and rooted into the meat of the skin island.

"I *was* trying to put your friend's legs back together, you bloated sac!"

CHAPTER THIRTY-EIGHT

During Mandatum in the Skin-Land Vast, many hardships may occur that cause the destruction of your fellow Demons. In rare cases, these instances may interrupt the command structure of your Cantavit. Strict protocol has been put in place for dealing with these types of situations. In the event that the commanding Praefectus is lost, command of the Cantavit is transferred to the Assistant Praefectus. In the event that the Assistant Praefectus is lost, command is transferred to the highest ranking Demon, and so on. This protocol has been developed to ensure the continuity of the Mandatum, which is the highest priority for the Cantavit, and the Devil.

—From "A Demon's Handbook"
By Delta-Haldon

M ontly dragged her hand across a brittle portion of bone wall as she slowly walked through the caves. Her skin-bound feet shuffled without enthusiasm across the stark white floor. Only the echoes of the Canem broke the silence as they scampered from cave to cave, searching for what they would never find: Delius. So far, she'd only turned up a few pieces of ragged skin, a makeshift bone knife, and many piles of dung. All of this Montly suspected was from the Unbroken who'd been hiding there in the days before their capture. The search seemed ridiculous. She knew of the rumors, the old stories of the Deltas' disappearances, and now she had one of her own to tell. As she continued her long, fruitless search, she found herself terribly bored, and her mind began to wander.

Still, tucked deep into the folds of her brain, were thoughts of this Unbroken man she had Stemmed. It seemed that somehow he'd left something inside her. Like a thick cloud, when Montly investigated closer, it became ethereal, absent of form, a drifting fog. Yet something lay there, a memory, an experience this Unbroken had. It stuck hard, and Montly knew that it couldn't be ignored. Her thoughts broke as she exited the caves, hearing a screaming argument coming from camp.

The rest of her fellow Demons stood in a circle near the huge bone boulder. Montly could see arms waving back and forth, punctuated by heated words. She waited a few moments for the Canem to emerge from scattered parts of the caves, then made her way to camp.

"Did you find anything, Montly?" Lopex asked.

"Nothing, sir, only leavings of the Unbroken," Montly said as she joined the group.

"Then we need to get back to the Sled immediately!" said Lopex. "If we wrap up camp now, we can move out before Heaven-Fall. Then, in a day, two at most, we'll be back at the Sled to report Delius missing."

Zaavan shook his head, his arms and wings folded tight in anger. "For what, Lopex? For what? We've not completed our Mandatum. We've not reached our quota! In fact, because of

Delius, we have *two less* Unbroken!"

"Zaavan, you don't know that Delius had anything to do with the two missing Unbroken," Reese interjected.

"Don't I?" Zaavan bellowed. "If you think him innocent, you're a blood beer-soaked fool!" Zaavan turned to Chalt. "Chalt, what was the condition of the Drums guarding the Unbroken pen?"

Chalt replied quickly, "Three of the Drums had been put to sleep. The pressure points on the tops of their heads were activated, and they were unconscious when I found them."

"Unconscious Drums. Three of them! With pressure points activated!" Zaavan screamed even louder. "Tell me, Reese, are you saying that you think two beaten-down Unbroken were able to climb up seven-foot-high battle-hardened Drums, and knock them out using a pressure point they didn't even know existed?"

Reese dropped his head in silence and looked to Lopex.

"I don't know," Reese replied. "I just don't want to believe that."

"It doesn't matter what you want to believe! What do you think the Daughters will say when we return with no Delius and only these few weak Unbroken?" Zaavan paused for effect. "They will label us failures! We'll never see another day out in the Skin-Land again! Each and every one of us will be stuck in the hot stench of the Sled for eternity!" Bore and Chalt nodded their heads in agreement. Reese kept his head down in thought, and Montly, sidelined by the intensity of the conversation, observed silently.

"You think too much of your position, your future, Zaavan," Lopex responded. "Be careful. Ambition led the Devil to his Great Fall."

"You dare quote philosophy to me!" Zaavan said, unfurling his wings and arms. "This from the pupil of a traitor!"

"*I* am the Assistant Praefectus," Lopex said with a strength that exceeded his size. "And *I* am in charge of this Cantavit in the absence of the Praefectus!" He paused, looking over the group. "We've lost Delius under strange circumstances. We found an Angel and have no idea why it was here. We must get back to the Sled and report these things to the Daughters."

Reese nodded his head in agreement, while Bore and Chalt looked to Zaavan for a response. The winged Zeta took a moment and cracked his massive wings.

"*Strange circumstances?* Delius was lost under *strange circumstances?* You can't be serious," Zaavan said. "For the past one thousand years, the Deltas have disappeared under *strange circumstances.* Every one of them! *You* know that! *I* know that! Every Minion who spends a day on the Sled *knows that!* He took the coward's way out of Hell just like every Delta has!"

Lopex lunged at Zaavan, his coat rippling behind him. He stopped one inch from the Demon's face, and with every ounce of temperance and restraint, quietly whispered to Zaavan, "I will allow you that one outburst because this is a stressful time for all of us. But if you question the honor of Delius again, I will have your wings cut off and ground up into the next batch of grist!"

Zaavan took a half step back and extended his wings in silent defiance.

Lopex straightened his coat, calmed himself, and began his instructions.

"Bore and Chalt, bind the Unbroken to the Drums, then break down the tents. Reese, dismantle the kitchen and load the wagon. Montly, make sure the Mauss are fed what's left of the grist and ready them for travel. I'll map our trip back to the Sled. And Zaavan, take perch on the boulder to make sure the Skin-Land is clear. We're going to be moving fast, and I don't want any delays. Questions?" Lopex stood for a moment, letting his orders sink in, then turned, walking briskly back to his tent as the group dispersed.

Montly and Reese walked quickly to the makeshift kitchen.

"Look, kid," Reese began, "just follow Lopex's lead, okay? It's only gonna be a few days back to the Sled, but I don't think they're gonna be easy days. You understand?" He began collecting his gear.

"Whatever you say, Reese. I just can't believe Delius is really gone."

"Well, believe it, but don't dwell on it. Stay sharp, and keep these Sapiens in working order so we can get back as fast as possible. The less time we spend out here with Zaavan and his lackeys, the better."

"Right," Montly said, and began scooping out the sloppy remnants of grist from the ground pots into a wide skin sack for the Mauss.

Reese reached up to the boulder that flanked his makeshift kitchen and ripped down a large skin sheet he'd set up for backing.

Instantly, Montly had a flash of memory that was not her own. In her vision, she could see the silhouette of the Angel Zaavan had killed. Like a stencil etched with light, Montly could see the shape of his lean body, the arched span of his wings, even some of his delicate feathers.

"Tragen," Montly said. "His name was Tragen." The sound came from her mouth with no direction from her own mind.

"What did you say?" Reese asked.

"I don't know. I just . . ." She paused, the cloud in her mind flashing for only a fraction of a second. "The name of the Angel, his name was Tragen."

"What in Hell are you talking about, Minion?" Reese responded as he went back to work.

But in the depths of Montly's mind, deep in the thick cloud injected into her by the Backwash Stemming, the semblance of Silton's memories began to take form.

CHAPTER THIRTY-NINE

1. *Your work is with human stock, not a person. Use human stock to further the whole, not the individual.*
2. *An Engineer who is damaged is of no use to anyone. Your first priority is always to keep yourself in perfect working order.*
3. *Pain is of no use to the Engineer; always ensure your subject is comfortable. Pain causes struggle, and struggle will impede your work.*

—From "The 100 Tenets of a Master Engineer"
(Multiple Authors Credited)

Silton held Mariella in his arms as they both lay on the edge of the tiny island. For the first time since he'd met her, she had a smile on her face—a liquid, hypnotized smile, but a smile. Her chest rose and fell in shallow breaths, and a gummy elastic feeling pervaded her limbs. If not for her open eyes and the smile pasted on her face, Silton would have thought her unconscious.

"Are you okay, Mariella?" Silton asked.

"Oh yeah, I'm doing great, Soldier Boy." Her voice sounded deeper than usual, and she hung on the ends of her words, stretching out the syllables.

"What did you do to her?" Silton demanded to the half-man rooted in the middle of the skin island.

The half-man didn't respond at first. He was preoccupied, hunched over and fingering his torso of exposed bones, tendons, and muscles.

"You cracked two of my ribs, Minion! Do you realize that?" He reached into his midsection and pulled a rib out from under a thin sheet of light red muscle. "I haven't had a broken bone in over one hundred and twenty years." He twisted the rib to show a sharp crack along its edge.

"Lucky it's just a crack," he said as he pulled the muscle sheet over the rib and tucked it back inside himself.

Silton dismissed his shock and pushed his question. "What have you done to my friend?" he asked louder.

"I'm fixing her legs, you stupid Minion! Are you so ignorant that you can't see that?"

"Why is she . . . why is she so confused?" Silton asked, this time with less aggression, as he could not deny that he'd helped Mariella.

"Always, always, always push the dopamine before repair—always. If you don't push the dopamine, the subject will struggle and cause more damage before repair can be completed. It's the third tenet of the Master Engineer. How old are you, Minion? What is your job function?"

"Why do you keep calling me Minion? And what job?" Silton asked. Mariella began to move, struggling a bit in his arms. She bent her exposed knee. A few cracks came from the joint, but she moved it freely without dislocation.

"Oh my God, you fixed it! It's back in place." Mariella bent her knee over and over again, testing it, and with a few more flexes she tried to get up.

"Oh no, no, no, Minion! Don't get up just yet. I need to fix your other knee. Try to be still, come over here, and let me work on you a bit more," the man said.

Silton stayed Mariella, holding her tight to his chest. "You're not doing anything else to her!"

"Oh, I'm not? Fine. Fine with me. We can just sit here. Or you can go. Take your friend, swim back to land. Carry her out into the Vast, and go wherever you want, stupid Minion. But soon, your muscles will get tight, your blood thick, and your joints unbending. Next, the albumin will separate, turning your skin yellow and dry. And one day, one day very soon, you'll go stiff, frozen as the blood in your body gets tired and goes to sleep."

The half-man stretched his arms up over his head, as if casually rising from sleep. "And then you'll ask yourself, when you're frozen on the warm belly of Skin-Land, 'Why didn't I listen to that Master Engineer when I had the chance? Why did I crack one of his ribs? Why didn't I let him help us?' And what answer will you give yourself then, Minion? What answer, as the Skin-Land swallows you down, hot and sticky, will you say then?"

Silton kept Mariella close as his confusion grew. This thing knew his symptoms. It knew how he felt.

"How do you know that? How do you know that my muscles get stiff?"

The half-man mustered a disappointed look to Silton.

"You have no heart, Minion! No heart, no blood movement. No blood movement, and muscles get stiff. Even if you try and refresh it, old blood will still lay in your legs, your feet. It gets thick and bored, and then that is the end. They didn't tell you that when they took your heart?"

"No one took my heart," Silton snapped back.

"No? You mean the Devil isn't collecting hearts anymore? That's strange, I guess he's completed that project of his."

"What are you talking about? No one took anything," Silton said.

The half-man of bone and muscle caught himself for a moment, wondering if his observations could be in error.

"How long have you been here?" the half-man asked.

"About a week," Mariella said, interjecting herself into the conversation.

"A week? Both of you? A week? But ... you're sin stamped. Your tenderlings, they're gone. Are you not Minions?"

"I don't know what you're talking about," Silton started, but Mariella's drug-induced enthusiasm cut him off.

"We got captured. Captured by these horrible things. They ... they burned us. Burned us up through the crotch, all of us. Then they stuck something into our heads and branded us with ... with ... our sins." Her voice was still deep, saturated with the dopamine that so dulled her senses.

"You are not Minions?" The half-man paused, bewildered and considering his words. "You're Unbroken people? Free Unbroken people? How? How could you be out here alone, without your Demon holders?"

"One of them helped us escape."

"Mariella!" Silton said, stifling her. "Be quiet! We have no idea what this thing is."

"No, I won't be quiet, Silton! We've been doing things your way, and it's gotten us nowhere!" Mariella said defiantly.

"We were trapped. Trapped with a bunch of other people, but this Demon, this big Demon named Delius, he let us go. He just let us go. Then he drowned himself. He just walked out into the lake and drowned himself!"

The half-man sat silently and digested what Mariella had said.

"So, it has begun. I can't believe it. It has begun." He curled his spine into a crouched sitting position, put his hand to his bony chin and thought for a moment. "You must understand; I've been here so long. I... I've lost some of my manners, I think."

"Been here so long? Why?" Silton asked.

The half-man ignored his question. "So, Delius helped you escape?"

"Yes, he was huge, with—" Mariella began.

"Stop talking, Mariella!" Silton demanded again.

"No, Silton! No! You shut up! You don't tell me what I can and can't say, damn it!" She pushed herself away from his embrace, sliding across the patch of skin toward the half-man. "I've been crippled, crippled and dying from the pain all this time. And now he's helping me, and you don't want to answer his questions?"

Her face flushed hot. "I'm going to talk to him. I'm going to tell him what happened. And I'm going to let him help fix me, damn you. What choice do I have? What other choice? To be carried by you to this Sled place? So we can find your wife? I don't think so. I'll take my chances. I'll make my own way now." She defiantly wiped away a hurt tear.

"The Sled?" The half-man said, as a smile broke across his face. "You know about the Sled? And you want to go there? Brave Unbroken... brave and very interesting. And how exactly are you planning on finding the Sled?"

"We'll find it. I have to find it." Silton replied, his voice firm.

"Well, little Unbroken man, this is your lucky day."

"And why is that?" Silton asked, suspicious.

"I know exactly where the Sled is," the half-man said.

CHAPTER FORTY

Fat comprises a relatively small percentage of the total mass of Hell, yet due to its density compared to other body substances, most of the fat in Hell rests in gelatinous pits at or near the surface. Alone, fat is not a hazardous material, but it is extremely hard to detect. If one were to step on an area of skin covering a fat pit, the skin could break under the stress, causing one to sink rapidly. Due to the viscosity and depth of fat pits, escape from this phenomenon is extremely difficult.

—From "Hell Geographica"
By Doctorem Delta-Lindicus

Zaavan circled high above the Cantavit, skimming through the low, green clouds, the pungent, vaporized acid stinging him like a thousand pins. He reveled in the pain it caused, the heat that burgeoned deep inside him, and the fire of anger it so stoked.

The group trolled across the Skin-Land back toward the Sled, with the slow Unbroken limping in the rear and the Canem distantly scattered in front of them. Zaavan turned around, flying over the convoy, facing the bone caves and the flat blood lake. Far off to the horizon, he took one last look at the Arm Forest and the void in the sky that fed it. Almost invisible to him now, he couldn't help but think of the human stock left behind due to Lopex's cowardice.

He panned back, picking up a hot, acrid gust of wind that pushed him higher, past the Cantavit. The Vast stretched out, undulating then flat, with only the occasional patches of thick hair breaking up the various colors of skin. And then he saw it: glistening in the distance, it looked like a heat mirage. Zaavan flapped his wings, striding fast toward the anomaly, and pressed his Compound Eyes, stretching his corneas to concave so he could see it clearly.

Below him lay a wide, deep patch of fat. From the ground, it would be invisible, but from Zaavan's vantage point, he could see through the thin layer of skin that covered it to the semi-hardened white cake and the depth of warm fat that no doubt rested below.

"Flawless," Zaavan said, with the hot wind passing over his face. "Absolutely flawless." Zaavan curled his left wing and started back down to the Cantavit.

Montly strode proudly next to Lopex as they walked their Mauss across the Skin-Land. She thought the view from the front of the group so much more magnificent. The deep colors of the sky seemed brighter, the sounds clearer. But most of all, the putrid smell of the Unbroken and their seemingly constant defecation no longer itched at her nose. For the first time, Montly could envision herself as a full Demon.

"Thank you so much for letting me ride up front," she said to Lopex. Lopex chuckled in response.

"Think nothing of it. This is where you belong. Who else

would I have at my side but my pupil?" He smiled at her, and Montly returned the smile. "Also," Lopex continued, "We need to stay together. Reese, you, and me. The Zetas, they're an unpredictable bunch, and as you've seen, Zaavan doesn't take well to orders from me."

"I know," Montly replied. "He seems . . . unstable sometimes. But I don't understand why. Cantavit protocol is clear on these issues. Even I know that."

"It is, but you will see as you spend more time on the Sled that people who only think of increasing their position often allow ambition to cloud their thoughts. When you think of nothing but yourself, how can you truly serve Hell?"

"I understand," Montly said, dancing around the edges of what she really wanted to talk to her teacher about. She gathered the courage and began. "There's something I wanted to ask you. It has nothing to do with Zaavan, but I . . ." She hesitated, careful with her words.

"Ask me, Montly. You can ask me anything."

Comforted, she felt her inhibition fade away.

"Ever since the Stemming, I've felt . . . well, not really felt, but I've been seeing things. Actually, more like remembering things. Memories that aren't mine are stuck in my head. I see them, very clear sometimes, and other times it's as if I'm reaching out to grab a thought, then nothing." Montly thought her explanation ridiculous, but had no other way to describe it.

"What kind of memories? Memories about what?" Lopex asked.

"The Angel mostly. The Angel you had me bury."

Lopex kept his Mauss at stride, but now Montly had his undivided attention.

"Go on. What exactly are you remembering about the Angel?"

"I know this is going to sound absurd, but ... I know his name. And it's not like I'm guessing his name, or that I think I know it. I *know* his name. I can hear his voice. I can see his mouth moving when he says it. Like he is telling it to me."

"Go on."

"His name is Tragen. It doesn't make sense. I told Reese, but he didn't really believe me—"

Lopex stopped Montly cold. "Have you mentioned this to the Zetas?"

"No ... no, I just told Reese," she said. Lopex turned his head back to the Skin-Land, deep in thought.

"Then it is even better that we're heading back now. You must be experiencing backwash from Stemming that Unbroken. He must have spoken to the Angel, and somehow that memory got pushed into you. And now he's escaped. This is not good."

He turned back to Montly. "Try your best to stay away from those memories. They can fragment your mind, make you think you're someone you're not. You have to do your best at that. When we get back to the Sled, we'll have to get you to the Engineering floor. We'll have to Stem you again, and see what else that Unbroken left in your mind."

For the first time, Montly felt scared.

"Am I going to be alright? Is this going to get worse?" she asked, fear trimming the sides of her words.

"Yes, you'll be fine. But you must stay away from those memories until we can get you the help you need." Lopex hoped that he was right. He didn't know much about the effects of Backwash Stemming, but he did know that often the afflicted were destroyed.

Zaavan dropped down in front of them, his huge wings wafting up a billow of air that rushed into Lopex's and Montly's faces and stopped the gait of their Mauss.

"Up ahead," Zaavan began, "we have some dangerous terrain. It looks like some weak skin. I could see through it from the sky. If we veer south, we'll avoid it. And we won't be off our pace too much."

"How bad is it?" Lopex asked.

"It's probably nothing the Mauss can't handle, but the wagon and the Unbroken, they may get stuck, even sink. And I don't want to go back to the Sled with nothing to show from this failed Mandatum," Zaavan said snidely.

"Fine, fine. Mark the change in direction, and Montly and I will lead," Lopex replied.

Zaavan did so, and moved to Lopex's side, letting them both pass. He patiently waited for the Cantavit to go by, heading in the new direction he'd pointed out. Reese rolled past him silently on his wagon, and a few lengths behind, the Zetas brought up the rear, the Drums and Unbroken in trail.

"I can't believe we're on Unbroken duty, Zaavan," Chalt said, her eyes slit with anger. "It stinks back here."

"Smell," Bore droned, his dumb face twisted with disgust.

"Silence, Zetas," Zaavan whispered. "You won't be back here for long. Watch for my signal, and when you see it, stop. Hold the Drums back, and keep the Unbroken at bay. Do you understand?"

"Yes, Zeta-Zaavan, we understand perfectly," Chalt said, crisping a smile of pure white bone against her tumor-plated black lips.

CHAP+ER F⊕R+Y-⊕NE

Beneath the dermis of Hell lies a network of nerves called the
Inner Ganglion. This network has grown over many thousands
of years, and is suspected to cover the entire surface of Hell. In the
times before The Great Fall, the Devil used the Inner Ganglion
as a rudimentary communication system, allowing him to send
messages to disparate outposts. The ganglion can only be accessed
through a deep spinal connection that roots members of Hell into
the structure. Here, the rooted member can "feel" vibrations on
the surface of Hell, and if trained, "see" the location of large objects
both stationary and in motion. As one of the many consequences
of The Devil's Great Fall, access to this system has been disabled.

—From "Hell Geographica"
By Doctorem Delta-Lindicus

T he half-man moved the edge of his bone finger through
Mariella's kneecap and checked the tiny strands of
tendon he'd attached before being struck by Silton. Liking the
quality of his work, he sliced a small hole into the Skin-Land
island and scooped up a palm-sized glob of yellow fat.

"This will pad the area until it heals. It'll be swollen for a day or so, but don't worry, the fat will melt into your leg and soon you'll have full motion in the knee." The half-man smeared the fat into the open area of the kneecap, filling in the empty space like mortar in loose bricks.

"I can't believe it. I can feel it staying in place, finally. Thank you. Thank you so much. I . . . I don't even know your name," Mariella said, graciously.

The half-man paused.

"I haven't been asked that in so long. Almer Almericus is my name, but call me Almer."

"Thank you, Almer, thank you so much," Mariella replied.

Silton, suspicious but impressed, pushed into the conversation.

"You're sure that will hold?"

"Oh, of course. These are her own tendons. They will seal much faster to the bone than if I got them from somewhere else. Hopefully her other knee is the same, but if not, I can always improvise with some—"

Silton interrupted him. "So where is this Sled?"

"Ambitious, this one," the half-man snapped. "First, tell me why you want to go there. It's not a very nice place for Unbroken like you."

"Don't worry about that. Just tell us, and we'll be on our way," Silton said.

"You don't have any idea what you're getting into, do you?" Almer said. "Only a week here in Hell, and you want to seek out the Sled? On purpose? You know that there are Unbroken who spend eternity running from the Sled? Unbroken who spend eternity trying to escape the Sled?"

"He wants to rescue his wife. He thinks she's there,"

Mariella said, drunk from the dopamine painkillers rushing through her blood, and tired of Silton hiding his intentions.

"Rescue?" Almer laughed. "Naïve Unbroken. So naïve." He pulled a flap of skin over Mariella's knee. "I'm going to need some veins to close this up. Then I can start on your other knee."

"Just tell me. Where is it?" Silton pressed.

"So anxious. I can hear it in your voice. You were a very determined individual in the life-times, yes?"

Silton ignored him. "Are you going to tell me?"

"Of course I'll tell you. It means nothing to me whether you know or not. But will you at least fetch me some vein so I can patch up your friend here? I saw a flesh rain just before you arrived, so there must be many pieces of human stock laying around, plenty over there for me to work with."

"Yes, fine, but first tell me where the Sled is," Silton pressed.

"Unbroken, Unbroken, it's not that easy. the Sled is constantly moving, constantly traveling across Hell. But I can feel it. Under me, I can feel the vibrations of that huge monstrous thing moving. It's unmistakable. I can always feel it. That's my punishment." Almer paused for a moment, eyes closed, then spoke again. "The Sled is northeast of here. Moving west. If it keeps course, but you—"

"Northeast from here? Good, how far?" Silton pressed.

Mariella, still high on painkillers, interrupted. "Punished? What were you punished for?"

"My dear Unbroken, I was punished for doing what I am doing right now—helping. Helping poor, desperate Unbroken like you."

"Why? Who would punish you for that?" Mariella asked.

"There is much you don't understand about this place. About the Devil. He doesn't see you as people. That's why he has us call you Unbroken, Broken, Sapiens. He only sees you as tools, tools to help him hurt God. Not the individuals you are. It's the first tenet we are taught as Engineers, to not see you as people, just as human stock, even if you're perfectly fine, like the two of you."

Almer leaned back, coiling his spine to sit. "I never quite understood that lesson, even though I was one of the best Engineers on the Sled. I made Demons, for Satan's sake! But when I was tested for Master Engineer, I failed. I wasn't able to see you Unbroken as meat. I see you as I see myself. Compassion was my failure. And this . . ." He stretched his skeletonized arms wide. "This is what happens when you fail the Master Engineer test—banishment. They tell you that it's only temporary. So you can spend a thousand years thinking about why you failed. Why you were wrong. They tell you that they'll be back, but they never came back."

Mariella turned her head, saddened and empathetic to Almer's predicament. "You've been here for a thousand years? How could they be so cruel?"

"You have no idea, my dear. How is the pain? Would you like me to make it go away again?" Almer asked.

"Oh yes, Almer, please make it go away. It's starting again." Mariella replied, grateful.

The half-man stretched his hand to the back of Mariella's head and fingered inside the hole. Silton watched him closely as he seemed to touch some delicate section of her brain. Mariella closed her eyes, let out a low, relaxed hum, and a smile broke on her face.

"There you go, dear, that should hold you for a while. Now

tell me, Silton, what will you do once you get to the Sled?" Almer asked.

"I'm going to find my wife. I know she's there. And I'm going to get her out."

"How? How could you know she is there? Are you just guessing?" He said in a patronizing tone.

"The Demons, they got into our minds. They pushed this knife-thing into the backs of our heads and—"

"I know what they did to you," Almer interjected. "It's called the Stemming. It's to identify your sins. It happens to everyone."

"But *I* got into the *Demon's* mind, and I saw my wife. I watched the Demon's memories, and I saw her."

"Are you sure?" Almer said. "I will tell you what you are describing is quite rare. You must have a strong will for an Unbroken."

"So, I have to go," Silton continued. "I have to find her and get her out of that place."

Almer nodded his head.

"Love. I remember love, I think. I think in the life-times I knew love. You should know that love might destroy you here, Silton. I hope you know what you are risking. There are not many places in Hell worse than the Sled. Thousands of Sapiens, hundreds of Minions, and then there are the Demons. That's where they are made. I know, because I made them there. To get in and out with one of their Unbroken, to even find who you seek, it's almost impossible." Almer said.

"I don't care what *is* or *isn't* impossible. I never have," Silton replied.

Almer looked into Silton's eyes and saw clearly that his determination would not be averted by logic. He let out a huff of acrid air, his lungs visibly shrinking under his rib cage.

"I'll make you a deal then," Almer started. "You get me out of here. You pull me up and take me off this island, and I'll see that you get to the Sled."

"Why do I need your help? Now that I know where it is?" Silton pushed.

"Why do you need my help?" Almer paused and smiled. "Without me, your friend won't walk. Without me, your heartless body will stiffen up before you get there. And if you do make it, the first Demon you run into will rip your arms off and beat you with them."

"How can I trust you?" Silton asked.

"You're right, you're right. As a show of faith, I'll fix your friend. Make her able to walk again. I'll even help you, make you a match for the Demons you will inevitably encounter. Then I will take you to the Sled."

Silton considered the offer for a moment, until he realized he had no other option.

"Deal," he said. "What do you need to fix Mariella?"

"Not much. The other knee is probably like this one, most of the tendons still intact. I'll only need some fresh veins so I can stitch her up. There should be plenty of it around the edges of the pond, where the flesh rain collected." Silton rose and looked to Mariella, she gave him a sloppy nod.

"If you do anything to her while I'm gone, I'll take your head off and kick it into this blood pond! You understand?"

"I'm sure you will, Unbroken, I'm sure you will," said Almer chuckling.

Silton walked into the blood pond and made the swim to shore quickly. He climbed over the wall into the piles and piles of flesh that rested on the ground. He combed through the sticky mess and gathered a tangle of veins. Some had already collapsed, so Silton pulled them out, leaving only strong, thick purple cords. He wrapped them around his arm like rope and made his way back to the island.

It only took Almer a few minutes to complete the stitching of Mariella's knee. His hands moved with deftness and speed, using a thin needle of bone to lace the skin together. Silton could see Almer's knowledge of anatomy easily eclipsed his own, and the half-man moved with precision and practice that rivaled any surgeon.

"Now, dear Unbroken, I am going to start on the other knee. How's the pain?" he asked.

"It hurts a little," Mariella said, wafting in dopamine.

"Well, let me fix that." Almer fingered her brain to release more endorphins, pushing her into a dream. He began work on her other knee, and soon two long lengths of purple laced down Mariella's kneecaps. "Who fixed your bones here?" Almer asked as he pointed to the hard skin casts on her legs.

"I did," Silton replied.

"Nice work, very nice work."

"I'm a medic. I mean, I was a medic. I've fixed countless broken bones. Hers were no different."

"A skill that will serve you well here, Silton. We have more in common than you think." Almer's repairs finished, he turned to Mariella. "Now, try to stand. Your tendons will attach quickly. You may not be able to run, but they'll hold. In a few hours, it will be like nothing ever happened."

Mariella rose, feeling a pinch as she applied pressure. Silton helped Mariella up, holding her by the arm. She tensed, let her full weight down, and began to cry.

"It's incredible. I can't understand how it works so fast," she said.

"This is the best and worst thing about Hell. You, your body, and every other piece of flesh and bone that surrounds us are immortal. A sad, terrible sentence," Almer said.

"Thank you," Silton said. "You've been true to your word, Almer."

"Good. Now rip me off this island, and let's get to dry skin. If you're going to be foolish enough to make the trek to the Sled, you're going to need a few alterations of your own."

Silton and Mariella took position, each with a hand under the stringy muscle of Almer's arms. They pulled and strained, ripping the bone of his spine from the meaty anchor of the skin island. Soon they waded out into the blood pond toward the land that surrounded it, having uprooted a creature that had been imprisoned on that tiny skin island for over a thousand years.

CHAP†ER F⊕R†Y-†W⊕

Mutiny is the most heinous offense a Demon can commit. It is an immoral act against one's own Demon brothers and sisters and an affront to the sacrifices made by all of us. Most of all it erodes the bond between brethren, and insults the gifts Hell has given us. Those Demons responsible for mutiny will be exiled and made Sessile, resigned to spend eternity alone in the Skin-Land Vast.

—From "A Demon's Handbook"
By Delta-Haldon

Heaven's Eye crested bright and blue over the Cantavit as it reached the highest point in the yellow-green sky. The Canem ran, scattered across the moist skin, lapping up puddles of morning sweat. Montly guided her Mauss in a wide arc around to the rear of the Cantavit and slowed to a trot as she came up behind the convoy. The dry Skin-Land broke easily in this area of Hell. The Mauss and heavy wagon ripped holes in its surface, and a trail of crimson painted the landscape behind them. Montly silently counted the Unbroken—only nine remained. The three men captured first seemed to be doing the best. They'd developed a bond. They walked together, leaned on each other when needed, and even occasionally carried one another. These three were in near perfect physical shape, and Montly thought they would fit nicely into the Herd.

The rest of the group wasn't doing nearly as well. The preacher wouldn't stop coughing, a terrible hacking cough that often made him stumble. *Zaavan must have pressed the collar brand around his throat too hard,* Montly thought. Now blood and pus leaked into his lungs, making it hard for him to breathe. They would have to be replaced once they got to the Herd.

The doctor had taken to crying, not an unusual response after a Scrotting, but he didn't seem able to stop. Every few steps, he could be heard talking to himself, a murmur about this all being a dream. His transition to the Herd would be a hard one. The other Unbroken pushing the Sled didn't take too well to those who cried. They would no doubt shun him, and this would make his time there more difficult.

The three women also looked to be bonding. The two healthy ones held up the woman Bore had accidentally lobotomized, guiding her and picking her up when she fell. But unfortunately, they seemed to have stepped on some exposed bone along the way. All three women had deep cuts on their feet and ankles. Montly hoped they weren't in too much pain. Those types of superficial injuries wouldn't be fixed when they got to the Herd.

But worst off was the martyr, the man who'd arrived in Hell with one of his arms blown off, the one Chalt had struck during the Stemming having been so disgusted with his sins.

His walking pattern looked as if he were drunk. But his eyes told the most awful part of his predicament: There was nothing left of him. Montly had seen that look before, the vapid emptiness of a man erased. His faith and sacrifice so ill-placed during life, his interpretation of God's word so fundamentally wrong. The realization of this had taken away all of his hope, and Montly was quite surprised he'd not begun to sink yet. Even if he did make it to the Sled, there was no doubt his body would be used for parts.

Montly cantered up to the Zetas, who rode silently, dragging the Unbroken behind them. She smiled at Chalt, and as always, Chalt ignored her completely. Montly knew that she was jealous, but what could she do? She had no control over her field promotion since the loss of Delius. So she brushed away the fantasy of having Chalt as a friend and confidante.

She passed Reese on his squeaking wagon, his white chef's coat stretching in tight bands across his round belly.

"You're doing great, kid!" Reese said as Montly passed, and she blushed at the compliment.

Montly rejoined Lopex at the front of the Cantavit. His eyes alternately looked to the horizon and up to Zaavan circling above.

"How are they doing?" he asked.

"I'll say this much, I finally understand why the Herd Praefectus is always in a poor mood after taking possession of Unbroken from the Vast."

"And why is that?" Lopex asked.

"Well, sir, they're a mess. Most of them will make it, I'm sure of that, but some are in need of serious work. The one with a missing arm will most likely be labeled as stock."

"So, eight, then—eight out of a quota of twenty-five. Damn!

I knew that number was too high, even if we hadn't lost Delius."

"I never asked. How are you doing with that?" Montly said.

"I just want to get back to the Sled. I need to report all of this to the Daughters. I don't know what to think." Lopex pushed the thoughts from his mind. "How are the Zetas?"

"Quiet. Very quiet," Montly responded.

"Yes, well, from here on out, stay close to me. We've only another day to go, and we aren't going to stop to make camp. I don't want Zaavan or his Zetas dwelling on this power shift for too long."

"Agreed," Montly said.

Zaavan circled the sky in front of the Cantavit. Lopex had taken his suggested change in direction perfectly, and the short caravan made a straight line right for the middle of the weak Skin-Land that spanned a deep pit of liquid fat.

"Time to set the trap," he said to himself as the wind filled his wings. The Zeta took in a few deep breaths, expanding his acid lung sacs over and over again, distending them to their fullest capacity. He dropped down to the surface several hundred feet in front of the Cantavit, and gently landed on the Skin-Land, careful not to pierce it. Zaavan waved his arms and wings frantically, pumping his hands and giving the signal for the Cantavit to stop.

"Something's wrong," Lopex said, seeing Zaavan's signal. "Reese! Cantavit! Halt!" he yelled.

"What is it?" Montly asked.

"I'm not sure. There must be an obstacle. I'll check it out," Lopex said.

"Let's go," Montly said anxiously.

"No, you stay here with the Cantavit," Lopex replied.

"Oh, come on, why not? Isn't this the job of the Assistant Praefectus?"

Lopex chuckled. "It is. Okay, let's go." He turned to Reese. "Stay put while we see what's going on, and don't aggravate the Zetas while we're gone."

"I make you no promises, Brother Eta!" Reese joked. Lopex smiled and nodded to Montly, then the two rode off.

Zaavan stood firm, with his feet shoulder-width apart and his wings folded halfway, ready for flight. He compressed his eyes and looked to the Cantavit. Chalt and Bore returned his stare, knowing their master's plan was in motion.

Lopex and Montly pushed their Mauss to a fast gait. The majestic beasts' bone-carved hooves dug deeply into the Skin-Land, but their dexterity made the change in surface imperceptible to their riders. The pair approached Zaavan, who held up his hands for them to stop.

"What's the problem Zaavan?" Lopex asked.

"It's the Skin-Land. I don't know if it's strong enough here, so I wanted you to see it for yourself before I suggested we divert the Cantavit again."

"Right," Lopex said while dismounting. Montly did the same.

Their feet pressed deep into the elastic ground, and they could feel it give much more than normal.

"I think it's fine for us to walk on," Zaavan added, "but I don't think it will take the weight of the wagon, or even the Drums, and the Unbroken will most likely have difficulty."

"I thought we were supposed to be avoiding all of this?" Lopex said.

"So did I. But the fat pool must be wider than I thought. We may even have to double back."

Lopex shook his head, disappointed and frustrated. He bent down and pressed his hand to the skin, testing its strength.

"We might be able to fashion the wagon with runners," Montly said as she bent down as well, feeling the skin's elasticity.

"Maybe—" Lopex started, but Zaavan interrupted him.

"You know, on the Sled they talk about your Demon class, Lopex. Everyone does. No one quite understands the Etas," he began.

"What?" Lopex said, perplexed. "What are you talking about?"

"No one understands why the Etas were made. No one. You just don't seem to fit in anywhere. I mean, think about it: The Alphas, they were sent down here with the Devil, his mighty army that almost defeated God. Then the Betas. The incredible Betas that tamed the Skin-Land and built the Blood Palace. And of course, who could forget the Gammas, the mighty Demons who rescued the Devil from his Great Fall. No one can deny their place in history."

Lopex rose slowly, still confused by Zaavan's speech.

"Then the Deltas, the grand first class in Hell's New Order—you don't need reminding of their contributions. The Master Engineer Demons, the Epsilons, responsible for the construction of the Sled, along with countless miracles made from human stock. Then of course, there is my class, the Zetas, the fiercest weapons ever created in Hell. Our history is being written with every Heaven-rise.

"And then we have your class, the Etas. What were you even designed for? To be cooks like Reese? To fill Sapien Bay with laborers? Or with bureaucrats like you to curry favor with the Daughters? Or perhaps you were just made to admire the work of Demons greater than yourself? We are all so confused by this, Eta-Lopex, so please tell me, what *are* you good for?" Zaavan finished.

"What's going on?" Montly asked.

"What's going on is that you should have never taken this position," Zaavan retorted. "It was supposed to be for my protégé, Chalt. You belong in the Herd, with the rest of the stinking Unbroken."

Lopex moved in front of Montly, pushing her behind him slowly. His instincts, carved from hundreds of years in Hell, told him of Zaavan's intentions.

"Think, Zaavan. Think. Don't let your pride command you. Pride leads to The Fall, Zaavan, every Demon knows that."

"That . . ." Zaavan paused, fuming with anger. "That is the last time you will *ever* preach to me, Eta-Lopex!"

Zaavan let out a massive cone of acid from his lungs directly into Lopex's chest. He fell back, on top of Montly, and they both broke through the thin skin into a bath of warm fat. The two Mauss bolted, and in seconds, they too had broken through the skin. Zaavan flapped his wings once and burst a few feet into the air as the ground around him dissolved into a green-beige soup of flesh.

The Skin-Land shattered across a huge expanse. The deep lake of milky fat enveloped everything—including the faint shadow of Lopex and Montly as their bodies disappeared.

CHAPTER FORTY-THREE

Adding to your body can be one of the best ways to gain an advantage in Hell, either by harvesting parts from the landscape or by directly harvesting from another person. Simple additions like muscle fibers or bone knives can be done marginally well with little practice. But more sophisticated alterations, like blood plumbing or limb attachment, should not be attempted by the untrained.

—From "Hell: A Survival Guide"
By Delta-Delius

The swim to shore with the half-man proved more difficult than Silton expected, and although Mariella helped, he'd done most of the work. Now Silton lay exhausted on a cushion of flesh-covered bones against the blood brick wall that surrounded the pond.

Almer scooped through all the organs, veins, and other stock, while Mariella spoke about her work as a nurse, and how impressed she was with his surgical skills. The two chatted casually, like old friends might. Silton was bothered by this.

"I've spent a lot of time in the OR, and I've never seen anyone do a full knee reconstruction that fast," Mariella complimented.

"I was one of the fastest in my class. Back on the Sled, I once pulled out an entire nervous system down to the very last cluster in only a day. Even my teacher was impressed," Almer reminisced as he quickly separated the flesh into organized piles of muscle, bone, and organ.

"So, all this stuff, it fell out of the sky. Why? What causes that?" Mariella asked.

"It's called flesh rain. It happens when there's a mass death event in the life-times, some horrible multi-dismemberment, a killing, or accident. Anything like that."

Almer stopped talking for a moment and smiled, having found a full, thick flap of pristine muscle. He then continued, "When the pieces of people come through the portal from the living world to Hell, everything gets jumbled up, then it just falls, usually across large areas. Sometimes a few pieces would land on the island, but not often." Almer found another large piece of muscle and tossed it on the growing pile.

"You said you made Demons. You made those things that caught us, and tortured us?" Silton interjected with a sharp tone to his voice.

"I wouldn't say I 'made' them, more like enhanced them," Almer answered. "A Demon is made through their training. We Engineers just add the parts they need to do whatever their job might require. And, by the way, what they did to you wasn't torture. It's just the normal indoctrination into Hell. It's a process we all went through, moving from Unbroken to Broken."

"Castrating us isn't torture? Branding us isn't torture?" Silton's voice rose, becoming angry.

"No, as a matter of fact, it's not." Almer stopped digging through the flesh for a moment. "'Castration,' as you call it, or the *Scrotting,* has been done for thousands and thousands of years. It happened to me. It happens to everyone. The purpose of it is to take away temptation. And not only your temptation, but the temptations that others may have toward you."

Almer looked to Mariella. "As for the 'branding,' or the Sin Stamp, it's critical to classify everyone with the sins that brought them here. That's the first step toward redemption, my friend. When most Unbroken arrive, they think it's some kind of mistake. They don't have any idea what they could have done to deserve being sent to Hell. The Stemming and the Sin Stamp answer that question."

Almer went back to his piles. "Let me ask you, Silton. Did you think that this was where you'd end up when you killed yourself?"

Silton was taken aback by the question. Almer was the first one to confront him with his most intimate failure.

"No, I didn't think I'd end up here," Silton admitted.

"Then, there you go. It's a system, and I'm sorry to have to tell you, but it works. If I'm going to help you do this, you're going to need more than just a few alterations and some fresh blood. You're going to need to start understanding this place for what it is. Whether you agree with it or not." Almer looked hard at Silton, letting his words sink deep, then went back to sorting stock.

"Almer?" Mariella said.

"Yes, my dear," Almer responded.

"My knees are a little achy. Can you do that thing in my head again, please?"

"Of course I can, dear. Come over here. I don't move so fast."

Mariella quickly scooted over to Almer through a sticky pile of discarded flesh, and once again he reached his bony finger into the orifice in the back of her head.

"Do you think that's such a good idea? Doing that, Mariella? It's like pushing drugs on a patient," Silton scolded.

"Oh, shut up. You're not the one whose feet feel like they're on fire. You didn't scream with every step, or have to fight to keep from crying while being dragged across the ground in a skin hammock!"

Silton didn't respond.

"It's the third tenet of the Master Engineer, Silton. I have to do everything in my power to make sure my subjects aren't in pain. What about you? I'm almost ready to start working here. Would you like me to settle your pain, too?" Almer asked.

"I don't think so. And you're not doing anything to me until we go over it in detail first."

"Of course, of course, I would never. Not for an Unbroken like you, so learned in the flesh arts."

"Oh relax, Silton," Mariella started, her voice drunk with endorphins. "He knows what he's doing. He's been doing it for a thousand years," she said in a lofty, dreamlike tone.

"Yeah, right," Silton said, suspicion coating his words like sap.

"The first thing we need to do is patch up those heart valves of yours. It won't be any help to give you more blood if it's just going to drain out through your chest. Next . . ." Almer reached into a wet pile of reddish-brown organs. "I'm going to put two of these spleens I found behind your shoulder blades, just under a few layers of muscle. I'll fill them up with fresh blood, and attach them to your piping. Then, when you start to feel that sluggish feeling when your muscles get stiff, you can bend over, flex down with your arms, and squeeze that reservoir of blood into your body. I'll build you a thick tube, with a one-way valve, and loop it up so it comes out near your mouth. Then you'll be able to refill the spleens by pouring blood into it when you have the opportunity."

"That sounds terrible," Silton said as his stomach turned with the thought. "Why don't you just replace my heart?" he asked.

"I would if I could," Almer replied. "There are some pieces of heart here, but unfortunately, it's an organ that has to be intact to work. The spleen option behind the shoulders works well as a substitute. It's high enough on the body to take advantage of the downward pressure. Trust me on this one, I've done it hundreds of times."

"Trust you, huh? What choice do I have?" Silton muttered.

"None!" Mariella yelled, then started laughing, deep under the spell of her own dopamine.

"All of this is great, Almer," Silton said. "But if I'm going to get to my wife, I know I'm going to run into a few of those Demons. The last time that happened, things didn't work out so well for me."

"Yes, well, they are impressive. Designed with purpose and trained with purpose."

"Yeah, I'm not worried about the training part. I've got the training. What I need is speed. Strength would be nice too, but speed most of all. What do you do to them to make them so fast? I encountered one. Twice my size, and it moved faster than anyone I've ever seen."

"Speed, yes, yes. That was a great leap in Demon development. It's quite a procedure, but one I am very familiar with.

There are a few . . ." Almer paused. "A few drawbacks to adding speed, though."

"Tell me," Silton demanded.

"The only way to make you faster is to increase the communication between your nerve endings. We need to make the synapses between nerves more robust, basically instantaneous. The only way to do that is to redirect the acetylcholine in your brain so it pushes more of it into your nervous system."

"Brain surgery?" Silton stopped him. "I don't think so."

"No, no, it's not brain surgery. I've found plenty of brain matter here. I can do the work on one of these pieces, then insert it into the hole they made for your Demon Stem. The brain piece will attach, and the redirection will start to take place. Easy."

"Easy, huh? What else? What else about the drawbacks?"

"Well, to start with, any increase in communication in your nervous system works both ways. Nothing can be done about that. You'll be able to move faster, but if you receive any stimulus through your nervous system, any pain, any feeling at all, it will be greatly magnified."

"So, I'll feel pain more?" Silton clarified.

"You'll feel everything more."

"Fine, I don't care about that. What else?"

"Then there is the heat. That's just a function of the mechanical action of your body. You'll get hot, very hot. I don't have the time or the technique tools to skin you and tuck all of your veins and arteries sub-muscular. That's what we do to solve the problem with Demons, but you're just going to have to deal with it."

"Okay, fine. Anything else?" Silton asked.

"Well, there's one more thing." Almer paused again.

"Tell me."

"With any diversion of a neurotransmitter, there are always . . . trade-offs. Neurotransmitters do a lot in the body, so when you repurpose them for one thing, it changes other things."

"Keep going, Almer, keep going," Silton pressed.

"Acetylcholine is one of the main chemicals responsible for memories. We've seen Demons who have had this done, and sometimes they lose memories."

Silton remained silent.

"And . . ." Almer said.

"*And?*" Silton questioned.

"Acetylcholine is also responsible for critical thinking, logic, verbalization of thoughts. In the Demons that I've done extreme re-routing of acetylcholine, we've observed them becoming, well, dumb. There's no other way to put it."

"So, for the speed, I feel more pain, I'll sweat profusely, and it'll eventually make me dumb? Did I get all of that?" Silton said, forcing sarcasm.

"The body doesn't decompose here. It is beautiful and immortal, but it still has limitations."

"Can you balance it? Can you give me some of the benefits without all of the downsides?" Silton asked.

"Sure, I can try. But it's not exact, each brain is different. Who knows—if you make more acetylcholine than normal, you might not even notice the effect. You may experience more of one, and less of another. This is one of the reasons Demons go through so much training. It's to help them deal with these . . . these side effects."

Silton didn't know what to make of Almer's proposal, but

he knew that if there was any chance to save Kay, this was it. For the first time, he felt what he could only describe as the pull of humanity, like a cord that anchored him to some semblance of being human, a rock where the idea of himself rested. To do this, his humanity had to be sacrificed. The thought ran through his head, bouncing off of his logic, his passion. And then, in the back of his mind, like a voice forcing itself to be heard, came the memory of Delius's speech of the fault of physical pride:

"This is what happens when you think that you are your body! You are not the flesh and bone you've known in your lifetimes! You are much more!"

"Do it," Silton said.

"Yes, yes, good decision, Unbroken Silton, good decision. Now lay on your stomach, over here. And my dear Mariella . . ."

"Yes, Almer?" she said.

"I could use your help. Can you hand me that cord of vein over there?"

"Of course I can, Almer."

Silton slid down to a clear patch of Skin-Land and lay down. Carefully, while Almer went for the vein cord from Mariella, he reached into his chest hole and pulled out the blood-soaked feather, tucking it deep into his fist.

"You're sure you don't want me to curb the pain?" Almer asked. "If you struggle, if you move, I'll have no choice but to push your endorphins."

"Don't worry, I won't."

Almer nodded, then threaded a thin needle at the tip of his boney fingers and began to sew up the meaty valves where Silton's heart once was.

And Silton didn't move a muscle.

CHAPTER FORTY-FOUR

Absorption into the Skin-Land is a harsh reality that faces all of Hell's inhabitants. Little is known of this phenomenon, but some recorded cases of near-absorption describe a feeling of oneness with Hell, a feeling that the body is stretched into an infinite, blended immortality. This is not to be feared, fellow Demons. Instead, revel in it.

—From "The Demonic Encyclopedia"
By Delta-Haldon

Montly drifted down slowly as her lungs filled with viscous fat. While the brilliant light of Heaven's Eye dimmed, warmth spread through her body, pulsing tingles out to her floating limbs. Her mind played out frantic memories as she began to give herself up to Hell, dissolving into its rich, tepid bowels.

She remembered her initial fall to Hell. She remembered her years pulling the Sled, watching her fellow Sled-mates' bodies fall apart like brittle branches. And she remembered the day the Herd Praefectus gave her the tumor necklace she always wore, the only gift she'd ever been given here.

As her thoughts meandered over the past, she tried to remember anything about herself before Hell. Montly found nothing. It was as if she didn't exist before she existed here. She pressed harder into her past, wanting to remember something of her life-times before she gave up to the innards of Hell. But Montly could not remember anything.

Instead, when she searched hard, she only found the misty cloud of thought the Unbroken Silton had left in her mind: the hazy scene of Tragen and the muted conversation they had that Montly could not discern. Her body began to convulse as the fat seeped into her, and she could feel the skin of her arms and legs become tender as she floated down. The misty cloud in her mind began to clear, and Silton's memories started to come into focus. As Montly drifted in the warmth, giving in to the entirety of Hell, she had a stark vision. She could hear Silton and Tragen speaking, and the conversation became perfectly clear: a conversation about hope.

"Take this."

Montly heard the Angel speak to Silton as he handed him a large white feather.

"Let this be a reminder to you that hope is the only weapon you have against them, against this place. It is the only thing they can't take from you, and the only thing that will stop this place from swallowing you whole."

Hope, Montly remembered. The only thing that helped her survive and make it through the years and years in the Herd. She repeated the ancient chant she held so close: *Hope has no lungs, yet it breathes. Hope has no heart, yet it beats. Hope has no legs, yet it travels. Hope has no mind, yet it knows all.* Montly's own thoughts forced the memory to play, and she could hear Tragen speak once again.

"It is our job to take them to Heaven. A rescue Mandatum is to take place in two days. I've scouted for their arrival. They're on their way, more Angels than have ever descended to Hell before. And they're going to redeem the many trapped here by the Devil in his massive construct."

A stiff jolt wrenched Montly's arm. Her shoulder cracked in response and she was yanked out of her vision. She felt the swift flow of warm fat and skin pieces wafting across her face. Soon her eyes, still foggy, began to see light again. Just as Montly's arm felt as if it'd be torn off, she broke through the surface of semi-hardened fat.

"Montly! Montly! Can you hear me!" she heard a voice say. Still half-entrenched in the memory, she thought the Angel Tragen was speaking again. But something familiar about this voice forced another conclusion. She flopped onto the soft Skin-Land, and before she could wipe away the yellow fat from her eyes, she felt a massive push on her chest. A thick stream of fat spewed out of her mouth. The trauma shook Montly back into the stark reality of Hell.

"Montly!" she heard again, followed by a sharp slap to her face. She raised her hands up, wiped her eyes, and saw Lopex's face staring down at her. "Can you hear me?" he said.

"I can! I can ..." Montly took in a deep breath of acrid air and choked out the last of the fat in her lung.

"Just stay calm. You're okay," Lopex said as he took her under the arms and dragged her from the edge of the wide fat pit.

Montly got her wits, shook away the foggy vision, and came back fully to consciousness.

"I thought I was ... I thought *we* were ... I could feel myself melting. I could feel Hell taking. How did you ...?

How did we . . . ?" Montly could hardly find the right words to ask a question.

"Zaavan," Lopex growled. "That bastard Zeta scum! He tried to sink us!"

Montly sat up, still amazed she was on the surface. "But how? He sprayed you with acid. How are you still . . . still here?"

"He forgot that we Etas have our hands into everything. He forgot that my class is in charge of just about everything on the Sled, including the Clorix Basin. The Etas make that acid he is so fond of using, and we know everything about it. I visited my brother, Eta-Hotund, at the Clorix Basin before we left, and he gave me a Basin robe for just this type of betrayal."

Lopex pulled at the stomach-lining garment plastered to his body. A deep green stain covered the front, but the rest of Lopex was completely unharmed. His remaining clothes, however—his coat, his shirt, his pants—were liquefied.

"But how did you know?" Montly asked.

"I trust a Zeta to be a Zeta—overly ambitious and full of pride. I put it on under my clothes as soon as I took over the Cantavit." Lopex paused. "Can you walk, Montly?"

"I can." She pushed herself up with Lopex's help.

"Come on! We have to get to Reese." Quickly, the pair ran back to the Cantavit.

But several feet from where the Cantavit was supposed to be, Lopex and Montly stopped running. Lopex hung his head and covered his face. There were only a few pieces of Reese left: a half torso still wrapped in his white chef's coat, a hand minus its fingers, and the wagon, which was completely sunk into the fat pit.

"Zaavan!" Lopex screamed, shaking with an unbridled anger.

"I'm going to sink you deeper into Hell than Jesus did the Devil!"

The Unbroken were gone, the Drums were gone, the Canem and all the supplies were gone. Only their Mauss remained, having escaped the edge of the sinking fat pit. They looked confused and bewildered.

"Brother Reese... Eta-Reese..." Lopex dropped to his knees and pounded his fists into the skin.

"I'm so sorry, Lopex, I'm so sorry." Montly reached out and put a hand on her teacher's shoulder. She waited a moment, not sure when or how to tell him of her vision. But knowing that there would never be a good time, and that time was short, she spoke. "Lopex, I need to tell you something. I... when I was under skin. I had... I was able to see. I went to that place you told me not to. The memory, the memory that Unbroken pushed into my head. I know what it is now."

"Montly! What? I told you that you can't—"

"Stop! Just stop! I know what you said! I know what you told me, but..." Montly paused carefully, knowing that her next words would change everything. "They're coming. The Angels, they're coming. They're going to attack the Sled, more Angels than have ever come down to Hell before. That's what the Unbroken knew! That's what the Angel told him!"

"What!" Lopex yelled. "When? Did he say when?"

"He said in two days' time," Montly answered.

"Two days?" Lopex thought for a moment. "But two days... that would make the attack today!"

CHAPTER FORTY-FIVE

Once muscle has been successfully grafted onto your body, either directly to bone or to a base of existing muscle, you will experience what is called the Second Skin effect. The added pieces, although physically connected to the bone or muscle fibers, will not "feel" like they are a part of you until your nervous system can fully communicate with the added tissue.

—From "The Demonic Encyclopedia"
By Delta-Haldon

Silton's eyes snapped open to the hazy color of beige skin, his head feeling distant and faint. Instantly, he looked to his clenched fist, still hiding the blood-matted feather. A wave of unbearable heat washed over him, and he felt drops of sweat run down his sides like tiny rivers. He started to get up, but a strange feeling pervaded his body, like a dozen thick blankets wrapped tightly around him. As he moved his arms up underneath his chest, a shrill tickle fired up his spine, and every nerve ending in his body sizzled. Silton let out an audible gasp.

"Oh, he's finally conscious," Almer said.

"Good. I bet he's starving," Mariella joined in.

Silton grunted, "I . . . I can't move." He labored under a new weight, as if his body lay inside another body. He struggled for each movement.

"That should only last a minute or two. Your nerve endings are jumpstarting all of that new muscle," Almer said. "Concentrate on moving your fingers and toes. That should push the impulses through quickly."

"What did you do to me?" Silton grumbled as he tried to turn himself over.

"Mariella, my dear, can you help your friend please?" Almer said. "Sit him up so he can see us. So he can see himself."

"Of course, Almer," Mariella said.

Silton felt Mariella's hands grab him, and a shock struck through his core.

"It hurts," Silton said.

"No, it doesn't hurt, Silton," Almer said. "That's just your brain acclimating to the boost in your nervous system, that's all. It's not pain, just . . . just a hyper awareness of sorts. You'll get used to it."

Mariella turned Silton over, then hoisted him up against the blood brick wall.

"How do you feel?" Mariella asked him.

Silton could barely respond as he took in the full view of her. "Mariella, you . . . you look . . . What happened to you?" Silton asked as he perused her body.

Mariella stood tall and proud above Silton, her hands on her naked hips, a smile across her tanned face. Her thighs were now twice as large as before, and her calves were the same. The skin around her legs formed a mismatched pattern that was not her own, held together with bright purple vein stitching.

The skin on her arms was stitched as well, and packed with rippling cords of muscle Mariella didn't have before.

"What happened to me?" Mariella responded. "I'll tell you what happened. I'm stronger than I've ever been! I feel great! I haven't felt this strong since college." A huge smile spanned her face. "But forget about me. *You* look incredible!"

Silton bent his neck slightly and saw a band of black skin covering his chest and tucking into the hole where his heart once was. He moved his hand to touch it, but felt a tight mass of muscle in his arms.

"I told you, Mariella," Almer started. "His chest looks great with that onyx skin matted through his heart hole. Do you see what I meant, now?"

"I do, I do! It looks so striking. The hole is so smooth. Almer did a wonderful job on you," she said.

Silton pushed back against the blood brick wall, now feeling full control over his limbs, and stood up. He felt the added mass of the muscle immediately, but he felt no added weight. Looking down, he could barely see over his own chest. His arms were thick, his legs were plump and swollen, and he felt two itchy lumps on his back, like he was carrying a satchel.

"So, what do you think?" Almer asked.

"What have you done to me? What did you do!" Silton bellowed.

"What did I do?" Almer said, shocked. "I did what you wanted me to do. I made you ... well, better. Making things better is what I do best."

Silton roiled with anger and denial. He put his hands to his head, and out of frustration, kicked the blood brick wall hard with his foot. The wall disintegrated, sending pieces of brick sailing across the blood pond.

"I guess the muscle took," Almer said, and smiled heartily to himself.

"Silton!" Mariella screamed, storming over to him. She grabbed his hands, took them down from his head, and looked him hard in the eyes. "You'd better calm down! Do you hear me, Soldier Boy! Get it together! Stop acting like a child!" she scolded him. "You want to get to your wife? Do you? Did you see what you did to that wall? Did you? Now calm down!"

Silton breathed heavily, the massive black band of his chest rising and falling like a rabid animal. Another wave of heat washed over him, and he could feel sweat escaping his body, rolling down his ultra-sensitive skin. Silton became woozy, and his huge body started to wobble. Seeing this, Mariella took him by the arm and sat him on the edge of the wall. Silton regained his composure, and started breathing slow and rhythmically again.

"What did you do, Almer? What *exactly* did you do?" Silton asked in a calmer tone.

"Well . . ." Almer started. "First off, I stitched up your heart hole veins so you won't lose blood. Then I had to patch up all that exposed flesh on the inside. I couldn't find anything to stuff the hole with, like a shoulder or hip joint, so I just layered the black skin on the inside. I think it looks very original. You'll never forget what you did to yourself to get here, but I like that. It's poetic."

Almer uncoiled himself so he could stand as tall as a man with no legs could. "Then I added the spleens—they were much easier than I thought they'd be. You have great wide veins. Next, as you can feel, I reinforced the muscle fibers of your arms and legs. When I was done with that, you looked a bit unbalanced with a normal chest, and since I had some leftover muscle and a nice swatch of black skin, I added that as well. All of the fibers and tendons joined perfectly. The only hard part was putting in your blood tube. It's a bit sloppy, but it'll work." Almer pointed to Silton's right side.

Silton looked down to his right shoulder and saw what looked like a tube coming out of the base of his neck. It was stiff, and he could feel where the tube ran across his back to the spleens.

"Mariella actually found it. It's a trachea. I couldn't have asked for a better body part. It already has a one-way valve."

"You made me . . . You made me a *monster!*" Silton said.

"I did. Yes, I did. Quite a beautiful monster, I'd say. Especially considering what I had to work with. Now, do me a favor. Just before you woke up, I put in your acetylcholine diverter. That's probably what shook you awake. Try moving around a bit. You know, fighting. I want to make sure it took," Almer said.

Silton didn't quite know what to think or what to do. He walked a few feet, feeling an effortless spring to his steps. He only had to put the most minor thought into moving, and it happened instantly. Silton took a fighting stance and threw a typical three-punch combination. His hands flew out in front of him with blinding speed. Before he could register that he'd thrown the first punch, he'd completed the combo.

"No," Silton whispered to himself. "That can't be." And then he punched again. His hands moved like a blur. Silton stepped forward, twisted his torso, and swung his elbow in a curving strike. The power behind the blow, so strong and so fast, took Silton off balance as if he'd just swung a sledgehammer.

Amazed, Silton walked back to the wall he'd destroyed. A few pieces of petrified blood bricks lay on the ground. He picked up an armful and began to throw them. He launched them all the way across the pond, almost out of the shallow skin valley entirely.

"Now you're getting it, aren't you, Silton?" Mariella asked, a huge smile still stretched across her face.

"It's amazing. It's like the muscle's always been there," Silton said.

"I know," Mariella agreed. "We've worked on the human body all of our lives, thinking we knew what we were doing. How could we ever know it was capable of something like this? It's like we belong here."

"I wouldn't go that far, Mariella," Silton replied.

"Okay. Great, you two are getting accustomed to your additions. We should eat before we get going," Almer suggested. "I know it's not much, but I was able to scare up something for us." He motioned to a patch of skin where he'd separated some muscle, jellied marrow, and cleaned skin strips for their meal.

The three ate heartily, the muscle and marrow tasting much better than the soup the Demons had made for them. For a time, no one spoke; they just reveled in the calm before their journey. And then, Silton broke the silence.

"So, Almer, how long will it take us to get there? To the Sled?"

"Not more than a day. It's very slow. Constantly moving, but very slow. It's north of us, but moving to the west, so it's not getting further away. We'll know we're close when we pick up the blood ruts. They'll be easy to see, like two red rivers that run behind it. Besides, the way you two are outfitted we'll get there in no time. You'll be almost as fast as a Mauss," Almer said, before ripping off a piece of muscle with his bony teeth.

"I'm stronger than normal with all this new muscle, but I still need to figure out a way to carry you, Almer," Silton replied.

"Oh no, don't worry about that," Mariella interrupted. "I'm going to carry him. We've already worked that out."

"Don't be foolish, Mariella," Silton objected. "Of course I'll carry him. I'm stronger."

"That's exactly why you shouldn't carry me," Almer said. "We need you ready if we run into anything out there. You can't have some legless lump on your back if we get into trouble."

"Besides, Silton," Mariella said. "Almer already made me a sack to carry him in. It fits perfectly, and with my legs fixed now, it'll be easy for me to keep up." Mariella looked over at Almer, and the two smiled at each other.

"Yes, it'll be easy for you, dear. And if your new legs cause you any pain, I'll be able to fix that for you too," Almer said, smiling.

Silton watched the two of them, and an instinct of jealousy pinched his stomach. Almer and Mariella had grown close so quickly. Too close, he thought. And Silton was liking their relationship less and less with each second that passed.

CHAPTER FORTY-SIX

Angel Fall has occurred sporadically over the past two thousand years since The Great Fall. Know that it is a most dangerous time, a time when the very fiber of Hell is at stake.

—From "A History of Hell"
By Delta-Holt

The plodding sounds of hoof on skin broke the silence between Lopex and Montly as they pushed their Mauss hard toward the horizon. Neither of them could find words. Both, lost in thought, attempted to understand their new reality.

The majestic Sapiens began to tire, and their wide, flat, keratin hooves tripped occasionally on the skin.

"We should take it easy," Montly said over the loud slapping strides of the beasts. Lopex didn't hear her, not because she wasn't loud enough, but because anger overflowed his senses.

"We should take it easy!" Montly yelled this time, meeting his eyes. Lopex slowed his Mauss.

"What?" Lopex responded.

"They're getting tired. When they get tired, they get sloppy. When they get sloppy, they slip. And I know we don't have time for me to fix a broken Mauss leg," Montly said sternly.

"You're right. How long do we have to slow them down?"

"Let's walk through this valley. It's flat, so it'll be an easy break for them. Then we can push them back to stride."

"Fine, if we must," Lopex conceded, grateful to have Montly to challenge him. "But we have to get to the Sled as soon as possible." Lopex paused. "Angel Fall . . . If we can't warn the Sled in time . . ."

Lopex shook his head, trailing off in worried thought.

"I've never seen Angel Fall before," Montly said.

"It's a horrible thing," Lopex recalled. "They've gotten stronger, smarter, over the centuries. They take more and more of our slaves each time. They are the reason monsters like the Zetas were made." Lopex patted his Mauss, hoping to speed its recovery. "I've seen them attack twice. Both times we almost lost the Sled, and lost many of our fellow Demons as well. If what you're saying is true, and they're going to come at us with more than they ever have before, we might not have a home left if we don't warn them in time."

Montly considered her next words carefully.

"What about me? What about the fact that I let an Unbroken into my mind, the Backwash? That I let him know things. That I . . ." Her voice stammered with fear.

"That's the least of our worries right now," Lopex said sharply. "If we can get back, we can warn them. How we learned of the Angel Fall won't matter. At least, I hope it won't matter."

Montly felt fear wave over her. It penetrated her muscles and leached into her blood. It occurred to her that the coming days could very well be her last. Montly reached under her jacket and pulled out the tumor necklace that always brought her comfort in times like these.

But the necklace offered no such relief.

CHAP+ER F⊕R+Y-SEVEN

4. *Hearts are the most precious of organs and must be saved at all costs.*
5. *No Sapien, Minion, or Demon shall have more heart than they need to operate.*
6. *All unused hearts are the Devil's hearts and shall be commandeered immediately.*

—From "The 100 Tenets of a Master Engineer"
(Multiple Authors Credited)

Silton's body heaved as his bulk moved easily across the Skin-Land. The fluid movement of his joints surprised him, and the responsiveness of his muscles seemed lightning quick, even with so much flesh added to them. Silton felt stronger than he had the day he joined the Army, and just as confident.

Mariella seemed much better too. At times, her pace was a bit faster than Silton's, and he had to press himself to keep up with her. Almer bounced along on her back, encased in a skin sheet that covered his muscle-wrapped skeleton, save his neck and head. He loomed over Mariella's right shoulder, and every once in a while Silton caught him whispering in her ear while he tickled the orifice in the back of her head. This only stoked the angry embers itching in Silton's psyche.

"I have to apologize for thinking you two were Minions when we first met," Almer said. "Such an insult to you and completely my fault. I've just been alone for so long, and Silton has no heart. I thought for sure you were Minions."

"Why would you think that? Just because I don't have a heart?" Silton asked.

"The Devil's been collecting hearts for so long. I just assumed that he'd collected yours. Only those who absolutely need hearts have them on the Sled," he answered. "In fact, I only have half of one."

"Why does the Devil collect hearts? What does he need them for?" Mariella interjected.

"No one knows, my dear. Some say it's a way of the Devil owning a piece of you forever. Others say it's his way of keeping you bonded to the Sled, committed to being fixed, treated, and bound to him. And some say he's building something."

"Building something?" Silton asked skeptically. "What could you build that would need so many hearts?"

"I don't know. I was almost a Master Engineer, and I never knew of anything that would require such a provision." Almer switched subjects. "But never mind that, Silton. Tell me. Exactly how are you going to get to your wife? You know that the Sled is teaming with Sapiens, Demons, and Minions, all of which will not take too kindly to you and your plans."

Unsure if he should trust the half-man but knowing that he'd probably need his help, Silton reluctantly answered.

"When I was in that Demon's mind, when she invaded me with that thing, that 'Stem,' I saw a weakness in the Sled."

"A weakness? In the Sled? Oh, do tell," Almer said excitedly.

"That Sled, it's pulled by people, like a huge team of horses, only it's thousands of people—thousands. It takes coordination for a team of horses to pull something. If one or two break stride, the load stops. It has to work the same way with the Sled," Silton said. "If I can cut off some of those people, maybe just disrupt a group of them, I think I can slow the Sled down. If I can do that, I'm betting that no one will care about us or what we're doing."

"But how can you be sure? How can you be positive they won't just, I don't know, just kill you on the spot?" Mariella contested.

"Because I've seen it work," Silton replied.

"What do you mean, you've seen it work?" Almer pressed.

Silton took in a breath and stretched a bit, pushing a few liters of blood from his new spleens into his body. "When that Demon was attached to me, I saw in *its* mind. I saw what I just explained happen. A few people escaped—only a few of them ripped off their lashings and ran. And the whole mess of people pulling the Sled almost fell apart." He paused. "I'm telling you, it's like a team of horses. We only need to get a few of them skittish, to peel off the herd, then all hell will break loose."

"That is, if you can get to them," Almer said.

"Yeah, well, that's why you made me into this monster, isn't it, Almer?"

"I guess it is, Silton. I guess it is."

"I think that with Almer's help, there's nothing we can't do here," Mariella said, her words coated in artificial happiness.

"That's so nice of you to say, my dear," Almer replied, and patted Mariella on the head like a loyal pet.

CHAP+ER F⊕R+Y-EIGH+

Angel Fall is normally preceded by a loud thunderclap. It has been hypothesized that this is the air compressing in response to Angels quickly crossing the threshold between Heaven and Hell.

—From "Hell Geographica"
By Doctorem Delta-Lindicus

Heaven's Eye shone hazy and obscure above Lopex and Montly as they strode slowly up a sharp hill in the Skin-Land. The sky bled a sick yellow-green haze down upon them in a phenomenon Lopex had not experienced before.

"The air . . . do you feel that?" Lopex asked.

"I do feel it. It's thicker," Montly replied. "Why?"

"I don't know, but I can't help but think it has something to do with your vision." He heeled his Mauss to trudge stronger up the steep hill, and Montly followed his lead.

The pair crested the smooth hill where a tuft of coarse black hair lay matted along its top.

"Thank the Devil!" Lopex exclaimed.

Montly reached the precipice and her eyes widened. The Sled, huge and clumsy and beautiful, sliced across the Skin-Land leaving two thick canals in its wake.

"I'll make straight for Sapien Bay," Lopex started. "You go to the Herd. Find the Herd Praefectus and warn her of Angel Fall. She'll no doubt push speed. I'll get to the Daughters as quickly as I can. Don't let anyone stop you from—"

"Lopex!" Montly interrupted. "Look!" She pointed north, beyond the trudging slave Herd to a small group traveling toward the Sled. It was Zaavan and his Zetas.

Lopex pressed his eyes, stretching his vision across miles of skin patches to see his would-be murderer.

"He still has the Unbroken," Lopex observed.

"They must have slowed him down," Montly said, "and we caught up with him."

Lopex considered the options as a waft of berserk anger welled up inside his bones and blood.

"Change of plans," he started. "You get to Sapien Bay. Warn the Daughters. Be sure to tell them directly."

"But what if they ask me how I know? Will they even believe a Minion like me?"

"You can't worry about that, Montly. The Sled is all that matters now."

"Lopex, what are you going to do?"

"I am going to kill that Zeta. I'm going to sink him into the Skin-Land and make him swim with flesh for the rest of eternity," he said, darkness coating his words.

Montly took the seconds that passed to remember what Delius had told her. To be an advisor, to tell her master not what he wanted to hear, but what he needed to hear.

"You can't do that," Montly said abruptly.

"What?"

"You can't do that! You know that I need to tell the Herd. And you know that you can get to the Daughters faster than I can, and that they will believe you. Besides, Zaavan will—" Montly stopped mid-sentence.

"Zaavan will what? Zaavan will what? Tell me, Montly!" Lopex pushed.

"He'll destroy you! You know you can't match him!" she said, the words paining her as they left her lips.

Lopex stared at her. Reality swam around his mind, sketching out the confrontation between him and the Zeta—the battle class.

"None of that matters. No matter what happens today, Zaavan cannot survive. Not after what he did to us, to Reese."

"You're letting emotion strafe your thoughts, teacher. You must see that," Montly implored.

"And so I have," Lopex said. He took in a deep breath, flexing the band of muscles that spanned his chest, and locked in an extra set of vocal cords behind his throat.

"Zaavaaaaaaan!" Lopex roared with the deafening sound of a Canem. The scream traveled across the smooth Skin-Land, announcing his presence.

Zaavan looked up from his Mauss, compressed his compound eyes and pulled in the view of Lopex and Montly on the top of the steep hill.

"What is it, master?" Chalt asked.

"Take the Unbroken to Sapien Bay. It appears that the Eta class is more resourceful than I gave them credit for."

As Zaavan finished his words, the sky cracked, and a bellowing roll of thunder boomed from the thick, yellow-green clouds above. It shook the Zetas, the Unbroken, Lopex, and

Montly. It shook the Sled, the Skin-Land, and every corpuscle that strung the meaty flesh of Hell together.

CHAP+ER FOR+Y-NINE

Bonding to other individuals in Hell can be a very effective
survival technique, but understand that dependence on another
in Hell can be more than just a temporary arrangement.

—From "Hell: A Survival Guide"
By Delta-Delius

A sound that could only be described as thunder shook
Silton to his very core as he pushed up a steep hill of
craggy skin. Mariella dropped to her knees in response, clutching
the ground to keep her balance.

"I could feel that in my legs!" she said with a quirky smile.

"Does that mean it's going to rain again?" Silton asked.

"Something like that," Almer replied.

Silton reached over to help Mariella up, and she pushed his
hand away with a scowl.

"I'm okay. I can do it myself!" she said in a deep, drugged
voice as Almer crouched on her back.

Silton pressed on, his massive arms easily getting him
up the steep incline. He gripped a tuft of coarse black hair

that covered the top of the hill and used it to pull himself up.

And there he saw it: a massive construct that looked like a city made of flesh and bone slicing across the meat of the Skin-Land.

"My God!" Silton said, stunned.

The size of a city block, and stretching up at least ten stories, the flesh city teemed with activity. Layers of multi-colored skin walls covered the outside, and expertly carved bone scaffolding stabilized the structure. Huge white bone spires erupted from the center, topping the flesh city like a pipe organ. Silton thought for a moment that it looked beautiful, a fantastic creation born from the minds of demented masters. He shook this feeling as he realized that this building was made of people like him. People in search of redemption in Hell, but now were a permanent part of the brick and mortar that housed the Devil and his Demons.

"Ahh, the Sled," Almer said, as he and Mariella crested the hill. "I wasn't sure what I'd feel when I saw it. Hatred? Joy? Now that I'm here, it's both."

Silton ignored him, continuing to survey the scene.

"Over there." He pointed. "That's it. I think that's where she is."

In front of the Sled, a riotous group of bodies swarmed like a massive colony of ants. Silton surmised that at least ten thousand people were there, all connected by a stringy lattice-work of translucent material webbed to the front of the Sled.

"Yes," Almer said. "If your wife's still above skin, that's where she'll be. Everyone is tied to the bone yokes, strung together with sinew. Very tough stuff. But don't worry. If you work at it, you shouldn't have any trouble ripping it apart."

"So many people ... I had no idea," Silton said in awe. "I

didn't think that it would be that many. How am I going to find her?"

"I'm not sure," Almer said. "Maybe she'll remember you, maybe she'll—wait, that's strange," he said, interrupting his own thought.

"What's strange?" Silton asked.

"Those columns, those white spires." Almer pointed to the center of the Sled. "Those are new."

"So, what? I'm not planning on getting anywhere near them," Silton said.

"But they're odd. I don't understand what they would be used for," Almer said, almost to himself.

Silton realized that Mariella hadn't spoken a word since reaching the top of the hill. She hadn't gotten up, either; she still just knelt there, on all fours, her head drooped down.

"Mariella . . . Mariella!" Silton said. "Hey, we're here! Get up. We need to get moving." Silton reached down for her arm to help her. Again, Mariella slapped it away.

"What's wrong with you?" Silton asked forcefully.

"Nothing's wrong with me! Nothing at all," she said, her voice low and deep. "But I'm not going with you."

Silton stood silent. He didn't understand.

"What do you mean, you're not coming with me?"

"I think she means that we're together now, Silton," Almer said as Mariella straightened her arms and lifted her head to an awkward position. The skin sheet covering the half-man fell away. Silton couldn't believe what he saw underneath. Almer's spine had completely fused into Mariella. The bony snake of veins drove itself into her like a fat tree root to the ground, merging entirely with Mariella's back.

"What have you done to her!" Silton screamed, and lunged

for Almer's head. Mariella wound up her body and struck Silton square in the jaw with a strength so great a crack came from his mouth and he spilt over to the ground.

A trickle of blood and saliva ran down his face as he looked up at Mariella standing over him, her eyes soaked in dopamine, her arms puffed out with aggression. Almer's head arched over her shoulder and stared down at him.

"I don't *need* your help! I don't *want* your help!" Mariella said, her fists clenched, ready to strike him again.

"Mariella, he's done something to you. All of that playing inside your head ... he's changed you! Don't you see that? He's attached to you, he's controlling you ... you must see that!"

"And what if I do?" Mariella yelled. "You have this belief that people need your help, that people want your help. Well, I don't! I've told you things. Things I've never told anyone before. And in a way, you know me better than anyone else ever has. But don't for a second think you understand me!"

"Don't you see what he's done? He's using you! Like a slave!"

"And so what if he is? So what if I'm to be a slave here?" she said defiantly. "That's the difference between you and me, Silton. I *know* I belong here. I *know* I deserve to be here. You just haven't figured that out yet."

Silton pushed back so as not to be a threat to her and picked himself up, still stunned at the monster Mariella had become.

"Goodbye, Silton. And good luck," Almer said.

A tear of disbelief escaped Silton's eye.

"There was a part of me that fell in love with you here, Soldier Boy. But I still hope you find your wife. I hope you aren't chasing a ghost. And if you find her, tell her ..." Tears trailed down Mariella's cheeks. "Tell her I'm sorry."

And with that, Mariella-Almer dropped down on all fours and scampered down the steep hill like a horse and rider, leaving Silton alone to face the Sled.

CHAP+ER FIF+Y

After His crucifixion and ascension to Heaven, Jesus demanded His Father let Him visit Hell before returning to Earth. Jesus, although merciful, had been angered by the Devil's efforts to tempt Him away from His Father's love. Jesus was also troubled that the Devil could move so easily between Hell and the world His Father had created for man.

During the three days Jesus spent in Hell, He dismantled all of the Devil's works, including the bridge to Earth. In the end, He determined that the Devil could never again reach such a powerful state. So, He cursed the Devil: If he should ever stop moving, ever stop traveling the surface of Hell, he would sink like a stone into its fleshy depths. Jesus hoped this would cripple the fallen Angel, allowing Hell to become the purgatory His Father had always envisioned.

Upon the execution of this curse, the Devil sank into Hell. This event is thusly called: The Devil's Great Fall.

—From "A History of Hell"
By Delta-Holt

Lopex strode hard across the Skin-Land, his Mauss huffing acrid air through its many nostrils. A wave of deafening sound echoed from the sky, compacting his muscles as he kicked the Sapien harder to speed. The Angels would be upon them soon, but not before his time with Zaavan, the Demon murderer. Lopex's clothes flapped in tattered, acid-soaked ribbons around him, but his Basin robe remained intact. Lopex could only hope that it would protect him once more.

Zaavan dismounted his Mauss and slapped its hind-quarters, sending it off to the familiar Sled in the distance. The Zeta stretched his wings and took in a few deep breaths, expanding his acid sacs to their fullest capacity.

Lopex broke his Mauss's stride, stopping twenty feet from Zaavan. He pulled up the hood of his Basin robe, cinched it tightly around his head, and put on the pair of vitreous jelly goggles that his friend Eta-Hotund had given him.

"Are you surprised to see me, Demon Murderer?" Lopex scowled as he dismounted.

"I am always surprised to see you, Lopex. I would have thought Hell would swallow up someone as weak as you centuries ago. Every day you're above the Skin-Land is astonishing to me. But I can fix that," Zaavan said as he finished stretching.

"Imagine how surprised you'll be when you sink into Hell where you belong," Lopex countered.

"And why is that?" Zaavan asked. "Why do I deserve to be destroyed? Please, as your last words: What makes you so righteous, Lopex?"

"You sank Reese. You tried to sink me, and you probably had something to do with Delius. You're a Demon Murderer. There's nothing worse, nothing that insults the true nature of Hell more," Lopex said as he circled.

"Ahh, Delius, your master. Not that it matters now, but I didn't destroy him. I was *supposed* to destroy him. But I didn't. Do you understand that, simple Eta? The Daughters told me to destroy Delius. They told me to sink that ancient, twisted wretch into the Skin-Land. That was my secret Mandatum. And you think that you know the true nature of Hell? Do you know better than the Daughters? Better than the Devil himself?"

"You lie! The Devil owes everything to the Deltas. Why would he want the last of them destroyed?"

"Oh, Lopex, you're so naïve. I bet you were even more pathetic than this in the life-times. Did you ever think that perhaps it is exactly *because* the Devil owes the Deltas everything that he demanded the last of them be destroyed? You know so little of the world around you. I will miss your playful ignorance. I promise you that."

"Your treachery will not be missed, I promise *you* that, Zeta-Zaavan."

"Treachery? I don't think so. I just consider myself fortunate that your coward master destroyed himself for me. Why don't you do the same?"

And with those biting words Lopex sprang forward, bouncing off the Skin-Land with terrific speed. Zaavan instantly exhaled a cloud of acid between them, and Lopex dove straight through. The caustic green haze ate away every piece of flesh not covered by the Basin robe. As Lopex emerged skeletonized from the cloud, he hit Zaavan square in the chest. The pair tumbled to the ground in a blur of melted skin and blood.

✠ ✠ ✠

S I L T ⊕ N bounded across the Skin-Land, his enhanced legs

pushing as fast as a horse's gallop. The monstrosity of the Sled drifted in front of him. Its spires, its walls, looked dizzying, but he ignored the intimidating structure and made a straight line to the massive horde of people lashed to the front of the Sled. He flexed his shoulder spleens and felt a wash of fresh blood course through his body, invigorating him with strength and speed.

"*Tell her I'm sorry,*" he thought. Mariella's last words haunted him.

Out of the corner of his eye, Silton saw an object moving at tremendous speed. He glanced over to see a mounted rider on a direct course with his path. In a moment of hesitation, Silton stutter-stepped, but his momentum made him stumble. The surprised rider also hesitated, heeling the Sapien it rode, and the two glanced off each other, narrowly avoiding a collision. The rider flew off the beast, tumbling to the ground, and Silton tripped, landing on his back.

Silton shook the daze from his head quickly, his eyes focusing on the yellow-green sky above as best they could. He slowly got to his feet, his legs rubbery and unsteady, then looked to see whom he'd collided with. A form lay a few feet away, also slowly rising, and Silton readied himself for battle. His eyes cleared with concentration. There before him stood the Demon who'd invaded his mind, and whose mind he had invaded in return.

"You!" Silton screamed, and he lunged unsteadily toward her. Montly, barely having her wits about her, quickly side-stepped and fell to the side. Silton, still dazed, missed entirely and fell across her, landing face down on the Skin-Land.

Montly ached as part of Silton's massive body fell on her. Still stunned, she sat up and tried to scramble away. Silton got to his knees, took his massive arm, and gripped Montly by the neck, slamming her back down. He straddled her hips and began to choke her. He raised his right hand to a fist as she desperately tried to gurgle out words.

Silton locked eyes with Montly, and instantly the two of them washed back into each other's memories.

Silton saw the scene clearly as if it were his own experience: this Demon running down Kay while she tried to escape, then catching her, pulling her up, and taking her back to the massive herd.

Montly too was thrust into vision. She saw the Angel Tragen, heard his voice of warning for the coming Angel Fall, and saw him melted away by Zaavan.

And in those joined moments, the two of them shared the violent ebb and flow of Backwash Stemming fully. Their collective consciousness tore strength from both of them, and they settled into the knowledge that the two of them were connected.

Silton let go of Montly's throat, and they stared astonished into each other's eyes.

Montly caught her breath. "Silton! You're the one whose mind I've been in. You... It shouldn't have happened that way. I've... You... you warned us of Angel Fall!" Montly said, stumbling over words.

"My wife! My wife, Kay! You know her! You know where she is!" Silton yelled.

Knowing exactly what Silton meant, Montly replied. "I do. I know who she is ... and somehow, I know what she means to you. And I know why you have to find her," Montly said, feeling the power of Silton's emotions as if they were her own.

"You have to take me to her! You have to take me now!"

Montly fought hard against these new feelings, this leaking emotion of love pressed into her. She felt close to this man, closer than she should. The Sled must be warned the Angels were coming—but she would never have known of this without him. In her mind, she tried to justify helping him. Her thoughts drifted through the shifting logic of Demon, Unbroken, and Hell's purpose. Then Montly resolved to do what she thought was right.

"We don't have much time, Silton. Come with me now!" Montly said as she mounted her Mauss, and the pair tore off toward the bellowing mass of people pulling the Sled.

✛ ✛ ✛

EVERY inch of Lopex's skin not covered by the Basin robe had liquefied and now rested in a viscous pool where the two wrestled. His hands, naked white bone held together by pale tendons, struggled to keep Zaavan at bay as the pair tumbled over one another. Zaavan's strength was incredible, far more than Lopex expected, and soon he found himself underneath the Zeta, fielding blow after blow to his face. The vitreous goggles cracked, sending a few shards into the jelly of his left eye. Lopex felt his cheek shatter into a spider web of fractures. He lifted his left arm to protect his face, only to have Zaavan's sharp talons reach into the bare muscle of his forearm and rip it from the bone.

"Now you see, weak Eta-Lopex!" Zaavan tossed the flap of muscle to the side. "Now, in your final moment, you will understand the true nature of Hell!" Zaavan took both of his massive wings and wrapped them around Lopex's body, trapping him in a cocoon of dark skin. Zaavan pulled in tight, squeezing

Lopex closer, stealing away the movement of his arms and legs. The Zeta Demon took his forehead and smashed it into Lopex's face, crumbling the bone, caving in his cheek. Shards of bone fell into Lopex's throat, stifling his breath and forcing blood to spew from his mouth.

The pain ran across the inside of Lopex's skull like fire, burning every nerve ending to maximum agony. He cried out a guttural whimper and choked on a bone shard as it dug deep into his esophagus.

"Now, to add a few more pounds to Hell!" Zaavan screamed as he arched back and took in a deep breath, looming over Lopex.

Struggling with near helplessness under the Zeta, Lopex slipped his free hand into the pocket of his Basin robe, feeling the tiny brain organ Delius had given him still safe. But now he knew the memories of his master would be lost, forever sinking in the Skin-Land along with him.

I am so sorry, Delius. I am so sorry I failed you, Lopex thought.

Zaavan exhaled a cone of thick green as he pulled his wings up into a massive canopy.

The acid settled in, and Lopex lay shuddering as his Basin robe slowly gave up on its duties. The left side of his skull melted, and the caustic acid crept into his mouth, sizzling the flesh inside. Out of his weeping right eye, he could see the deep yellow-green of the sky of Hell waver like a thick ocean as tiny drops of pure white emerged from the clouds. At first, they were only dots, but soon the sky was filled with them. Lopex could see the white forms sprouting wings, and quickly the horizon filled with Angels, thick as a blizzard. As his body quivered in a pain so great it could yield no scream, he smiled.

It was the most beautiful thing Lopex had ever seen.

✝ ✝ ✝

S I L T ⊕ N sprinted easily alongside Montly and her Mauss as the pair strode across the Skin-Land parallel to the traveling Sled. The huge mass of the Herd could be seen in the distance, churning up a cloud of blood and feces as it pulled against a tangle of bone yokes and vein rope. Silton thought that he should be suspicious of his new companion, but there was something gentle about her. Sharing their minds through the Backwash had made them close. Silton trusted her—counter to his instincts, he trusted her.

Montly looked down at him from her mount, shocked that he kept pace so easily. She could see that he'd been altered. Only a few days before he'd been half this size. *But how?* she wondered. His body, sleek and matted with muscle, was formed as perfectly as a Master Engineer would do for a Demon. Montly felt a bond with him in a way she'd not known for some time, and she wondered if this was the insight that Delius had told her about.

Montly pulled her eyes up, looking to their line toward the Herd. Then, without warning, she heeled her Mauss to halt. Silton mirrored, and skid his massive body to a stop. His skin ran heavy with sweat, just like Almer said the acetylcholine enhancement would do to him.

"What? Why are we stopping?" Silton demanded.

"We . . . we have a problem," Montly said, stuttering as she looked to the left.

"Oh, I'd say you have more than one problem," said a familiar voice. Silton couldn't see over her enormous Mauss, so he walked around to get a better vantage. There, on the top of a slight hill, stood Chalt and Bore, black and red, shining bright, looking down on them from their mounts. Behind them, the captured Unbroken wheezed, heavy and tired, still shackled to the Drums.

Chalt began in her typical demeaning tone, "First of all, you are consorting with an Unbroken. Second, that Unbroken is *our* property! And last, well." Chalt glared snidely at Montly. "Just like your master, you *just won't stay sunk.*" She laughed to herself. Bore, hesitating from confusion, chuckled in a dumb mimicked fashion.

"You ... you killed Reese!" Montly said, terrified, but defiant.

"Reese? Oh, don't you worry about your friend Reese," Chalt said. "We treated him properly. We figured since he was always so passionate about food, we turned him into his own final dish." She turned to the Unbroken behind her. "You all liked Reese very much, didn't you?" There was cruelty in her voice as the Unbroken winced at the memory.

"Didn't you!" Chalt screamed, demanding a response.

"Yes, Master Chalt," they said together in a warped, beaten tone.

"You are going to pay for that, Chalt!" Montly said with a bravery that surprised even her.

"I really, *really* hope you make me pay for it," Chalt said, and led her Mauss down the slight hill, followed by Bore, blocking their path to the Herd.

"We don't have time for this," Silton said to Montly.

"There's no other way, not now," Montly replied as she dismounted.

The group shooed away their Mauss and squared off: Montly with Chalt, Silton with Bore.

"You ... remember you ..." Bore stammered to Silton.

"Yeah, well, I won't be *exactly* what you remember, big boy," Silton said as he flexed his shoulder spleens, flushing his body with blood.

"You change. You look like Demon. You think you Demon now?" Bore asked with slow stupidity.

With a sudden flex of his legs, Silton crossed the distance between him and Bore with a speed that looked as if he'd vanished. He landed a forearm with curled elbow directly into Bore's bone-plated head. The square white bone cracked in half, sending part of it in one direction and Bore flying off in the other.

"A Demon? No, but something like that," Silton said as Bore arced through the air.

Chalt jumped at Montly, striking her hard in the face. Montly turned on her heels from the hit and flailed her arms in clumsy swings that found no mark. Three more hits to the face and body with Chalt's black-matted fists, and Montly couldn't tell which way was up.

"Oh, come now," Chalt said. "You better give me as good of a fight as Bore will get. If not, I'll have to feed *you* to the Drums. They are your old friends, right? I think they'd like the taste of their handler, don't you?" Before Montly could get her wits, Chalt kicked her in the side, doubling her over, and fired a tumor-coated knee into her face, crushing her nose and sending Montly to her back.

Meanwhile, Bore tumbled onto the Skin-Land in what looked like an awkward fall, but the Demon used the momentum to rise to his feet into a perfect fighting stance.

"Bore okay... Bore okay..." the dumb red mass said, feeling his throbbing head. He ran his fingers over the now jagged edge of his broken head plate, and was astonished to find half of it gone, exposing part of his face. His black eyes narrowed, tunneling his vision at Silton. He flexed his arms, legs and torso, and his red, bone-dusted skin flushed bright with blood. Bore looked as if he were on fire.

Silton readied himself, twisting his feet into the soft Skin-Land, and Bore came at him in a streak of blood and fury. Bore struck him hard with his shoulder, and Silton hinged like a door. Taking some of the force, he swung Bore around, gripping his arm and tossing him to the ground. But he miscalculated the red Demon's strength, and the two rolled together in a topple of flesh.

Silton felt a burning in his hands and arms anywhere he touched Bore. It was as if Bore were covered in razors. Soon the pair were coated in Silton's blood from the cuts. Bore slid from Silton's grip and edged behind him, grabbing his right arm. Bore twisted Silton's arm against his back, immobilizing it, and rubbed his razor skin all over him, slicing open wounds wherever he touched.

Silton struggled, realizing Bore's true strength as the skin cast was ripped from his arm. He tried to break Bore's grip, but the slippery blood allowed him no traction. He tried to struggle to his knees, but the massive weight of the Demon wouldn't allow even his enhanced legs to move. Silton tried every combat tactic he knew of to wrest his arm from Bore. None of them gave him even so much as an inch.

And then it dawned on Silton: *I am not my body.*

Silton reached over his torso with his left hand, grabbed his right elbow by the cusp, and heaved with every enhanced muscle he had. His right forearm cracked right in the place where he'd first broken it, and it released his shoulder and elbow.

Then Silton began to tug with all of his weight and strength.

The skin and tendons of his arm ripped apart in gummy pieces. Silton separated from his forearm and hand in a second, embracing the pain, slipping away from Bore, leaving the dumb demon holding a bodiless appendage. Bore froze in confusion as Silton jumped to his feet. Then Silton began to pummel him. From the left side, a solid, balled fist crushed him. From the right side, a bloody stump of a jagged bone stabbed him. Over and over in a blur, Silton struck left and right for what seemed to be a torrid eternity, until the only thing left was a bloodied, headless torso that was once Zeta-Bore.

Chalt lifted the dazed Montly to her feet, gripping her worn coat by the collar, putting them face to face.

"I'm so glad you escaped. I'm so glad you'll let me destroy you myself!" Chalt said in a sadistic whisper. "You don't belong here. You don't belong with the *real* Demons, with the *real* keepers of Hell." She shook Montly from her daze to ensure that her gloating would not go unnoticed. As she shook Montly, the tumor necklace popped out from her coat. Chalt saw it, and ripped it from around her neck.

"But I won't miss that stupid story about this ugly necklace!" Chalt tossed it to the ground. "Now give me some space so I can show you how a true Demon destroys someone." Chalt spun around on her heels, holding Montly by the collar, and tossed her with all her strength. Montly flew through the air and landed against the solid flesh of a Drum.

Montly could only see a beige blur and a streak of black in front of her. Her eyes were drenched in sweat, her breath panicked and frenzied, her fearful muscles denying her control at every effort. Montly could see the black streak getting closer, and she pressed herself up against the Drum as if it would give her some escape, some protection from the Demon.

Some protection? Montly thought in a flash of clarity.

Montly took her hand and gently reached up the Drum's body. She felt the seam where the torsos were stitched together and followed it slowly up the giant's form. The Sapien was distressed by the violence, but Montly's kind touch calmed the beast for a moment, and she softly made her way to the underarm of the stitched joint. There, Montly caressed the soft button just under the skin, the adrenal. She watched as the black blur of Chalt became larger, and when it was all that Montly could see, she pressed the Drum's adrenal, ducked down under its arm, and rolled away as far as she could.

The Drum snapped like a thousand bones breaking all at once. The three-headed Sapien let out a scream, part rage, part desperation, and flailed its six arms in a madness inspired by the activation of its three adrenal glands. It stormed forward, taking with it the priest and one-armed martyr tied behind it. The Unbroken men became a fleshy morning star, striking Chalt as the Drum swung them around and closed in. A thick strand of the vein rope lassoed Chalt, and she found herself tangled with the Unbroken, screaming and wailing in terror. Montly watched as the Drum made its way to Chalt. The tumor-plated Demon put her arms up as protection from the berserk Sapien, but soon she disappeared into a pile of flesh and bone.

Montly walked over to where Chalt had thrown her necklace and picked it up.

"You never understood the necklace, Chalt," she said as the Drum beat Zeta-Chalt into a black pile of sludge.

"So, we're done here, right?" Silton asked Montly, joining her at her side.

"I'd say so," Montly replied.

"So, we let the rest of them go, okay?" Silton said.

"Yeah, yeah, we do," Montly replied. "But your arm."

"Oh, don't worry about it. I'll get another one," Silton said.

The two released the rest of the tattered Unbroken, mounted a pair of Mauss, and made for the driving Herd in the distance.

✛ ✛ ✛

ZAAVAN panned in flight over the crippled Lopex, and breathed in deeply to finally sink this Eta forever. Selfishly preoccupied with his victory, Zaavan didn't see the horizon filling with Angels. It was only the desperate howl from the Sled, the howl of every Canem, Minion, and Demon raising the alarm that forced him to look up.

The Zeta's tiny heart dropped when he saw it: a sky full of Angels from edge to edge. He looked back to the Sled, seeing his fellow Demons scattered and confused as they prepared, but the Angels were nearly on top of them already. Zaavan looked down at Lopex, who crawled aimlessly in a soup of skin.

"You're as good as sunk," Zaavan said, and sprinted up toward the Angel Fall.

A group of a dozen Angels, naked, black, white, brown, and all pristine with shining, alabaster wings, dove down into the mass of people pulling the Sled. In seconds they plucked away Broken slaves from their lashing and flew upward, carrying the redeemed under the arms.

Zaavan took a hard line straight above the Angels as they flew awkwardly with their newly rescued people. He hovered for a moment, waiting for them to come into range, and expelled a massive cloud of acid directly into their path.

The Angels' feathers melted instantly as the cloud engulfed

them, and the group of two dozen fell down into the trampling Herd. Zaavan turned to see three more groups of Angels making their dive, so he flapped his meaty skin wings and flew directly up into the fray.

Zaavan reached out and slashed at a passing Angel, ripping his perfect skin open at the rib and leaving a trail of falling blood. He quickly turned, following another Angel who passed, and dove down toward him. Zaavan drove his knees into the Angel's back, shattering his white wings. The Angel turned to see his foe, and Zaavan gripped him by the ears and twisted his head off. The Zeta flapped his wings to flight and let the Angel's headless body fall twitching to the Skin-Land.

Zaavan searched to find his next target, but was overwhelmed. Angels were taking the Broken up into the air, far beyond where he could reach them. They dove past him with terrific speed, in a blur so fast, he couldn't make out one Angel from the next. His fellow Demons had started to engage, but they were outmatched three to one. Another group of Angels began their ascent with at least five Broken slaves. Zaavan inhaled and flew into position to once again spray his acid. Then he was crushed from behind with a blow so hard it cracked his tumor chest plate.

Zaavan tumbled out of the sky, twisting over in a blinding, midair fall. The Angel had him wrapped tightly, pinning one of his wings, and Zaavan could do nothing. The pair landed on the Skin-Land, breaking through the top layer into the blood below. Zaavan exhaled blindly, hoping to burn his attacker enough to get some space for fight. The Angel melted away in Zaavan's grip, screaming with a tender Angel cry not often heard in Hell. The Zeta, covered in a thick soup of blood, feathers, and organs, pulled himself out of the shallow skin hole. He shook his wings clear of the viscous stuff, and felt sick at the scene in front of him.

The Angels, too many and too fast, picked away from the Herd at will, taking the souls they had worked so hard to find, to keep, to enslave. A wave of hopelessness washed over the arrogant Zeta-Zaavan as he realized the cacophony of battle was well in the hands of the Angels.

✚ ✚ ✚

A SILENT calm hovered over Silton and Montly as they rode hard toward the Herd. Silton tied off his amputated arm so that only a sharp, jagged piece of forearm bone protruded from his elbow. He found the pain from his wound intense, but manageable. Perhaps his time in Hell had made him tolerant to such injuries.

A horrible echoing of howls erupted from the Sled, and when the pair turned to look upon the massive construct, they saw a bevy of activity bustling as they rode past.

"What was that?" Silton asked.

"It must be the alarm. They see Angel Fall," Montly replied.

The horizon quickly erupted into battle as Angels dove down into the Herd and lines of Demons scampered across the Sled to meet them.

"How are we going to find her in this mess?" Silton asked.

"Don't worry about that. I know the Herd better than I know anything. We'll find her," Montly said confidently.

The two pressed on as the scene became chaotic. Bodies fell from the sky like rain; Angels screamed across the yellow backdrop, followed by trails of red blood; Demons toppled to the Skin-Land, beaten by groups of white-feathered warriors.

Silton and Montly rode through the turmoil, seemingly invisible to those battling for the redeemed. They arrived near the front of the starboard side of the Herd, where a crowd of no less than ten thousand Broken men and women screamed, begging the Angels for rescue.

Silton heeled his Mauss, his Sapien mount restless from the pandemonium. As he looked into the horde, he observed the deepest heart of Hell. Some people were helplessly dragged; others, strung together with only the slightest bits of skin and bone, hobbled along; and others still pushed against their yokes, terrified and bewildered. Silton shuddered with horror, knowing that his wife Kay lay somewhere inside that madness.

"Now what?" Silton screamed over the bedlam, but Montly didn't respond. The Herd she'd commanded for so long, nurtured and shaped for a hundred years, was coming apart at the seams. The Angels were too many, too fast, and although the Demons dispatched them at will, it wasn't nearly enough. The Angels slowly picked away at the flesh engine that moved the Sled, and Montly knew exactly what that meant.

"Montly!" Silton screamed. "Montly! Now what? We can't stay here!"

Montly shook herself out of the mental conflict, knowing she had a promise to keep to Silton.

"This way! To the second yoke at the front of the Herd. She's up here," Montly said, and started a gallop.

Massive columns of white bone yokes stretched across the slaves of the Herd. Each one of the fat posts had no less than five hundred Broken lashed to it with vein rope.

Montly pointed to the second column, almost at the very front of the Herd. A Broken man on the end of the row looked up at her and screamed in terror.

"You . . . not you!" the Broken man yelled at Montly.

"Eyes down, slave!" Montly screamed instinctually, and raised her hand in a motion to strike him. She caught herself, lost in the automation of her previous duties.

Silton watched her, wide-eyed, as she chastised the poor man. In that moment, his image of her cracked: *Is she my friend? Someone to help me? Who is she really?* he thought.

"What's wrong with you?" Silton asked.

Montly paused. "I . . . I don't know . . . You . . ." Montly looked to the sky, the Angels dropping down, taking Broken so fast they left a swirl of feathers behind them. She looked to the base of the Herd, to the place where the long, vein ropes met at the Control Platform.

She compressed her eyes to see across the distance, and there she saw her old master, Shelle, the Praefectus of the Herd. Shelle struggled against the writhing yokes, trying to control the messy motion of the Sled. The Demons who should be protecting her in such a situation were preoccupied with the mass of Angels, and had left her alone. Seeing this, an Angel dropped down from the sky and struck her hard in the head. Montly's old master flew off the platform and was quickly trampled by the Herd she commanded.

"No!" Montly screamed, reaching out to the air. The Herd, now unmanned, broke stride, and a long terrible crack could be heard as the Sled began to slow and list to the side.

"Montly! Let's go! Show me now!" Silton yelled.

Thoughts bounced from one end of Montly's head to the other, from her hundred and fifty years in the Herd to the depths of what she'd seen inside Silton's mind. Confused, her thoughts edged to a precipice where they would no doubt shatter, and she searched across the valley of her soul to see who she really was.

And then she knew.

"I can't," she replied to Silton. "I can't go with you."

"What? Stop this. Let's go," he said.

Montly reached around and took off her tumor necklace. "Take this!" She handed it to him.

"What? What is this?" he asked as they clasped hands.

"Just listen to me. We all have our place here, we all do. No matter how horrible things are, no matter what you become."

"What are you talking about?"

"Silton, your wife is down this row. Go to her."

"But I thought that . . . I thought that we were . . ."

"Just don't forget: *Sin follows you. It does not lead you.* Don't ever forget that," Montly said, and she gripped Silton's hand tight, the necklace tucked inside. With that, she stormed off, driving her Mauss back toward the base of the Sled and the platform where her old Praefectus had been trampled.

Confused, Silton slipped the black skin covering his chest hole aside, and dropped the necklace near where the feather lay. Then, he dismounted and pushed himself into the riotous meat of the Herd.

✢ ✢ ✢

ZAAVAN dove through the busy sky, slashing at every Angel in reach. His remaining tumor plate and exposed muscle were covered in a sticky mess of red blood and white feathers. He and his fellow Demons dispatched dozens of Angels in their fighting flight, but as he looked to the sky, it was as if they'd done nothing.

A heavily muscled Angel hidden in Zaavan's blind spot rammed him hard in the back, sending his wings to flutter. He lost flight, dropping to the ground with a hard slap. Zaavan peeled himself off the Skin-Land, aching with the weariness of battle, and looked to the sky, seeing no less than twenty of their hard-fought Broken slaves being taken up to Heaven. Zaavan sighed with exhaustion, and forced himself to go on.

To his right he heard a familiar creaking sound, and the ramp of Sapien Bay opened.

"What's this?" he asked himself as the ramp slapped down onto skin. Out from the bowels of the Sled came a barrage of Sapiens. The Canem led the way, several hundred of the ravenous dogs, then throngs of fat Drums crawled out like caterpillars. Finally came the Mauss, ridden by wingless Demons and Minions alike, all carrying bone spears and glaives. They tore the Skin-Land bloody, and filled up the beige ground with their legions.

"Fools," Zaavan said. "They can't reach the Angels. They can't fly. This is all for naught." The Zeta felt an uneasiness, realizing their counterattack would be useless.

Then, as the Zeta rose to his feet, he heard another awful drone as the sound of the battle horn cracked across the warring sky. He looked to The Sled, perplexed by the horn's second sounding, and saw a massive tube drop from underneath the floor and sink into one of the deep blood canals. Zaavan had never seen this thing before. The tube's girth was wider than he was tall, and it extended from the floor of Sapien Bay into the fresh blood below. Zaavan looked to the Sapiens, Demons, and Minions that now surrounded him, and noticed they were all looking up, waiting anxiously for something to happen. And then a deep basal thump sounded and the flesh tube throbbed as it wavered, sucking blood up from the channel beneath.

The beast Sapiens screamed and roared as they looked up at the Sled for something soon to come. The tall white spires began to tremble, and near the center of the Daughters' tower, the tower where the Devil himself resided, a huge sheet of skin burst open, revealing a mass of bright red hearts stitched together as one.

The hearts thumped, sucking in a torrent of blood from below, and from the top of the pristine white towers a cascade of blood exploded into the sky, showering the Skin-Land in thick, red rain.

The Angels closest to the Sled began to drop from the sky. At first, one at a time, then in groups, as their blood-soaked feathers could no longer command flight. The waiting mass of Sapiens below tore them apart in heaps of bloody carnage. The Canem ripped at their wings; the Drums, berserk with strength, crushed their ribs and skulls; and the mounted Demons ran down any who tried to escape. Not one Angel who fell lasted more than a few seconds on the Skin-Land.

Zaavan looked down and watched as the thick red rolled easily off the tanned skin of his wings. He smiled, the blood trickling through his bone teeth.

"Never underestimate the wisdom of the Devil!" he said as he laughed, then took flight into a sky filled with blood and Angels.

✠ ✠ ✠

SILTON struggled to muscle his way through the tight row of bodies lashed to the yoke of the Sled. The men and women, slaves to the constant pushing, had their hands tied and twisted to the wide bone column with lengths of bone piercing their wrists. Thinking him a Demon, the Broken shirked away from Silton, but couldn't move more than a few inches from their locked position as he squeezed by.

A fat man, his body stretched from obesity and branded with a G on his forehead, blocked Silton's way. He turned to see Silton and almost lost his footing in shock.

"No! Please don't! No!" the fat man screamed, fearing some unknown torture. "It's okay. It's okay. I'm not one of them," Silton said, but the man seemed not to understand. As Silton reached out to console him, the man slipped on the slick Skin-Land and fell. The man's weight ripped his hand off, leaving it there hanging, amputated on the bone column. Silton winced at what he'd inadvertently done, and in an effort to help, he lifted up his wounded arm with the jagged bone protruding and cut away the vein rope lashing the fat man's other arm to the Sled.

The fat man fell to the ground, free from his bonds.

"Are you okay?" Silton asked, but again it was as if the fat man could not understand. He just wobbled along the ground, smiling.

"I'm free! I'm free!" the man bellowed. He regained his footing, muscled his girth, and rushed past Silton, almost knocking him over as he burst through the row of people from where Silton had just come, escaping from the Herd.

The masses around Silton saw what he'd done for the man, and began to cry out, begging with inhuman shrieks for the same. Silton, stunned by the voices, ran the thought through his head. He could move through the row easily if these people were gone.

"*De Oppresso Liber,*" he said. "To Liberate the Oppressed.

There's never been a truer example . . ." And with that, Silton began to slash away at the vein rope with his jagged arm, freeing the Broken from their bonds while he cleared the path in front of him.

Then, Silton heard a deafening bellow of sound from the Sled that crashed like a sonic wave over the Herd. A few seconds later, a shower of blood fell from the sky, drenching the scene in red as every man and woman screamed in terror.

Silton wouldn't let this distract him. He slashed away at the bonds of every person in front of him. Some of the Broken hugged him briefly as they escaped, others ignored him completely as they ran, and a few fell to the ground in weakness, trampled by the rows and rows of people behind them as the Herd pressed on.

Silton quickly approached a blockade of large veins holding together two massive pieces of bone that made up the columns. He struck it hard with his jagged bone, and slowly the veins began to split open. In an instant, the pulling force of the Herd tore the weakened veins apart. The whiplash force snapped Silton to the ground, and the entire column of bone bent away from its position, making a deep cracking sound as it twisted from the force.

Silton pushed himself up, slipping on the blood, and saw the thick bone column begin to splinter. And then it split. The shock wave from the massive break kept Silton on the ground as shards of white bone showered him, some biting into his skin. The Herd began moving in two different directions, and Silton knew he'd broken its rhythm. The Sled behind him started to slow, its two thick bone blades no longer slicing easily through the skin. All at once, the momentum stopped, and soon the entire construct was sinking.

People ran in all directions, some still lashed to pieces of bone, dragging them away to escape. The Angels plucked out a few of the redeemed, and clumsily flew away with blood-covered wings. Silton relied only on his instincts, and shut out the confusion while he trudged through the bodies and soft Skin-Land farther into the screaming crowd.

Blocking his way was a huge log of broken bone, with three women still tied to it. They struggled under its weight, their slight frames not able to move the massive piece. Silton took up his jagged arm and freed the first woman, then the second. He reached up to cut away the third, but her body lay hunched, awkwardly covering the vein lashings. She had deep open cuts on her back that seeped with pus. He reached to her shoulder and gently pulled her upright.

His eyes filled up with the face of the woman: Long, blood-soaked hair covered her head, her cheeks were silky white, and her lips soft. Silton knew that all of these belonged to the woman he loved: Kay. Although dazed and whipped with exhaustion, it was Kay.

"Kay!" Silton yelled, his face inches from hers. "It's me!"

She recoiled in shock, her hands still pinned to the bone column. Silton made quick work of her bonds, then grabbed her with all his strength, hugging her to his body.

"It's me, baby. It's me!" he said in her ear, feeling her struggle away from him, confused in his arms.

"Don't hurt me. Don't hurt me again, please!" Kay cried. Her voice etched into his soul with the piercing familiarity of a loved one.

"I'm not here to hurt you, baby. It's me. It's Silton, your . . . your husband." He gave her some room to pull away slightly so she could take him in fully. She stared into his eyes for what seemed like an eternity as reality soaked in. Kay touched Silton's face, his shoulders, even caressed the black hole in his chest.

"Silton?" Kay whispered, more to convince herself than anything else. "But how? How are you here?" she asked in disbelief.

"Never mind that, baby. Are you okay?" he asked, then realized the absurdity of his question. "I've been here. I've been here looking for you. I'm going to get you out of here."

Kay started to cry in deep painful sobs and embraced Silton hard, nuzzling her head into his shoulder.

"I can't believe it. I can't believe it," Kay said over and over again, muffled by his body.

The masses freed from the Herd passed them like water around a rock, and the two held the embrace for a long moment, blocking out the pandemonium that encircled them.

Silton eased his grip and let Kay lean back so he could see her fully. Her eyes drenched in tears, her naked body covered in blood rain. He reached easily to her face and wiped away the matted hair.

And there it was, burned into her forehead, thick with deep scar tissue: the capital letter A.

✚ ✚ ✚

ZAAVAN watched as the Angels caught in the streaming arc of blood from the Devil's heart machine dropped to the Skin-Land. He flew easily through the rain as the Angels struggled on the ground, being chewed up one after another. Most of the Angel intruders held steady on the outskirts of the blood rain's canopy, taking turns diving through as quickly as they could to snatch away the Broken before they became too soaked. But the Angels' numbers lay shattered, and they could no longer attack the Sled in force. The Zeta made a slow arc over the scene, marshaling the winged Demons for a counter-attack, when he heard a terrifying sound come from the Herd.

He looked down to see the second row of the main yoke explode into pieces. Zaavan couldn't believe his eyes as he watched the Herd separate and Broken slaves flee into the Skin-Land. He knew that without constant forward motion, the Devil's curse would return, and another Great Fall would surely ensue, ending all civility in Hell.

Zaavan curled his wings and dove down into the teeming chaos of the shattered column.

✠ ✠ ✠

S I L T ⊕ N couldn't reconcile himself with this revelation.

"You . . . you cheated on me? On us?" he said in a whisper.

"I'm sorry. I'm so sorry. I was going to tell you . . . but I . . ." Kay dug her head once again into his shoulder, but Silton rebuffed her.

"But what? But what, Kay!"

"But I died, damn it!" she screamed. "Okay? Are you happy? I died! Hit by a car only an hour after I . . . after I . . . did it . . ." Kay started crying again, but fought hard to speak. "I got what I deserved! Are you happy with that? That's why I'm here! I know I deserved it."

Kay paused. "I know what I've done to you, to us. And I'm sorry. But understand me: What I did was a mistake. I knew it was a mistake to cheat on you the moment it happened, but I never had the chance to tell you." She melted into tears.

Silton felt destroyed. For the first time since his fall, Hell had become too much to bear.

"I killed myself because of you," he whispered. "I killed myself because you were gone." He understood for the first time the irony of the heartless hole in his chest.

"Oh, Silton," Kay cried. They held each other, covered in blood and their shared punishment.

A waft of cold air and the sound of flapping wings interrupted them.

"It's time!" said a voice, tender and clear, like music. The couple turned to see an Angel standing next to them, huge and perfect in form. His arm stretched out, and they saw his wings were lightly covered in blood. "We don't have another second. Come now. You are ascended!" the Angel urged.

The two, covered in confusion, looked at the Angel.

"Ascended?" Kay asked. "Ascended?"

"To Heaven," the Angel said.

Silton rose with Kay, smiling behind tears, and reached out to the Angel's hand.

"No... Not you!" the Angel said as he pushed Silton's hand away. "Just her."

Silton slapped the Angel square in the jaw, sending him spinning on his heels.

"What are you doing?" Kay screamed.

But Silton didn't know. It was instinct, a reaction from having been rejoined with his wife for only a few moments, now to have someone try to take her away. The Angel moved back slightly, raised his hand, and kept his eyes on Silton. In an instant, three more Angels pounced from the sky, piling on top of him. The Angel scooped up Kay, writhing against his strength, and began the effort to fly.

"No!" Silton screamed. "Take me! Take me too!"

"Let me go! I love you, Silton!" Kay yelled, struggling in the

Angel's arms. "Let me go!" She shrieked as the Angel's wings labored against the blood rain.

Silton twisted to his knees, and threw up an elbow behind him that crushed the jaw of one of the Angels.

"I am *not* a Demon!" Silton said in a guttural voice as he thrashed, releasing himself from their collective strength. Silton got to his feet, reached into his chest hole and pulled out the blood-soaked feather.

"Look! Look at this! One of your own gave this to me! I am *not* a Demon!" he yelled.

"We know!" the Angel holding Kay said. "We know you are not a Demon."

"Then take me up with her! Take me now!" Silton screamed.

The Angels moved slowly away from Silton, the injured one adjusting his broken jaw.

"We know who you are, Silton. We know," the Angel said. "But it's not your time. You are not redeemed."

"*I am not redeemed?*" Silton screamed. "Look what I've done for you!"

"And we are thankful. *God* is thankful," the Angel continued. "But you will not ascend today."

"How dare you! How dare God!" Silton boiled with anger, but a flash of memory reminded him of something he was charged to do. "I'm supposed to give you a message. I'm supposed to tell you that Delius is destroyed. The last of the Deltas is destroyed! Isn't that enough?"

The Angel froze. He looked to the other three, who also stood stunned by Silton's words.

"It has begun," the Angel said with deep reverence. "Listen to me, Silton. God has a plan for you, a plan for you *here*. That plan is now taking shape *here in Hell*. He needs you to serve

Him *here,* to understand your sins fully *here.* Keep the feather safe, and try to know the Father better—and above all, Silton: *You must survive."* The Angels pulled back, dragging the screaming Kay with them, and with a burst of their wings, took flight, streaking into the blood-rained sky.

Kay cried and cried, soaring above the battle, held under arm by the Angels as they escaped the canopy of blood. The acrid yellow air stung at the open cuts on her back, but as the light of Heaven's Eye filled her with warmth, it slowly erased all of the injuries Hell had done to her.

✛ ✛ ✛

ZAAVAN landed hard on the Skin-Land near the front of the Herd and surveyed the scene. The battleground had settled, and Angels could only be seen in the distance, fluttering away with their catch. Any remaining descendants of Heaven were just heaps of flesh being toyed with by Canem and Drum alike.

Zaavan looked in disbelief at the shambles of the starboard side of the Herd. The Sled barely moved forward, and slowly the heavy weight of the Devil's curse began to take hold. Zaavan looked to the side and saw one of the bone blades sinking into the Skin-Land, and the massive flesh city began to lean.

Zaavan ran into the depths of the shattered bone yokes, hoping to find the broken column so that he might repair it, or if he had to, pull it himself. They'd lost at least two hundred Broken slaves. Some to the Angels, but most had escaped across the Skin-Land during the confusion of battle.

But how? he thought. *No Angel was strong enough to do this.*

Zaavan entered a flat clearing littered with splintered pieces of bone. And then he saw him: a blistered mass of a man sitting with his head hung down, missing a hand, with that telltale hole through his chest Zaavan knew all too well as one of their Unbroken.

"*You!*" Zaavan said as Silton turned to him. "*You* did this?"

Silton rose to his feet, his eyes soaked in tears, his face exhausted from emotion.

"And so what if I did?" Silton replied without fear.

"You have no idea what you've done here, Unbroken!"

"What?" Silton said as he wiped away some blood from his face. "I think it's an improvement."

Zaavan, enraged, circled Silton in silence, in awe of this Unbroken's arrogance.

"I'm *not* going to sink you into Hell, Unbroken," Zaavan started. "No. I won't let you escape that easily. You've just volunteered to be my new Artifex. My personal slave. Once I saw down your arms and legs, you'll find your chores difficult while crawling on your belly for eternity!"

"I'm gonna pass on that," Silton said, and sprang forward with terrific speed directly at the Zeta.

Zaavan twisted to his side, flapped his huge wings, and moved out of the way in an instant. Silton, not able to stop his momentum, missed the tackle and landed face first, sliding a few feet on the Skin-Land.

"You may think you have the strength of a Demon," Zaavan said. "But inside you're still a weak, pathetic Unbroken." The Demon sucked in deeply and sprayed out a cloud of acid. Silton put up his jagged arm to shield his face, and the green fumes melted away everything it touched, leaving his right arm and leg naked of skin, his muscles sizzling in pain.

Zaavan leapt up with the help of his wings and planted his

feet squarely onto Silton's chest, flattening him to the ground. A fraction of a second later, Zaavan landed a blow to Silton's face that shook his body to the core. With Silton dazed, Zaavan wrapped his wings tightly around his arms and body, pinning him to the Skin-Land.

"Now, my little Artifex. I just need to burn out this aggression of yours. I'll need to get through your skull, put a hole in your brain. It shouldn't take more than a moment or two." Zaavan opened his mouth and let a thin stream drip down onto Silton's forehead. The acid sizzled and burned his skin as it began to eat into the bone of his skull.

Silton fought against the pain, screaming between his teeth.

He pushed his chin down to avoid the acid, and saw Zaavan's huge body and cracked tumor plate glistening black and wet above him. He struggled against the Demon, but even his enhanced strength offered him no advantage in this position.

Then, in a moment of inspiration, his mind went back to his training as a Combat Medic in the Army. Silton imagined Zaavan's Demon anatomy underneath his armor: the muscle, the tendons, and the curving ribs that protected his acid sacs.

Zaavan rose to inhale, taking in air that would birth a stream of acid to puncture Silton's brain. In that second, Silton felt the slightest relief on his skeletonized right arm. Having only a bit of muscle left, his arm was little more than a stump, but it was a sharp stump. Silton righted the crippled arm upward, positioning it toward the space that would slip through the crack in the tumor plate and between Zaavan's ribs.

Zaavan began to exhale, pressing down upon Silton in a massive rush. Silton thrust the jagged forearm up, puncturing the skin under the Demon's massive weight. The bone slipped between the gate of Zaavan's ribs and stabbed into the Demon's bloated acid sac.

An audible pop sounded, and instantly the smoke of cooking flesh burst from Zaavan's core as his body shook to spasm. A wash of green erupted inside Zaavan's abdomen, and the Zeta let out a scream that made the howls of the Canem seem a whisper. Zaavan's eyes flew open wide as his own acid spilt through the tumor plate, rendering it to black paste.

Silton rolled away, snapping his arm off at the bony shoulder and leaving it inside the Demon. The acid spattered onto Zaavan's right wing, eating away holes wherever it touched. Zaavan choked hard, spitting up as much of the acid as he could from the punctured lung. The Demon looked down to see his right side completely gone, and a huge glob of acid dropping down from between his legs, eating a hole right through the Skin-Land. The Demon fell straight down as he struggled against his own devastating weapon. Soon, Zaavan's body was just a stick figure of bone scaffolding and tendons, slowly melting into misshapen jelly.

✢ ✢ ✢

SILT⊕N rose from the battle, his right arm gone, still burning with fumes of thick green acid. He took in a slight breath of relief within the pulses of excruciating pain, lifted his left arm to his forehead and wiped. The thin, flat skin that held his Sin Stamp "S" sloughed off from his skull, falling to the ground.

In the distance, Silton could hear a commotion, the sound of many approaching the bare bone columns absent of any slaves to pull them. He assumed the Demons and Sapiens were on their way. Silton sighed, knowing he couldn't fight them off, knowing his destruction was mere moments away.

A horn sounded, a third deafening echo that rumbled across the shredded Skin-Land, followed by a voice.

"All Demons to the Sled! Devil Fall! Devil Fall!"

Silton, exhausted, looked up toward the voice in the distance and saw someone standing on a platform, waving a skin flag with a black X. Soon the sound of the oncoming Demons died away. Someone, someone who sounded so familiar to Silton, was calling them back.

He pressed his eyes, looking harder at the platform, and there he saw her: Montly. She waved a black crossed flag, back and forth, commanding the Demons assist her with pulling the sinking Sled out of the Skin-Land.

Silton couldn't see Montly's face with such a great distance between them, but he could feel her. He could feel their shared fear drifting away, he could feel the connection between them becoming something permanent, he could feel a pinch of sadness for having to leave her. Silton silently mouthed "Thank you," and smiled. Montly, waving the black X flag with frenzied strength, nodded, and shared the smile.

Silton surveyed the carnage around him: the hobbled Sled desperately being held afloat, the bloody piles of Angels and Demons littering the landscape, the hundreds of freed slaves disappearing into the Skin-Land Vast, and on the horizon, the last of the white wings taking the redeemed to Heaven. Taking Kay to Heaven.

"Almost perfect. Almost fucking perfect," Silton said to himself.

He walked from the scene, into the endless depths of Skin-Land, choosing to leave behind his flesh and his feelings alike.

Just like when he arrived in Hell, Silton was alone. Alone except for his sin, the cause of his damning, the burden that he had to carry, the plague of his life-times. And although heavy, the pain of his sin was beginning to give him a familiar comfort.

Silton finally understood this sin to be the only companion he would have here in Hell, for it was the only companion he truly deserved.

"Sin follows me, it does not lead," Silton said in a moment born from epiphany.

✚ ✚ ✚

AND watching from above, in the bright blue depths of Heaven's Eye, God smiled.

THE END

EPIL⊕GUE

L opex bobbed helplessly, half of his form sunk into the Skin-Land, half of his form sinking. The pain had all but subsided, his nerve endings having no more strength to tell his acid-soaked body of injury. The Eta could feel his faculties melting into Hell, into the oneness of the billions that made up this place. In the blurring vision of his only remaining eye, he saw someone walking toward him. A huge body, stacked with strength, missing an arm, with a hole right through his chest.

"You've seen better days," Silton said sarcastically.

It took Lopex a moment to focus and place the Unbroken Silton for who he was.

"Amazing," Lopex coughed up a deep, viscous red. "How? How can you be . . . how can you be here? How?"

"I had some help. A lot of help, actually. Your master, the big one with the tentacles, he let me go."

"Delius let you go? Impossible," Lopex said, taking every ounce of strength he had to keep himself above skin.

"Well, he did. He wanted me to give the Angels a message, but a lot of good that did me." Silton wiggled his stump of an arm.

"To tell the Angels? Tell them what?" Lopex strained.

"Not that it matters, but he wanted me to tell the Angels that he was gone, that the last of the Deltas was destroyed. Doesn't make any sense to me. But the Angels sure thought it interesting."

Lopex roiled with thought, confused, bewildered in his final moments.

"But why... why would he do that? Why would the Angels need to know?"

"No idea, but maybe you can ask him when you get down there. He sank himself in that lake you found us at," Silton informed him.

"No, never. Delius would never do that," Lopex whispered in disbelief.

"Okay then, have a good one. I'm sure you'll understand if I don't help you." Silton began to walk away.

"Wait!" Lopex said as loud as his voice would let him.

"What?"

Lopex dug into his pocket, now submerged into the soup of skin he lay in, and pulled out the piece of brain given to him by Delius.

"I can't let this sink with me. I can't." He reached out to Silton as far as his crippled hand could. "If Delius trusted you to give the Angels a message, I can trust you to take this."

Silton bent down into the shallow pool and looked at the little organ.

"What's this?"

"It... it's the memories of all the Deltas. It's a precious thing. A very precious thing. There is something inside it, something that terrifies the Devil, something the Devil wanted destroyed. I can't... I can't let it sink with me. Take it... please," Lopex pleaded.

"Something that terrifies the Devil?"

And Silton took the tiny organ gently into his hand.

ABOUT THE AUTHOR

Fabrice Wilfong has been writing fiction since he was 15 years old. His works have consistently leaned toward the dark side of human experience, where he uses characters and philosophy to challenge our shared interpretations of life.

For most of his professional career, Fabrice has been in the Healthcare Industry where he's learned to love human anatomy and the systems of the body. He feels the body remains a frontier that we are all forced to explore with little understanding of how things will unfold.

His works consistently push the reader to a deeper knowledge of themselves both mentally and physically, while daring into the fantastical and bizarre.

Fabrice lives in San Diego where he and his wife enjoy the beach, hikes, and the occasional wine festival.